Until Next Summer

"*Until Next Summer* is the book equivalent of catching fireflies on a warm summer night, and I couldn't put it down. Full of charm, nostalgia, and swoon, Ali Brady's newest release is best consumed by the light of a glowing campfire."

—*New York Times* bestselling author Lynn Painter

"*Until Next Summer* is a heartfelt and hilarious frolic through a nostalgic landscape of Color Wars, first kisses, and toilet-paper porch decor—with a cocktail in hand. Whether you're a 'camp person' or not, I defy you to read Ali Brady's latest without glowing from the inside at this tender and hopeful exploration of friendship, romance, and the magic that only a very special place in the woods can hold."

—Shelby Van Pelt, *New York Times* bestselling author of *Remarkably Bright Creatures*

"For fans of every single good thing—friendship, romance, summer camp, and reclaiming your authentic self—this book is a complete winner. It's redemptive and romantic in the most perfect way."

—Annabel Monaghan, bestselling author of *Same Time Next Summer*

"Get ready for an extra dose of nostalgic summer feels—with a side of steamy romance—in this delight of a novel by authors Alison Hammer and Bradeigh Godfrey, who write together as Ali Brady. You'll fall in love with plucky Jessie and earnest Hillary as the two women—whose friendship fractured a decade ago—try to find their way back to trusting each other, all while trying to save the summer camp that meant so much to them as kids. Throw in a hot, conflicted camp chef and a sexy, brooding writer holed up in a camp cabin with his dog, and you have yourself a recipe for two spectacular summer flings—and maybe even more. But just like the calm waters of the fictional Camp Chickawah's lake, there's more depth than you might expect beneath the surface, and you'll find yourself laughing and crying along with Jessie and Hillary as they host several weeks of adult campers and are forced to discover what it really means to save the day—not just for the camp, but in their own lives, too. *Until Next Summer* charms with crackling summer romance, the magic of true friendship, and an against-the-odds story of discovering the things that matter—and finding the courage to fight for them."

—*New York Times* bestselling author Kristin Harmel

"*Until Next Summer* is an absolute must-read! This novel beautifully captures everything that's magical and marvelous about long summer days, away camp, best friends, first kisses, and finding your people and the place of your heart. When everything the Chickawah campers love is placed in jeopardy, our protagonists try everything they can think of to save the day. Rarely have I been so completely invested in the outcome of a story. In a word, it's Chicka-wonderful! Hey, if you know, you know, and if you don't know, you need to read *Until Next Summer*!"

—Jenn McKinlay, *New York Times* bestselling author of *Love at First Book*

"Thank you to Ali Brady for taking me back to sleepaway camp. First loves, shower shoes, Color Wars, the camp play, best friend necklaces . . . you didn't miss a detail about what makes camp a place where time moves differently and the outside world is a galaxy away. *Until Next Summer* is an irresistible frolic through the joys of summer, friendship, and young romance, but also a reminder of the heartache that comes along with that unforgettable time in life. This book is for anyone who still thinks about their first crush, their first friend, or their first sip of bug juice."

—Elyssa Friedland, author of *The Most Likely Club*

"Ali Brady is back with a can't-miss vacation-in-pages. Two estranged friends come together to celebrate the last season at their favorite place with the best idea of all time: adult summer camp! Whether you're a former camper or could simply use an escape, run, don't walk, to pick up this charming, fun, and utterly poignant novel about the pieces of our younger selves that are always waiting to be rediscovered. Ali Brady captures the feel of carefree childhood days so vividly that you can practically smell the s'mores. *Until Next Summer*, like camp itself, brims with summer romance, forever friendship, and, maybe most of all, finding who you're meant to be. As a camp fanatic, I give this one five huge stars—and now I want to go to Camp Chickawah, too!"

—Kristy Woodson Harvey, *New York Times* bestselling author of
The Summer of Songbirds

"*Until Next Summer* grabbed me with its summer camp nostalgia, the deep friendship between its protagonists, and two simmering romances. I was rooting for every single character to find their happily ever after, especially Camp Chickawah!" —Jessica Saunders, author of *Love, Me*

"While the romances have their steamy moments, this story is ultimately proof that platonic soulmates are just as important as romantic ones. A fun, sun-drenched homage to camp memories." —*Kirkus Reviews*

"*Until Next Summer*, the sweet, steamy third novel by Ali Brady (*The Beach Trap*), celebrates the magic of summer camp and the glittering potential of second chances both romantic and platonic." —Shelf Awareness

"Summer nostalgia, friendship, and romance meld in *Until Next Summer*." —*Woman's World*

Praise for

The Comeback Summer

"This uplifting story will have you cheering for sisters Hannah and Libby as they push past the boundaries of their comfort zones. The dual narrative lets the readers experience Hannah's and Libby's compelling journeys, both of which unfold at a perfect pace throughout the story. The prose, character development, and romance are a ten out of ten in *The Comeback Summer*." —Suzanne Park, author of *So We Meet Again*

"Both heartful and so much fun, *The Comeback Summer* finds two sisters at forks in their roads and challenges them to consider the path not taken: in love, in family, in life. A delightful confection all about reinvention."

—Allison Winn Scotch, New York Times bestselling author of
The Rewind

"In this lovely story of sisterhood and summer, self-discovery deftly entwines with two sweet romances. Full of warmth, complexity, and charm, The Comeback Summer is the perfect read."

—Emily Wibberley and Austin Siegemund-Broka, authors of
Do I Know You?

"The ultimate vacation read. I didn't want to put it down. The duo deliver a stunning story about the love between sisters and soulmates, and for one's self. Heavy topics such as body positivity and mental health are handled with a light, humorous, and heartwarming touch, and The Comeback Summer will leave you grinning from ear to ear."

—Denise Williams, author of Do You Take This Man

"Lighthearted and endearing."   —Parade

"Another winsome and winning tale that neatly pivots between the two sisters' viewpoints and delivers the maximum measure of sharp humor and smoldering romance, all while insightfully underscoring the importance of the bond between siblings and the rewards found in embracing new challenges in life."

—Booklist

Praise for
The Beach Trap

"Full of beauty, and hope, and reminders that it's never too late to roll up our sleeves and rise above the mistakes we made. I cheered, I cried, I swooned while reading about Blake and Kat, and their journeys to finding love, to finding themselves, and to becoming the sisters they were always meant to be. Take this book on vacation with you, and let its heart and humor sweep you off your feet!"

—Ali Hazelwood, *New York Times* bestselling author of
The Love Hypothesis

"A unique and fun twist on the enemies-to-lovers trope, *The Beach Trap* features two half sisters who hate each other, but are thrown together one fateful summer to save their family's beach house. It's *The Parent Trap* meets *Flip or Flop* (with not one, but two hot handymen). In other words—the ultimate vacation read."

—Colleen Oakley, *USA Today* bestselling author of
The Invisible Husband of Frick Island

"*The Beach Trap* is both a celebration of sisterhood and an unflinching examination of how where we come from shapes who we become. . . . With an HGTV-worthy plot, heaps of family drama, and a side of romance, *The Beach Trap* hits the nail on the head when it comes to the perfect summer read. Don't forget to pack this one in your beach bag!"

—Sarah Grunder Ruiz, author of *Love, Lists, and Fancy Ships*

"From the deft manner in which the authors shift the narrative between their two protagonists to the dual romances that unfold with just the right dash of snarky wit and sexy sizzle, readers will find *The Beach Trap* to be an absolute delight."

—*Booklist*

"A juicy beach read!"

—Motherly

"Ali Brady . . . hit the ball out of the park with their debut—the story is just so well done. The writing is vivid, and I felt like I was transported to the beach or living in the beach house. *The Beach Trap* is a sweet and uplifting story that had me cheering for Kat and Blake to resolve their differences and come to terms with their family's sordid past. It will be the perfect book to take to the pool or the beach this summer."

—The Buzz Magazines

"If you're a fool for HGTV and sibling rivalry novels, toss *The Beach Trap* into your bag."

—*The Augusta Chronicle*

Berkley Titles by Ali Brady

The Beach Trap
The Comeback Summer
Until Next Summer
Battle of the Bookstores

Battle

of the

Bookstores

Ali Brady

BERKLEY ROMANCE
NEW YORK

BERKLEY ROMANCE
Published by Berkley
An imprint of Penguin Random House LLC
1745 Broadway, New York, NY 10019
penguinrandomhouse.com

Book design by Alison Cnockaert

Library of Congress Cataloging-in-Publication Data
Names: Brady, Ali, author.
Title: Battle of the bookstores / Ali Brady.
Description: First edition. | New York: Berkley Romance, 2025.
Identifiers: LCCN 2024048202 (print) | LCCN 2024048203 (ebook) |
ISBN 9780593640845 (trade paperback) | ISBN 9780593640852 (ebook)
Subjects: LCGFT: Romance fiction. | Novels.
Classification: LCC PS3602.R342875 B38 2025 (print) |
LCC PS3602.R342875 (ebook) | DDC 813/.6—dc23/eng/20241021
LC record available at https://lccn.loc.gov/2024048202
LC ebook record available at https://lccn.loc.gov/2024048203

First Edition: June 2025

Printed in the United States of America
1st Printing

The authorized representative in the EU for product safety and compliance is Penguin
Random House Ireland, Morrison Chambers, 32 Nassau Street, Dublin D02 YH68,
Ireland, https://eu-contact.penguin.ie.

For the book people—the readers, the librarians, the booksellers, and anyone who gets lost in big books, big feelings, and big, beautiful endings. This one's for you.

Reading is escape, and the opposite of escape; it's a way to make contact with reality after a day of making things up, and it's a way of making contact with someone else's imagination after a day that's all too real.

—Nora Ephron

Battle

of the

Bookstores

1

Josie

WHEN I TELL people I'm a bookseller, I'm sure they imagine me curled up in a cozy chair reading for hours, sipping coffee and discussing books, or hobnobbing with famous authors at literary events. You know, living the ultimate bookish dream, every breath filled with that intoxicating tang of fresh ink and crisp paper.

What they *don't* imagine are the endless hours on my feet, my back aching from hefting twenty-pound boxes of books, or my stomach knotting from the constant stress over razor-thin profit margins and climbing overhead expenses.

Still, there's nothing else I'd rather do. I love flicking on the lights each morning and gazing at the shelves and stacks, all neat lines and sharp corners. I love unpacking shipments of glossy new hardcovers and recommending my favorites to customers.

But the best part—the absolute, hands-down, best part of running a bookstore—is getting to read books before they come out.

Several months before publication, publishers send galleys to booksellers, advance reading copies that arrive in brown paper packages, covers adorned with glowing blurbs, in the hopes that we'll read and recommend (and hopefully stock multiple copies of) this new title.

A while back, a publicist at one of my favorite imprints emailed to ask if I'd consider reading an upcoming release and providing a quote, if I liked it. And did I? Well, I stayed up until three o'clock in the morning reading, and my tears left damp spots on the final pages. I spent days writing and rewriting the perfect paragraph to encapsulate the essence of this epic, heart-wrenching story.

Last week, I got an email from said publicist telling me that advance copies were being sent out, and oh, by the way, they'd used my quote on the back cover (cue internal squeeing!). This morning, that package arrived. My hands shake as I rip open the brown paper, my eyes scanning until—

"A stunning meditation on grief and betrayal. . . .
Worth reading and cherishing for years to come."
—Josie Klein, bookseller
Tabula Inscripta, Somerville, MA

My breath rushes out. They only used a fraction of the paragraph I sent.

But: It's my quote. My name. I've spent the past five years becoming the best bookseller I can be, determined to prove that a college dropout can make something of her life. I may be a bookish little introvert, but I've got ideas and opinions to share. Someday, I hope readers throughout the city—maybe even the country—will turn to me for book recommendations.

Someday, my voice will matter.

Desperate to share my excitement, I grab my phone and

pull up BookFriends, a website with discussion forums for booksellers across the country.

> **BookshopGirl:** Guess who got an ARC with her first blurb printed on it?!

I post it in the Celebration subforum, where any user can read it, but I'm hoping to reach one specific person. Biting my lip in anticipation, I wait—and when I see the username I'm looking for, my heart soars.

> **RJ.Reads:** What?? Congratulations! That's amazing! Just wish you could tell us the title so I could see it.

I wish I could, too, but the forums are strictly anonymous. That way, booksellers can share honest opinions about publishers and authors without fear of negative blowback.

Grinning, I switch over to our DM thread.

> **BookshopGirl:** There's only one other bookseller quoted on the back of this ARC and guess who it is?

> **RJ.Reads:** PAW?

> **BookshopGirl:** You got it!

RJ knows all about my adoration of Penelope Adler-Wolf, owner of Wolf Books in Providence, Rhode Island. PAW is a bookseller of impeccable taste and vast influence. If she endorses a book, it's gonna be *Big*. My goal in life is to be just like her.

My phone lights up again with a reminder: MEETING WITH XANDER.

I sigh. Xander Laing has spent the past few years buying up the entire block, including the coffee shop next door, though he doesn't care about books or coffee—just his bottom line. When he bought Tabula Inscripta, Xander questioned if "a girl with nothing but a high school diploma" could handle being the manager. I convinced him to give me a shot, and since I pull a profit each month, he keeps me around. Still, I always feel like I'm on thin ice.

I send a message to RJ, wishing I could chat longer.

> **BookshopGirl:** Gotta go—have a great morning!

> **RJ.Reads:** You too. And congrats again. I'm so happy for you.

After that, I lock the door behind me and step into a crisp, sunlit morning. My bookstore is right in the heart of Davis Square, my favorite neighborhood in the Boston area—tree-lined streets, brick-paved sidewalks, charming shops, and eclectic restaurants. It's late May and the day is already warm, the air filled with the gentle hum of traffic and the occasional *ting* of a bicycle bell.

I step into Beans, where I breathe in the life-giving aroma of coffee. Xander's not here yet, thankfully.

"Josie!" Eddie Callahan, the manager, calls. His classic Southie accent, tattoos, and gruff exterior hide the fact that he's a total softie. "Good mornin', sweetheart. The usual?"

"Yes, please," I say, smiling as I walk up to the counter. "How's the morning rush going?"

"Nearly over, thank god." Eddie motions over his shoulder at a blonde barista, who's struggling with the complicated espresso machine. "You know how it is—you hire someone, hoping to get some help, and it ends up taking ten times as much energy to train 'em." He shakes his head. "I shouldn't complain when you're staffing that place alone seven days a week."

"My sister helps when she can," I say.

Eddie gives me a worried-uncle look. "You're gonna burn yourself out, kid. Let's get you an extra shot of espresso and a cheese croissant. On the house." He winks.

He fusses over me like a mother hen in a way my own mom never did, and his concern unexpectedly makes my throat tighten.

"You're the best," I say.

"That's a fact." Another wink. "I'll have Mabel bring your order. Good luck with the boss man today."

I thank him and turn. Xander's arrived; he's seated at a table next to a man whose back is to me.

"Good morning," I say as I pull up a chair.

Xander—short and balding and with a perpetual irritated frown—gives me a curt nod, then motions between me and the other guy. "I assume you two know each other?"

"No," I say, as the guy turns and says, "Yes."

I blink, confused. He does seem familiar, but I can't place him. He's around my age, with messy brown hair and tortoiseshell glasses. He's wearing a brown cardigan and a pink lanyard stuck all over with colorful pins. I assume the lanyard holds a name tag, but it's flipped around, so that's no help.

Xander is introducing us, but I only snap to attention as he says, "—and this is Josie Klein, who manages Tabula Inscripta."

"I'm so sorry," I say, embarrassed. "I don't remember meeting you before."

This isn't unusual for me—sometimes I'm so deep into a book that even when I'm not reading, my mind is stuck on the story and I can have a whole conversation and hardly remember it.

The guy blinks at me from behind his glasses, a confused smile tugging at his lips. "I manage . . . Happy Endings?"

He points to his right, the opposite side of the coffee shop from my store.

It all clicks, and my stomach drops. He's the tall guy who runs the romance bookstore on the other side of Beans. Eddie once told me he made some comment about how there's "not enough caffeine in the entire coffee shop to keep people awake while reading the books sold at the Tab." Eddie thought it was funny, but it hit a nerve. I grew up being teased about my adoration for books that put everyone else to sleep. And sure, literary fiction isn't everyone's cup of tea, but coming from a fellow bookseller? That stung.

"Oh, right," I say. "The massage place around the corner?"

It's supposed to be a joke, and maybe a little payback, but the man's smile drops abruptly.

"It's a bookstore," he says.

Apparently, this guy can dish it out, but he sure can't take it. Or maybe I'm "not that funny," as I've been told plenty of times. Guess that's what happens when you spend your formative years inhaling books rather than learning how to, you know, people.

"I—I know," I say awkwardly. "You just sell romance."

His jaw tightens, and I realize my error—I didn't mean *just romance* like I'm disparaging the genre, I meant romance is the only genre he sells.

This is going all wrong—I'm operating at peak social awkwardness today; usually I enjoy making connections with other people in the industry.

"Let's start over," I say, sticking my hand out. What did Xander say his name was? Brian? "It's nice to officially meet you, Brian. I'm Josie."

He gives me a tentative shake. His hand is huge, engulfing mine. "I know who you are, and it's—"

"Great, we all know each other," Xander says, interrupting. "But I've called you both here for a reason."

I turn to face him, pull out my notebook, and write the date in the top right corner. I consider writing *BRIAN*, too, so I can commit the name to memory, but I'm worried he'll see it.

"Here you go!" a cheery voice says, and I look up to see the new barista, Mabel. She sets a drink in front of me. "An iced white-chocolate-chunk macchiato with two extra pumps of vanilla, miss."

"Oh, this isn't mine," I say, handing it back to her. "I had an Americano?"

Mabel gasps. "I'm sorry! Eddie said to bring it to this table, I figured since you're the only woman here—"

"It's mine," Brian mumbles.

Xander chuckles. "Should've been obvious—he's the one who works at the girly bookstore."

Mabel scurries off as Brian's ears turn pink. My stomach

clenches. I know how it feels to be on the receiving end of Xander's digs.

"Xander," I say, "that's not—"

"And your coffee order is like your books, right, Josie?" Xander continues, grinning. "Boring and bitter. What'd you call her store, Lawson? A bleak wasteland of existential dread?"

He laughs and nudges Brian, who huffs out a half laugh before stopping himself. But he doesn't correct Xander.

I press my lips together, seething. I won't make the mistake of feeling bad for him again.

Xander's phone buzzes on the table and he answers it, holding up a finger to indicate that we should wait. Then he stands and walks a few steps away, barking into his phone about a construction project.

Mabel reappears with my drink. "Here you go— Americano, no milk, no sugar."

"Thanks," I say.

Brian's lips twitch, like he's trying not to smirk. Probably thinking his good pal Xander really nailed me: *Boring and bitter.*

I know I should ignore him, but this guy is getting to me. So many people see a buttoned-up bookseller and assume I'm timid. But when it comes to defending my store—and the stories within it—I don't hold back.

I face him. "Excuse me?"

"I didn't say anything."

"Well, you sure seem to have an opinion about my coffee choice." *And my books.* "Please, do share."

Brian blinks and licks his lips. "Just wondering . . . does anyone actually enjoy that kind of drink? Or do they order it because"—his eyes flick toward my store—"they think it impresses other people?"

My jaw tightens. I've always believed that book people are the best people, but there's an exception to every rule.

"Maybe I've learned to appreciate complex, nuanced flavors," I say, and take a sip of my Americano. It burns my tongue, and I wince.

His eyebrows lift.

"It's hot," I say, too defensively.

"Okay." He takes a long, long sip of his drink and I suppress a sigh, telling myself not to let him get under my skin.

When Brian sets his cup down, there's a dot of whipped cream on his upper lip. My eyes zero in as his tongue slips out and licks the cream away. Something prickles across my skin, like static electricity.

I shake myself and look away.

"What?" he says.

"Nothing. Just seems like you're really enjoying your drink."

"I am."

"Great. It's important to know what you like, Brian—"

"You have no idea what I like," he says, eyes flashing. "You don't even know my—"

"Can we keep moving?" Xander says, returning to his seat. As if we're the ones who interrupted the meeting.

"Absolutely," I say, picking up my pen again and facing him. The sooner this ends, the sooner I can go back to avoiding Brian. "You had something to talk with us about?"

"Yes," Xander says. "I'm combining your stores and Beans."

Brian chokes on his drink.

I stare at Xander. "Combining . . . *our* stores?"

Xander nods. "It's been my plan all along, and the pieces are finally falling into place. This neighborhood doesn't need two bookstores so close together. It's bad for business, built-in competition."

I'm about to tell him that my clientele is entirely different from that of a romance bookstore, but Xander's still talking.

"And you know what people like to do when they shop for books? Drink coffee. Eddie says customers are always coming here and reading. So I figured, hey, let's combine it all. One big bookstore with a coffee shop in the middle. People can get Harry Potters and parenting books and spy thrillers and sit right down and read them. You know?"

I'm speechless. Appalled. A little nauseated.

Tabula Inscripta has always been a small boutique bookstore focusing on literary fiction and select nonfiction. I spend hours each season curating my selection, just as the prior owner, Jerome, taught me. I imagine his bushy gray eyebrows rising in horror at all these changes.

"But our bookstores are totally different," Brian says.

"Yes, completely different customer bases," I say, nodding. "We're not in competition."

"Well, you'll figure it out," Xander says. "I mean, one of you will."

I blanch. "What?"

"No reason for me to pay two managers for one store."

"So—one of us is out of a job?" Brian sounds horrified.

"Who?" I ask, instantly sick. Xander is a man's man. I know he's going to choose Brian—the two of them already seem chummy.

"I'm not deciding right now," Xander says. "Here's the plan."

He launches into a detailed explanation, and I do my best
to take notes, even though my head is spinning. Construction
will start in a couple of weeks, and the stores will stay open
during the process. Xander anticipates the process taking
three months, and the manager who earns the most profit
during that period will be the manager of the new store. The
other will be looking for a new job.

"So you'll hire either Brian or me, based solely on
financials?" I hate the idea of being judged by profit—if Xander
knew anything about bookselling, he'd know that owning an
indie bookstore will *never* make him rich—but at least it's an
objective measure.

Brian frowns. "It's actually—"

"Exactly," Xander interrupts. "I anticipate making my
decision by Labor Day."

I sneak a glance at Brian. I can't get a bead on him. The
cardigan, lanyard, and tortoiseshell glasses are giving "small-
town librarian," which isn't a terrible vibe for a bookseller. The
messy hair, I'll admit, bothers me; he can't take the time to
comb his hair before work? But maybe that's a good thing—
maybe he's a mess in other aspects of his life, including his
managerial skills.

Brian's eyes flick over to meet mine. My skin prickles again.
Behind his glasses, his eyes are warm golden brown, like dark
honey, and my stomach coils tight with the strangest sensation.
For one split second, I get a flash of us sitting at this table, each
with a coffee and a book, reading together.

Ha. No way—he'd probably make snarky comments about
my book being better than Ambien.

Plus, he's my competition.

Brian shifts his weight, which makes his lanyard slip

forward, revealing some of the colorful pins. They say things like MORALLY GRAY >>>, BOOK WHORE, IN MY SMUT ERA, SPREAD THOSE PAGES.

And one that I cannot for the life of me understand: STFUATTDLAGG.

Focus, I tell myself. This man has disparaged my books, my store, and my personality. Now he could end up with my job? Everything I've worked for in the past five years, the reputation I've built, the clientele I've cultivated—all my goals for the future are riding on this. I've pulled myself out of the humiliating hole of my past to create a career I'm proud of.

I can't let this guy take that away.

At least my chances of winning are decent. I mean, how many books could a romance bookstore sell, anyway?

2

Ryan

SHE'S CALLED ME Brian three times.

Make that four.

I always figured Josie—see, I know *her* name—didn't like me. She gives me the cold shoulder every time I see her at Beans. Acts like she doesn't know who I am.

Maybe it's not an act?

Which would be crazy. She's worked at the Tab almost as long as I've been running Happy Endings. I know she orders an Americano with three shots of espresso in the morning and herbal tea in the afternoon. And a cookie if she's having a bad day.

Although, TBH, it always looks like she's having a bad day.

Maybe her bun is too tight. I get the sense Josie never lets her hair down—literally or figuratively. I don't think I've ever seen her without a thick book in her hands. It's like she carts them around to make sure everyone knows she's Smart with a capital *S*.

It's obvious she is. She's also really pretty, in an unapproachable, ice-queen way. Dark hair and sharp green eyes, wearing heels so high they could be used as shivs.

Which is why I've never had the balls to talk to her.

And I probably won't have the chance to ever again after Xander's comment. I did *not* describe her bookstore as "a bleak wasteland of existential dread." I said her bookstore is bleak—an objective fact—and her books fill *me* with existential dread. Also true.

Okay, so maybe that's not any better. I still wish I'd corrected him.

"I'm glad you two are being good sports about this," Xander says.

Josie has her arms crossed over her chest, her jaw clenched tight. I can't tell if she's scowling or trying to hold back tears.

"Doesn't seem like we have a choice," I say.

Xander laughs as if I've made a joke. This whole meeting feels like a joke, and we're the punch line. I can picture him with his smug grin, lying naked in a California king bed, counting his money and thinking of ways to make his monkeys dance.

I don't want to dance for him or anyone else, and I don't want to compete against Josie for our jobs. I wish there was a way we could both win and no one would lose their store.

But the world isn't all happy endings, dickwad.

I shake my head, trying to clear my older brothers' words from my mind. They'd probably be happy to see me lose and get a more "masculine" job, one that won't make them question my sexuality or the fact that I'm single.

The store must be crawling with hotties.

If I were you, I'd be banging a different customer every day.

Sometimes it blows my mind that we grew up in the same

house with the same parents and ended up with such different
ideas about love and sex.

"All right, then." Xander scoots his chair back so abruptly it
screeches against the floor. Josie cringes, revealing a dimple
I've never noticed. She really is pretty, even when she's upset.
"May the best bookseller win."

And with that, he's off.

I turn back to Josie, hoping for a moment of shared
commiseration, but she's eyeing me like *I'm* the enemy.

I should say something to break the tension, but I don't
have a clever bone in my giant, awkward body. Especially
around a woman who's as intimidating as she is striking. *The
Hating Game* comes to mind, and I wonder what Josh
Templeman might say to Lucy Hutton in this situation. But I'm
no Josh, and I don't have Sally Thorne drafting my dialogue.

My silence seems to annoy Josie even more. She stands in
a huff and hurries back to her store, leaving me with a table
full of dirty dishes and a familiar, soul-deep discomfort.

Growing up as the youngest of four boys, *everything* was a
competition. Who could eat the most the fastest, who could
hit the hardest, who could pee the farthest from the toilet
bowl. Who was the oldest (that one didn't make any sense).

I came in last for every single one.

Not that I ever really tried to win. I've always gotten more
pleasure from doing an activity than coming in first. What was
there to even win? Bragging rights?

Now, though, the stakes couldn't be higher.

I glance at the wall dividing my store from the coffee shop,
which currently displays artwork for sale by local artists. I try
to picture it gone, seeing right through to Happy Endings,

looking in on my employees, all blissfully unaware that everything is about to change.

Eddie and the new girl both look busy, so I bus the table and leave the dirty dishes on the counter before leaving.

THE BELL ON the front door of Happy Endings chimes as I enter, and a wave of nostalgia hits me. Elaine, the store's original owner and my first and only boss, created this little corner of the world to be a haven for the tenderhearted: those who love love but don't always feel deserving of it. She'd be proud of how we've grown, carrying the books to back up our motto—Everyone deserves a love story.

If Happy Endings closes . . . No other bookstore in Boston carries such a diverse selection of romance. Our customers won't have anywhere to browse without judgment, to sit and read in cozy nooks, to connect with themselves and each other.

There's so much at stake, and not just for me.

"Boss!" my assistant manager shouts, even though I'm steps away from her.

"Cindy!" I say back in mock excitement. Her eyebrows furrow, and I realize my mistake. "Cinderella!"

For the life of me, I can't get used to calling my buxom, middle-aged, bottle-bright-red-haired assistant manager Cinderella. And it's not like she identifies as a humble, hardworking woman waiting for her prince—she just got a free name change after her divorce was final. Most people, I assume, change back to their original name, but Cinderella isn't most people.

"I got you something," she says, her eyes sparkling.

Cinderella places a light blue pin on my open palm with such tenderness you'd think she was handing over the Heart of the Ocean.

The white letters read: NONPRACTICING ROMANTIC.

"Get it?" Her smile lights up her face. "You'd be a practicing romantic if you ever went on a date."

"How about I'll start dating when you do?"

Cinderella blushes and shakes her head. I don't think she's been on a single date in the seven years since her divorce—right about the time she started coming into the store. Every day, she'd sit in a nook and read, crying over the happy endings. She treated her book therapy like a job, and eventually we gave her one.

I don't regret hiring Cinderella, but I do regret telling her I loved the BOSS BITCH pin she gifted me on her first day. Last I counted, I had nearly two hundred pieces of "flair." I fear the day she gives me a second lanyard.

"I saw the pin on a customer's jacket and knew it was meant for you," Cinderella says. "She didn't want to part with it, but she finally agreed to a little barter."

Persephone purrs at my feet until I pick her up. She always seems to know when I could use cheering up—unlike Hades, who keeps his distance unless I pop a can of tuna.

"A barter?" I ask, afraid to hear the details.

Cinderella shrugs. "I gave her the ARC of Ali Hazelwood's next book. I figured since we'd both read it already . . ."

"Absolutely," I say, grateful she didn't trade a book we could've sold. This penny-counting stuff is new for me—we're going to have to step it up. Tighten our bootstraps. Our belts?

Whatever the metaphor, we need to do better than Josie's store and all their hardcover books with price tags as big as their authors' vocabularies. With those profit margins, she'll only have to sell half what we will.

The bell on the front door chimes, and two regular customers walk in, laughing and smiling.

"Hey, handsome." Michael is dressed as himself today, not as his alter ego, Ginger, the star of our monthly Drag Queen Story Time for teens. "I'm ready for a new book boyfriend."

"I know just the guy!"

And with that, I switch gears and do what I do best: match readers with stories to help them realize they deserve the kind of love people write books about.

SEVEN HOURS LATER, I'm headed home, having finally finished my closing duties, including vacuuming up all the crumbs the teenagers left after camping out all afternoon in "their" reading nook.

Not that I minded. The busywork kept me from ruminating over worst-case scenarios.

Instinctively, I slow down outside Josie's store. I can see her through the window, her hair still in that severe bun, head bent over a book. I'm tempted to go inside and ask what she's reading, but I'm probably the last person she wants to talk to.

It's just . . . she looks so lonely in there.

Or maybe that's because the store is so sterile and organized it feels more like a museum than a bookstore. I shiver at the thought of her taking over Happy Endings and destroying the inclusive, beautiful selection of novels I've worked so hard to curate.

Across the street, a group of drunk college students pile out of an Uber, making enough noise to wake the dead. And attract Josie's attention.

I look away a beat too late, and as I hurry toward the Davis Square T stop, I try not to think about her sad, beautiful green eyes.

It doesn't work. I'm still thinking about them when I get home to my studio apartment in Charlestown. I pour a big glass of wine and break into the "better than sex" cookies a customer brought me today.

Desperate for a distraction, I grab my laptop and open BookFriends, the review site for booksellers and librarians. At first, I didn't understand the strict anonymity rules, but after a popular YA author made homophobic jokes at one of my events, I realized how grateful I was for a place where I could share a warning without fear of blowback.

But my favorite thing about BookFriends is the reviews people share. It reaffirms the saying that there's a lid for every pot. What one person thinks is pure drivel is another's literary masterpiece.

There's one woman whose reviews I always look forward to. BookshopGirl reads big books like the ones Josie sells. But BSG (as I think of her) isn't a snob. Her reviews are thoughtful and inquisitive; I can tell she puts a lot of time into them.

A couple months ago, we had a lively discussion on a thread about Lily King's *Writers & Lovers*—one of the few books we've both read. The question at hand: Can a book be both literary and a romance novel? My answer was one hundred percent unequivocally yes, and after much cajoling, I got her to agree.

Someone commented and told us to "get a room"—so we

did. BSG started a private message chain, and we've been chatting regularly since. In the spirit of the site, we haven't shared our names, locations, or any other personal information. Although it doesn't get more personal than sharing the books you love.

I'm relieved to see a green dot by her name; she's online. I pull up our chat and pick up where our last conversation left off: What page are you on now?

> **BookshopGirl:** 376.

> **RJ.Reads:** So you're what? Halfway done?

> **BookshopGirl:** More like two-thirds. I've got about 150 left.

I shake my head. A few romance novels have left me wanting more, but not three hundred pages more.

Good book? I ask, feeling the tension in my shoulders finally start to dissipate.

> **BookshopGirl:** Technically speaking, yes. The prose is beautiful and the characters are well developed.

> **RJ.Reads:** And not technically speaking?

> **BookshopGirl:** The author is a bit pretentious—but I know that from

personal experience, so I'm trying to
keep an open mind about the book.

RJ.Reads: How diplomatic of you.

BookshopGirl: I try. How about you?
What page are you on?

RJ.Reads: Page zero. Finished an ARC on
the way home and haven't picked my
next book yet. Got a suggestion for me?

BookshopGirl: Hmmm.

As I watch the three dots appear and disappear, I smile at
the prospect of reading a book of BSG's choice. Based on the
books on her Favorites shelf, it might take me the whole
summer to read whatever she picks, but I can always get an
audio copy. Or I can do what I did during my remedial English
classes in high school—google reviews and cobble together
enough information to make it sound like I read the book.

Not my proudest moments.

The dots stop, then start again. I'm on the edge of my seat.

BookshopGirl: Sorry, my sister called.
I've got to run, but I'll get back to you
soon on a five-star book. Goodnight!

And with that, her green light turns red, and I'm left
wondering what BookshopGirl's eyes look like. If they sparkle
like Cinderella's, or if they're sad and lonely like Josie's.

BOOKFRIENDS

May 22, 6:47 AM

BookshopGirl: Morning! I hardly slept last night, and unfortunately I don't have a book rec for you yet, but I can share a controversial opinion inspired by recent events.

RJ.Reads: Ooh, do tell.

BookshopGirl: Books are better than people. There, I said it. Literature >>> humanity.

BookshopGirl: Now, before you think I'm a total misanthrope, I'm not saying books are better than ALL people. And it's not like I'd throw a person in front of a moving train to save a book.

RJ.Reads: But would you throw a book in front of a train to save a person?

BookshopGirl: Hmmm, depends on the person. And on the book. (Kidding. Mostly.)

BookshopGirl: I mean, I've never met a Barbara Kingsolver novel that let me down—or a person who didn't, at least a little.

RJ.Reads: I get that (though for me it's Abby Jimenez novels).

BookshopGirl: Books are more dependable than people. They don't stab you in the back, they don't gossip about you or insult you. Also, bonus— they won't judge you for spending the whole day in pajamas crying over the death of a character.

RJ.Reads: Or for laughing out loud in the middle of a funeral (which people definitely judge. Ask me how I know).

BookshopGirl: You read during funerals?

RJ.Reads: Just once. In my defense, it was my great-great-aunt's, and she was 102.

BookshopGirl: I'm not judging. I'm impressed.

BookshopGirl: That's another great thing about books: they're always there for you, and they'll never get sick of your company.

RJ.Reads: They'll also never complain about being ignored when life gets stressful or overwhelming.

BookshopGirl: Exactly! No matter how long it's been, books are waiting with open pages, ready to whisk you away on an adventure or comfort you after a rough day. People may come and go from your life, but books? Books are forever.

RJ.Reads: Amen to that.

3

Josie

GROWING UP, COUNTLESS well-meaning adults urged me to get my "nose out of that book" and go outside to "experience real life." But from what I've seen, reality is vastly overrated.

My earliest memory is of reading *Where the Wild Things Are* to my sister, trying to drown out my mom's shouting match with her latest boyfriend—I couldn't even sound out all the words, but I needed to take us somewhere, anywhere, that was magical instead of messy. By second grade, when playground dynamics started to feel way too complicated, I'd spend recess lost in the pages of a chapter book. For my eleventh birthday, I invited my entire class to a Readathon party—I even reserved a room at the local library—but no one showed up. I stayed anyway, grateful for the librarians who always welcomed me. When I got to high school, I longed to go to the football games and parties everyone talked about, but I was usually home babysitting my sister. Mom wasn't exactly reliable, so someone had to be—but hey, at least I had books to keep me company.

For better or worse, my library has always grown faster than my social circle.

Managing a bookstore has forced me out of my shell, helping me grow from a shy bookworm into someone who can confidently navigate conversations and recommendations—at least, in the safety of these shelves. Out in the world, I may be quiet and reserved, but here, I've found my voice.

Except now, Xander Laing has put all that at risk.

But it's not just *my* future, my livelihood—it's the customers I've served for five years. Like Beatrice Glaybold, who moved down to Florida but trusts me to send her any book I think will strike her fancy, or Michael Liu, who writes a literary column for the *Boston Herald* and bases his reading on *my* recommendations. Or James Kendall, who lost his wife last year and comes in weekly to buy a new book and chat.

If I lose this job, I lose them, too—and we all lose the store, this quiet refuge of words and stories.

When the bell on the front door chimes, I'm sitting in the back room of the shop, surrounded by boxes I haven't opened. All I can do is stare into the middle distance while panic churns in my stomach.

A voice calls, "It's me!" and a huge sigh of relief rushes out of my lungs. It's my little sister (for her, I'd throw every book I own in front of a moving train—plus myself, for good measure).

"I'm in the back!" I call.

The front door closes, followed by the familiar *step-step-tap* as she makes her way across the polished wood floor.

"I brought rugelach," Georgia says. She sets her cane against the desk, puts down a white to-go bag from Mamaleh's in Cambridge, and finally her backpack. She's heading to class at Tufts after this, and I feel a pinch of envy.

"Thank you, dear sister," I say, grabbing one of the pastries.

Georgia takes a bite, too, and we chew in silence. It tastes like buttery chocolate comfort. Our neighbor, Mrs. Goldstein, would bring rugelach over when our mom was having one of her "hard times"—though I doubt she had any idea how scary things could get. Georgia and I have kept up the tradition, buying it whenever one of us has a bad day.

My sister is a more relaxed, optimistic version of me, with the dark hair and green eyes we got from our dad (before he skipped out of our lives when I was five and Georgia was a baby)—but my sister's hair is loose and wild, curling from the early summer humidity. We both have the soft curves we inherited from our mom, but I'm in a tailored pencil skirt, while she's wearing a floral dress that flutters to the floor, partially obscuring the brace on her right leg. She's fearless and unguarded and fun—my opposite.

"So . . ." she says. "Didn't sleep much?"

I grimace; she's also *too* perceptive. Ever since she started graduate school in psychology, she's adopted a new tone that sneaks out when we're talking. Concerned; professional. Like she's trying to burrow into my brain and analyze me.

"I'm stressed," I say. "But I've been brainstorming ways to win this competition."

Georgia picks up my notebook and reads: "Number one: Cut expenses. Number two: Sell more books." She raises an eyebrow. "I hate to break it to you, Jojo, but those aren't exactly actionable strategies."

"I know," I say, sighing.

"How are you going to cut expenses? You already run this place pretty lean."

She's right. Since my part-timers left, I've been doing it all: buying, receiving, and stocking; paying the utilities; managing the website. I even clean the toilet in the back room. Georgia helps out, but she won't let me pay her. She says she "owes me for saving her life," which isn't technically true, though I appreciate the thought. What she doesn't know is that I set aside what I would have paid her in an account she can use if and when she needs it.

"And how are you going to increase your sales during the summer?" she continues. "That's not a big season for literary fiction."

Again, she's right. This time of year, people want beach reads: light, engaging, easily digestible. I get it—sometimes people just want to unwind. What's-his-name at Happy Endings probably sells a boatload of books in the summer.

(Brian, I remind myself. Brian, who wears cardigans and weird pins and hates my bookstore. Brian, the man who has been given the power by *another* man to ruin my life.)

"Why couldn't this happen in the fall?" I say. My highest season for sales—aside from the holidays—is September through November, when publishers release their most anticipated titles. "I'd be unbeatable."

"Maybe you should lean into that," Georgia says. "Target people who prefer reading books that require you to have a dictionary on hand?"

She's teasing me, but it's not a bad idea. "Maybe I could host a literary salon where people can discuss books they're reading?"

A banging sound distracts us: someone knocking on the

glass door of the store. When I step out of the back room, a man is peering in the window. He waves, so I head to the door and open it a crack, trying not to let the AC escape (Strategy 1: Cut expenses).

"Hi there, we're not open yet—"

"I need to return a book." He's the picture of impatience—crisp suit, shiny shoes, probably on his way to a Very Important Meeting—and I decide it's easier to do the return than tell him to come back later. He's not a regular customer, but if he has a good experience, maybe he'll become one (Strategy 2: Sell more books).

I give him my most welcoming smile. "Of course. Come on in."

He follows me to the register and plunks the book down. It's the latest Oprah's Book Club choice; I've sold dozens of copies.

"I'll just need your receipt," I say.

He frowns. "It was a gift."

"I'm sorry, but we only accept returns or exchanges with receipts." I point toward the printed sign next to my register.

"You have copies of the same book right there." He nods at the display. "Can't you refund me your current selling price?"

I smile and stick to my guns, repeating the policy.

He exhales in frustration. "Where's your manager?"

"I'm the manager, actually."

Cue the usual response: eyeing me suspiciously as the wheels turn in his mind. *This small, young woman cannot have any sort of actual influence or authority.* I am in fact thirty years old and of average height, but I was cursed with a baby face that makes me look at least five years younger—which is why I dress professionally and always wear my hair up.

"I mean the head manager," he says. "Is he here?"

My smile freezes. "You're looking at her."

He huffs. "This is ridiculous. The book was—" He flips open the cover and points. "Twenty-nine ninety-nine! Plus tax! That's an absurd amount of money for a book."

My jaw tightens. The foil accents on the dust jacket, the deckled edges on the paper . . . it's a freaking work of art! This man clearly has no appreciation for the craftsmanship that goes into creating a beautiful hardcover.

"Sir, I don't set the prices, but—"

"I want a refund. Now. I don't have time to argue with a checkout girl. Understand?"

The words are a swift kick to my chest. I'm proud of what I do; my job is so much more than running a register.

"Oh, I understand," I say, my smile disappearing. "But if I give you twenty-nine ninety-nine—plus tax!—for a book that may not have been purchased here—"

"It was—"

"Even if I do sell it at some point, I won't make any profit. Furthermore . . ." I take off the dust jacket and inspect the book; the spine is visibly cracked. "This book has been read."

"That's not—"

"So technically speaking, it's not in sellable condition." My hands shake as I hand it back to him, but I keep my voice calm and cool. "If I give you twenty-nine ninety-nine plus tax for this unsellable book, I will lose that money. And if I do that for other customers, I will not be able to afford to keep the lights on and replace the paper rolls in my register and pay my own meager wages, and eventually this store will close, and you, sir, will have contributed to the demise of one of Boston's most beloved literary establishments, a store that has stood in this spot and served this community for over sixty years."

He's flustered, pink in the face, and for a moment I think he's going to start yelling . . .

But then he wheels around and stomps away. Before leaving, he turns back and shouts, "I will never set foot in this store again!"

"We'll miss you terribly," I say.

"Bitch," he mutters.

My stomach bottoms out, but he's already gone.

Behind me, my sister slow-claps. "That dude just got Josie'd," she says, grinning. "It's been a while since I've seen that."

She must not have heard the last thing he said. I sigh, trying to shake off the nastiness of that final insult. I hate that I'm now questioning myself, wondering if *I* was rude. It's a constant tightrope act, running a business as a woman, wanting to be respected for my abilities but knowing that no one will take me seriously unless I'm *nice*.

"He was just . . ."

"Oh, he deserved it," she says. "But if you have the emotional energy, it may be useful to explore why you react like that when people disparage your career."

"Because it's incredibly rude!" Though of course, it's much more than that. It's the fear that maybe they're right, that I'll never amount to anything of importance and I don't deserve this job anyway.

"Yes," Georgia says, "*and* maybe it's a wound you haven't fully healed yet?"

I purse my lips and remind myself that I am absolutely, positively thrilled that my sister is studying what she loves.

"You know what? I think it's time for coffee," I say, and head out into the early morning sunshine.

BEANS IS BUSTLING. Eddie's new hire, Mabel, takes my order (an Americano for me, a dirty iced chai for Georgia), smiling nervously as she promises to get it right this time.

"Is she scared of me?" I ask Eddie, who's wiping down a table.

"No, she's scared of *me*. I gave her a lecture about not assuming someone's gender based on their coffee order." He gives me a concerned look. "You okay?"

I slump into a chair, the word *bitch* crawling around my mind like an ugly spider. "I had a terrible customer."

"Already? You're not even open!"

"I know!" I tell him the story, and he looks appalled. "It just felt so . . . belittling. Xander does the same thing."

Eddie gives my shoulder a sympathetic squeeze. "Try not to let the bastards get to ya."

Something occurs to me. "Wait—how does Xander's plan affect Beans?"

He shrugs. "My guess is I'll be working under the head manager."

I hear the disappointment in his voice. Eddie enjoys being in charge as much as I do.

"If I win, I'll make sure you get to keep running it the way you want."

He hesitates a beat too long before saying, "Thanks, darling."

Hang on. Does he not think I'm going to win?

"Eddie," I say, leaning forward, "what do you—"

"Oh, would you look at that line—I better help Mabel before she dissolves into tears."

He rushes back to the register, and I sit back, stung. Eddie's my friend—and he underestimates me, too? Maybe he knows something I don't. He's like the Mayor of Davis Square, keeping tabs on everything. He sees how many people go into Brian's store compared to mine and how many walk out with purchases. Meanwhile, I don't know much about Happy Endings. All I know is that the clientele is mostly women (judging by the customers I've seen holding the store's pink-and-gold bags), and I think the employees are, too.

"Josie?"

I stand and run smack into a solid chest. A hand grips my arm to steady me. I look up; it's Brian.

He's shockingly tall this close—even with my four-inch heels, he towers over me. I have to tilt my chin way up, giving me a view of his jaw, covered in light brown flecks of stubble. The heat of his hand gripping my arm radiates through the sleeve of my blouse.

"Excuse me," I say, taking a step back.

He releases me and clears his throat. "Sorry. I was . . . uh, hoping we could chat?"

Today, Brian's wearing a gray cardigan, along with his pin-studded lanyard and tortoiseshell glasses. His hair's still a mess, though if he was a hero in a romance novel it would probably be described as *flowing chestnut locks that partially obscure the piercing gaze of his mahogany eyes.*

I'm not sure what he wants, but I'm not having this conversation while he's looking down on me.

"Sure," I say. "Let's sit."

He seems surprised, but nods, and we both pull out chairs.

My eyes catch on another pin on his lanyard: WHEN I THINK
ABOUT BOOKS, I TOUCH MY SHELF.

It takes me a moment to get it. When I do, the song by the
Divinyls starts playing in my head, sparking a memory: my
mom, dancing around the kitchen, deep in the throes of
another love affair with another man she swore was the One.
Little Georgia, dancing along, hope sparkling in her eyes.
Forgetting that in a few weeks, this boyfriend would dump our
mom and she'd be back in bed, crying with the curtains
drawn, forgetting that her two young daughters needed meals,
clean laundry, and help with homework.

Shaking that away, I refocus on Brian. He's staring at me,
his eyes drifting across my face like I'm a book he's reading.

A *boring, bitter* book.

"You wanted to talk?" I say.

He blinks. "Oh, yeah. About this whole Xander thing. I
mean, there's no reason for us to be enemies."

"Agree," I say, though I'm wary. I'd love to feel like we're on
the same side, united by mutual loathing of our evil boss.
Unfortunately, it seems that Xander and Brian are bros, united
in their mutual scorn of *me*.

*What'd you call her store, Lawson? A bleak wasteland of
existential dread?*

"Great, that's great," Brian is saying. "Because, um, after
Xander combines the stores, it's going to be a lot to manage
and—and it's going to require a lot of work."

"Yes," I say, unsure what he's getting at. Does he think I'm
not capable of it?

"I've been trying to think of what I could do . . ." He
brushes his hair out of his eyes, hesitating. "So you aren't out
of a job when—"

"What do you mean, *when*?" My voice squeaks on the last word.

"I mean, *if*," he corrects quickly.

"You said *when*." I swallow the surge of dread. Did Xander say something to him? Maybe this whole competition is a farce and Brian's already got it in the bag? "Word choice matters."

"It was a slip of the tongue."

"A Freudian slip, maybe."

He blinks at me from behind his glasses. "Well, I apologize."

He doesn't sound apologetic. He sounds irritated, which isn't fair—he's the one who implied I was going to lose.

Exhaling, I glance at my phone. Almost time to open. "Thanks for the chat, Brian, but I—"

"STOP CALLING ME THAT."

I rear back, shocked. "Excuse me?"

He mumbles something I don't catch.

"Hmm?" I say.

"Ryan," he says more clearly. "My name? It's . . ."

He turns the lanyard around: RYAN LAWSON. MANAGER, HAPPY ENDINGS.

My cheeks heat with embarrassment. I've been calling him the wrong name for *days*.

But before I can apologize, he stands. He's looming over me, a mountain of a man, and I scramble to my feet and try to muster a confidence I do not feel. "Is there anything else?"

"Yes, if you'd let me finish." He huffs out a frustrated sigh. "All I'm trying to say is that *if* I win . . ." He bites his lip, then blurts, "You could be my assistant."

Indignation sparks through me. "Your *assistant*?"

"I mean, I could hire you as an assistant manager so you

wouldn't be out of a job." The expression on his face is all, *See what a nice guy I am?*

"Wow, that's great," I say.

"Yeah?" His eyebrows lift.

"I mean, you're the man, you should be the boss."

"Uh . . ."

"And all us little women should work for you, right?" I'm gathering steam, letting the frustration I didn't unleash on that awful customer surge out of me. "I bet that's why you love managing a bookstore. Hordes of women asking you to tell them what to read? And hey, if those books happen to reinforce the message that women aren't complete without a man, that's a bonus! Patriarchy at its finest."

"I . . ."

I step closer, poking a finger at his chest, saying what I wish I could say to every single person who has ever underestimated me.

"I'll never be your assistant, Mr. Happy Endings. And you'd better polish up your resume, because I'm going to win this battle. And the first thing I'll do? Fire you."

With that, I turn and walk off.

I wish saying all that made me feel better. Instead, I'm left feeling like no matter what I do, if I stay silent or stay in control or let everything out, I'll always end up in the wrong.

4

Ryan

WHAT IN THE ever-loving hell was that?

I'm blinking at the spot where Josie stood just seconds ago. I thought she'd be happy to know she wouldn't lose her job, even if she lost Xander's stupid competition.

The last thing I meant to imply was that I think she's beneath me.

Cue my brothers' voices in my head, suggesting that very thing: Josie, beneath me.

Fat chance of that happening. The fact that her eyes sparkle like emeralds when she's angry and she smells like a lavender field on a rainy day is irrelevant. I have no doubt that if Josie Klein could summon lightning like Violet Sorrengail, I'd be a pile of ashes on the floor.

If she'd given me a second to explain, maybe she'd realize I'm not the enemy, Xander is. I'm the one person who understands that our jobs mean so much more than a paycheck, that we'd be lost, rudderless, without our bookstores.

It's true for me, and I bet it's true for Josie, too. She's *always* at the Tab, from open to close seven days a week. Other than that young woman with the bedazzled cane, I never see anyone helping her. Another advantage: her profit margins won't take the hit of any staff salaries.

I think of my employees and sigh. I can't protect them from this news much longer. After all, they might be back on the job market come September.

"Don't take all that with Josie personally," Eddie says from behind the coffee bar.

My cheeks burn; of course he saw the whole thing. Everyone in here probably got a kick out of seeing that spitfire of a woman dress down the giant, awkward dude.

"Yeah," I say, trying to brush it off. "That was something."

"She's got her reasons for being prickly," Eddie says. "Try and give her a break."

"Give *her* a break?" I repeat. "She's the one who accosted me."

"She had to overcome a lot to get here." Eddie sounds oddly protective, and I don't get it.

"What do you mean?"

Eddie shakes his head and starts wiping the counter. "Not my story to tell. I only know the bare bones, anyway." He gives me a long, hard look. "Just . . . don't give me any reason to spit in your drink, 'kay?"

"Okay," I agree, wondering who or what Josie had to overcome.

Stop being such a pussy. My brothers' voices are back.

But they're right. Josie Klein may not be my enemy, but she is my competition.

And it's about damn time I start acting like it.

"THE LAST TIME we had an emergency meeting, you told us Elaine had died," Cinderella says, her voice pitchy with nerves.

"No one's dead," I say, locking the door and switching the sign from OPEN to CLOSED. I sent out an all-staff email this afternoon, asking everyone to come by before closing.

Hearing Elaine's name summons up an image so clear, it's almost as if my old boss is beside me, people-watching the couples walking by and predicting who'll be getting lucky and who'll be left with blue balls.

Elaine was a walking contradiction—she looked like a grandmother but swore like a sailor. She had a take-no-shit attitude that made me believe her when she said everything would be okay. It was true back when I was fifteen and she caught me shoplifting, and it was true the day she told me she was retiring and leaving the store in my "strong, manly hands."

I still wonder what she saw in me: a lost, lonely teen who claimed to hate the very books he tried to steal. Of course, I didn't hate them. I hated that I had such a hard time reading them.

Who knew reading out loud to a parrot named Esmerelda who had a thing for romance novels—the smuttier the better—could change all that?

Elaine, apparently.

"But it's bad news, right?" Cinderella says, settling into the worn leather couch where she spends a good chunk of time reading, on and off the clock.

"It's news," I say, taking a seat on the purple wingback chair, commonly referred to as Persephone's throne. The cat is here now, perched on top, a paw resting on my head as if she's anointing me. "And I'll tell you more as soon as we get through the fishbowl."

I'm met with a collective groan, even from Indira, who confided in me that she secretly loves these icebreakers. Personally, I'm not crazy about them, but I'm not about to mess with Elaine's traditions.

"Nora, why don't you do the honors?"

I pass the glass bowl to our senior staff member, who works one shift a week. Nora is seventy-nine and resembles a stylish Mrs. Claus with a snowy white bob. She claims to work for the employee discount, but I think it gives her an excuse to binge-read historical romance.

Nora sets aside her crochet project and reaches into the bowl, pulling out a folded slip of paper.

"Share your anti-kink: something that turns you off in an otherwise good romance novel." She looks up, her eyes twinkling. "Mine is when they make elderly characters out to be sexless. We might need a little blue pill or some good lube, but we're not dead yet! Eliza?"

We all turn and look at Eliza, who is going to be a senior—in high school. Her cheeks are flushed, either from the mental image of horny grandparents or from her soccer scrimmage. She came here straight from the field.

"My anti-kink is when YA authors talk down to readers," Eliza says. "Like we couldn't possibly understand the complexities of love and sex."

"But you don't read YA," Cinderella says.

"Exactly," Eliza says before passing the question to Indira.

"This one's easy." Indira's voice is loud and clear as she says, "Arranged marriage."

We all nod, understanding her complicated feelings toward the Indian tradition that brought her parents, grandparents, and great-grandparents together. Indira hasn't said so directly, but I have a feeling one of the reasons she dresses in black, from her lipstick down to her combat boots, is to make herself less appealing to all the "aunties" looking to marry her off.

"My anti-kink is stories with men who cheat," Cinderella says, "even if it's just a setup to get the heroine into the arms of the hero. There's enough of that in real life, you know?"

We do. Even the IT guy who comes in every few months is familiar with Cinderella's tale of woe.

I'm up next, and I consider giving a fluff answer, but decide to be as vulnerable as my staff. Elaine knew what she was doing when she started this tradition; sharing literary preferences can reveal a person's own story, the scars they're trying to heal.

"I've got two," I say, pushing my hair out of my face. "First is the whole tall-man fetish—what's the big deal about a few extra inches?" The women on my staff make eyes at each other. "Don't answer that."

"What's your other one?" Nora asks, looking up from the tiny animal she's crocheting—it looks like a meerkat.

"This might be controversial," I warn, "but nothing pulls me out of a story more than an enemies-to-lovers trope."

Everyone gasps; this is blasphemy.

"It normalizes toxic behavior and romanticizes serious issues that shouldn't be glossed over," I say, while the others groan and roll their eyes. "Hear me out: if someone's really your enemy, you wouldn't fall in love with them. It's not plausible."

"But monster sex is?" Cinderella says.

"Or vampires and werewolves?" Indira adds.

"I can suspend some disbelief. And sure, enemies can have

hot hate sex—but if they're really enemies . . ." My mind drifts to Josie's fiery eyes, and I shiver. "Feelings that deep don't change. Love is love and hate is hate."

Cinderella harrumphs, and I have a feeling she's already making a mental list of her favorite enemies-to-lovers books to change my mind.

But as fun as this interlude has been, I called this meeting for a reason.

The mood in the room deflates as I fill my staff in on everything: the competition, the profit goal; how at the end of the day, only one manager will be left standing.

"What does that mean for us?" Cinderella asks, a slight wobble to her voice.

"If Josie wins, I can't promise what she'll do. If she'll keep everyone on, or if she'll want to hire her own staff."

Silence settles over my group of misfit booklovers.

"It's going to be okay," I say, attempting to channel Elaine's unwavering optimism. "We'll find a way to finish on top."

"That's what she said," Nora quips, and the tension is replaced with laughter.

For everyone but Cinderella. "What are we *actually* going to do?" she asks.

"We're going to sell as many books as we can," I say, hoping I sound more confident than I feel. Elaine had a *Field of Dreams* strategy—if you stock the books, the readers will come. It's always worked for us.

"But how . . ." Cinderella prods.

"Let's brainstorm," I say. "See what we can come up with together." It's got to be better than what my head came up with alone: pretty much nothing.

Persephone slinks down the chair and settles in my lap,

nudging my hand with her head. I run my fingers through her soft coat, grateful I decided to keep Elaine's cats around despite all the shedding.

"My soccer team had a bake sale last month," Eliza suggests.

If only that wouldn't compete with Beans. But since nothing kills a brainstorm faster than a Negative Nancy, I give her an encouraging smile.

"I'll take notes," Indira says, reaching for the journal she's always scribbling in. I know her MFA classmates give her flak for working at a romance bookstore. They'd probably respect her more if she worked at Josie's store—but Josie doesn't have a staff.

Apparently, she doesn't need anyone. She can do it all herself.

I'm ashamed of the *na-na-boo-boo* tone in my head; this competition is already bringing out the worst in me.

"We could host more author events?" Nora suggests.

"So many people bring books they bought online," Indira says, shaking her head. "It's like they don't realize bookstores need to make money to stay in business."

I nod—we had forty people show up to our last author event but only sold twelve books.

"What if we hosted different kinds of events?" Cinderella says.

"Weddings!" Eliza lights up, but Indira effusively shakes her head.

"One word," she says. "Bridezillas."

"How about funerals?" Nora suggests. "The customers can't complain if they're unalive."

Everyone titters except Cinderella, who looks as if she's actually at a funeral. "Can we please take this seriously? The future of Happy Endings is at stake!"

"We've got three months and a lot of good ideas," I say. "Let's keep them coming, okay?"

"I've seen some cute romance-themed crochet patterns," Nora says, holding up her half-finished creature. "I could make some for us to sell."

"What about blind date books?" Indira suggests. "I could write poems using the tropes!"

"Ooh—we could host a safe sex night!" Eliza says. "Sex ed at school is so lame—it would be great to discuss consent and protection. And we could feature books showcasing that."

"Maybe a panel with sex experts?" Nora says. "Like the author of that *Tickle His Pickle* book."

That derails us into a lengthy conversation about what makes someone a sex expert—whether it's the actual having of sex or the scientific knowledge—until Indira gets us back on track, suggesting, "What about a 'good vibes' night, where we give away a vibrator with every book?"

"We're trying to make money, not give it away," Cinderella says, wrinkling her brow.

"Maybe we can get a company to donate them," Nora says. "It would be good advertising for them, and it's not like people only need one vibrator."

Everyone agrees.

Over the next hour, we fill Indira's journal with ideas— several of them good, a few of them great. By the end of the night, I feel almost optimistic. Josie may not have the additional overhead of a staff, but she also doesn't have a team. A team that feels like family. A family that's going to do whatever it takes to win.

This battle is on.

BookshopGirl: To celebrate making it through an exceptionally shitty day, would you like to play a game?

RJ.Reads: Always.

BookshopGirl: Badly describe one of your favorite childhood books. Go!

RJ.Reads: Let's see. A bear with a binge-eating disorder, a pig with generalized anxiety, and a donkey with clinical depression have adventures in a forest.

BookshopGirl: Winnie the Pooh?

RJ.Reads: Yep! My mom read it to me when I was little.

BookshopGirl: Lucky. I have no memories of my mother reading to me. But she only read bodice rippers, so that's probably a good thing. Anyway, my turn! Let me think . . .

BookshopGirl: OK, got it. Misanthropic chocolatier lures children to factory powered by forced indigenous labor, resulting in the death and/or injury of nearly all the children while said indigenous laborers sing cautionary songs.

RJ.Reads: Charlie and the Chocolate Factory.

BookshopGirl: Ding ding ding! Too easy?

RJ.Reads: My 4th grade teacher read it aloud to us. Thinking about it brings back memories of prepubescent body odor.

BookshopGirl: Yuck?

RJ.Reads: It's funny, because at the time I thought Willy Wonka was this magical whimsical guy . . . but now I think maybe he was the villain.

BookshopGirl: Wonka wasn't the villain. The real villain is Grandpa Joe.

RJ.Reads: What?!?

BookshopGirl: The man lies in bed for twenty years, allowing his poor daughter-in-law to break her back caring for him! Until Charlie gets that golden ticket. Then Grandpa Joe jumps right out of bed and dances a fucking jig.

RJ.Reads: Damn. I never thought about it that way.

BookshopGirl: He's a lazy, malingering freeloader who tagged along with Charlie and nearly ruined everything. Tell me I'm wrong.

RJ.Reads: You're not wrong.

BookshopGirl: I knew I liked you.

5

Josie

I'VE SPENT THE past two weeks feverishly pulling together thoughtful, inspiring programming to bring more people into my store. Tonight, I'm hosting the first strike in my crusade: Pages and Pairings, featuring three new releases, each paired with a wine to capture the essence of the book. I've never hosted an event like this before—I've always felt too socially awkward to even try—but now, with my job on the line, I have to push myself.

Registration includes a tasting glass of each, plus a copy of one book of the customer's choice—but I hope they'll fall in love with the other books and buy those, too. Thirty-two people have registered. If all goes well, I'll make a tidy profit.

Take that, Ryan of Happy Endings, Upholder of the Patriarchy.

His comment—*You could be my assistant*—continues to niggle me, pricking at my self-doubt. I'm determined to use it as motivation. The store looks beautiful, with a display of each book and its corresponding wine. Customers are milling about. Soft music tinkles in the background, an instrumental playlist I found on Spotify. Georgia has class tonight, so I'm on my own, but seeing familiar faces helps me relax.

"So glad you could come," I say to Kevin O'Rourke, who teaches English at the nearby high school.

"Lara and Lana—good to see you! Love the outfits," I say to the sixty-something twins who dress identically and read books together (literally, at the same time!). They both beam and say thank you (in unison).

Alfonso Canino, my sweet nonagenarian customer, gives me a dry kiss on the cheek and presses a box into my hands. "You shouldn't have!" I say, delighted; he always brings cannoli from his family's restaurant in the North End.

Over and over, I apologize for the dust. Construction has started, beginning with knocking down the wall between our back rooms. Now I have to worry about running into Ryan-not-Brian of the Messy Hair and Stupidly Tall Height every time I unpack a shipment or fetch supplies.

Fortunately, that hasn't happened. Maybe because the storage area for Beans is between us; maybe because he wants to avoid me as much as I want to avoid him.

Unfortunately, I can't avoid the sounds ricocheting through our connected back rooms. You'd think Beans would be the major culprit, what with the coffee grinders and blenders. But no, it's the customers and staff at Happy Endings. The squealing. The laughing. Even, a few times, the *moaning*.

Which is why I planned this event for later in the evening, after construction has ended for the day and Happy Endings is closed. I don't want anything to disrupt us.

The sommelier, a lanky guy with an exaggerated French accent I hired from Spoke, a nearby wine bar, is describing how he paired a novel set in Spain with a light and bubbly cava. Apparently it has notes of almond and leather—not that that means anything to me. I'm a total noob when it comes to

this stuff; the only wine my mom drank was of the boxed
variety or Manischewitz at Passover.

But as they say, fake it till you make it.

"This is a beautiful event," someone says, and I turn to see
a gray-haired couple, each with a glass of wine. They're not
regulars, and I'm thrilled to see new faces.

"I'm so happy you're enjoying yourselves!" I say, smiling.
"I'm Josie Klein, manager."

"Robert and Ingrid Schwartz," the man says, shaking my
hand. He's a retired attorney, he tells me, and his wife is on the
board of the art museum.

"I had no idea this place was here," she says, showing me
her stack of books—a copy of each of tonight's selections, plus
a few others. "What a gem! You can be sure I'll be back."

I beam. "Thank you so much."

"Every aspect of tonight has been curated to perfection,"
her husband adds. "The books, the wine . . . and as Ingrid
knows, I'm a huge fan of Itzhak Perlman."

"*Huge* fan," Mrs. Schwartz says, nodding.

I smile as I try to figure out what they're talking about. "I'm
not familiar with his work. What has he written?"

Mr. Schwartz gives me an indulgent smile. "He's a violinist.
Extremely well known."

At my blank look, his wife adds, "You're playing his music. I
think my husband assumed—"

"Of course!" I say, laughing awkwardly. "I'm a huge fan,
too. So nice to meet you both."

I excuse myself, hoping they don't notice my flushed
cheeks. It's a reminder that I am, indeed, still faking it—and I
haven't made it yet.

The sommelier begins his presentation about the rosé he

paired with another selection, and I smile while watching everyone nod along.

But then a ripple passes through the crowd. People take a step back. There's a gasp, a shriek, and the sickening crash of breaking glass.

Heart in my throat, I push through the group to see a huge black cat leaping from the display table, leaving toppled-over books, broken wineglasses, and a wine bottle shattered on the floor. The sommelier shouts some expletive in French, and a woman exclaims loudly that her shoes are now covered in wine.

Horrified, I lunge for the cat, but it slinks away, tiptoeing across a shelf, and I follow it, tossing apologies over my shoulder to my customers and promises to return as soon as I can. How the hell did a cat even get in here? It slips through the slightly open door to my back room—did someone leave the door to the alley open?—and on, past stacks of boxes.

I ease closer, reach down, and carefully pick it up. It rears back and hisses and—

"LET GO OF MY CAT!"

A monstrous figure materializes out of the shadows. I shriek as the cat twists out of my hands and leaps away from me . . . right into the arms of my adversary.

"This is *your* cat?" I shout, wincing at the scratches on my forearms. "What was it doing in my store?"

"He's just exploring!" Ryan says, cuddling the cat to his chest. It scrabbles away and leaps onto a nearby shelf, scowling down at us with fierce yellow eyes.

Ryan has earbuds in—probably listening to a smutty scene while he works—but he pulls one out as he looks at the cat.

"It's all right, Hades," he says in a soothing voice. "Did the mean lady scare you?"

I put my hands on my hips, facing Ryan. "Scare *him*? That cat ruined my event."

"What a shame." Ryan narrows his eyes. Lurid red scratches are blossoming on his neck, but he doesn't seem to notice. "I'd hate to inconvenience those highbrow customers of yours—"

"Did you send him over on purpose?"

Ryan shoves his messy hair out of his face. "Why would I do that?"

"Because you're so desperate to beat me you're willing to play dirty?"

"I won't need to play dirty to beat you," Ryan snaps, leaning down until we're eye to eye.

We lock eyes for the length of a breath, then another.

"When I win," he says in a low voice, "it'll be fair and square. But I will enjoy watching you squirm."

I swallow, my throat suddenly thick. "I don't squirm."

"We'll see."

Then his gaze flicks to my mouth and stays right there.

The air between us crackles. Now I'm staring at *his* mouth and remembering the whipped cream on his upper lip and that glimpse of his tongue when he licked it away—

I take a step back, clearing my throat.

"Listen," I say, smoothing my skirt, "Xander put us in this situation, but we should at least act like adults."

He folds his arms, a sulky look on his face. "I'm not the one throwing around ridiculous accusations."

"And I'm not the one who allowed my pet to sabotage someone else's event!"

He huffs. "I didn't—"

"No interfering with customers," I cut in, taking a calming breath. "They're off-limits."

"Fine," he says. "So are my staff. I won't have you treating them badly to get at me."

I scoff. What does he take me for? "I would never do that, Brian."

His face contorts in disgust. "It's *Ryan*."

"Is it?" I arch an eyebrow.

"You know my name."

"Do I?"

"*Yes!*" he roars.

I smirk; he's way too easy to rile up. "My mistake. By the way, you owe me for the broken bottle of wine and three broken glasses."

Ryan's face reddens, and he reaches into his pocket for his wallet. "How much? Twenty bucks? Forty? Here, have a hundred and let's call it good."

He thrusts the bills at me, and the fabric of his T-shirt strains across his chest and shoulders. He's not wearing his usual cardigan, I realize, and he's . . .

My mouth goes dry. I didn't know he was so . . .

Well. Broader and thicker than I would've expected. My mind fills with an image of him grabbing a full box of books, the sleeves on his T-shirt tightening around his arms as he easily hefts something that would take all my strength to lift.

I flick the thought away and pocket the cash.

"Now if you'll excuse me," I say, "I need to get back to my customers and clean up your mess."

LATER THAT NIGHT, after I've swept up the glass, put away the books, and paid the sommelier, I walk the four blocks to my building—a triple-decker Victorian—and climb the stairs to my apartment, where I flop onto my sofa without turning on the lights.

I'm exhausted. Mind, body, and soul. After the debacle with the feline god of the underworld, my event never got back on track. Half the customers were gone by the time I returned, and only a handful ended up buying additional books.

My phone vibrates with a text from my sister:

> How did it go? I'm heading out with friends but I want to hear everything!!

I'm not going to bug her with more of my problems—she deserves to have some fun. She's been so focused lately, so serious. Georgia was such a happy kid, always smiling and laughing, twirling around our apartment in her tutu and ballet shoes.

Until the accident.

Unbidden, my mind slips back to the evening I got the call. I was in my dorm room at Emerson with my roommate. My phone rang: my mom, her voice hysterical.

Your sister's been hit by a car.

She's at the hospital.

They don't know if she's going to make it.

The next hour was a blur: rushing to the hospital, racing through the hallways to my sister's room. Georgia had just come out of surgery. I'll never forget the sight of her body, tiny and broken in the hospital bed.

I thought that was the worst day. But somehow the worst part came later, when I was back at school and Georgia called to tell me that our mom had taken off with a guy.

After that, everything fell apart. I don't regret choosing my sister over my own plans, but it took me years to crawl out of that hole. To create a life I'm proud of, even if it's not what I always hoped for.

And now that life feels fragile. Like those wineglasses shattered on the floor.

Trying to brush the memories away, I pull my laptop toward me, the glow of the screen illuminating my dark living room as I navigate to BookFriends. RJ.Reads has added a new book to his Read shelf—an ARC I finished a month or so ago—but no rating or review yet.

> **BookshopGirl:** Hey! I saw you read that new debut that's getting all the buzz. What did you think??

His light turns green; he's online. For the first time in hours, I smile.

> **RJ.Reads:** Oh my god, so good. It made me cry. Four times.

> **BookshopGirl:** Only four? I cried at least nine times.

> **RJ.Reads:** Well, one cry session encompassed the last hundred pages.

I laugh, my shoulders relaxing. We don't often like the same books—RJ tends to go for lighter fare than I do—so it's extra fun when we find common ground.

Of course, it's also fun when we argue.

BookshopGirl: So . . . what did you think about the structure?

RJ has a knack for identifying the structural reasons a story did or didn't work: inciting incidents, plot points, dark moments, etc. This book bucked convention, but I thought it was effective.

RJ.Reads: It was unique, I've got to hand it to the author. But the pacing was a little slow to start.

BookshopGirl: What?? That first section was crucial to setting up the entire storyline! You're just impatient.

RJ.Reads: It could of been streamlined.

RJ.Reads: *could have (sorry)

RJ.Reads: But my point still stands: the beginning was slow.

BookshopGirl: Fine, okay. What did you think about the ending?

The tension of the day releases as I relax into the familiar, comforting world of fiction.

I wish I could stay here forever.

6

Ryan

PLAN A BUNCH of events, they said.

It'll be easy, they said.

The last two weeks have been a flurry of emails and missed calls and conversations about budgets and community outreach and scheduling. Our store calendar looks more complicated than a treasure map—but if there's any chance these events will lead to a chest of gold, then I have to be all in.

The first one starts in an hour: a Knitting and Knotting circle. Thirty-seven people RSVP'd to bring their knitting projects and discuss the Omegaverse, a subgenre of speculative romance with a caste system of characters, usually featuring werewolves.

My phone buzzes in my pocket—a DM from a friend from the RomSquad, my romance bookseller group.

> **Gretchen:** I have a proposition for you.

> **Ryan:** Before you go any further, you texted me. Ryan Lawson.

Gretchen: LOL. I know who I texted.

Gretchen: I'm not the one who keeps calling you Brian, Ryan.

Ryan: Touché. What can I do for you?

Gretchen: You mean what can I do for you?

Ryan: ???

Gretchen: Can I call you?

The second I send a thumbs-up, my phone rings.

"Okay, so you know how I'm opening a bookstore on the Cape?"

"That sounds vaguely familiar," I tease. Between Gretchen deciding to buy and convert an old ice cream shop in Provincetown and my Xander-drama, the RomSquad—a group chat with romance booksellers across the country—has been more like group therapy than book talk.

"Well, I'm in over my head," Gretchen says. "And since you might be out of a job soon . . ." I wince. So much for having my friends' support. "Anyway, I thought, maybe you could help me with the store?"

"I'm not moving to the Cape."

"You could commute."

"Over three hours?"

"Please," Gretchen begs. "You know we'd make a great

team. And even if you win, the new store won't be Happy Endings."

They're right—it'll be a store that carries a bunch of genres I know nothing about. I sigh and shove my hair out of my face. "I'm not ready to give up."

"Of course," Gretchen says. "Just . . . think of me as your plan B."

It's not a bad idea to have a safety net that doesn't involve moving back in with my parents. Boston has dozens of bookstores, but would they want a bookseller whose expertise starts and ends with romance? Then I think about my staff and how hard they're working. How *this* store feels like home in a way nothing else ever has.

"I don't know," I say. "I'll think about it."

"Bless you," Gretchen says.

We say goodbye and I hang up. I *will* think about it, but I'll also channel everything I've got into this competition.

"Welcome to Happy Endings!" I say as two customers walk in—an older woman and a teenage girl. With any luck, they'll be in and out before all the sex talk starts.

"Let me know if I can help you find anything," I add.

"We're here for Knitting and Knotting," the older woman says, chuckling to herself. "So clever."

My eyes go wide. "Indira!"

She appears moments later, wearing a black shirt that says: INTROVERTED BUT WILLING TO DISCUSS THE OMEGAVERSE.

"We have a problem," I say through a smile. "Remember how I said people might think this was a PG event?"

Indira follows my gaze and laughs. "I've got this," she says, clearly not thinking about all the ways this can go wrong—including our store getting canceled. All it takes is one offended customer posting online, and *bam!* Forget profits, Xander won't trust me if we get bad press.

I pretend to busy myself straightening a new display. Indira's girlfriend works in visual merchandising, and she suggested moving things around to increase the average basket value per customer.

"Are you guys here for the event tonight?" Indira is asking.

"Yes!" the girl says. "My grandma taught me how to knit."

I groan inwardly, wishing we had opted for a name that was less clever and more clear.

"And my granddaughter introduced me to the knotting trend," the older woman says. "My late husband was an alpha, if you know what I mean." She nudges Indira with her elbow, and I exhale in surprised relief as the woman's granddaughter rolls her eyes.

I should know better than to make assumptions about a person's kinks. Elaine taught me that. I wonder what she'd think of how the genre has evolved. I have no doubt Esmerelda the parrot would have gotten a kick out of it—that bird was especially vocal during the steamy scenes.

I chuckle at the memory of my "punishment." In hindsight, I got off easy. Not only did I do a shit job of stealing the dirty book my so-called friends dared me to take, my oversized, clumsy ass knocked over a whole display of erotic glass figurines when I tried to make my escape.

Instead of calling the police—or worse, my parents— Elaine agreed to let me work off the damage. Every day for three months, I reported to the bookstore after school and read a romance novel out loud to her parrot. She said Esmerelda was lonely, plucking out her own feathers, and needed company.

Those afternoons at Happy Endings helped me discover my love of reading—and by proxy, I got the keys to a sex education other boys could only dream of. In the early days, I was so embarrassed by the words I was reading out loud—*his quivering shaft of desire; her tender petals of feminine delight*—that I forgot to be embarrassed by the fact that reading was such a struggle. The parrot didn't care how slowly I went or if I mispronounced a word—she was just happy to have someone reading to her.

By the time Elaine informed me that my debt had been cleared, I was hooked—on the books, the stories, the customers, and yes, even the parrot.

Since I had no intention of stopping, Elaine started to pay me and give me more responsibilities. I kept working at Happy Endings through high school and college, where a kind professor suggested I get tested for dyslexia.

I always thought dyslexia meant switching letters around, but apparently there are a lot of different types. For me, reading feels like hard work, like I have to focus all my attention on every single letter of every single word. I make stupid mistakes with spelling, especially words that sound the same but have different meanings. And in general, I have trouble maintaining attention with printed words.

Once I got the diagnosis, it made sense why Elaine's "punishment" helped me so much—reading aloud (to a persnickety parrot or quietly to myself) helped me understand—and enjoy—books for the first time since my mom read them aloud to me as a kid.

After I graduated from UMass Boston, Elaine assumed I'd want to move on—but the bookstore was my home, the staff and customers my family. So Elaine promoted me to assistant manager, then manager. Her kids held on to the store for a few years after she passed, but eventually Xander made them an offer they couldn't refuse, and I was grateful he kept me on.

"We've got a small problem." Indira's voice breaks me out of my reverie, and I realize the store is overflowing with an eclectic group covering every decade, gender identity, and sexuality. The one thing we don't have is enough chairs.

NEXT DOOR, BEANS is relatively empty.

"Hey, hot stuff," Eddie says from behind the counter, giving me a wink.

"Any chance I can borrow a few chairs for the next hour or so?"

"For your little knitting event?" a familiar, condescending voice says from behind me.

Eddie tries—poorly—to suppress a smile.

Josie and I haven't seen each other since she accused me of sending Hades to ruin her event—which, from the looks of it, wasn't nearly as crowded as ours is tonight.

"Knitting is only half of it," Eddie says, handing Josie her drink.

It's late in the day for her to have caffeine. And she looks tired—her eyeliner is smudged, and wisps of hair are coming out of her bun. But I quickly dismiss any sympathy. It's not my fault if she's been up all night with stress. Xander may have made this a competition, but she's the one who made me her enemy.

"What's the other half?" Josie asks, a mocking lilt to her voice.

Behind her back, Eddie catches my eye and makes a

spitting motion into an imaginary drink, his unspoken warning clear.

Message received; I will be perfectly pleasant.

"Knotting," I tell Josie.

She blinks. "Like crochet?"

"Sweetheart," Eddie says. "We are not talking about yarn."

Josie's eyebrows arch. "What, then?"

"It's a sex thing," Eddie says nonchalantly. "In the Omegaverse."

"The omega what?"

"The Omegaverse," I repeat, grateful Indira gave me a rundown last week. I've read a few books in the genre, but the speculative stuff has never been my jam. "There's an A/B/O character system—alphas are dominant, betas are neutral, and omegas are submissive."

"Like S&M?" Josie asks. I'm surprised she's not more flustered. If I had to guess, I'd bet she's the closed-door, lights-off, missionary type. I get a flash of her, lying beneath me, her hair falling around her shoulders, and the thought is enough to make my dick twitch.

I adjust myself discreetly and force the image out of my mind.

"It's basically werewolf porn," Eddie explains. "And knotting is when the base of the penis swells after penetration, so it kind of gets locked up in there."

He hooks his pointer fingers together and pulls to make the point. Josie chokes on her coffee.

"It can last up to an hour," I add. "Until the swelling goes down."

"Sounds . . ." She trails off, clearly at a loss for words.

"Kinky?" Eddie suggests. "I'd definitely bang a werewolf, wouldn't you?"

"Chairs!" Josie exclaims, a non sequitur if I ever heard one. "You needed chairs."

She's right; that's why I came over here. And the event is starting any minute.

"Take whatever you need," Eddie says. "And if there are any werewolves in the crowd . . ."

"I'll send them your way," I promise. Then, to Josie: "You want to come listen in?"

"Absolutely not." She turns on her heel and walks off.

Smiling, I have a sudden urge to howl like a werewolf before heading back to the store with chairs for what promises to be an . . . interesting evening.

7

Josie

KNITTING AND KNOTTING? Gross. Ridiculous. Idiotic.

Intriguing?

Nope. I shut the thought down as I head out the door of Beans. This is exactly why I don't read romance. It's not—as one ex-boyfriend suggested—that I'm boring and closed off when it comes to sex (he was just bad at it). And it's not—as my mother suggested—that I hate love and don't believe in relationships (she was just bad at them).

Nor is it because I look down on the genre, as Ryan seems to think. I firmly believe there's a book for every reader and a reader for every book—it's just that romance doesn't speak to me. I love literary fiction because it's gritty, raw, and complicated, like real human experiences. No guarantees, no tidy conclusions.

No false hopes, either.

I'm shaking my head as I walk back into my store, where Georgia has arrived to help me set up for tomorrow's event. She's dressed like a seventies flower child thrust into the modern world—wavy hair parted down the middle, round pink glasses, flowy sundress with no bra, Birkenstocks, and of course, her bedazzled pink cane.

"What's wrong?" she asks, pushing her glasses up onto her head. "Your face is all red and blotchy."

I pick up the sign I made to advertise tomorrow's event. "What do you think?"

She knows I'm changing the subject, but she allows it. "The Literary Collective," she reads. "A.k.a., the book club for people who believe the best novels are the ones that only make sense after being read three times."

"Ha ha. At least it isn't Knitting and Knotting, like at Happy Endings."

She coughs out a laugh. "Like, *that* kind of knotting?"

I eye her. "You know what it is?"

Her cheeks turn deep crimson. "I may have wandered through the Omegaverse on occasion."

"George!"

"But not lately, given that I'm swamped with classes. Remind me again why I wanted to take summer term?"

She grabs a broom and I grab a dustpan, and together we start cleaning up the bits of drywall and dust left behind by the construction crew.

"To get your degree faster," I say. "I told you to enjoy your last summer of freedom, but you didn't listen."

"I should have. I keep thinking back to when we were kids during summer break. Remember how we'd go to the pool at the JCC—"

"And the park."

"And the library!" She smiles. "Your favorite."

She's right; our city library was a half mile from our

apartment, and we'd walk there together. We'd each take a backpack and check out the limit—fifteen books each.

"You'd get all those big chapter books, then go home and read for hours," she says. "I loved when you read to me."

I'm happy to hear that; I'm not sure she fully understands why I did it, though. Each book was a doorway to another world, transporting us away from the chaos at home. Reading wasn't just an escape; it was a lifeline.

"You know who else could read for hours and hours?" Georgia says, leaning on the broom. "Mom."

I stiffen at the comparison.

"The difference is that she'd lose herself for days at a time and forget she had two daughters," I say. Meanwhile, I always made sure Georgia was taken care of.

Georgia sighs. "I know."

"Instead of facing her responsibilities like a grown-up, she wanted her Prince Charming to swoop in and turn life into a fantasy—just like in those books she read." I try to keep my voice steady, but it's not easy. "I don't need a degree in psychology to know that isn't healthy."

It happened after every bad breakup: Mom would pull out her paperback romances, the ones with clinch covers featuring bare-chested men embracing women with heaving bosoms, and she'd hole up in her room for days at a time like they were an escape hatch from reality.

It was terrifying, but I had to pull myself together for Georgia's sake. I'd make meals, walk her to school, do our laundry—even when I was barely big enough to reach into the washing machine in the basement of our building. Mom was fired from her job more times than I could count. Sometimes we ran out of food and I'd have nothing to feed Georgia but stale saltine crackers and cream of chicken soup. Once, Mom forgot to pay the gas bill and we spent a frigid night in January wearing three layers of clothes and shivering in bed.

After a while, Mom would emerge, thin and pale, and declare that she was "ready to find love again." Soon enough, she'd have "met someone real nice," a man that would treat her "better than those other awful guys."

And the cycle would start all over again.

"She's doing better now," Georgia says, her voice tentative.

"You've been talking to her?" I say, horrified. I stopped returning Mom's calls a couple years ago, when the drama became too much to handle. As far as I knew, Georgia had done the same.

"No—well, a little." Georgia shrugs. "She called me a few months ago, and I picked up . . . She's working as a receptionist at a dentist's office. I helped her find a therapist, and she's moved into a new apartment and . . ."

I fold my arms. "And?"

"And she's dating someone—"

"George!" I burst out.

"He sounds nice."

"They always do."

My sister turns, looking at me with mournful eyes. The same way she looked at me when I came rushing home from college after her accident, because our mom had taken off after her latest boyfriend.

"I wish you'd give her a chance," Georgia says quietly.

My throat tightens. I know she wants to believe our mother can change, and I love that about her. Unfortunately, it's never going to happen, and the last thing I want is for my sister to get hurt again. So many popular novels showcase big, sweeping character arcs—but that's the author's imagination. Fictional.

In real life, people don't change, not enough to make a difference.

"I—I need to unpack some boxes," I say, and head into the back room.

THAT NIGHT, AS I'm closing the register, my mind drifts back to that conversation. Not about giving our mom a chance, but Georgia's comments about how I used to read as a kid. When I'd get sucked into a book so thoroughly, hours would feel like minutes. And when I put the book down, reentering reality would feel like surfacing from underwater.

On a whim, I grab my phone and pull up my chat with RJ.Reads.

> **BookshopGirl:** Do you read for fun?

His username lights up. Maybe he has an alert set for my messages, like I do for his. The thought makes me smile.

> **RJ.Reads:** Of course. Is there any other way?

> **BookshopGirl:** I remember reading for pure enjoyment as a kid. It hasn't felt the same as an adult, though.

> **RJ.Reads:** What did you read as a kid?

This is the first time we've discussed something other than book recommendations, book pet peeves, or reviews. It's still book related, but it seems more personal.

> **BookshopGirl:** Anything I could get my hands on. Harry Potter, of course. Percy Jackson. Anne of Green Gables. Old Nancy Drew books. Newbery Medal winners, like Tuck Everlasting, The Westing Game.

> **RJ.Reads:** And now?

> **BookshopGirl:** Well, I read upcoming and new releases in order to recommend them to customers, or if I'm asked to blurb something. I try to keep up with the broader literary conversation, you know? Buzzy books, bestsellers, award winners.

> **RJ.Reads:** To be honest, it kind of sounds like you think of reading as a job.

I sit back, stung. He's right. Reading is still my favorite activity—but somewhere along my journey through adulthood, it's started to feel more like a task on my to-do list than recreation.

> **RJ.Reads:** Hey, sorry. There's no right or wrong way to read, as long as you're enjoying it.

BookshopGirl: No, it's fine. That's my point—since it IS my job, maybe that's taken some of the joy away? I'm reading books I think I should read, not necessarily what I want to read.

RJ.Reads: Like forcing yourself to eat your vegetables because you know you need the vitamins and fiber.

BookshopGirl: Ugh. Am I the reader equivalent of the person at restaurants who orders a salad with dressing on the side, says no to the bread basket, and skips dessert? No one likes that person.

And I don't want RJ to think of me as that person. Uptight; rigid. I've been called that before.

RJ.Reads: Not at all. I'm saying that any balanced diet should include desert.

RJ.Reads: *DESSERT. (Sigh. Why doesn't this damn website have an edit feature??)

BookshopGirl: I knew what you meant ☺. And I see your point.

I'm remembering the rugelach Georgia brought. The sugar crystallizing on my tongue, the sensation of comfort as it settled in my stomach.

When's the last time I felt that way about a book? Not in years.

> **BookshopGirl:** So do you have a rec for me? Something . . . well, fun?

No response. The minutes tick by, and I'm surprised at how disappointed I feel.

Which is silly. I'm sure RJ has plenty of other things to do.

After ten minutes, I head home, heat up a microwave dinner, and crack open a sparkling water. I eat my sad little meal while reading an ARC that arrived earlier today, but it's not grabbing me, so I set it down and get ready for bed.

As I'm about to turn off the light, my phone chimes.

> **RJ.Reads:** Sorry, took a while because I was brainstorming titles that would be "fun" for the one and only BookshopGirl. Something superlong (obviously), complex and layered, with thought-provoking themes, and a satisfying but not-too-neat ending. I finally settled on one of my brother's favorite books that he made us all listen to on a road trip. It's a backlist title, you can probably get it at the library. Are you ready?

> **BookshopGirl:** After that introduction? I'm on pins and needles.

> **RJ.Reads:** Ha. I'm sure.

> **BookshopGirl:** So what's the book???

> **RJ.Reads:** 11/22/63.

I stare at his message, confused. Is that the pub date? I do a quick Google search.

> **BookshopGirl:** By Stephen King? I'm not really a horror fan.

> **RJ.Reads:** This isn't horror, it's a blend of science fiction and historical fiction. With an incredibly unique and intricate plot. And a protagonist you can root for. And a love story, but not a typical one. It's like a fully balanced meal in one eight-hundred-page book—meat and potatoes, vegetables, and dessert.

A smile tugs at my lips.

> **BookshopGirl:** Okay. I'll give it a try.

THE NEXT MORNING is Saturday, which means it's time for my inaugural meeting of the Literary Collective.

Today's selection is a literary thriller about a small-town sheriff who's secretly a serial killer investigating his own crimes. What makes it special is the spare, almost bleak prose, so devoid of emotion that it invites the reader to use their imagination to embroider events, heightening the sense of terror unfolding on the pages.

I loved it. (And so did PAW. She blurbed it.)

Judging by the discussion, so did many of our readers. About two dozen people attend, many of them familiar faces, though several have brought friends. There's also a group of five middle-aged women wearing matching sparkly pink shirts. I'm pretty sure they're in the wrong place, but it's too late to let them know.

We're discussing the main character, and Marc Stapleton—a fifty-something regular with a bushy brown beard—raises his hand. "I know the sheriff is a murderer, but experiencing the story through his eyes turns everything upside down. I started to doubt my own judgments about morality."

"That's fascinating," I say. "Other thoughts from the group about the main character?"

In the back of the room, one of the women in pink raises her hand. "Did anyone else think he was kind of hot?"

Two people turn to stare at her, horrified. Georgia, who's sitting in the front row to support me, stifles a smile.

"Well," I say, my cheeks heating with embarrassment, "he murdered twenty-three people—"

"I could have changed him," the woman sitting next to her says, and the women in her group dissolve into giggles.

The other customers shift their weight, clearly uncomfortable. I try to keep us on track, leading the discussion back into less unhinged territory, but the women in pink continue with the bizarre interjections. Georgia takes note of my panicked expression and slips to the back row. As one of my regulars talks about how the flashback scenes to the killer's past build compassion for him, I overhear Georgia whispering to the women—introducing herself, asking where they're from. Blessedly, this distracts them.

The rest of us carry on, but I'm having trouble concentrating. Then I hear one of the women whisper, "A bookseller over at Happy Endings told us about this, and we thought it would be fun to branch out of our usual genres."

Ryan. He sent them to deliberately ruin my event.

My embarrassment flames into anger. Hands clenched into fists, I stand and head over to Georgia, whispering in her ear, "I'll be right back—keep going."

She nods, a confused look on her face, as I slip outside and past Beans, storming into Happy Endings, scanning the place for a giant man in a blah-colored cardigan with his hair flopped seductively over his eyes.

But when I get a few feet into the store, I stop short.

The place is a disaster. Overflowing shelves of various colors and styles fill the room; more books are stacked on the floor in messy piles. Mismatched chairs are wedged into every corner, with books spread face down over the arms (broken spines! I cringe). The entire back wall is ripped down to the studs, and the floor is partially removed in one corner, which contributes to the madhouse vibes. A candle is burning somewhere in the back, a floral scent that makes my throat itch—and gives me instant anxiety. An open flame around books?

Claustrophobia hits me in a wave. It's too much like our apartment growing up. When I came home to help Georgia after the accident, the place was a safety hazard: spoiled food in the fridge, trash overflowing, junk everywhere. It took a week of decluttering and cleaning before Georgia could navigate her wheelchair from room to room.

My chest tightens, my breath coming in short, fast bursts.

"Can I help . . ." a voice calls.

Ryan. His smile drops when he spots me. "Oh. It's you."

My frustration flares again, and I march toward him, fighting the aggravating sensation that I'm shrinking as my eyes are forced up—way up—to meet his. He's holding a grayish-white cat in his arms.

As I near him, I see a button on his lanyard that reads, IT'S NOT SMUT, IT'S CLITERATURE, and my face flushes.

"We said no sabotage!" I say.

He looks bewildered. "What are you talking about?"

"Those women you sent over to ruin my event! They're asking ridiculous questions. 'Did anyone else think the serial killer was hot?' Complete lack of social propriety, no respect for the gravity of this novel."

Slowly, understanding dawns on his face. "Oh. The Sluts."

"Huh?"

"Five middle-aged women in matching pink T-shirts?"

"Yes."

"Those are the Book Club Sluts—their name for themselves," he adds hastily. "They join all the Boston book clubs. They've never come to your store before?"

"No."

He shrugs, as if to say, *Well, that's kind of sad.* "They were at Knitting and Knotting—they must've seen your sign advertising the event."

"But that was just yesterday." I pause, my frustration cooling. "Though I guess that explains the inappropriate questions—they didn't even read the book."

"They read fast. But they also pregame before most events. They're probably tipsy." The corners of his eyes crinkle, like we're sharing a joke. It might be cute, on anyone else. On him, it looks like he's mocking me.

"But it's eleven a.m.!" I say.

"Mimosas at the Painted Burro," a voice chimes in. It's a middle-aged woman with cartoonishly bright red hair, emerging from the labyrinthine book stacks.

I blink at her, confused, then turn back to Ryan. "They said a bookseller at Happy Endings told them about my event."

The red-haired woman stifles a laugh, and Ryan shoots her a surprised look. The cat wriggles in his arms, and he kisses the top of her head before setting her down. Again, cute— from anyone but him.

"Well, it wasn't me," he says, "though I bet those Sluts buy a hundred dollars' worth of books each."

"Oh," I say, feeling somewhat better. But then I look around at the chaos, and claustrophobia hits me again. The words slip out under my breath: "How can anyone stand this place?"

Ryan's expression turns rock hard. "What's that supposed to mean?"

I shift my weight uncomfortably. "Nothing. It's just, it's so . . ."

"Lowbrow? Unsophisticated?" His eyes flash.

"That's not—"

"Just because we don't cater to the 'literary elite' doesn't mean we're worthless or stupid or embarrassing, okay? At least my store isn't cold and lifeless—"

"Lifeless?"

"Soulless. Joyless. Devoid of any warmth or magic." He takes a step into my space, crowding me against an ornate purple bookshelf.

He's so close I get a whiff of his scent, warm and masculine, and my knees nearly buckle. I'm acutely aware of our size difference, how he's twice as broad as me and a foot taller, how easily he could pick me up and press me harder against this bookshelf and—

I clear my throat and sidestep away. "Just because my bookstore is clean and orderly doesn't mean it's boring and pretentious."

"Just because *my* bookstore is cozy and homey doesn't mean it's dirty."

"That's not—" I fight the urge to scream. Two nearby customers have paused their browsing to watch our exchange. "Why do you take *everything* I say in the worst possible way?"

His jaw tightens. "You're the one insulting my store—"

"I didn't mean it like that!" I protest. "I like things neat! That's all I'm saying!"

"And I'm saying that there are enough people out there who judge this store. We don't need it from you, too."

He folds his arms, staring me down like a bouncer. His outrage is ironic, coming from the guy who made rude comments about *my* bookstore to Eddie and Xander and probably plenty of other people, too.

"I think you should get back to your event," he says. It's clear from his tone that he means *now*.

Shaking my head, I move to the door. Near the exit, I notice a sign that reads, THANKS FOR VISITING! YOUR THE BEST.

My right eye twitches. *Don't do it*, I tell myself. *Just walk away*. But it's like an itch that'll drive me bonkers if I don't scratch it.

I whip the pen out of my bun and add an apostrophe and an *E*, so it reads YOU'RE. When I look back, Ryan is still staring me down—but his cheeks are now flushed.

Without another word, I leave.

BookshopGirl: I'm finally home and need to get my mind off some work stuff. Are you up for Bookish Never Have I Ever?

RJ.Reads: Sure!

BookshopGirl: Perfect! I'll share a commonly used expression, and if you've ever experienced that in real life, you have to drink.

BookshopGirl: Example: "Never have I ever let out a breath I didn't realize I was holding." If you HAVE let out a breath you didn't realize you were holding, you drink. Got it?

RJ.Reads: Got it, and I have a drink poured and ready.

BookshopGirl: Okay here goes: Never have I ever . . . bit my lip until I tasted blood.

RJ.Reads: Nope, haven't done that either. Sounds violent. My turn: Never have I ever felt wetness on my cheeks and wiped it away, only to realize I was crying.

BookshopGirl: 🍷

RJ.Reads: Really? How did you not realize your crying?

RJ.Reads: *you're

BookshopGirl: It's called emotional repression, RJ. You clearly had a healthier childhood than I did.

BookshopGirl: My turn: Never have I ever clenched my fists until my nails left marks on my palms.

RJ.Reads: 🍷

RJ.Reads: YOU clearly never wanted to punch your older brother in the face but restrained yourself because you knew he'd clobber you.

BookshopGirl: Nope, no big brothers. Just one sweet little sister.

RJ.Reads: LUCKY. Never have I ever heard screaming and then realized it was me.

BookshopGirl: Never have I ever padded softly across a room.

RJ.Reads: Never have I ever gripped the steering wheel so tightly my nuckles turned white.

RJ.Reads: (*knuckles, obviously)

BookshopGirl: 🍷 You must not live in a place that has black ice.

RJ.Reads: Or I know gripping the steering wheel that tightly isn't going to help?

RJ.Reads: Never have I ever watched a muscle in a man's jaw tic or watched an Adam's apple bob slowly as he swallows.

BookshopGirl: 🍷🍷

RJ.Reads: Really? Jaw muscles? Adam's apples? That's what does it for you?

BookshopGirl: Oh yeah.

RJ.Reads: Interesting.

8

Ryan

I WOKE UP this morning with a hard-on and the remnants of a dream. The details were sparse, but the memory was more than enough to get me off before I had to get up for work.

In the dream, I was in the back room at the bookstore, only I was a werewolf, and I had Josie pressed against the shelves.

Her skirt was up around her waist—so unsophisticated—and her legs were wrapped around my hips. Dream Josie was warm and as tight as that perfect little bun on top of her head. I had an animalistic urge to devour her, to control her and make her mine. To show her who was the boss.

Then she reached up, removing the elastic around her bun so the dark waves of her hair cascaded down, releasing the scent of her floral shampoo. I loved seeing her unravel, shedding her prim and proper exterior. She was no better than me.

But then her eyes flew open, and whatever she saw in me made her shut down. Gone were the desperate pleas for me to go harder, faster, deeper—and in their place was the stuck-up ice queen I've come to know all too well. Dream Josie pushed me away, pulling up her panties and lowering her skirt, mumbling excuses about having to get back to her store. She had important, intelligent books to sell to important, intelligent people. She had to make money, so she could beat me and fire my staff and turn my bookstore into a cold, bleak literary hellscape.

That part didn't feel like a dream. It felt like a premonition.

"Hey, Romeo, I think that one's got enough tape on it."

I snap to attention and glance down at the blind date book I'm wrapping in brown paper. Cinderella's right—there are six pieces of tape where I only need one.

"Mind's somewhere else," I mumble.

Cinderella smirks as if she knows what I was thinking.

Her hair is now a vibrant green, like the M&M's that were rumored to make you horny back in the day. Too bad there wasn't another color that could turn it all off and stop you from thinking inappropriate thoughts about your newly sworn enemy.

The dream was confusing for more than the obvious reasons. I've never been into the paranormal stuff; I prefer stories that could really happen. Books where I can picture myself as the main character meeting the LOML, having that instant spark that makes people say, "When you know, you know."

Although the last time I thought I "knew," the other person did *not*. I have no intention of getting myself in that position again, but I still love seeing it play out in fiction.

"Your mind's been somewhere else a lot lately," Cinderella says.

"There's a lot going on," I tell her. "With the store."

"Mmm-hmm." She narrows her eyes as she tapes a sloppy

corner on another book. If only she paid as much attention to her job as she does to my personal life. "Things got a little heated with you and that Tabula girl yesterday."

"Yeah, well."

"It's not like you to let someone get under your skin like that."

She's not wrong. When I'm around Josie Klein, I can go from completely fine to pissed to turned on in the length of a heartbeat. But I can't explain why, so I shrug and say, "It's not every day someone comes into my store and disrespects my customers and staff."

This seems to satisfy Cinderella, who moves on to wrap another blind date book.

"Speak of the devil," she says a moment later, nodding toward the front of the store.

Confused, I follow her gaze. Josie is standing outside, checking out our new display windows. She looks past one of the mannequins reading in a suggestive pose and her eyes lock with mine. I give her a wide, unabashed grin and wave because I know it will piss her off.

Her eyes grow as wide as they did in my dream, and she disappears again, back to the safety of her boring store and its vanilla window display.

"You want to bone her," Cinderella says in a know-it-all voice.

"Do not," I say, although it's hard to sound convincing when the memory of my dream is so fresh.

Cinderella shakes her head. "I wanted you to *read* enemies-to-lovers books, not find yourself in the middle of one. That's what this reeks of. The two of you, pitted against each other, only then—"

"—only then the assistant manager gets back to work," I say, handing her another book to wrap.

"I saw what I saw yesterday. And that's how the story goes—one day you're ripping each other's heads off; the next, you're ripping off each other's clothes."

"The blind date books have been a big hit," I say, desperate to change the subject.

And it's true. The success of this program has shattered everything I thought I knew about what makes people buy a book. Apparently, they don't need to see the cover, back cover copy, or blurbs.

The coolest part is the books we've been selling. We've included a few bestsellers, but it's mostly been old stock, backlist titles that didn't get as much attention as they should have.

I was talking about this just last night with BookshopGirl. We kept chatting until almost one a.m. after our Never Have I Ever game. I was tipsy by the end and making even more spelling errors than usual. Luckily, BSG has never once made me feel dumb about them (unlike Josie Klein, the High Priestess of Intellectual Snobbery). Anyway, she and I both agree it's impossible to really know what will sell and what will collect dust on our shelves.

Personally, I think the whole thing is random. Publishing companies throw books at the wall like spaghetti to see what sticks. BSG seems to have more faith in the system, believing that publishers look to tastemakers and other literary elite to help predict what readers will like.

If that's the case, I don't fit the mold of that literary elite. Which tracks.

The bell on the front door chimes, and I look up to see

Eliza, wearing a hoodie from her soccer team. School's officially out for the summer, but she still has practice most mornings.

"Perfect timing," I say, tossing her the roll of Scotch tape. She catches it with one hand, grinning.

"Ooh, blind dates!" She joins Cinderella, and I head back to shelve the shipment that came in this afternoon. I could delegate this task, but I enjoy deciding where the books go. At the moment, I have a whole shelf featuring the "only one bed" trope, and another section featuring love interests named Josh. My system isn't neat or logical—Josie seemed revolted by it—but our customers love to browse and explore, discovering books they might have otherwise walked by.

I'm debating where to shelve a new M4M young adult title that's gained popularity thanks to social media, when the front door chimes again.

"Excuse me, is RJ working today?"

The familiar voice stops me in my tracks.

"I'm sorry," Cinderella says. "We don't have an RJ here."

"Oh." There's disappointment in her voice. The voice that belongs to a woman I haven't seen in more than a decade.

I could easily stay back here and let another decade pass, but I know that's not what Jack would have wanted. I look down at the novel in my hands, wishing my best friend could have lived to see the day when he could walk into a bookstore and buy a book like this. A love story he could imagine himself in.

"Mrs. Palmer," I say, stepping into view.

"RJ." Her eyes shimmer, and I know she's not seeing me. She's seeing the shadow of her son. RJ and JR—best friends since first grade. Our birthdays were a day apart, and we celebrated every milestone together—until senior year of high school.

After everything happened, the Palmers sold their house and moved away. Somewhere they wouldn't have to see me getting older while my best friend, their son, stayed forever seventeen.

"I think you can call me Brenda now," Mrs. Palmer says, walking toward me. "I heard you were still working here."

"I'm running the place now," I say, and the pride in her smile makes me stand even taller.

"That's really something. How are your parents doing?"

It's the kind of small talk reserved for familiar strangers, even though I used to think of Mrs. Palmer—Brenda—as a second mom.

"They're great," I say, happy to report the truth. "They're throwing a big party for their fiftieth anniversary in a few weeks—I'm sure they'd love to see you."

"We'll be back home by then. In Florida."

So that's where they went.

"How about you?" Brenda / Mrs. Palmer asks. "Anyone special in your life?"

Cinderella chuckles, and I shoot a glare in her direction. At least Eliza is pretending not to eavesdrop, wrapping a blind date book with excellent precision.

"Not at the moment. I'm too busy helping other people find their love stories." I hold up the book, expecting her to blanch at the cover image of two young men wrapped in an embrace, but she doesn't.

"Is that a good one?" she asks.

"It's excellent," I say, holding it out for her to take.

She accepts it, turning it over. I wait for her cheeks to burn bright as she reads the back copy about the lovers, two young men from families who didn't accept them for who they are, who ran away and found family in each other. To her credit, she doesn't.

"This does look good," she says. "I think I'll get it."

"It's on the house," I say, ignoring the way Cinderella's jaw drops. Last week, after another "barter" incident, I laid down the law: no more trades or freebies. I'll run my credit card for this later; the thought of Mrs. Palmer reading that book is worth far more than $17.99 plus tax.

"Thank you." Her eyes well with tears, and I know she's trying to find the right words to make a graceful exit.

"It was good to see you, Mrs. Palmer. Brenda." I give her a hug, aware of how strange it is to be looking down at this woman I used to look up to. "Please don't be a stranger."

She gives my arm a loving tap before turning to go, and I wonder what she'll find if she comes back in another decade. If I'll still be here, managing whatever this store becomes. Or if she'll find Josie behind the counter, the LGBTQ romance section confined to a tiny back corner.

If there is one at all.

How can anyone stand this place?

The memory of what Josie said turns my sorrow into a rallying cry, a reminder that it's not just myself and my staff I'm fighting for. It's for the girls and guys and gays and theys who deserve the support and solidarity my best friend never got.

I couldn't save him, but I can save this place for them.

9

Josie

"I HONESTLY DESPISE him," I say to my sister. "It's more than a superficial dislike. It's loathing. Disgust. Like, on a soul-deep level."

"I don't blame you," she says. "Especially after how he treated you."

We're talking about Ryan, of course, he of the Loud Yelling and Defensive Reactions, as we walk toward Tabula Inscripta after grabbing breakfast at Davis Square Donuts & Bagels. Georgia's munching on a Boston cream donut, and I've got a sesame bagel with honey walnut cream cheese. The warm sun filters through the trees lining the brick-paved sidewalk, and the distant melody of a street musician's guitar mingles with the sounds of traffic and pedestrian chatter. It's almost pretty enough to distract me from the twitchy feeling I get whenever I think about Ryan.

Not quite, though.

"He's the antithesis of everything I value," I continue. "He's unkempt, disorganized, anti-intellectual, vulgar, and has serious issues with emotional reactivity."

I'm hyperbolizing, and we both know it, but one of the best

things about Georgia is that she's unequivocally on my side. Bonus: she's now psychoanalyzing him with zero evidence other than my highly biased recounting of our interactions. But what else are sisters for, if not to join in mutual hatred?

Another bonus: if she's analyzing *him*, she's not analyzing me and why I'm so fixated on him.

Which I am also trying to avoid analyzing.

"I bet he's uncomfortable with successful women." Georgia's channeling a fairy princess today, her hair in a braid crown dotted with tiny flower pins, loose tendrils framing her face. "We had a whole discussion about this in my Gender Dynamics class. When men feel emasculated, they compensate with increasing hostility, sexism, homophobia—all sorts of toxic traits."

"He's definitely hostile." Backing me into the bookcase, for example. Yelling at me. Ordering me to leave his store.

Although *maybe* I can see how he saw my comments as insulting, even if I didn't intend them to be. I'll give him some props for being protective of his store—though, come on, he insulted *mine*, too. He called it soulless and joyless. Organization is plenty joyful!

"Let me guess, he has short-man syndrome," Georgia says.

"Well, no," I admit. "He's tall. Like, really tall. And big. Not in a gym-rat way, more like a sturdy, farm-boy kind of thing. Like he could heft a bale of hay in one hand and a sick baby cow in the other, walking three miles uphill, without breaking a sweat."

Georgia eyes me. "That's . . . specific."

Oops. Before she can ask why I've spent so much time thinking about Ryan Lawson's body, I say, "He's probably *overconfident* because of his height, you know?"

Nodding, she takes a bite of her donut. "If it's not short-man syndrome, it's probably small-penis syndrome."

I choke on my bagel.

"It's a real diagnosis," Georgia insists. "Well—it's a type of body dysmorphic disorder. Men with anxiety about their penis size have increased rates of erectile dysfunction and lower intercourse satisfaction."

My cheeks warm. I'm remembering the feeling of being crowded against the bookcase, Ryan's eyes blazing with fury as he glares down at me.

"That sounds about right," I say, though somehow, I know it's not. There's a coiled intensity in Ryan's muscles that speaks to some level of confidence in bed, and my mind flashes to an image of him shirtless, those honey-brown eyes burning with desire instead of rage.

We're almost to Tabula Inscripta, which is good, not only because I need something else to think about, but because Georgia is limping a little. I know she won't want me to mention it. She's fiercely independent and, as she likes to remind me, has surpassed all medical expectations following her accident.

Still doesn't stop me from worrying about her.

"All things considered," Georgia says, "he strikes me as a basic run-of-the-mill asshole. Avoid him."

"I'm doing my best," I say as we stop in front of my store. I fish out my keys, unlock the door, walk in, and flick on the lights.

We both gasp.

The walls separating Tabula from Beans, and Beans from Happy Endings, are gone. All that's left are a few vertical studs and drywall dust on the floor.

I knew a bunch of construction happened last night—the contractor asked me to close the store early so his guys could work late, and he left behind some tarps for me to cover my bookcases—but I didn't expect this.

Beans is open and bustling, and I can see past the throngs of coffee-craving customers into Happy Endings: the motley assortment of bookcases, the multicolored chairs, the haphazard stacks of books. I even catch a glimpse of the damn black cat.

Turning to my sister, I can tell by her horrified expression that she's thinking the same thing I am:

Avoiding Ryan the Repugnant just got a lot harder.

GEORGIA LEAVES FOR class, and I remove the protective tarps and straighten my shelves, hyperaware of what's happening on the other side of Beans. Ryan walking in, his feet stomping on the floor. Ryan calling good morning to his staff, his voice somehow rising above the coffee shop chatter and noise.

He's not just big, he's loud. And his voice is like sandpaper, scraping against my brain.

The whole vibe of my store feels off. My customers come here to browse in peace and quiet, which is impossible now. The tinkling chime of the Happy Endings door makes me want to stick cotton balls in my ears. And there's the smell, thick and musty, like someone is burning incense, mixing with the familiar scent of coffee. It reminds me of one of my mom's old boyfriends, a white dude with dreadlocks who wore Rastafarian colors and texted my mom "Every little thing's gonna be all right" when he dumped her.

The memory—and the scent—makes me feel nauseated.

I find myself counting the customers leaving Happy Endings (carrying their pink-and-gold bags) compared with those leaving my store (with our made-from-70%-recycled-material bags).

They're beating me four to one, and my panic rises. I try to calm myself: Xander is paying attention to net profit, and Ryan's overhead is higher than mine. He has three other staff members working today, and his larger store means higher utility costs. Plus, his paperbacks are cheaper than my hardcovers.

Still, I'm worried.

I'm ringing up a customer (Sandy Bartholomew, a regular, purchasing James McBride's latest), when Ryan's thunderous laugh makes me flinch.

"Are you all right?" Sandy asks.

"Yes," I say. "Just . . . the noise over there. Sorry about that, I know it's irritating."

She shrugs, peering across the space. "Oh, it's fine. Is that another bookstore?"

"They only sell romance." I know Sandy's tastes don't lean that way.

But she lights up. "Really? My daughter adores romance. Thanks—I'll head over there next."

My heart sinks as I watch her cut through Beans into Happy Endings, where Ryan greets her. I despise the way my eyes seem magnetically drawn to his body, to his broad shoulders and narrow hips, his thighs in those jeans. Somehow, he makes a cardigan and old Levi's look undeniably—the word pops into my mind before I can squelch it—*sexy*.

"Welcome to Happy Endings," his voice booms. "What kind of love story can I help you find?"

And then he leads *my* customer away, his head bent toward hers as she tells him that her daughter adores Christina Lauren and Alexis Hall and Talia Hibbert, and can he help her find some new releases by similar authors?

My jaw clenches so tight my molars hurt.

Ryan glances back and our eyes lock. When his mouth twists in a cocky grin, a hot *zing* runs through me, and I whirl around. It's irritation, this reaction I keep having to him. It must be. Not the fact that his lips are kind of lush and pouty and—

I grab a spray bottle of cleaning solution and furiously polish my counter.

BY EVENING, THINGS have quieted down. This is one of my favorite parts of the day, a chance to recharge until it's time to start my closing duties. Happy Endings is still open, but Beans is closed. With the lights off and my back turned, I can almost forget that one side of my store is a gaping hole.

Smiling, I pull out *11/22/63*. It's not high literature, but the plot is intriguing, the characters well drawn. I can't stop turning the pages.

A soft, glowing warmth spreads over me as I read. There's something intimate about recommending a book to someone, so to have someone choose a book for me, a book that's exactly what I need after a challenging day? A true gift. *Thanks, RJ.*

A burst of applause startles me, and I jolt back to reality. In the far corner of Happy Endings, a group of people in chairs are facing a woman wearing a purple dress. Another event?

My body twitches with irritation, but I return to my book, only to be interrupted by laughter. Most of it is high pitched and feminine, except for one deeper voice, booming above the rest.

Against my will, I'm thinking *shoulders, thighs, pouty lips*, and fury sparks through me. I cannot spend the rest of the summer dealing with this. I have an event later this week with a local poet leading a guided meditation. I need some kind of barrier from the chaos. And from him.

My eyes land on two bookshelves. They're the kind with locking wheels, though I've never moved them before . . .

I head over to the first one, unlock the wheels, and push. Nothing happens, so I lean my shoulder against the side and shove with all my might. The bookcase shifts an inch, the wheels sending out a rusty *screech*. Over at Happy Endings, everyone goes quiet. Undeterred, I keep my head down and push again. *Screech, screech, screeeeeeeeech*. I've moved the shelf approximately three inches.

"What are you doing?"

I jump at the sound of Ryan's furious whisper behind me, and my skin prickles. I don't look up. "Well, hello to you, too, Brian—"

"My name isn't—"

"I'm just moving these shelves," I say, giving the bookcase another push. *Screeeeeeeech*.

"You can't do it later?" he hisses.

"Are you saying that"—I shove again, grunting—"it's annoying when noise"—shove, grunt—"from another store bothers your customers?"

He huffs in frustration, and I imagine him running his hands through his messy hair.

The first bookcase is now halfway into position, and I'm sweating and breathing hard. I realize with horror that the sounds I'm making are mildly pornographic, and I try my best to stifle them. I push again and flinch at the piercing shriek of the wheels.

"You know what, Brandon?"

"That's also not my—"

"If I'm annoying you so much, you could help me."

He huffs again, this time in disbelief. "Why would I do that?"

"Because I'd be done faster." I give the bookcase one last shove and straighten, wincing. "One down, one to go."

Ryan watches me as I head over to the next bookcase. His arms are folded across his stupid brawny chest, the expression on his face half grumpy toddler and half smirking douchebag. Like he knows he could push the shelf into place with little to no effort, but he'd rather watch me break my back.

And that's exactly what he does. The wheels aren't as squeaky on this one, but they're stiff. With each shove, my feet scrabble on the polished wood floor, and I'm cursing under my breath by the end—but he doesn't move a muscle.

My simmering frustration spikes into red-hot anger. It's like he enjoys seeing me struggle. Like he wants to humiliate me.

Or . . .

I twist around to see his face: lips parted, pupils dilated, eyes focused on my butt. He straightens and glances away.

"Were you staring at my ass?" I snap.

"You wish." His eyes flick to my chest for a half second before sliding away.

Heat sizzles down my spine—the heat of rage, I tell myself. Pure, scorching *rage*.

I march toward him, steam practically coming out of my

ears, and he stumbles back, bumping against the shelves behind him. He thinks he's the only one who can back someone into a bookcase?

He's towering above me, so I grab his lanyard and tug him down to my level. His eyes flash with surprise and something else—red and hot—and I realize what I've done: his mouth is inches from mine.

"You have something to say?" His voice is a husky rumble.

I can't meet his eyes; I'm breathing hard, fixated on his mouth, that full lower lip. "I hate how tall you are."

"Do you?" His tone is mocking. Like he's thinking, *Liar.*

"Yes," I snap. "I hate how you always look down on me."

"Want me to get on my knees?"

Fury zings through me, and I clench my thighs together.

"What I want," I say, "is for you to stop staring at me like you can't decide if you want to kill me or fuck me."

His eyes flash with heat. "Too bad," he whispers.

He's looking at me with blatant hunger, like he's daring me to pull him the rest of the way down. Just a couple of inches and his mouth will be on mine. My grip tightens on his lanyard. And for a split second, I think, *Why not?*

A burst of laughter sounds from his side of the store—like a bucket of cold water hitting me. I release his lanyard. He straightens up.

Taking a step back, I smooth my hair and attempt to pull myself together, knowing there's nothing I can do about my flushed cheeks. Flushed from *anger*—it must be. The alternative is too awful to even consider.

When I look up, he's smirking again, like he knows how much he rattled me. Like this is all part of his strategy to crush me into oblivion.

"I think you should go," I say, lifting my chin.

"Yeah," he says, releasing a dark laugh. "I would have if you hadn't—"

"Just go."

His jaw clenches, and he turns and stalks away, and I'm involuntarily staring at his butt, at the way his worn jeans hug everything *just right*—

"My sister was right about you," I call after him, and he pauses. "You're just a basic run-of-the-mill asshole."

His body goes rigid for one second, then two. But he doesn't turn around, doesn't reply. He just keeps on walking, disappearing behind the new bookcase-wall and into his store.

10

Ryan

A BASIC RUN-OF-THE-MILL asshole.

Even now, two days later, I can't get over the banality
of Josie's insult. Or the memory of her grabbing my lanyard,
her eyes glittering green fire. At that angle, I could see right
down her shirt, and the image of Josie Klein's cleavage
cupped in a bloodred bra will forever be tattooed on my
brain.

I'd think she was trying to screw with my head and get an
advantage, but she looked as out of control as I felt. Like we'd
been caught in some magnetic field and thrown together.

Until she broke the spell with that pathetic insult.

Simple as they were, her words stung. Maybe because she
wasn't wrong. Not about the asshole part—Josie is the only
one who brings that out in me.

But I've spent my entire life trying *not* to be ordinary or run
of the mill.

As the youngest Lawson brother, I got the leftovers of my
parents' DNA. I wasn't a good athlete like my brother John, I
wasn't funny like Robert, and I didn't get good grades like
Paul. The start of every school year was always the same—

when teachers realized I was one of *those* Lawsons, their expectations skyrocketed.

Which made their inevitable disappointment even worse.

For years, I tried to be athletic and academic, but around the time I became "friends" with those kids who dared me to shoplift a dirty book, I stopped. It was easier to give up than it was to keep failing.

If it hadn't been for Elaine, I may have never found my calling. To run this bookstore, and—

"Boss, can you come hang this for us?"

—and be the tallest person in almost any room.

"Sure thing," I say, heading over to hang the MAZEL TOV banner. Love is in the air today, along with a never-ending shower of dust motes from the construction. But I'm focusing on the bright side.

Today we're not just selling romance, we're playing a part in one.

Barb and Eva have one of the best second-chance love stories I've ever heard. Both women are in their eighties; they fell in love when they were in college and had to keep their relationship a secret. In the decades since, they each got married, raised families, and lost their husbands. They reconnected last year, and now the world is ready to celebrate their love.

A proposal like this would be a big deal at any time—but especially now that our days could be numbered. If Josie wins, love will come here to wither and die, not blossom.

The bell on the front door chimes and Indira walks in, carrying a Tupperware container.

"What've you got there?" I ask, grateful for a distraction.

Indira blushes. "Kansar." She opens the lid to show me

what looks like sweet confetti. "It's traditionally served at Indian weddings, but it's supposed to be a good omen, and I thought . . ."

"Eva and Barb will love it. We've got a table set up in the back if you want to put it there."

Indira smiles, and heads toward Cinderella, Eliza, and Nora, who are helping the couple's friends find hiding spots around the store. When you're loved by as many people as Barb and Eva are, it's impossible to keep things small.

And it will be impossible to keep them quiet.

As if on cue, the door opens again, and Alan, Barb's son, walks in, carrying his guitar. When Eva said he wanted to play a song for the couple, how could I say no?

The fact that it might cause a little disturbance for the meditation event Josie's been hawking all week is unfortunate. Maybe those big bookshelves will mute the sound.

And if not? #SorryNotSorry.

I'm not sorry our customers were having so much fun the other night that they got a little loud and disrupted her and all of her . . . oh, wait. There weren't any customers in her store. I'm also not sorry that I took so much joy watching Josie get all sweaty and breathless as she struggled with the shelves.

I *am* sorry that I stared at her ass (though it is an objectively gorgeous ass). Partly because it's disrespectful, but mostly because I *hate* that she affects me so much. My dick has not gotten the memo that Josie isn't someone we want to get closer to.

Maybe it's a good thing she made that bookshelf barrier. Out of sight, out of mind. Except I'm still thinking about her.

My phone buzzes: Gretchen.

> **Gretchen:** Hi, friend! It's a beautiful day on the Cape!

The photo attached is a close-up shot of two men wearing very tight Speedos.

I reply with the laughing emoji, and Gretchen comes back with: Have you thought more about my offer?

I'm telling the truth when I say, Yes . . .

Gretchen's "plan B" has been on my mind more than I'd like to admit. In the dark moments when I doubt myself—not just my ability to win the competition, but my ability to manage this entire bookstore if I do.

> **Gretchen:** And . . .

So many ands: And Lawsons aren't quitters. And Boston is my home. And Happy Endings isn't just a bookstore that could be replaced or replicated. And . . .

> I'm not ready to throw in the towel yet.

> **Gretchen:** Fair. Don't hate me if I check in again in a few weeks. You're a hot commodity. xx

Before I have a chance to reply, another text comes in. This one is from Eva: they just got off the T and are on their way to "pick up a book" they preordered.

"They're almost here!" I call out, and everyone hides.

"Hi, ladies," I say when they walk in a few minutes later.

"I hear you've got bookmail for us," Barb says.

Behind her, Eva catches my eye and grins—she's curled her hair and is wearing a dress for the first time I can remember.

"The new Casey McQuiston," I say, trying to tamp down my smile. "It's in the back. And, Barb—there's a new collection of poetry over there I think you might like."

"Ooh!" Barb heads to the front of the store, unaware that a photographer friend is standing outside, ready to snap photos through the window.

I give Eva a good luck squeeze on the shoulder, then join Cinderella and Indira behind the Hot Priest/Rabbi shelf.

We hear Barb's voice: "What in the—?"

And I know she's turned to find Eva down on one knee.

"Barbie, my love," Eva says, clearing her throat. "I haven't stopped loving you since the day we met sixty years ago. I don't regret the years we spent apart; they gave us our beautiful children . . . But now . . . now . . . I don't want to go another minute without making our love official. I want to be your wife, and I want you to be mine. Will you marry me?"

I peek around the bookshelf to see Barb, now also down on her knees, kissing Eva as tears spill down their cheeks.

Tears fill my eyes, too, as I'm pulled back to a memory I'm usually able to suppress. Having grown up under the shadow of my parents' love story, I went through high school and college with my eyes and my heart open, waiting for my own lightning-strike moment when I'd meet someone and know she was the one. It finally came on the day I moved into the dorms sophomore year.

Or so I thought.

For three wonderful years, Kate and I had a storybook

romance. Until she dumped me for her chemistry class TA. I was blindsided: I'd already started saving for a ring. When I asked her why, what this guy had that I didn't, she shrugged and said, "When you know, you know."

Based on her Instagram, she *did* know. They've been married for seven years and have two adorable kids. Meanwhile, I have two bookstore cats—one of which doesn't even like me—and a job I might be on the verge of losing.

But the most devastating part wasn't losing Kate, it was losing trust in my own intuition. If I was wrong about something that felt so right, how could I ever trust that feeling again?

Which is why, over time, I've realized that my purpose isn't to have my own love story, but to help other people find theirs.

"She said yes!" Eva calls out, and the room erupts in cheers as everyone jumps out to congratulate them. Cinderella pops a bottle of champagne, and I help the newly engaged couple back onto their feet. Kevin launches into a rousing rendition of Bruno Mars's song "Marry You."

It's a moment of pure, unbridled joy—until it's interrupted by the sound of someone clearing their throat. I turn to find Josie, her cheeks red, fallen tendrils of hair framing her face.

"Can I speak to you for a moment?" Her voice is flat, but her eyes are blazing. She's pissed, and I'm not in the mood to get lectured.

"If you have something to say, you can say it right here."

Josie surveys the scene, then huffs out an impatient breath. "I have twenty people over there trying to meditate." Her voice wavers, and I realize her eyes aren't shimmering from anger, but because she's on the verge of tears. "I planned this event for when you were closed so this wouldn't happen!"

Suddenly, I feel like the basic asshole she accused me of being. I knew her event was starting at seven; I could have asked Eva to plan the proposal for six instead.

"Josie, I'm—"

"I know you hate me," she cuts in. "I know you hate my books and my store. But I thought a fellow bookseller would have some respect for my *customers*. They're booklovers, just like the ones who come here."

She's right, and I feel a twinge of guilt. "Listen, I—"

"Not to mention the author leading the event has terrible social anxiety; he's in the back room hyperventilating into a paper bag." Josie breaks off, breathing heavily herself. It's obvious how much she cares about her customers and the anxious author, just like I would.

I am definitely the asshole here.

I'm about to apologize when Cinderella bursts in: "We're celebrating!" she says, lovably oblivious to the tension between us. "Here, have some champagne."

Josie shakes her head and pushes away Cinderella's hand. Champagne slops out of the glass and onto Cinderella's shirt, and my assistant manager backs away as if she's been slapped.

My protective instincts flare: Cinderella's been putting on a brave face, but I know proposals make her think of her own broken vows; of the husband who left her in the most generic way possible: falling in love with his much younger secretary.

I turn back toward Josie, who has her hands on her hips,

looking like a very beautiful, very rude nuisance. Still, I decide to be the bigger person and apologize.

"Josie," I say, "I really—"

"Do you even have a liquor license?" she asks, somehow forgetting that she recently hosted an event with wine. "I could call the cops on you. Drunken and disorderly behavior and disturbing the peace!"

Any sympathy I have for Josie Klein and her stupid meditation event evaporates faster than the champagne on Cinderella's shirt.

"Hey, Alan," I say, keeping my eyes focused on Josie's. "Why don't you play another song. And make it loud."

RJ.Reads: Just saying hi! Haven't talked to you in a few days!

BookshopGirl: Hi back! And yes, sorry, I've had a lot going on.

RJ.Reads: Hopefully good things?

BookshopGirl: Ughhhhhhh.

RJ.Reads: That bad?

BookshopGirl: You have no idea. And to top it all off, my final customer today was the living embodiment of one of my biggest pet peeves as a booklover.

RJ.Reads: Go on . . . *grabs popcorn*

BookshopGirl: So this customer, she's not one of my regulars, but she came in right before closing and started asking me for recs—which I LOVE giving, of course. She seemed genuinely interested, so I told her about all my recent favorite reads. I mean, maybe I was waxing poetic, but if you can't do that in your own bookstore, where can you? Anyway. She looked overwhelmed, then she said, "Wow! You sure read a lot. That's great that you have so much free time. I couldn't possibly read that much—I have responsibilities."

RJ.Reads: No. She. Did. Not.

BookshopGirl: Right? First of all, it's my literal job to know the product I sell, but also: I actually don't have a lot of free time, Janet. (Her name wasn't Janet but whatever.) I work open to close, seven days a week. And by the time I get home, I'm so tired I want to pull a Grandpa Joe for the next twenty years. But when you love something, you make time for it. You give up sleep, you say no to social engagements, you squeeze it in between your other tasks. If YOU don't like reading that much, JANET, just admit it. But don't you dare walk into MY bookstore and make ME feel like there's something wrong with me because I prioritize my favorite activity on the planet!

RJ.Reads: *SLOW CLAP*

RJ.Reads: I wish you'd said that to her.

BookshopGirl: Me too. Unfortunately, I just stood there gaping until she scuttled away.

RJ.Reads: Now I'm wondering how many books you read in a year. If that's not too personal to ask?

BookshopGirl: Usually between 250 and 300.

RJ.Reads: DAMN. Okay, you've got me beat. And you read big books. How do you do it? That's a genuine question—I want to know your technique.

BookshopGirl: The main thing is to not have any social life or other hobbies. But the other trick is to always have a book with you. Example: I have a Purse Book, in case I'm waiting in line or at an appointment. Then I have my Register Book, sitting behind the counter at work. My Kitchen Book, the one I read while I'm cooking (usually an ARC so it's okay if I get spatters on it). There's my Nightstand Book (not too riveting/ disturbing), and my Toilet Book (sorry, TMI), and my Bathtub Book (different from the Toilet Book because the

Bathtub Book is for relaxing reads). Plus there's a precarious pile on the end table in my living room, staring at me reproachfully for not getting to them yet.

RJ.Reads: Whoa whoa whoa. You're reading multiple books at the same time?

BookshopGirl: Well, yeah. It's rare that one book can keep me fully satisfied.

RJ.Reads: Maybe you're just meeting all the wrong kinds of books.

RJ.Reads: *reading. I mean READING the wrong books.

BookshopGirl: Ha. So you only read one book at a time?

RJ.Reads: Usually, yeah. I guess I'm a serial monogamist. I like to give my current book all the care and attention it deserves.

BookshopGirl: I bet your book appreciates that.

11

Josie

MY MONTHLY MEETING with Xander is today.

Last night, I dreamed that I was forcibly removed from my store along with my beloved customers, favorite authors, and hundreds of beautiful books, all of us chucked in the dumpster while Ryan watched, rubbing his hands together and cackling like a cartoon villain.

I'm terrified that it was a premonition, that Xander will tell me his good buddy Ryan is so far ahead, he's going to call it right now and hire him.

My phone chimes, and I'm grateful to see a message from RJ.

> **RJ.Reads:** Did you finish 11/22/63?

> **BookshopGirl:** Yes . . .

> **RJ.Reads:** And . . . (he says, nervously holding his breath).

> **BookshopGirl:** I loved it. I'm still thinking about that ending—glad he didn't cop

out and give us an unrealistically happy conclusion. It was SO satisfying. And who knew Stephen King could write such a compelling love story? Thanks for the recommendation.

RJ.Reads: I RECOMMENDED A BOOK TO BOOKSHOPGIRL AND SHE LIKED IT! I feel like I won a gold medal at the Olympics!

A customer walks up and I trade my goofy grin for a professional smile. Chatting with RJ feels almost like reading a good book, the kind you can't wait to get back to—but even better because we're writing it together as we go. There's no pressure, no awkward pauses; I can take my time with my replies and savor every word of his. We're characters in a story of our own making, with no real-world complications to muddy the waters. It's comfortable and exciting all at once—and unlike anything I've felt in my life. When I'm finished ringing up my customer, I send him another message.

BookshopGirl: Do you have another rec for me? I've forgotten how relaxing it is to turn your brain off and live in another world.

RJ.Reads: You want something to take you to another world? Hmmm . . .

RJ.Reads: Have you read The Princess Bride?

BookshopGirl: I've seen the movie.

RJ.Reads: The book is always better, but in this case, the book is a GAZILLION times better. I think you'll get a kick out of a literary device he uses. It's another won of my brother's favorite books.

RJ.Reads: *another ONE (sorry)

BookshopGirl: Are you ever going to suggest one of your favorites? The best way to get to know someone is to read their favorite books.

RJ.Reads: Yikes, that's kind of personal! I need to test the water before being that vulnerable. What if you hate my favorite book? I'll be forced to cut you out of my life, which would be a real shame.

BookshopGirl: Ah, yes, the literary obligation to hate people who hate your favorite book.

RJ.Reads: The #1 commandment of readers: Thou shalt despise all those

> who despise thy beloved books, for they show contempt for the treasures of thy heart and the wisdom therein.

I'm grinning as I go through my day; it's busy, but after a particularly maddening customer, I can't help sending another message.

> **BookshopGirl:** A customer asked for help finding books for his wife's birthday— classic "One has a blue cover and the other one starts with M" scenario. I found them! But then . . . he ordered them online. RIGHT IN FRONT OF ME.

> **RJ.Reads:** NOOOOOO. Why do people do this?

> **BookshopGirl:** RIGHT?? Like, "yes, I will use your mental labor for my benefit and not compensate you in any way."

> **RJ.Reads:** He clearly doesn't know that the #2 commandment of readers is "Thou shalt not exploit the goodwill of the independent bookseller only to forsake them for an online mega-store."

He manages to make me smile again, even though I'm still seething inside.

I needed that sale.

Fortunately, I have an event tonight that should help me take a huge leap ahead in this competition. It's with someone I've admired for years: Kenneth Michael Rutherford, international bestseller, short-listed for the National Book Award for his debut novel, *Tell Me No, Tell Me Yes.*

His second book came out two days ago, and I—yes, I, Josie Klein of Tabula Inscripta—have booked him for an author event this evening.

It's a coup. A miracle. How did I manage it? After trying (and failing) to get a response from his publicist, I decided to take matters into my own hands. I sent a message through the Contact Me page on his website, gushing about his first book— and about his latest, which I haven't read (his publisher didn't send an ARC). I said I'm his biggest fan, and if he has any openings this summer, I'd be delighted to host him for an author event. To my shock and delight, he replied and said he had an opening during pub week. This all happened ten days ago, and since then, I've been feverishly planning.

After Rutherford posted about the event on his social media, hundreds of orders poured in for signed copies, which I received yesterday via rush delivery from the publisher. And now it's happening. I, Josie Klein, college dropout and humble bookseller, am hosting one of the most respected literary authors of the twenty-first century.

I can't help sharing the news with RJ after setting up chairs for the event.

> **BookshopGirl:** I'm hosting an author this evening and I'm SO nervous.

> **RJ.Reads:** Who?

I pause; if I tell him, he can easily find out where Rutherford is appearing tonight, and then he'll easily find me.

The thought sends a ripple of discomfort through me. If RJ knew who I really was, I'd feel pressure to be the persona I've created over the past five years here at Tabula—the polished, professional bookseller who never lets her guard down. I'd start second-guessing everything I share, censoring myself. It would never be the same.

> **BookshopGirl:** Oh, never you mind. ;) But it's someone I really admire.

> **RJ.Reads:** You'll do great. And remember, you're doing a favor to the author. There grateful to be their, talking to people who care about there book.

> **RJ.Reads:** *they're. *there. *their. (smacking forehead repeatedly)

> **RJ.Reads:** Sorry. typing too fast.

> **BookshopGirl:** ☺ It's not a big deal. I appreciate you listening.

> **RJ.Reads:** Happy to. And thanks for not judging my typos.

> **BookshopGirl:** How could I judge you when I'm worried I won't be able to form

> a coherent sentence when I meet this
> author?

> **RJ.Reads:** If you're half as well spoken as
> you are well written, everyone will be
> impressed. You've always impressed me.

His words give me a warm burst of confidence. I vividly remember when Penelope Adler-Wolf hosted Kenneth Michael Rutherford at her store two years ago. She live-streamed the event, and I watched the whole thing, not only because I loved Rutherford's book, but because I wanted to memorize how PAW moderated: her command of the crowd, her ease around an author who'd leave me stammering.

That was the moment I decided I wanted to be just like her, a literary tastemaker, facilitating important discussions of books. And here I am, taking another step in that direction.

BUT FIRST: MY meeting with Xander.

We meet at Beans, and I give him the good news about the sold-out event tonight while he checks his phone and nods vaguely. Then he launches into his news.

"Josie, your profits are up compared to last June," he says. "I'm impressed."

My heart leaps; I know this—I've been tracking every penny—but it's nice to hear him confirm it.

"Unfortunately, you're slightly behind Ryan," he says, and my heart drops. "It's close, though, and you have time to make a comeback. But you better pull out your A game."

"Of course," I say through a smile, though internally, I'm wilting.

Xander rattles on about profit margins and expenses as I try not to burst into defeated tears. I've been working myself to exhaustion, but it hasn't been enough.

Thankfully, Xander is never one to linger. He stands, calling over toward Happy Endings.

"Lawson?"

Ryan appears from behind a bookshelf. "Ready when you are."

Xander glances at his phone, then waves a hand. "Something came up—I'll call you tomorrow."

And he's gone. Ryan looks over at me, one eyebrow cocked, like he's asking how my meeting went. I give him an easy-breezy smile, and his face falls. *Good.* Soon enough, he'll get the news that he's slightly ahead of me, but until then, let him simmer in worry.

Thank goodness I have this event tonight. It might even help me take the lead.

Ryan turns and walks away, and I squeeze my eyes shut so they don't watch his backside as he retreats, the way his broad shoulders fill out his cardigan, how he's wearing another pair of jeans that look so worn and soft I want to rub my cheek against them.

I need to focus on my objectives: meet one of my favorite authors, schmooze the hell out of the sold-out crowd, and sell a shit ton of books.

FIVE MINUTES INTO the event, and I'm queasy. Not because of nerves—but because something weird is going on here.

The place is packed, with every seat filled and more standing in the back. Rutherford was gracious as I helped him sign all the orders, plus more stock for the store, and my introduction went off without a hitch.

But I'm getting an odd vibe.

"I'd like to talk about the inspiration behind this newest novel of mine," Rutherford is saying. "I'm heartened that so many are willing to come hear about something that isn't . . . well, comfortable."

Three or four people in the crowd chuckle knowingly, and that's when it hits me: every person here is a white man. That's not typical for my events.

Maybe it's just a coincidence?

"As many of you know, this novel has been somewhat . . . controversial," Rutherford goes on.

Controversial? I discreetly pull out my phone and do a search for the novel title, plus the word "controversy."

I gasp.

The men in front of me turn, and I try to cover the noise with a cough. When they turn back around, I return to my phone and read, *Award-winning author Kenneth Michael Rutherford slammed for "ableist" views in recent novel.*

Heart sinking, I skim the headlines—there aren't many; his book just came out. The few reviews posted on retailer websites are either glowing five-stars praising his "forward thinking" or one-stars calling him "disgusting."

I google his publisher; it's a vanity press, which means the author fronts the costs of publication. The only reason a bestselling author like Rutherford would go that route is because no other publisher would work with him.

Up front, Rutherford is still talking: "From the beginning of the human race, those who were unable to contribute to the group were left behind. Our ancestors understood that to succeed as a species, they had to ensure that only the fittest individuals would survive and reproduce."

Sickened, I try to block out his voice as I pull up BookFriends to message RJ—but stop myself. Aside from the anonymity issue, I'm not sure I want RJ to know I invited this vile human into my store.

Instead, I post in the literary fiction forum, where I never see RJ: Anyone know what's up with Kenneth Michael Rutherford?

Answers from booksellers across the country appear right away:

> **DallasBooks:** I heard his latest book endorses sterilization of individuals with disabilities.

> **BeautyandtheBook:** No one knew about it until the book came out two days ago, because his publisher didn't send out ARCs or submit for trade reviews.

> **IlikeBigBooks:** There was a whole discussion about it yesterday in the PubDay forum

How did I miss that? I click over, and my dread grows. Sure enough, Rutherford's novel promotes forced sterilization and outright eugenics of anyone with mental or physical disabilities, "for the good of the race." The wording gives me horrified chills. My sister has a disability. This man would like to erase her from the face of the earth?

I fire off a text to Georgia.

> Kenneth Michael Rutherford is a horrible human and I didn't do my homework on his new book and now he's in my bookstore.

I have to stop this. But before I can figure out what to do, my phone vibrates in my pocket.

> **Georgia:** I just looked him up. He's DISGUSTING.

> **Josie:** I feel horrible for inviting him. For ever supporting him!

> **Georgia:** How could you have known? The book just came out! It's not your fault.

But it is my fault—it's my literal job to know these things. I've been focused on winning this competition and beating Ryan, rather than keeping up with the literary community.

> **Josie:** I'm going to ask him to leave. I can't sit here and allow him to keep spouting this disgusting rhetoric.

> **Georgia:** WAIT!

> **Georgia:** Looks like he's supported by some scary people—white supremacy organizations and a group that wants to

legalize corporal punishments for disobedient wives. You don't want to upset these people. They could be dangerous.

Josie: I need to do something!

Georgia: Not while you're alone. Is there anyone at Beans who could stand with you while you ask everyone to leave?

I peer through the bookcases forming the makeshift wall between my store and the coffee shop. Mabel is the only one working, and she's busy ringing up a late-evening customer.

Josie: No

Georgia: What about at Happy Endings? That awful Ryan guy is tall and intimidating, right?

I almost scoff out loud. Yes, Ryan is at his store—and every glimpse I get of him brings back memories of his mouth, inches from mine, the mocking lilt in his voice, and his smirky smile. There is no way I'm asking him for a damn thing.

Josie: He won't help me. He hates me. He'd rejoice in my downfall.

Georgia: Then just sit tight. It'll be over soon.

Rutherford talks for another fifteen minutes, then does a Q&A, followed by a meet and greet. I spend that time looking up organizations that support individuals with disabilities—I'll donate tonight's profits to them. There's no way I can keep this money.

And if Xander asks what happened? I'll be truthful, even though it might ruin my chances of getting the head manager position.

RJ.Reads: How did the big event go??!? I've been sending good bookish thoughts your way all day.

BookshopGirl: I don't really want to talk about it if that's okay.

RJ.Reads: That bad? Did no one show?

BookshopGirl: No, there were plenty of people there.

RJ.Reads: I hope you at least sold a lot of books? (he says, not sure how to get out of this conversation that his friend clearly doesn't want to be having)

BookshopGirl: It wasn't just the event, though that was awful. The whole thing brought up some stuff from the past. I've been thinking about it all day and can't seem to stop.

RJ.Reads: I'm sorry.

BookshopGirl: Thanks.

BookshopGirl: You know how characters in books always have a wound from their childhood that drives their growth and the plot? Do you think all people have that, too?

RJ.Reads: I think we all have many, many wounds. Some that we don't even understand. That's why therapists have jobs.

BookshopGirl: True. What do you think your wound is?

BookshopGirl: Never mind—that's none of my business. Sorry!

RJ.Reads: No, I don't mind sharing.

RJ.Reads: Mine probably comes back to never being enough. I was the participation trophy kid in a first-place family.

BookshopGirl: I can relate.

RJ.Reads: No way. You were probably the smartest person in your high school.

BookshopGirl: Maybe—but then I went to college where everyone was the smartest kid in their high school. I didn't have what it takes to finish. I had to drop out during my senior year.

RJ.Reads: I'm sorry. I bet that was rough.

BookshopGirl: It was awful. Not just because I dropped out, but because of everything that led up to it.

RJ.Reads: Like . . . ?

RJ.Reads: Sorry, you don't need to tell me. Just letting you know I'm open to hearing more if you're wanting to share.

BookshopGirl: Maybe another time. I guess my point is, I can't shake this deep-rooted fear that I don't have what it takes to succeed. Not at college. Not in my job. Not in life.

RJ.Reads: For what it's worth, everything I've ever seen of you has made it clear that you're smart, hardworking, and passionate. I get the sense that you have the ability to overcome whatever life throws at you.

BookshopGirl: Thanks. I hope that's true.

BookshopGirl: Anyway, that's probably my wound.

RJ.Reads: Thanks for trusting me with it.

BookshopGirl: Thanks for listening.

12

Ryan

I'M SITTING IN my second-favorite nook before the store opens, about to push play on an audiobook, when my phone rings. It's Xander.

"Lawson," he says, and I cringe. I hate the machismo bro-y vibe of the whole last-name thing, and the fact that it implies some level of history or friendship. Xander Laing and I are not friends. "Sorry I had to jet yesterday," he says. "You know how it is."

"I do," I say, even though I don't.

"Listen," Xander says, getting right down to business. "Your profits are up compared to last June. I'm impressed."

"Thank you," I say, sitting up a little taller at the unexpected compliment. "I can't take all the credit. My team has been—"

"Unfortunately," Xander cuts in, "you're slightly behind Josie."

"Oh," I say, my face falling. I'm such an idiot—of course my numbers being higher than normal doesn't mean anything compared to hers.

"It's going to be close," he says, giving me a tiny spark of hope. "So you'll have to pull out your A game if you want to keep your job. Hopefully that'll motivate your staff, too."

I try to swallow, but my throat's gone dry. "Their jobs will be safe either way, right? The profits are only going to determine the manager job."

"That'll be up to whoever's managing the store." There's noise on the other end of the line, then I hear Xander talking to someone else. "Gotta run," he says, back to me. "Keep up the good work."

I hang up and try to blink away an unsettling mental picture of the future: Josie handing out pink slips or making things so difficult my staff quits on their own. I have to figure out some way to get ahead.

Even still, I find myself pulling up this morning's message from Gretchen.

> Greetings from your plan B! Any update?

I hesitate, chewing on my lip, then type: Can I call you later? No decision yet, but I'd love to hear more details.

Gretchen texts back immediately: OMG! Really?! Yes of course—call anytime.

Their enthusiasm is gratifying, especially after Xander's news. At least someone thinks I have something useful to offer.

I slump back against the couch and open the Libro.fm app. I wish I was listening to a comfort read, something with a guaranteed happy ending. But right now, I'm listening to a book that I know won't end happily—after BookshopGirl mentioned the best way to get to know someone is to read their favorite books, I put a few from her Favorite Reads shelf on my TBR list, including this one—*Atlas Shrugged*. I was going to buy the hardcover, but it's more than a *thousand* pages. The audiobook is sixty hours, but still easier for my mind to digest.

I'm about to hit play when a message from BookshopGirl comes in.

> **BookshopGirl:** Good morning! Guess what? I started The Princess Bride after we finished chatting last night.

> **RJ.Reads:** And . . .

> **BookshopGirl:** And the one I got is apparently abridged. Do you know where I can get a copy of the original? It's OK if it's longer. When we read Les Misérables for English in 11th grade, our teacher assigned us the abridged version, but I read the original even though it's 1,463 pages.

A laugh bursts out of me, startling Persephone, who just got comfortable on my lap. She gives me an annoyed side-eye before falling back asleep.

> **RJ.Reads:** There isn't an unabridged version.

> **BookshopGirl:** Yes, there is, the author says right at the beginning that the original was written by S. Morgenstern. Maybe I should try a vintage retailer.

> **RJ.Reads:** Did you google S. Morgenstern?

BookshopGirl loves unique structures, so I figured she'd get a kick out of this one—but maybe I should've just come out and told her. The last thing I want is to make her feel stupid for not knowing.

But that's the genius of the book. The author (William Goldman, a legendary screenwriter) frames the entire novel as the "good parts" of the original history written by the fictional S. Morgenstern.

The longer I wait for a reply, the more nervous I get. She's probably rolling her eyes and promising herself she'll never ask me for recs again. Good thing I didn't suggest one of *my* favorite books—I wasn't kidding when I said I couldn't handle it if she hated it.

I'm about to give up when my phone pings again.

> **BookshopGirl:** WHAT THE ACTUAL FUCK.

> **BookshopGirl:** ARE YOU SERIOUS??

My stomach sinks.

> **BookshopGirl:** This author is either a genius or a total nutjob. Either way, I'm hooked.

A huge smile spreads across my face as I lean my head back against the chair, relieved.

RJ.Reads: I'd never steer you wrong.

BookshopGirl: Thank you. Really—it's just what I needed. It's been a rough few weeks, which is another reason why last night hit extra hard.

BookshopGirl: Got to go. Chat soon!

"*Holy fuckin' shit!*" I hear Eddie say ten minutes later. The whir of his espresso machine has almost blurred into white noise, but Eddie's voice—especially at its most dramatic—can cut through anything.

I glance up, less than half interested until I see the person he's talking to.

The warm and fuzzy feelings from my conversation with BookshopGirl evaporate, replaced by the irritation I always feel around Josie. I don't care what's going on with her. I shouldn't. But my curiosity—okay, my nosiness—gets the best of me.

I lift Persephone off my lap. "Sorry, sweet girl," I say, giving the soft spot between her ears a nuzzle before stepping into Beans. I've already had my morning frappe, but there's always room for another.

As far as guilty pleasures go, mine isn't that bad. I wonder what BookshopGirl's is, if she has one. And just like that, I'm back to thinking about her.

Is it possible to have a crush on someone when you don't know their real name or what they look like? Except I'm pretty sure BookshopGirl is beautiful. Smart, thoughtful, funny, and beautiful.

"Fuckin' hell, Ry—you won't believe what Josie just told me," Eddie says.

Josie's back is to me, and her shoulders stiffen. She's in full ice-queen mode today: tight bun, black pencil skirt that hugs her curves, and sky-high heels that make her legs look endless. She gives me a brief glance, then looks away—but not before I see her expression. Totally sour, like she's sucked on a lemon. Hard to believe that a week ago she had me backed against a bookcase, staring at my lips like she wanted to suck on *them.*

"It's no big deal," Josie says.

"Come on, it's a *huge* deal," Eddie says, before looking at me and adding, "The usual?"

He raises an eyebrow and I gulp, hoping my "usual" doesn't include a wad of spit. I've been on good behavior around him—unless Josie told him about the bookshelves . . .

"It's fine," Josie says to Eddie. As if she can't be bothered to have this conversation with me. "I just had a situation at my event last night."

"No one showed up?" I ask, unable to miss the chance to razz her. I know she had a full house; I was here working late, filling more than a hundred Book and a Vibe subscription boxes.

"No," Josie hisses, sounding not unlike Hades. "The event was sold out, thank you very much."

"Then what was the problem?" I'll have to ask Cinderella if Mercury is in retrograde—what are the chances that Josie and BSG both had bad events last night?

"The guest author was a racist-ableist-eugenicist asshat," Eddie says to me.

Josie's shoulders slump as she mumbles, "I really fucked up."

I'm not sure she meant for me to hear that last part; it's unlike her to show any sign of weakness. But I also can't imagine Josie Klein inviting a guy like that to her store. Just last week I saw her dress down a customer at Beans who made a nasty comment about her sister's cane.

"Why would you host him?" I ask, genuinely curious.

"His last novel was nominated for the National Book Award," Josie says, before quickly adding, "and I didn't read the new book first."

"Ah man, been there, done that," I say, remembering when a local author gave off subtle pedophilia vibes at one book launch we hosted. "Just say no if an author named G. T. Offman comes knocking . . ."

"Same goes with Kenneth Michael Rutherford," Josie says, a bite in her tone.

"Wait, you brought *that* guy into your store?"

Rutherford was trending on BookFriends last night. The Literary forums aren't usually my jam, but I came across the post since it was started by BookshopGirl. The things people were saying about this guy . . .

Josie presses her palms against her eyes as if she's trying to block out the memory.

"I hope you kicked him out on his ass," I say.

I would have liked to see that, someone else being on the receiving end of Josie Klein's death glare.

"She couldn't kick him out," Eddie says, shaking his head. "The crowd was all white guys—no offense."

"None taken," I say, confused by why that matters.

But then I remember that someone on BookFriends said Rutherford has been linked to a bunch of violent, bigoted organizations, and it makes sense. Josie nearly always works alone—of course she wouldn't feel comfortable standing up to Rutherford and his fans without any support or backup.

"She was afraid for her safety," Eddie continues, putting a hand over his heart. "I wish I'd been here to help you, Josie."

"Me too," Josie says quietly.

"I was here," I tell them both. "I could have helped." I feel a twinge of guilt, even though I had no idea what was going on.

Josie scoffs and turns to look at me for the first time this entire conversation. There's that death glare again. "Oh, come on. You wouldn't have helped me."

"Of course I would have," I insist.

"Would not."

"Would so," I volley back, cursing Josie Klein for luring me into this childish game.

"Give me a break, Brayden," Josie says, and her intentional use of another wrong name grates on my last nerve. "You would have just stood there and watched me struggle."

"That's not—"

"That's exactly what you did the other day with the bookshelves," she says, her voice rising an octave.

That twinge of guilt turns into a gut punch; she's right. I was an asshole. But the circumstances were completely different.

"Your life wasn't in danger!" I say, my voice matching hers in volume and intensity. "Eddie, tell her I would have saved her if she was really in trouble."

Josie lets out a bitter laugh. "Eddie, tell him to get over his hero complex. Not all women need to be rescued."

Ouch. Her words hit a nerve; it's not the first time the word "hero" has been used to describe me in a less-than-flattering way. Is it my fault that I like to help people?

Hell, Josie is mad at me for *not* helping her. Damned if I do, damned if I don't.

"Ryan," Eddie says, drawing out my name and looking at me somberly. "The next time you see a bunch of scary-ass white guys over at Josie's, go help her." He turns toward Josie. "Josie, the next time you see a bunch of white guys over at Ryan's . . . call me."

He laughs at his own joke, defusing the tension.

Josie looks like she's on the verge of laughing, too, until Mabel walks over and attempts to hand her my drink. "Here's your frappe," she says.

Josie's expression goes blank, but her ears turn even more pink.

"That. Is not. My drink." Her tone is deceptively flat, but her eyes are that fiery green color I've become familiar with.

I can't look away, my own eyes drifting across her face: the faint freckles on her nose, the curve of her lips, the clench of her jaw. A few strands of dark, curly hair have come loose from her bun, tickling the nape of her neck, where the skin is a creamy shade of peach. I imagine how it would feel to press my lips right there.

I feel weirdly hot. Claustrophobic. And when she turns on her heel and walks back to her side of the store, I can't decide if I'm disappointed or relieved.

"I would have helped her," I tell Eddie once she's gone.

"I know," Eddie says solemnly. Then his lips curve in a suggestive smile, and he shakes his head. "Oh, I know, Ryan."

Beneath her layers of anger and hurt, I hope Josie knows it, too. This guy she's made me out to be—her enemy—he's not me. I don't even like sports because someone has to lose. I run a romance bookstore, for Pete's sake. I'm not a bad guy.

But deep down, I know it's not all Josie's fault that she sees me this way. I should have helped her with those damn bookshelves. Of course, if I had, she probably would've accused me of upholding the patriarchy. No matter what I do, I can't win.

But I can't lose, either.

Not this competition, and not my store.

LATER THAT NIGHT, I'm doing dishes and listening to my audiobook when my phone chimes.

> **BookshopGirl:** Hey, how was your day?

I sigh; I'm still bothered by that argument with Josie—I hate that she thinks of me as that kind of guy. And that I've been acting like that kind of guy.

> **RJ.Reads:** I've had better.

> **BookshopGirl:** What happened?

I don't really want to get into it, but for some reason, I find myself sharing a little.

> **RJ.Reads:** Remember our conversation about wounds? Well, someone said something today that pricked at one of mine. Basically implying that I'm not a good person. I've always thought of

myself as a good guy. But around THIS person, I'm not, and it sucked to realize that.

BookshopGirl: If it's just around this specific person, I doubt it's your fault. It's probably theirs.

Maybe, maybe not. And blaming my behavior on Josie isn't the mature thing to do, even if she does needle me like no one else.

RJ.Reads: I have objectively not treated this person all that great. But I'm not sure if I can do anything to change our dynamic.

BookshopGirl: Maybe you can't. But my little sister (she's in grad school to become a psychologist) would say that if you can't directly make amends with this person, consider doing something kind for someone else. It won't erase what happened, but it can help shift your energy in a positive direction.

BookshopGirl: I know that sounds hokey. I'm not sure I believe it, but maybe it's worth a try?

Interesting. Though I have no idea how I'd do anything like that.

> RJ.Reads: Huh. I'm willing to give it a shoot.

I read my message and shake my head, irritated at myself, the way mistakes sneak in despite my best efforts.

> RJ.Reads: *shot

> RJ.Reads: So . . . can I do anything for you? ;)

> BookshopGirl: Ha. Idk. Like what?

> RJ.Reads: My helpfulness is limited over chat, but . . . anything you want to talk about?

> BookshopGirl: Maybe? Ever since our conversation the other day, I've been thinking about what I told you—how I dropped out of college. And I realized that I haven't ever talked about it. Like, ever.

Warmth creeps through me, and I leave the dishes to go sit on the couch.

> RJ.Reads: If you think it'd help to talk about it, then I'd be honored to

listen. And I mean that truthfully.
Not just to shift the energy.

BookshopGirl: Okay. Well. During fall
semester of my senior year, my sister
was in an accident—hit by a car while
walking home from school. She broke
eleven different bones in her body.

My stomach drops to the floor; she's sounded so protective
when talking about her sister. Now it makes sense.

RJ.Reads: Oh my god. That's terrifying.

BookshopGirl: It was. At first, they
weren't sure she'd make it. I hardly left
her side during the two weeks she was in
the hospital. Then she went home and I
went back to school. I thought she was
doing okay until my mom took off.

RJ.Reads: Wait, what? Your mom left?

It gets worse. BookshopGirl tells me the whole story:
apparently, this was something her mom did a lot, chasing
some guy, forgetting she had daughters to care for. In this case,
she was dating an asshole who got fed up with the fact that
BSG's mom was "distracted" caring for her injured daughter.
So her mom left, leaving her young, wheelchair-bound
daughter home alone.

BSG went home to help her sister, which doesn't surprise me at all. What does surprise me is what she tells me next, how she blames herself for the way it affected her schooling.

> **BookshopGirl:** I should have been able to keep up—I was an English major, so all I had to do was read and write. I could do that from anywhere.

> **RJ.Reads:** Except you were overwhelmed and scared. I'm having a hard time wrapping my head around the fact that your mom took off. You were just a kid yourself.

> **BookshopGirl:** Technically speaking, I was an adult. And I've spent my whole life taking care of my sister, so I'm used to that.

> **BookshopGirl:** Anyway, I tried to make it work, but I failed two classes and lost my scholarship.

> **RJ.Reads:** Didn't anyone at school reach out to you? Try and support you?

> **BookshopGirl:** Yes, but by the time the next semester started, my mom had been dumped by that guy and wasn't

functional even though she was technically home. My sister needed me, so I just . . . never went back.

BookshopGirl: It's fine. I've had to live with that ever since: the knowledge that I'm the kind of person who gives up.

Shaking my head, I type the words I wish I could say to her in real life:

RJ.Reads: No, you're the kind of person who sacrificed her future to care for her little sister when no one else would. Your mom failed you. You did not fail. You showed strength and resilience in the face of adversity.

BookshopGirl: My sister is the one who showed strength and resilience. She deals with the effects of that accident every day—and she hasn't let that stop her.

RJ.Reads: Neither have you! You've worked your way up to be the manager of your store. That's impressive.

BookshopGirl: Right now I'm only managing myself.

RJ.Reads: Doesn't matter. Bookselling is important work, BSG. I know you know that.

BookshopGirl: Of course I do. But it's not just the job, you know? It's about what it represents—a sense of purpose, of accomplishment. Things at work are a little tenuous right now, and if I lose my job? I don't know what I'll do.

I understand completely. Interesting that we're both facing the possibility of losing our jobs—though I suppose that's probably true for lots of indie booksellers.

RJ.Reads: If that happens, you'll get through it the same way you got through the situation in college.

BookshopGirl: By giving up?

RJ.Reads: No, by finding a new path, by adapting and persevering. You're more capable and resilient than you give yourself credit for.

There's a long pause, and I start to worry that maybe I said too much. But then three dots appear, followed by her reply.

> **BookshopGirl:** You're a good person, RJ. I know you said you grew up feeling below average, but everything I've seen is top tier. You're an excellent listener, a thoughtful bookseller, and a wonderful friend. I know that for sure.

I stare at her words, wondering how she's turned this around so that she's complimenting and comforting me. But after my run-in with Josie earlier, I needed to hear this, to remind me of the kind of person I want to be. The kind of person I know I can be, if I'm honest with myself about my behavior and make some changes.

> **RJ.Reads:** I appreciate that. More than you know. Chat tomorrow?

> **BookshopGirl:** Of course. The best parts of my days are chatting with you.

> **RJ.Reads:** Same.

13

Josie

I'M AT TABULA Inscripta, packing online orders for a local author's preorder campaign, when the door chimes. It's Georgia, cane in one hand and phone in the other.

"I just got to Josie's store!" Georgia says into the phone, flashing me a wide, hopeful smile.

And instantly, I know. She's talking to our mother. The only person on earth who makes my smart, confident sister regress to an eager-to-please teenager.

I shake my head as Georgia whispers, "Mom's about to leave for Mexico—she wants to say hello!" Before I can respond, she says into the phone, "Hey, Mom! Josie's right here!"

She thrusts it at me, and I reluctantly take it. "Hello?"

"Josie!" My mother's high-pitched voice fills my ear. "Sweetheart! How are you? Are you dating anyone? It's been so long since you dated anyone, Jojo."

It's true, Georgia mouths, and I roll my eyes.

My mom continues, "Georgie sent a picture of you two, and it looks like you're breaking out a little. I heard about a new acne cream that could help. Darrell can get it for you—he's a doctor!"

I sigh, not even knowing how to respond. "Who's Darrell?"

My mom's laughter peals through my ear. "My fiancé, sweetheart, you know that."

Fiancé? I mouth to Georgia, who shrugs. I'd bet good money Darrell isn't actually her fiancé. Or a doctor. Last time my mother was dating a "doctor," he was just a guy who worked at GNC.

Mom rattles on about Darrell and his time-share in Puerto Vallarta, how she got auburn highlights and bought a new sundress that accentuates her figure. I'm only half listening—until she says something about Georgia meeting her in Mexico.

What? I mouth to my sister, who gets a guilty look on her face and shrugs.

Mom has run out of topics to ramble about. "I'd better get back to Darrell," she says. "Love you! Kisses and hugs!"

"Love you, too," I say, but she's already hung up.

I sigh again; I do love her—but that doesn't mean I think she's a healthy person to be close to.

I hand my sister the phone. "You're going to Mexico?"

"Probably not," Georgia says, shrugging. "Flights are expensive, and I can't miss too many classes, but I want to meet Darrell. It sounds like this relationship is the real deal, Jo."

I grimace. "Which is what she always says. Please tell me you see that."

My voice is getting snippy—because I'm worried. Georgia, despite taking an entire course in family therapy, doesn't recognize how damaged our upbringing was. She loves our mom when she's like this, fun and enthusiastic, albeit a tad flighty and judgmental. But it's like she forgets that at any moment, Fun Mom could morph into Absent Mom, then into Heartbroken Mom, and there's nothing we can do.

I can feel my body tensing, like I'm bracing for impact. It's how I always felt growing up, constantly on guard, never able to fully relax.

"Darrell is good for her," Georgia insists. "He's got her playing pickleball, he helped clean out her apartment—"

"Poor man," I say under my breath.

Georgia's face is flushed. "She's going to therapy and taking care of herself and now she's met a great guy—"

"Like all the other great guys?"

She presses her lips together, then shifts into that exasperating professional tone. "Maybe you should explore why you're distrustful of relationships, Jojo—Mom's right, you haven't dated anyone for a while. And when you *do* date, you never let yourself get emotionally attached. Why do you think that is?"

I fold my arms and match her tone. "Hmm. What could possibly be the reason, Dr. Klein?"

Georgia swallows. "Okay, Mom wasn't exactly a shining example of healthy relationships. But this time is different. I don't understand why you're not happy that she's doing well."

Because I know what happens next, when the knight in shining armor leaves. She'll chase after this guy—and then she'll crumble.

My eyes fill with tears, and I blink them away.

"I hope you have a wonderful time in Puerto Vallarta, if you decide to go," I tell my sister.

And I mean it: I hope that when she arrives, Mom and

Darrell are still deeply in love. I hope Mom stays happy forever.
I hope she's found her One and Only and spends the rest of
her life with him, safe and secure and adored.

But hope without evidence to support it is a delusion.

Georgia leaves for class, and I turn my attention to my next
task: moving a table back to the front of the store where it
belongs, then stacking all the new releases on it. The plumber
asked me to clear that area so he could work on the pipes in
the ceiling, but he had to order parts that won't arrive for a
week, and I can't handle an entire week with the table in the
wrong place.

By evening, the store is empty, so I go into the back room
and heat a frozen dinner. When it's ready, I sit at the desk,
which is strategically positioned so I can eat while keeping an
eye on the store.

I pull out *The Princess Bride*. I wasn't lying when I told RJ I
think it's genius. Ridiculous, yes, but self aware—like the
author is having fun. It's pure literary dessert, as RJ might
say—and I'm savoring each bite.

I lose track of time as I read, occasionally pausing to look
up and scan my store. But it's drizzling outside, and no one is
shopping, so even though I have a million things to do, I allow
myself to get sucked into the story. The feeling reminds me of
being twelve years old, reading under the covers with a
flashlight because I had to know what happened next.

As Westley and Buttercup are making their way into the
Fire Swamp, I become aware of a new sound, a light
spattering. I glance into the store—it's still raining outside—
and keep reading.

But the spattering gets louder. Maybe the door is cracked? I
force myself to close the book and check it out.

My heart drops.

In the front corner, where the ceiling is exposed, one of the pipes is leaking water. All over my freshly arranged table of new releases.

"No!" I cry, running over. It's not a full-on stream of water, more like a spray, but it's covering a large area—the entire table, plus a few feet surrounding it.

Stacked with hardcovers, the table's too heavy to move, so I start grabbing books—only to realize that exposes the lower layers of books to the water, too. Frantically, I look around for something to cover the table. The construction workers have left plastic tarps here before, but of course, not today. I run into my back room, find a box of trash bags, and race back to the front of the store.

I groan. The top layer of books is dotted with water—the beautiful dust jackets ruined, unsellable. Trying not to cry, I yank trash bags out and spread them across the books. The spray coats my hair, dripping into my eyes and blurring my vision—though that might be tears, too.

"Why is this happening to me?" I wail, out loud.

Out of the corner of my waterlogged eyes, I see a large blur coming toward me.

"What the—?"

I step back and wipe my eyes to clear them, shocked: Ryan Lawson is here. In my store. Voluntarily.

He's bending at the waist, putting both hands on the heavy wood table and giving it a giant heave. The table moves a full foot across the floor, and he keeps pushing, grunting with the effort, until it's clear of the water.

Then he straightens up, brushing wet hair out of his face, and turns toward me. Our eyes meet, and it's like the entire world slows down. He's not wearing his glasses, his hair is swept back, and he's giving off serious Clark Kent vibes—only, like, midtransformation. It's unexpectedly appealing. Hot nerd meets superhero.

"You moved my table," I say stupidly.

He removes the earbuds from his ears. "Yes."

"Why?"

One corner of his mouth lifts. "Because it was getting wet? Like I said, I'd help you if you needed it."

He doesn't sound smug, though. He sounds awkward. I'm still staring at him, so I clear my throat and turn my attention back to the table. All these beautiful hardcovers, destroyed. Thousands of dollars of stock. My stomach twists.

"This is bad," I say quietly.

Ryan comes up next to me. "Xander has insurance, right?"

"Yes, but . . ." My throat swells with panic. One of the baristas at Beans once accidentally left a metal spoon in a blender, which caused it to explode. Xander decided not to file a claim because he didn't want to pay the deductible. He made Eddie eat the cost. "I don't think he'll use it for this."

"The plumber must have done something wrong—he should cover the damages," Ryan says, looking up at the ceiling.

I shake my head, despair creeping over me. "He told me to leave the area clear until he could come back next week, but it was blocking the flow of the store." I shrug helplessly. "It's my fault. That's how Xander will see it, anyway."

This will destroy my bottom line.

Ryan picks up a book. "The top layer of books might be ruined, but the ones underneath aren't bad." He takes off the dust jacket and peers at it. "Some might be salvageable. You couldn't sell them for full price, but maybe at a discount?"

His tone is so peculiar. He sounds . . . concerned?

"Here, let's get these off and see how it goes," he says, and starts removing dust jackets. "Do you have any towels? And something to put around that pipe?"

Robotically, I grab paper towels, duct tape, and more trash bags from the back room, then return to the table.

Ryan is taking the wettest books off and setting them on the floor. The books underneath the top layer just have a few water speckles on them, and the relief I feel is overwhelming.

As Ryan duct-tapes layers of trash bag around the leaky pipe, I call the plumber, who says he'll come soon to take care of it. Ryan and I turn our attention back to the books. Some are ruined, but fewer than I expected. Fewer than there would have been, if he hadn't come.

"Why are you helping me?" I ask, my voice wobbling.

Ryan looks up. Again, his face startles me. The strong jawline, the way his eyes catch the light, his easy, unguarded expression—it's doing things to me. "Because your books were getting damaged?"

"Yes . . . but I'm your competition. You could have let everything get ruined."

If our situations were reversed, I might have done exactly that. That's how badly I've wanted to crush him.

Ryan's forehead wrinkles; he looks genuinely upset. "Books are too important to be casualties in our war, Josie."

His words hit me in the chest, and I nod without speaking. We work silently, stacking the ruined books in the back room, removing the dust jackets from the damp ones and spreading them across the floor, arranging the dry ones back on the table.

Ryan is meticulous, handling the books with care in his big

hands, his eyes narrowed as he inspects the spines and pages. We don't talk, and I'm glad—my throat feels swollen and raw. I keep worrying that I might start crying, not because of the damage, but from relief. From the sense of solidarity, the comfort of having someone at my side who understands exactly how awful this is.

I wonder what would've happened if we'd met some other way, not as competitors but as two fellow booksellers. Maybe we could've been . . . friends?

After we finish, Ryan follows me to the back room with one last armful of soggy books and sets them on the floor next to my desk. I don't know how to express my gratitude for this unexpected kindness that I don't deserve.

"Ryan," I say, "I owe you—"

"Are you reading that?" he asks sharply.

Startled, I follow his gaze. He's staring at the paperback copy of *The Princess Bride* on my desk.

Instantly, my hackles go up. "Yes."

All that openness I saw earlier in his face? Gone. His eyes dart between the book and me.

"No way," he says, almost to himself.

"Are you judging my reading choices?" I demand, hands on hips.

He doesn't seem to hear; he's running both hands through his hair in agitation, staring at me with the strangest expression. Like he's seeing me for the first time.

"No fucking way," he says.

And without another word, he's gone.

14

Ryan

JOSIE KLEIN IS BookshopGirl. *BookshopGirl is Josie Klein.*

My brain is short-circuiting. I can't believe it—I don't want to believe it. No way my smart, interesting, funny, kind friend on the internet is the ice queen herself. My nemesis. The woman who, if she wins, will erase everything I care about.

I'm dizzy and disoriented, like I've stepped through a portal. The store feels claustrophobic, so I close up and start walking. The sidewalks are nearly empty because of the rain, but I hardly notice it. My mind is reeling.

That couldn't have been a coincidence, Josie reading *The Princess Bride.*

Oh god, I hope it's a coincidence.

Somehow, I've ended up in Harvard Square. I duck into the Dunkin' to dry off and recalibrate. As I scroll through my messages with BookshopGirl, my stomach turns to lead. There are countless clues I should have picked up on. Like how BookshopGirl and Josie both have a habit of saying "technically speaking." Only when BSG says it, the phrase comes off as charming and cute. Unlike Josie, who uses the words as if she's looking down on everyone who isn't as smart as she is.

Then there's the whole Kenneth Michael Rutherford ordeal. It should have been obvious that BSG posted about the ableist prick the same night he spoke at the Tab. And of course, the story of her sister's accident—she must be the woman with the cane I've seen helping Josie.

And BSG mentioned that her job is tenuous.

Fuck.

I have no doubt it's true, but I can't merge the two people in my mind. One is kind where the other is callous; one is funny, the other pretentious; one is my friend, and the other is my sworn enemy.

When we talked last night, BookshopGirl was so vulnerable; that couldn't have been an act.

Could it?

Desperate to escape my swirling thoughts, I get up and keep walking, hoping I'll tire out my feet and my mind.

THE NEXT DAY, I'm no closer to figuring this out. I've been going through my work tasks in a daze, trying to avoid Josie at all costs.

Because the other question I'm wrestling with is: What do I do now that I know?

I hate lying. Plus, I have no poker face. The next time I see Josie, she'll probably see the truth written all over me.

"For god's sake, spit it out already!"

I look up to see Nora, deceptively dressed like a sweet grandma, holding a basket of crochet projects in her arm.

"Spit what out?"

She tsks. "You've been moping around all day, staring at your phone like a lovesick girl waiting for someone to slide into her DMs."

"What do you know about sliding into people's DMs?"

Nora makes a sour face—nothing pisses her off more than someone implying she isn't hip.

"Is it that girl you've been texting?" she asks, taking a seat at the other end of the couch.

My eyes widen. I try to keep my messaging with BSG to nonworking hours, but a few times—okay, a lot of times—we had really good banter going, like, Emily Henry–level banter, and I couldn't wait to reply.

"Oh, don't get your panties in a bunch," Nora says. "I didn't see anything. But there's clearly someone."

When I don't respond, she shrugs and hands me a small, stuffed crocheted item.

"What do you think?" She smiles up at me, all sweetness.

"It's . . ." I turn the object over, trying to figure out what it is. When Nora said she'd make romance-themed crochet projects to sell here, I assumed she meant more of the little animals she makes for her grandkids. Maybe this is some kind of sea cucumber? It's light brown and oblong with two round—

"It's a ween," Nora says.

My hand yanks back, and it falls on the carpet.

"Good lord, don't be such a prude." Nora stoops to pick it up, but I reach down and grab it for her. "Now, if you don't like it . . ."

She sounds hurt, and I realize that the entire basket is full of them, all different sizes and shades, from light tan to dark brown. These must have taken hours to make.

"They're great!" I say, my voice high pitched. "So great! I really, really think they're great."

She gives me a skeptical look. "Well, I tried my best to showcase a range of styles. Cut and uncut, large and small, some a little curved—"

"There is someone," I blurt out, holding up my phone.

Nora's painted eyebrows start dancing. "I knew it! Who is she? How'd you meet?"

I wasn't planning on talking about this with anyone, much less my septuagenarian employee, but it's better than hearing a detailed description of the crocheted dongs I've apparently agreed to sell in the store.

"I don't actually know who she is," I say, which was true just yesterday. "And we met on BookFriends."

"You mean Book More-Than-Friends," she says with a wink.

"Just friends." Although I felt more of a spark for BookshopGirl than I have for any of the women I've gone out with in the last . . . well, since college. "But I'm not sure we can even be that anymore."

Nora frowns. "What happened?"

I shrug. "It turns out she's someone I know in real life. A person I don't like. Someone who's completely different from the woman I thought I knew."

"Ah," Nora says. "And you're not sure which version is real."

"That about sums it up," I say, slumping back onto the couch.

"The internet is a tricky place," Nora says after a moment. "It's easy to pretend you're someone you're not. All those catfishers. And the trolls, saying things they'd never have the balls to say to your face. But for most people, I think the truth is somewhere in the middle."

"Between a catfish and a troll?"

Nora nods solemnly. "People want to be seen as the best version of themselves. So maybe they pretend they're nicer or taller or richer—but it's still them, deep down. I'd say that's true for your book friend, too. I mean, what reason does she have to lie?"

One of our conversations comes back to me, when BSG said she's worked so hard to make something of herself, to turn her life around. Maybe Josie's icy exterior is just armor, protecting the part of her that still believes she's a failure. Hiding the warm, generous, tender soul I've come to know online.

"Give her a chance," Nora says, squeezing my shoulder. "If you don't, you'll never know what you could be missing."

She's got a point, although I can't imagine a world where Josie Klein and I are friends, let alone anything more.

"Now," she says, pulling her basket back on her lap. "I found some patterns for vulvas . . ."

LATER THAT AFTERNOON, the store is bustling with the after-school book club. Eliza's running a thoughtful discussion on Alyssa Cole's latest. I thought it might be too racy for the under-eighteen crowd, but Eliza insisted that it showcases healthy sexuality, and I agree that's important. She also called me a hypocrite and a prude.

I'm up front, handling the register, when the front bell chimes. The man responsible for the sound freezes, like he's been busted for being somewhere he isn't supposed to be. Judging by his neatly trimmed hair, pleated khakis, and button-down shirt, he's one of two things: a romance-curious man who wrongly thinks his interest says something about his masculinity, or a man on a mission to buy a gift.

"Welcome to Happy Endings," I say, smiling. "Can I help you?"

"I hope so." He sounds forlorn. "I'm looking for a birthday gift."

"Great—what kind of books do they like?"

The man blanches. "She. And we've only been dating a few weeks."

"We have gift cards . . ." Although it could have a short redemption window if I don't figure out a way to get our profits even higher.

"She thinks they're lazy gifts," the man says.

"Okay, then," I say. "What books do you like? Sharing a favorite book with a partner can be a very intimate experience."

Which makes me wonder: Would Josie have taken my book suggestions if she'd known I was the one making them?

"I don't read romance," the man says with the air of someone who looks down on the genre even though they've never read it. "My taste skews more literary."

This is a challenge I like. As much as I'd love to convince him to buy something spicy—he could benefit from his girlfriend reading a book like that—I know he's trusting me to help him choose something that will make him look good, and I don't want to disappoint. I flip through the card catalog in my mind, trying to think of a romance that leans literary. More of a love story than a traditional genre romance . . .

"How do you feel about cherry farms in Michigan?"

A few minutes later, I'm leading the man—his name is Brad—across the invisible barrier that used to separate Happy Endings from Beans and around the bookshelf barrier into Tabula Inscripta.

Josie's eyes widen when she sees me. It's moments like this

that make me wish I wasn't such a goddamn giant. I know my size can be intimidating, but I wouldn't hurt a cat. Not even Hades when he's acting like the devil he was named after.

"Can I . . . help you?" Josie's the epitome of a buttoned-up retail professional today: hair slicked back in a long, dark ponytail; crisp blouse and pencil skirt; glossy red lips that match her high heels. A new image comes barreling into my mind: Josie Klein in nothing but those shoes and a red lacy bra and panties, ordering me to get on my knees.

Flushing, I shove that thought away and try to picture BookshopGirl dressing like Josie. I can't—I've always imagined her as a soft, sweet woman who wears flowy skirts and cozy sweaters, her hair in a messy bun, ink smudges on her fingers.

But like Nora said, there's no reason for BookshopGirl to be anyone other than her real self online, whereas Josie has plenty of reasons for treating me the way she has. Not that they're valid. Still, maybe BookshopGirl is there, underneath all that ice . . .

"Did you need something?" Josie asks in a wary voice.

"Yeah, sorry," I say, shaking myself. "My friend Brad here is looking for a special gift for a special lady—any chance you have *Tom Lake* in stock?"

Josie's dark eyebrows draw together slowly, creating two tiny lines between them.

"Follow me," she says after a beat, but she still looks suspicious.

She leads us to a shelf at the front of the store, on the opposite side of the offending pipe—which I see has been patched up. I think back to the surprise in Josie's eyes when I came to help her, and the suspicion, like she was waiting for me to say or do something mean.

How would she have reacted if it had been RJ who came to help her?

"Ann Patchett . . ." Josie says, trailing her long, delicate fingers across the row of spines. Her nails are painted pale pink, the color so close to natural I didn't think she was wearing polish at all. My eyes, and my mind, drift down, and I wonder what color her panties are.

Stop it, asshole. I cough and mentally smack myself. I'm already turned inside out; I don't need these damn intrusive thoughts about Josie Klein's lingerie making me even more mixed up.

"Here you go!" Josie says to Brad, her voice brighter than it's ever been when she's talked to me.

Sure enough, there's the bluish-green cover, dotted with flowers. I'm impressed she managed to find the exact book she was looking for in less than thirty seconds. Maybe there is something to how organized her store is. Efficient, if not exactly inspiring.

"She's going to love it," Josie tells Brad. And then she smiles at him. It's the first time I've seen a real smile from her—open and easy, with a hidden dimple popping in her right cheek—and I'm stunned. The way her eyes are shining, she's radiating light. She is the sun, and for the first time, I can see a glimpse of my book friend.

Too bad she hates my guts.

THAT NIGHT, I lie awake, staring at the ceiling, considering my options. If I tell Josie what I know, she won't want to keep chatting with me, and the thought of losing my friendship with BookshopGirl makes my chest feel hollow.

But continuing to talk without telling her? That feels dishonest, a lie by omission. A betrayal.

I pull up BookFriends and read the latest message from BookshopGirl, sent after I didn't reply to her this morning.

> **BookshopGirl:** Hey, you must have had a super busy day! I did, too—but in a good way. Anyway, just saying hi, and I hope all is well. Goodnight! Chat tomorrow?

I stare at the screen, trying once again to merge my mental images. Josie Klein, sitting at her kitchen table and messaging me while eating breakfast; Josie Klein, asking for my book recommendations; Josie Klein, opening up to me about the worst experience of her life.

Josie Klein, sending me one last message before turning off the light and going to bed.

If there's even a chance the warm and lovely BookshopGirl could be hiding beneath Josie's cold exterior, isn't it worth the risk? Getting to know the real her, and letting her get to know the real me?

Only one way to find out.

> **RJ.Reads:** Sorry, it's been busy. And weird. I'm glad yours was the good kind of busy, though. So, I've been thinking, and I hope this isn't unwelcome, but I can't stop thinking about it so here goes: Would you ever be interested in meeting in real life?

After pressing send, I remember that she doesn't know I'm also in Boston. I shake my head and write another message.

> **RJ.Reads:** I mean, in person depending on if we live in the same city, which we don't know for sure, right? Ha. Or we could talk on FaceTime or Zoom? Or a phone call?

Shit, I sound desperate. Just one more message.

> **RJ.Reads:** No pressure, though. Let me know. Goodnight

15

Josie

I CAN'T STOP staring at the message from RJ.

> **RJ.Reads:** Would you ever be interested in meeting in real life?

He sent it late last night, but I haven't figured out how to respond.

Georgia is sitting next to me, behind the counter at Tabula—but she's working on something useful, a paper for class. Me? I'm freaking out.

I know it's silly, but it's almost like I forgot that RJ isn't a fictional character. He's a fully formed human with his own motivations and expectations. All I know of him is his avatar (a hand holding a small, leather-bound book) and his brief bio: *Bookseller x 14 yrs. He/Him. Good endings matter.* He could live anywhere in the country. He could be seventy years old or twenty. I'd bet money that we're similar ages, though—within five or ten years—based on his word choices, abbreviations, and references. Somehow, that's even more intimidating.

The thought of stepping out of the safety of our online world, of confronting the unpredictable reality of this individual I know nothing about—it terrifies me. What if I can't be the person I am on the screen? What if I'm a disappointment? What if *he* is?

> **BookshopGirl:** Sorry, I don't think that's a good idea.

I press send and immediately regret it.

"What's that look on your face?" Georgia asks, and I close my laptop.

"Nothing. How's your paper coming?"

She leans back in her chair and sighs. "Stuff like this makes me wonder why I decided to go to grad school. Maybe you had the right idea—you figured out what you wanted to do and didn't waste time in college."

My muscles tighten. I never wanted to make Georgia feel guilty when none of it was her fault, so I've always told her it was my decision to leave college. And that I've never regretted it.

Georgia returns to her paper, and my mind drifts back to my conversation with RJ about this very thing. It's like he helped me revise the story I've had in my mind all these years. My version isn't gone, but he's written in some edits, crossed out some lines, added an asterisk.

You showed strength and resilience in the face of adversity.

But if we met in real life, I'd know that *he* knows the most secret, shameful parts of my past. It was hard enough to share that under the cover of anonymity; I'm not sure I can handle that level of vulnerability in person.

Still, I hate the thought of hurting his feelings, so I type a follow-up message.

> **BookshopGirl:** Hi again. Just want to say that the last thing I want is to stop chatting with you here. But I'm going through some complicated stuff and I need the rest of my life to stay as uncomplicated as possible. Is it OK if we keep things the way they are?

It's a cop-out, but it's all I can do right now.

"Question," I say to Georgia, wanting something else to focus on. "Could you cover for me when I go to IBNE? It's the last weekend in August, and it's in Boston this year."

The Independent Booksellers of New England conference is one of my favorite events of the year—a chance to mingle with colleagues, meet publishers, and learn more about industry trends. I submitted an application to be on a panel— I've applied for the past three years but haven't ever made it. It's a huge honor to be chosen, and another one of my life goals.

"You mean I-*BONE*?" Georgia says, grinning. "Sure. Happy to."

I roll my eyes, smiling. "I won't be boning anyone, sorry."

Although it's true a significant amount of hooking up does happen—hence the nickname. Bring a bunch of socially awkward book nerds together, add free books and a bar, and sparks fly.

"Why not?" Georgia says. "You deserve a hot one-night stand with a brawny bibliophile."

Laughing, I shake my head, but my brain takes this opportunity to remind me of something: *Ryan will probably be at IBNE.*

Not that we'll be boning. Not that I even *want* to bone him (my inconvenient attraction to him notwithstanding). But after he helped save my books the other day, I thought we had a moment, a breakthrough; that maybe we could set down our weapons and figure out how to be civil to each other.

Except he reacted so bizarrely to seeing I was reading *The Princess Bride*.

Compounding my confusion is the fact that he did another nice thing: bringing a customer over and hand-selling one of my books. The man ended up buying four other titles, too—a huge sale. It's such a switch from our prior interactions that I can't help wondering why.

Xander's voice echoes in my mind: *Unfortunately, you're slightly behind Ryan.*

Ryan must know that, too. Does he feel bad for me now? Does he want to prove that he's a "good guy" as he crushes me?

Unless he actually *is* a good guy?

That thought sends an uncomfortable twinge through my chest. Regardless of his motivations, I owe him, big-time.

I glance again at my laptop to see if RJ has replied. He hasn't. I tell myself he's just busy.

But as the hours pass, he still doesn't respond, and I feel a growing sense of unease.

After closing the store, I know I ought to head home, but if I do, I'll just ruminate on all my uncomfortable thoughts: the lack of response from RJ, the weird obligation I now feel toward Ryan.

Eddie brought me leftover pastries before he left, so I grab one and head over to Happy Endings. Maybe if I give it to Ryan, that'll assuage some of my discomfort.

There's a book club tonight—a group, mostly women, seated in a circle, talking and laughing—but I immediately spot Ryan in the back corner.

He's sprawled in a purple-and-yellow floral armchair, his broad shoulders and long legs making the chair look comically small. The white cat is in his lap, and the black one is snoozing on top of the chairback. As usual, he's wearing a cardigan (navy blue) and glasses (tortoiseshell), and the effect is very Hot Mr. Rogers meets Adorable Cat Dad. He also looks tired. The specific, bone-deep fatigue from a long day working in retail, your feet aching from standing, your face tight from smiling.

I can almost see the invisible weight he carries as manager, a weight I know too well, and again I feel a strange tug of solidarity.

I walk toward him. He glances up and sees me, then stiffens.

"I made sure your store would be closed," he says quickly.

It takes me a moment to understand. He thinks I'm here to complain about the noise.

"No, that's not—" I hold out the pastry. "I brought you something."

He looks confused, peering over the top of his glasses at me. "Why?"

"It's not poisoned, if that's what you're wondering," I say.

He sighs. "Sorry, I'm feeling a little . . . Never mind." He takes the pastry but doesn't eat it. "Do you, I don't know—want to stay for a bit?"

To my surprise, I do. I tell myself it's so I can spy on his operations and figure out how to pull ahead. But I have a sneaking suspicion it has something to do with this peculiar *interest* I feel toward him—and not just physically. The common ground we share despite our differences.

I can't allow myself to feel that way, though. He's currently beating me, and maybe he actually isn't all that nice. Maybe it was the water in my eyes and the panic in my veins, and now that I'm dried out and calmed down, I'll see that he really is the arrogant, uncouth jerk I've imagined him to be.

Tentatively, I settle into the red-and-blue plaid chair next to Ryan and listen as the book club finishes their discussion. The women in the glittery pink shirts are here—the Book Club Sluts, Ryan called them. They're in their element, making inappropriate comments that make everyone laugh.

As the conversation turns to the themes and characters, I find myself getting pulled in. A few years ago, I was invited to join a friend's book club; I was so excited for my first meeting, I created a color-coded, annotated list of discussion points about the book—only to find out that no one else had read it, and the purpose of the gathering was to drink wine and chat. Which is great! Except that I felt like a total nerd.

But these readers? They're just as book obsessed as I am, even if their "favorites" shelf may look different from mine. And I have to hand it to Ryan: he's created an inclusive, supportive atmosphere here.

After the book club ends, I hang around for reasons I do not allow myself to examine too closely. Wanting something to do to keep busy, I grab one of the chairs and start moving it back into place.

Ryan comes over and takes it from me (lifting it more easily than I did). "I've got these. You can sit down."

"What, I'm not capable of handling your chairs?" I'm trying for a teasing tone, but it comes out sounding peevish.

"I'm afraid you're going to sabotage them somehow. Stick thumbtacks on the seats, maybe." He frowns as he carries the chairs back to their places. "Sit, Josie."

Instead, I find a broom and start sweeping the floor. When he returns, he takes that from me, too.

"How can I possibly sabotage you by sweeping?" I ask.

"You'll figure something out," he mutters.

While he sweeps, I go behind the counter and start taking out the trash. But he's right behind me again, grabbing the trash bag from my hand and giving me a confused look.

"What are you doing?"

"I'm trying to repay you!" I say, frustrated. "You've done two nice things for me, and I've been uncomfortable ever since."

"I—what?" He looks bewildered. "Why?"

I bite my lip, then let it out: "I hate being in anyone's debt, especially yours."

"Because I'm your nemesis." He says the words flatly, almost distastefully.

"Exactly," I say, latching on to that because I desperately need to keep him in that category despite the thoughts I've been having lately. "It's eating me alive. I can't handle it."

His expression darkens. "Well, then . . . as your nemesis, I ought to let you stay in your discomfort for a while longer, don't you think?" He ties a knot in the trash bag and tosses it into the back room. "So, uh, what did you think about your first romance book club?"

This is the first time we've had an actual conversation, rather than an argument. I lean against the counter and say slowly, "It was . . . unexpected."

"You thought it would be a bunch of girlies squealing about their new book boyfriend?"

I stiffen at his tone: teasing, but with a hint of defensiveness—and maybe some judgement, too. "You know, you make a lot of assumptions about me."

He blinks. "What do you mean?"

"Just because I don't read romance doesn't mean I can't appreciate a good discussion." There's a messy basket of crocheted objects next to the register, and I start organizing it so I have something to focus on. I can't tell what they are—brown and pink, I don't know . . . vegetables? Flowers?

When Ryan sees what I'm doing, his eyes widen and he rushes over, whisking the basket out of my reach. Bewildered, I put my hands on my hips. "Why can't I do anything to help?"

He hands me a jumbled pile of bookmarks. "You want to organize something? Organize these."

My fingers brush his as I take them, and goose bumps prickle down my arm. I take a quick step away and focus on the bookmarks, sorting them by type. I DON'T WATCH PORN, I READ IT LIKE A F*CKING LADY, one reads.

"So what is your deal with romance novels, then?" he asks.

"My *deal*?"

"Why won't you read them?"

"It's not that I won't, it's . . ."

My mind conjures an image of my mother, curled in bed with a book, lost in a world that wasn't ours. I don't blame the books, of course—it's not their fault my mom couldn't cope with reality—so what is it? Maybe I resent them, for capturing her attention when her daughters needed her. When I needed her.

But there's no way I'm telling Ryan that.

Instead, I shrug. "They're too predictable. You always know how the story will end: happily ever after, wedding bells, heart-eyes. Why bother reading?"

I know it's a lazy take on the genre. But it feels easier than admitting there's something deeper underneath.

"Because it's about the journey, not the destination," Ryan says. "You're willing to follow these characters to the darkest depths because you know everything will be all right in the end."

"But that's not how the world works." I'm aware of how cliché I sound: the cynic who doesn't believe in love. "Why don't people write about messy, complicated love affairs that end in tragedy or devastation?"

He narrows his eyes, but there's laughter hiding there, too. "You're kidding, right? There are plenty of books like that— *Anna Karenina*? *The Song of Achilles*? *Call Me by Your Name*? I could go on . . ."

"Okay, okay."

"By definition, a romance novel is about lovers falling in love. Kind of like how mystery novels are about solving a mystery. Fantasy novels take place in a fantastical world; historical fiction is set in the past; literary fiction features purple prose and depressing endings—"

"Come on," I say, rolling my eyes as an unexpected grin pulls at my lips. "If you think that's true, you haven't read much literary fiction."

"And you haven't read much romance."

He knocks his shoulder into mine—well, his upper arm into my shoulder—and the contact sends a zap of electricity through me.

I really need to get out of here.

His phone vibrates on the counter between us, and I take that as my cue to go.

"One second," he says as he picks it up. "Don't leave yet, okay? I—I need to talk to you about something."

I nod, confused, and wait, looking at the Blind Date with a Book display while trying not to eavesdrop. But Ryan's voice is loud, and it's hard not to overhear.

"Yes, of course," he's saying. "Before the cake cutting. I promise."

A wedding? He doesn't sound thrilled.

The person on the phone says something—a woman's voice, though I can't make out the words—and he sighs. "The answer is still no. and I'm fine—I got a room at the Star Inn."

Another pause, and when he speaks again, his voice is softer, the voice I imagine he reserves for people he knows well. People he loves. "Of course I'm excited. Uh-huh. See you soon. Love you, too."

He ends the call, and I turn away to hide my burning cheeks. Maybe his girlfriend? I bet she's easygoing and sweet. She probably adores Hallmark movies and gets her nails done every week so she's prepared for when Ryan proposes?

"Sorry about that," he says to me. "My parents are having a party for their fiftieth anniversary this weekend—my mom is firming up the details."

"That was your . . . mom?"

So maybe he's single. Not that I care.

He nods. "She thought that maybe if she asked for the fifteenth time, the answer would change and I'd be bringing a date."

"Ah," I say. "The mom-pressure—my sister and I get that, too. Why are they obsessed with their children's dating lives?"

"My parents have this epic love story . . ." He shakes his head. "Anyway, my mom wants that for her sons, and I'm the only unmarried one, so she's obsessed with my romantic prospects. Talks about it constantly. Makes it awkward at family functions."

The rush of sympathy I feel surprises me—I understand the pain of feeling uncomfortable around your own mom. "Would it be easier if you had someone with you?"

The words are out of my mouth before I realize what I've said.

His eyebrows shoot up. "Are you offering to come?"

"Of course not," I say quickly.

"It sounded like you were." His expression is serious, but there's laughter dancing in those honey-brown eyes. "Like you're dying to live out a Fake Dating trope at my parents' party."

"Ha," I scoff, strangely flustered. "Right."

He leans closer, the corners of his eyes crinkling. "You could play the part of a loving girlfriend, hold my hand, dance with me. Help convince everyone I'm not pathetically single. Sounds right up your alley."

He's messing with me, of course. But for some inexplicable reason, my mind conjures up an image of being pressed against him on the dance floor, his hand firm against my low back, my cheek resting on his chest. An overwhelming sensation of yearning rushes through me.

I blink; what the hell is wrong with me? He's scrambled my brain. Rattled me so thoroughly that I'm having fantasies of *dancing* with him. The ultimate form of sabotage.

Maybe I can flip the tables on him. Throw *him* off his guard.

"Sure," I say, looking up at him through my lashes. "We could even try for a steamy kiss in front of everyone, just to really sell it."

The laughter fades from his expression and his eyes crackle with heat. Suddenly, I can imagine it: his hand coming up to cup my jaw, pulling my mouth to his. We wouldn't be tentative, not with all these weeks of tension between us—his kiss would be punishing, almost vicious, drawing me closer, then pushing me away, leaving me breathless and aching in front of his entire family.

There's no way in hell I'd ever do that.

And yet, when he says, "Is that what you want?" in a low, smoky voice—

I hear myself whispering, "Yes."

He holds my gaze. "Great. It's in Maine, so we'd have to stay overnight."

My stomach clenches; this is spiraling out of control. Now I'm seeing images of Ryan, shirtless, tossing me onto a bed, pinning me down, devouring me.

I take a step back, shaking my head. "I was kidding, Ryan."

"Were you?" He's still holding my gaze, intense and focused. I shiver involuntarily. "I didn't think Josie Klein was the type to back out of a commitment."

"I didn't *commit* to anything!" I protest.

"You sounded pretty committed to me. We'll leave tomorrow after work and come home on Saturday. Or are you going to chicken out?"

We're in a standoff, facing each other like two dueling cowboys. Who's going to flinch first? Not me.

"*If* I come with you to this party," I say, putting my hands on my hips, "I won't be in your debt anymore. Agree?"

I'm simply calling his bluff. Nothing to do with this bizarre pull I feel toward him, the insistent whisper nagging me to figure out what makes him tick. And definitely nothing *whatsoever* to do with the way my body reacts to him.

"Fine, whatever," he says. He takes his glasses off and rests his forearms on the counter, leaning down to study me, as if the information he's looking for is somewhere on my face. "But this could get messy. Are you sure?"

He's giving me an out, like he knows I don't have the guts to follow through. And it's true: the thought of going to a huge party where the only person I know happens to hate me . . . makes me want to curl up in a ball and hide.

But there's nothing I despise more than being underestimated.

I force myself to think through the logistics. It's July 4th weekend—the store will be closed anyway. Boston goes crazy over Independence Day, fireworks and concerts and crowds, and I wouldn't mind getting away. Other than the car ride, I just need to hang out at the party with Ryan for a couple hours. I can get my own room at that inn he mentioned.

Meanwhile, I'll use this opportunity to gather useful information on him. Convince him that I'm not a threat, learn his secrets, and when we return—swoop in and crush him.

"Positive," I say.

His eyes narrow. "You're plotting my death. You're going to slip poison into my drink. Suffocate me in my sleep."

"That's always a risk," I say, cocking an eyebrow, trying to look confident and a little devious—rather than flustered and confused.

He huffs a half laugh; apparently he doesn't think I'm a

threat. "What happens when it's all over? We go back to trying to destroy each other's prospects for the future?"

"Exactly."

A strange expression crosses his face—almost like sadness. Then he shakes his head, like he's still bewildered by this whole turn of events. I know I am.

"Okay. Fine," he says. "I'll book you a room at the inn—"

"You don't have to—"

"I'm getting you your own room, Josie."

His voice is stiff, and my face flushes. That is *not* what I meant. "Thanks," I whisper, unable to meet his eyes.

"Meet me here tomorrow afternoon at four," he says. "And pack a dress you can dance in."

16

Ryan

JOSIE—BOOKSHOPGIRL—LEFT ten minutes ago. Having
her here, bustling around my personal space under the guise
of helping, was unsettling.

How many times did I wish my online crush would walk in
the front door of Happy Endings, giving me a secret smile that
would somehow let me know it was her? She'd tell me her
name—something literary and classic like Emma or Jane or
Anne—and I'd buy her a coffee at Beans (something sweet,
like her), and we'd sit and talk for hours.

I'd be able to open up and tell her the things I haven't been
able to talk about with anyone: That even if I get the manager
job, I'm terrified the store will change so much it won't be
recognizable. Or worse, that I don't have the ability to manage
a bookstore that sells other genres. How angry I am at Xander
for putting us in this position, for forcing me to be so
competitive and cutthroat.

Of course, in my fantasy, BookshopGirl was not the
manager of the Tab. Oh, how quickly a dream can become a
nightmare.

I could still tell Josie not to come this weekend, pull out

one of a million excuses: That it's too late to change my RSVP; that there are no rooms left at the hotel. That I'm harboring a secret—I'm the same guy she's been chatting with online.

It would be so easy to tell her the truth, just reply to the message that's gone unanswered all day. But BookshopGirl wants to keep things the way they are, which is the one thing I don't know if I can do.

With my fingers poised over the keyboard, I consider confessing my identity. She'll be as torn and confused as I am, and there's no way she'll still want to go on the trip.

And yet . . .

Before I can change my mind again, I type out a quick reply and hit send.

> **RJ.Reads:** Okay. If that's what you want.

I know it's the coward's way out. I also know that, deep down, it's what I want, too; to go back to the way things were before I knew.

The best I can hope for is that this trip will show me once and for all who Josie Klein is. If she's the ice queen, or the woman I thought I was developing real feelings for.

"YOU'VE GOT A lot of stuff in here," Josie says.

It's the next afternoon and I'm parked in front of Happy Endings, getting ready to head out—twenty minutes behind schedule. I appreciate that Josie's attempting to keep the judgment out of her voice, even if she's not entirely successful.

I'm cleaning out my car—which I had every intention of doing before work, but I slept through my alarm, then got stuck on a call with my mom, who is *"absolutely tickled"* to hear I'm bringing a date, even though I stressed that Josie's just a friend. If that.

"Hey, you never know when you're going to need a . . ." I stop when I see Josie holding a pink satin eye mask that says, DREAMING OF MY HEA, from an author event last week.

"What's a he-ah?" she asks.

"H-E-A," I tell her. "Happily Ever After. Surely you've heard of those, even if they don't exist in your big literary tomes."

Josie's cheeks flush. She breaks eye contact, and I catalog another difference between the two women. Where BookshopGirl seems eternally curious, excited to learn about new things, Josie can't handle looking like anything less than the smartest person in any room.

My mind flicks back to the story she told me about losing her scholarship and dropping out of college. The deep shame she still carries. Maybe I've been misreading her; what if it's not about wanting to look smarter, but she's genuinely insecure? My heart gives a teeny, tiny squeeze of sympathy.

Until she lets out an exasperated sigh and gathers the ARCs sitting in the passenger seat. Like it's such a burden to pick up a few books—I left them there so I wouldn't forget to bring them home for my mom and sisters-in-law, before I knew someone would be riding shotgun all the way to Maine.

Wordlessly, Josie carries the books to the open trunk. I bet she's cringing at the clutter—which makes my jaw tighten with irritation. Rushing back, I take the books from her arms and toss them inside, closing the trunk before she can get a good look. I don't want to have to explain the boxes of vibrators, ready to be sorted for next month's subscription box.

"I think we're all set—just need to grab your bag," I say, spotting the small duffel resting on the sidewalk.

Before I can reach for it, Josie has it in her arms.

"I've got it," she says. The edge of defensiveness in her voice makes my own defenses rise.

"Listen," I tell her, "you don't have to come. We can find another way for you to balance the scales, or whatever."

"I said I was going, so let's go."

This is going to be the longest two-hour drive of my life.

WE'RE BOTH QUIET as we head out of Davis Square, toward 93. Traffic is crawling, but I'm hopeful it will pick up once we get to the highway. Thanks to the late start, we're going to be cutting it close.

I steal a glance at Josie, who has her duffel bag resting on her lap. She's hugging it to her chest like it's a stuffed animal. I can't tell if she's uncomfortable or afraid her bag will get dirty.

The song on the radio ends and the DJ comes on the air. "That was 'Shut It Down,' by Marley Greene. Now for the traffic report, brought to you by Tabula Inscripta—where Boston gets lit. As in literature."

Josie looks from the radio to me, excited—until she realizes that her competition is behind the wheel.

"You ran ads?" I ask, even though she obviously did.

Josie shrugs. "Sometimes you've got to spend money to make money."

"Smart," I say, wishing I'd thought of that. No wonder she's winning.

We fall quiet again, and luckily the traffic dies down past Medford. I'm cruising at a respectable five miles over the speed limit as the trees blur past our windows.

"We should probably get to know each other," Josie says, out of the blue. "Otherwise, your parents will think you picked me up off the street like a stray."

"I was planning to tell them you were a hitchhiker."

I can feel Josie's fiery eyes on me, but I don't give her the satisfaction of acknowledging her glare. Safety first—gotta keep my eyes on the road.

"Please tell me your parents know I'm coming."

"They know I'm bringing someone," I say. "A friend."

"Friends know things about each other."

"*Wellll*, I know you've been working at Tabula Inscripta for about five years; that you have one sister; that you drink triple Americanos, you always wear your hair up, and you have a penchant for big books."

Now I steal a glance, and judging by how wide her eyes are, she's shocked at my astute observational skills.

"What do you know about me?" I ask, remembering how just a month ago she didn't know my name.

"I know you have a very loud laugh; you have two cats you can't control, a ridiculous sweet tooth when it comes to your beverages, and a *lot* of stuff."

I choose to ignore the thinly veiled insults. Mostly because I'm surprised that she actually *has* been paying attention to me.

"How about we fill in the blanks?" I suggest. "Where did you grow up?"

"Newburyport—but not the nice part. How about you?"

"Winchester. The nice part," I admit.

"Not Maine?"

I shake my head. "We vacationed in Kennebunkport when I was a kid, and my parents bought a place there once they became empty nesters. How about siblings? One sister, right?"

"Georgia." Josie's love for her sister is apparent in the way she says her name, like it's precious. Like she's precious. Understandably so, after the accident BookshopGirl told me about.

"And you?" she asks. "Any brothers or sisters?"

"Three brothers; I'm the baby."

"Ahhh," she says, as if that explains something—but I know enough about birth order to know I'm not as outgoing or free spirited as youngest children tend to be.

On the other hand, I would have known Josie was the oldest even without my conversations with BookshopGirl. She's a textbook firstborn—a hardworking, high-achieving perfectionist who believes it's her duty to take care of her sibling.

Again, I feel that reluctant squeeze of sympathy. I still can't believe her mother left her sister alone, forcing Josie to leave school. Even worse, it sounds like that was a pattern their whole lives. It's hard to imagine a parent doing that. Mine have always been there for me, even if I sometimes wish my mom would back off a little.

"So, what'd you do before working at the Tab?" I ask. "Where'd you go to college?"

And just like that, Josie shuts down, her body stiffening, her expression flattening. I curse myself for bringing up a taboo topic and putting an end to our conversational volley. It had been going pretty well.

She answers, a single word, devoid of emotion: "Emerson."

I can tell she's bracing herself for the inevitable next

questions: what did you major in or when did you graduate. But I'm not going there.

Before I can think of a way to pivot, Josie says, "I love this song," and turns up the radio.

She doesn't seem like the type to love Flo Rida, but I let it go.

AN HOUR AND twenty minutes later, I'm waiting in the lobby of the Star Inn, my foot tapping with nerves and impatience. We're late.

As soon as we arrived, Josie went upstairs to change in her room, which is actually my room. The hotel was full when I called, so I gave her mine. I changed in the lobby bathroom, and I'll crash at my parents' after the party. My complicated feelings can't handle an "only one bed" situation.

I'm checking my watch for the twentieth time when the elevator dings, and I look up.

"Wow," I accidentally say out loud.

Josie's hair, freed from that constricting bun, cascades in waves down to her lower back. She's wearing a dark blue dress that hugs her curves in all the right places. The full skirt looks made for twirling on the dance floor, and the halter top dips low enough to reveal more than a hint of her cleavage.

My mouth goes dry, and I get a flash of myself loosening the tie behind her neck, watching the dress fall to the floor.

The moment—and my view—is interrupted when the elevator doors start to close. Josie squeaks and sticks her hand out, stopping them. Then she hurries over, biting her lip as she looks up at me. The unexpected vulnerability in her expression hits my chest in a strange way. It's like I'm getting a glimpse of BookshopGirl.

"No cardigan tonight?" she asks.

"My mom wanted all her boys in suits," I say. "But what's wrong with cardigans?"

"Nothing. If you're a spinster librarian."

And now she's back to Josie.

"I'm not the one who wears a bun every day to work," I say. Her dimple pops, as if she's trying not to smile, almost like she's pleased that I fired back. "Shall we?"

The inn is close enough to the venue that we could walk, but Josie's heels are high, and it'll be faster to catch a ride in one of the electric golf carts my parents hired.

The ride is short, and I try not to notice the way Josie's hair blows in the breeze, releasing a scent of lavender and warm honey.

"I forgot to ask," she says. "What are your parents' names?"

"Mr. and Mrs. Lawson." Josie turns to me, an odd expression on her face. "Just kidding. They're Merrie and Jim."

Josie nods, her lips moving as she repeats their names, committing them to memory. It's oddly endearing. "And your brothers?"

"John is the oldest. Then Paul, Robert, and me. Ryan. Or Brian, if you prefer."

Josie shoots me a "don't mess with me" look. "And they're all married?"

I nod. "John married his college sweetheart, Michelle; they're both lawyers like my parents, with two boys and a girl. Paul's wife is Anna; he's a surgeon, she's a pediatrician, and they have two daughters. Robert and Sandra got married a year ago, and she's expecting their first baby. He's a nuclear engineer, she's a history professor."

Josie whistles. "Damn. No pressure there."

"Tell me about it," I say. "Now add in that all three of my brothers were college athletes."

She glances at me. "You didn't play sports? Not even basketball?"

I stiffen; I've heard this before. Thankfully, the golf cart pulls up in front of the Boathouse. "We're here," I say, stepping off the cart and offering Josie my arm.

When she takes it, her hand brushes mine, and her skin is so soft my dick jumps to half-mast. I wonder if she's this soft everywhere.

"Well," she says with a hint of impatience—or is it nerves? "Are we staying out in the parking lot all night?"

I shake my head and take a steadying breath, preparing myself for the onslaught.

The door opens, revealing a party in full swing. My parents went all out in honor of this milestone. A half century together. I can't imagine. Even if I found someone now and got married within a year, I'd have to live well past eighty to make it to fifty years.

I spot them on the dance floor, looking as spry and starry eyed as I imagine they were on the day they got married, fresh out of college. Mom sees me first—her face lights up, and she tugs Dad off the dance floor and over to where we're standing.

"Son," my dad says, giving me an aggressive pat on the back as my mom launches herself into my arms. "It is so good to see you, RJ—"

I squeeze her tighter, hoping to muffle the sound of my old nickname. Josie *cannot* hear her call me that. Not until I figure out how I'm going to handle this.

"Hi, Mom," I say, releasing her and glancing at Josie. She doesn't seem to have heard.

Mom beams at her. "Now introduce me to your stunning date!"

"Mom, Dad, this is Josie."

"It's so nice to meet you, Mr. and Mrs. Lawson," Josie says.

"Josie!" Mom exclaims, ignoring her outstretched hand and wrapping her in a hug. "Aren't you a sight for sore eyes. Please, call me Mom."

Josie flinches and gives me a wide-eyed look over my mom's shoulder.

"Mother," I warn. "Let's take it easy on Josie, okay? We don't want to scare her away, now, do we?"

"No, we do not," my mom says, shaking her head for emphasis.

"Merrie! Jim!" someone calls.

"Go, have fun," I say, and they head back to the dance floor, where I spot my brothers with their wives and kids—all looking like they're having a blast.

The next two hours pass in a blur of hors d'oeuvres, champagne and cake, teasing from my brothers and sisters-in-law, hugs from my nieces and nephews, and versions of the same conversation with dozens of my parents' old friends.

Ryan, good to see you! You are so tall!

You aren't still working at that bookstore, are you?

Do people even read books anymore?

Looks like you finally found your own love story! Your poor mom must be so relieved.

You really are tall, aren't you? Shame you never played basketball.

At half past ten, I scan the room for Josie—we got separated when my sisters-in-law dragged her off to dance to "Girls Just Wanna Have Fun."

"She fits right in," Robert says, nudging me, and he's right: Josie has been wonderful with my family. At one point, she even had my two-year-old niece in her arms. Now I spot her on the dance floor with Uncle Frank, my dad's pervy old college roommate. And his hands are drifting dangerously close to Josie's butt.

A surprising bolt of anger runs through me, and I head over, pushing my way through the crowd.

"Uncle Frank," I say, resting a hand on his shoulder.

"I'm busy, kid," he says, tightening his hold on Josie.

"Not anymore, you're not." I add pressure to my grip, and Uncle Frank sighs in defeat, but not before planting a sloppy kiss on Josie's cheek.

"Oh, thank god," Josie says, once she's safely in my arms. The relief in her voice makes me stand up straighter, and I find myself pulling her closer. To my surprise, she lets me, her body relaxing as she sighs, a sound that makes my collar feel tight.

This is the first time we've been on the dance floor together all night, and I wonder why I waited so long. Swaying back and forth with Josie in my arms is a hell of a lot better than schmoozing with my parents' friends.

Nearby, my parents are dancing, too, and Mom's beaming as she watches me and Josie. Two of my brothers and their wives are over at the bar, openly staring at us. I discreetly shake my head and return my attention to Josie. The material of her dress feels as soft as her skin, and I find myself mindlessly running my hand up and down her back, trying not to think of what's underneath.

Someone clangs a fork against a glass, and I'm disappointed when Josie releases my hand as my mom steps up to the front of the room.

"Hello, party people!" my mom shouts into the microphone. She's clearly been overserved but is having the time of her life. My dad chuckles and takes the mic from her hands.

"Thank you all for being here to celebrate our golden anniversary," he says. "Fifty years of marriage teaches you a lot about love, patience, and most importantly, the art of pretending to listen. Just kidding, babe."

The crowd laughs as my mom playfully elbows my dad. She looks at him with such love and adoration, even after all these years. They set the bar impossibly high, I'm afraid.

"Despite a few questionable decisions, like that mustache in the eighties, my gut hasn't steered me wrong." Dad pats his slight beer belly, and the guests laugh again. "Like they say, when you know, you know—and the moment I saw Merrie in our high school cafeteria with her golden hair and that yellow dress . . ." He pauses and looks down at my mom like he's still seeing that girl. "It was like the rest of the world faded to black and white, and she was the only thing in color. I knew that very moment she was the one."

There's a collective *aww* from the crowd. They all know, like I know, that the love my dad has for my mom is as authentic as it gets. None of this is for show.

"And just look at where that love has led us. We have four wonderful sons and three wonderful daughters-in-law." I inwardly cringe at this mathematical proof that I don't measure up. The youngest Lawson boy, still a disappointment. "Five grandchildren, with another on the way, and more friends than we can count."

Dad's voice cracks, and he pauses. My mom steps in to take the mic, and I marvel at the way they instinctively know what the other one needs. My chest tightens with the longing I try so hard to ignore—to have what they have. To know like they know.

"What my Jimmy is trying to say is that we love you all like crazy. Thank you for being on this ride with us. Now let's get back to dancing. DJ, hit it!"

The DJ starts playing "This Magic Moment." Mom throws her arms around Dad's shoulders, and they kiss as they sway to the beat. Other couples join in, and soon the dance floor is filled.

As wonderful as the moment is, it feels like too much. I lean down to Josie and whisper in her ear, "What do you say we get out of here?"

17

Josie

NONE OF THIS is going as planned.

I had it all mapped out in my mind: we'd make polite conversation in the car, head to the anniversary party—where I'd hang out in the background and *maybe* share an obligatory dance with Ryan while keeping a sizable distance between us—then call it a night and go to bed early.

I never planned on his entire family being so excited to meet "Ryan's new girlfriend" that I wouldn't have the heart to explain that we're not even friends. I never planned on them being so welcoming I forgot to be nervous, or dancing with his sisters-in-law and nieces and laughing myself silly.

And I certainly never planned on Ryan Lawson in a suit.

All night, I've been staring at him. His shoulders, how they seem even broader; the strain of his shirt buttons across his chest when he moves; the crisp white collar and the tie knotted just below his Adam's apple.

I meant to come here and tilt him off his axis, not the other way around.

I also never imagined this: walking down to the beach with him, holding my shoes in one hand while he carries a bottle of champagne and two plastic cups he swiped from the bar. The salty air nips at my bare arms; the sand is cool on my feet as we sit on a patch of dry sand.

Off in the distance, a few fireworks explode. I'm right at the earliest stages of tipsy—warm and relaxed, soft around the edges. The ocean breeze washes over me, crisp and a little smoky.

"Your family is great," I say. The kind of family I grew up envying: stable, successful parents; a whole mess of siblings.

"They are," he says fondly. "They're also a lot."

"It must have been fun growing up with all those brothers."

Though I found them a little intimidating, exuding success and masculinity in their tailored suits. Ryan left his tie and jacket at the party, and now he's unbuttoned his top button and rolled up his shirtsleeves. His hair, which was neatly combed at the start of the night, has reverted to its usual floppy state, and it makes him look more like himself. All evening, it's been difficult to remember that this handsome, imposing man is the same guy who wears tortoiseshell glasses and cardigans and a lanyard covered in ridiculous pins. The same guy I've been competing against for weeks.

Real life seems far away, here on a beach in the moonlight with the waves whispering against the sand.

"Fun is one way to put it," he says. "Being the youngest meant I was always the butt of the jokes. And now, being the only one still single . . ." He grimaces. "Champagne?"

"Please," I say. He fills a plastic cup halfway, then hands it to me before filling his own. "So I hate to bring up a sore subject, but . . . why *are* you single?"

Ryan chokes on his champagne. "Not you, too!"

"Sorry!" I say, laughing. "But it doesn't make sense. You're tall, you have a job, you have adequate personal hygiene—"

"Thanks?"

"—so maybe you don't want to be tied down? Is that it?"

"Oh, I'd love to be tied down."

I press my lips together, fighting an unexpected vision of Ryan, his giant body sprawled in bed with silk ties on his wrists. "Kinky," I murmur.

"Not like that." Even in the darkness, I can tell he's blushing. "I mean, I wouldn't be opposed to it, in the right scenario . . ." He shakes his head and sighs. "Okay, starting over. It's more that—well, you saw my parents together."

"They're cute." Smiling at each other with hearts in their eyes, even after fifty years.

"I guess I'm looking for what they have." He sounds wistful.

I take another sip of champagne, the bubbles tickling my throat. "What was it like, growing up with parents who adore each other?"

"Wonderful," he says immediately. "It's an incredible gift to give your children, a solid and healthy marriage between their parents."

"But . . . ?"

"But it's a lot to live up to." He looks out at the horizon, the moon hanging low over the water. "They're meant for each other. I grew up assuming I'd find that, too, that it would land in my lap and I would know, like my Dad did."

"And it hasn't?"

"No," he says flatly. "And I'd rather be single than put myself in that position again."

He doesn't elaborate, but the weight in his words says enough. I can't help wondering who broke his heart.

"Come on," I say, "there have to be throngs of women who'd love to date a guy who reads romance."

"And why would they want that?" He narrows his eyes suspiciously.

"Because they assume he knows what women like." My voice falters. "In the bedroom."

He's blushing again. It makes me want to keep going down this road. Or maybe it's the champagne; I'm more relaxed than I've been in ages.

"So you've never hooked up with a customer?" I say. "Never ever?"

"Not never *ever*," he says, and I swear, his blush deepens. "There's this whole thing in romance about big men and tiny women, right? Lots of women love that trope, and I get it—the pressure women feel to be small, the idea that smallness equals femininity, that kind of thing."

I nod, remembering how it felt when he cut in on the dance floor and rescued me. The instant relief of his large frame close to mine—and a jolt of attraction, too.

But like he said, that's probably because of his size. It's primal, something I can't control.

"So you're saying it's tough being the physical ideal of masculinity," I say with a wry smile.

"No, that's not—" He exhales and runs a hand through his hair. "It's more— Well, romance novels are about the escape, the fantasy. If someone wants to fantasize about being railed by an eight-foot-tall blue alien, more power to them. I just don't need to be used as the stand-in."

He smiles, but it looks forced, like he's trying to play this off as a minor irritation when it's much deeper.

"That's happened to you?" I ask.

"Yes." He's avoiding my gaze, drumming his fingers on his knee as he takes a sip of champagne. Long, thick fingers; big hands. "And I'm a man, so maybe they think I'd be thrilled, but honestly? It doesn't feel great to realize that someone sought you out for that purpose, then dropped you." He glances at me. "You think I'm overreacting."

"Absolutely not," I say. "No one deserves to be fetishized."

He nods, holding my gaze. There's a world of hurt behind those eyes. "I'm all for healthy sexuality, and romance novels allow people to explore their kinks in a safe way. That's great, but . . ."

"But it's not great to use someone else to explore those kinks without their full consent."

"Exactly." He leans forward, elbows on knees, which makes his dress shirt strain against his shoulders and broad back.

"But you still love romance," I say. "Despite all that."

"Because it's not just about the sex, it's about the connection. Elaine, the woman who started the store, she used to say that the fantasy is less about the woman getting seven orgasms and more about the man wanting to give them to her. Caring about her experience. Apparently, this is so rare that women had to invent an entire genre to get that."

I can't help it; I blush. "Okay . . ."

He leans back and glances at me, his eyes twinkling like he's enjoying my reaction. "Anyway. The reason I love romance, and why I'm so passionate about promoting diversity in the genre, is because I love helping people find love stories they can see themselves in." He tilts his head in my direction. "So why do you like literary fiction? To me, it's always seemed like homework or something."

"You're right, it's not easy to read," I say, and consider how to explain it. "It's like . . . like mining for diamonds, and sometimes you're stuck in the dark, chiseling through rock— but when you uncover those jewels . . ." I sigh happily. "It's so worth it, more so than if they were right out in the open."

I glance over at Ryan, hoping he didn't take that as me insulting *his* favorite genre. But he nods and says, "Interesting. For me, reading is for relaxation. Escape."

"It's an escape for me, too. Disappearing into a story, feeling the emotions of the characters, experiencing a different life—"

"So how do you handle it when the story ends badly?"

"Badly?" I repeat. "You mean, a tragic ending? Because those aren't bad if they're right for the story. When I was a kid, I loved books that made me cry—*Charlotte's Web, Where the Red Fern Grows, Bridge to Terabithia*—"

"I *hated* those books," he says, shaking his head. "Isn't life hard enough?"

"But reading is different—you always know you can close the book if you need to. Whereas if you're going through an *actual* tragedy . . ."

"You can't close the book," he says, nodding.

"Exactly." I smile over at him. How is this the same guy I called a basic run-of-the-mill asshole? *This* guy is articulate, thoughtful, and interesting.

"Now back to the prior topic," he says, and I refocus. "Have *you* ever hooked up with a customer?" When I wince, he grins, his eyes glinting in the moonlight. "You have!"

"I only made that mistake once."

"Details," he prompts. "I told you about the blue alien thing."

I laugh, then take a long sip of champagne, draining the cup.

"Let's just say that MFA candidates who idolize Vonnegut and write about the existential pain of being a white man in America are—shocker!—not great boyfriends."

"I can imagine," he says, smiling.

"You can't. Not unless you've been stopped in the middle of sex so he can grab his Moleskine and jot down a phrase he wants to use in his latest work in progress."

Ryan laughs—that big, booming laugh I always hear echoing from his store. It's like a warm hug, and I'm not sure why I ever found it irritating.

"I think he hoped dating a bookseller would be helpful once he sold his Great American Novel," I say. "But he figured out pretty fast that publishing moves at a snail's pace, so it would entail years of investment on his part—which he wasn't interested in. Not that I was, either."

Like Georgia pointed out, I don't tend to get emotionally invested in anyone I date. What's the point, when it's going to end anyway?

"Let me guess, he never sold his novel?" Ryan says with a grin.

"Oh, he did. To an obscure small press."

I stretch out my legs, digging my toes into the cool sand. "I mean, it sold better than I expected. I looked it up on BookScan once—sixty-three copies in the first year."

He bursts out laughing, and so do I, falling against him so our shoulders touch. I'm oddly disappointed when he straightens up, putting space between us. It's got to be the champagne. Or the fact that the night is turning chilly. He's warm; I'm cold.

"Anyway," I say, "I'm sure that only fueled his delusions of being a misunderstood starving artist living in his two-bedroom apartment in Beacon Hill."

"Because his parents pay his rent, of course," Ryan says, nodding.

"He deserves it! He's doing art!" I lift my cup. "I'm just glad he's not doing me."

"Cheers to that." Ryan clinks his cup against mine, and we both take a sip. My eyes zero in on his throat, watching his Adam's apple bob as he swallows.

"You're a mystery, Josie Klein," he says, turning to face me.

I refocus on his eyes. "How so?"

"Sitting on the sand, barefoot, drinking champagne out of a Solo cup, swapping stories about shitty relationships. But at the bookstore, you're this self-contained, buttoned-up woman—"

"Oh, so I'm uptight." I've heard these words before: Rigid. Ambitious. Cold.

"I thought so before," he admits, "but not anymore. I'm trying to figure you out."

My face warms as he watches me intently. It's unnerving.

"What do you mean?"

"You're so in control of yourself, your store, everything—"

"That's an illusion," I say, waving a hand.

"Why do you work so hard to maintain it?"

"I—I don't know," I say, forcing an awkward laugh. "My sister would say it stems from the lack of control I felt as a child."

"So now you never let yourself lose control?" His voice, a little husky, scrapes some long-forgotten place inside me.

"Never," I say. He raises an eyebrow. "Rarely," I amend. "What about you—do you lose control?"

"With the right motivation? Sure."

He holds my gaze, and I imagine what that would be like—to be the one to make him lose control. His body, his strength, fully unleashed. I remember the moment I had his lanyard in my fist, the hunger in his eyes.

Heat creeps down my spine.

"You've already seen it," he says, then clarifies: "I never yell. I never lose my cool—until recently. With you. I'm sorry about that, by the way. But you get under my skin in a way no one else has."

I swallow. "I guess I could say the same about you."

There's more to it than the fact that we're competing for the same job. From that first meeting, there's been an undercurrent of electricity between us—and now it's crackling to life.

Again, probably the champagne. Or the moonlight glinting on the waves, the pop and sizzle of fireworks in the distance. Or it could be the way he's watching me, like he's uncovering some long-buried artifact. My life back in Boston, our competition, feels like a distant memory. And I can't stop staring at his mouth.

"My what?" Ryan asks.

I blink; the champagne has definitely gone to my head. "Hmmm?"

"You said something about my . . . mouth?" He sounds amused—and a touch confused.

I consider brushing it off, but instead I find myself lifting my eyes to his and saying, "It's a very nice mouth."

His eyes flick to *my* mouth, and it's like an outside force takes control of my body as I lean in and press my lips to his.

I pull away, but his hand comes to my jaw, bringing me back to him, light presses of his lips against mine, warm and sweet and almost chaste. It's the exact opposite of what I would've expected after our prior interactions, the sharp words and heated glances. This is like sinking into the softest feather bed. The world around me turns hazy, and when he slides his hand into my hair, I can't hold back a sigh of pleasure.

He kisses me slowly, purposefully, all his attention on me, on our lips gliding against each other. I have the vague thought that this probably isn't a great idea, but that's drowned out by the fizzy sensation rising in my chest. The lush softness of his mouth, the gravelly hum he makes as I slip my hand into his thick, wavy hair. Involuntarily, I shift closer, trailing my other hand down his shoulder, feeling the tension in his muscles; there's something fascinating about that controlled strength. Knowing that he could take what he wants but is choosing to follow my lead.

Then his lips part, and his tongue meets mine, and it's like the first bite of the most delicious dessert—I am suddenly ravenous.

I pull myself even closer, deepening the kiss, my hands raking through his hair. My teeth catch on his lower lip, and a soft groan rumbles in his throat, sending sparks of pure lust straight through my core. His hand in my hair curls into a fist, a tight knot that's right on the edge between pleasure and pain, as he kisses me with an intensity that steals my breath. He's hungry and urgent, and I'm desperate and greedy. I'm practically climbing into his lap as he kisses my jaw and my neck, his stubble rasping against my skin, making me moan in a way that's maybe a little embarrassing, but I'm too far gone to care.

Soon I'm straddling him, and he's running his hands down my body like he's claiming everything he touches: my back, my waist, sliding down to my butt and pulling me against him. I gasp at the hard press of him between my legs.

Without thinking, I lean back against the cool sand, pulling him down with me; he follows, continuing to kiss me, his hand sliding up my rib cage, thumb grazing my breast. Another moan slips out of my mouth. I have never in my life felt such unexpected, uncontrollable desire for another human being.

Needing him closer, I tug him over me, parting my legs so he can wedge his thigh between them. The weight of him is overwhelming in the best way; I've never been under a man this big—he's bracing himself with one forearm against the sand, trying to be careful with me. I rock against him, and he seems to know exactly what I'm after, pressing his thigh right where I want it. The friction . . . it's almost too much. My hands slide under his shirt and up his back, his skin hot against my palms. I bury my face in his neck and inhale; he smells *divine*. And I want his shirt off.

My hands shake as I bring them to his collar and fumble with the buttons. Again, he's right there with me, reaching around to untie my halter strap, tugging the top of my dress down until my bra is exposed, still kissing me like his life depends on it. We're both nearly frantic, and I pull too hard on his shirt and pop the final button at the same time his hand moves under the cup of my bra. He's palming my breast as I push him up just enough to grab his belt and undo the buckle and—

"What's going on out there?" a man's voice calls.

A light flashes, and we scramble apart like two teenagers caught behind the bleachers. A figure holding a flashlight, walking toward us. Ryan tucks me behind him as I pull the top of my dress back up. I'm breathless and shaky, the blood rushing back to my head as it hits me: We were taking our clothes off. In the middle of a public beach.

"Sorry, Officer," Ryan calls out. "We didn't—"

"Aren't you one of the Lawson boys?" asks the man—a cop, apparently.

Ryan coughs. "Uh, yes, sir. I'm Ryan, the youngest. I apologize for—"

"No, no, this is great. I mean, not on the beach, but from what your mother's been saying, this is a long time coming. Just, you know—get a room."

A laugh bubbles out of me, and I stifle it. Ryan sighs. "Yes, sir. Sorry again."

The cop chuckles as he heads away. "You two have a good night."

When he's gone, Ryan turns to face me. His hair's a mess, his lips swollen, his collar half popped. I reach up and touch my hair: tangled, gritty with sand.

"Holy shit," I say, still breathless.

His eyes widen. "I didn't—that wasn't all me, was it? You had a lot of champagne—"

"That definitely wasn't all you," I say, and he's visibly relieved. Yes, I'm tipsy, but I was in full control of my faculties.

Only now my brain is catching up, and I'm mortified at my behavior. My desperation. The sounds I made.

"I—I don't usually do things like that," I say.

"Me neither."

I'm trying to keep my eyes on his face. But his shirt is open, and his chest is exposed, and my god, it's beautiful. Thick and muscled, but not too cut, slightly soft around his navel, with a trail of dark hair disappearing into his pants.

His pants that I tried to take off.

"I should get back," I say, scrambling to my feet. "To the room. *My* room."

He stares up at me for a beat before nodding and standing, buckling his belt.

As we head back up the beach toward the inn, I feel like I'm doing the walk of shame without any of the benefits. In silence, he walks me to my room; I use my key card, and the door swings open, giving a clear view of the bed.

Ryan's right behind me; I can feel his warmth, can still catch a whiff of his scent. For one split second, I have the insane urge to grab his arm and tug him inside.

"Where's your room?" I say, instead.

"This is it."

My breath catches and I whirl around to face him.

He's grinning, eyes twinkling. "When I called to book you a room, the inn was full. I'm crashing at my parents' place."

"Oh," I say, surprised by how let down I feel. *Sleeping with the enemy is a terrible idea*, I tell myself.

Only problem is, he doesn't feel like the enemy anymore.

"But—if you go back to your parents' house, they're going to think we had a big fight or something," I say, then bite my lip. *What am I doing?*

His grin slowly fades as my words hit him. His pupils dilate. "Do you . . ."

I swallow. Stare at his lips. Let my mind drift back to the

feeling of his body on mine, his weight pressing me against the sand.

"I think you should sleep here," I say. His eyebrows shoot up, and I blurt, "*Just* sleep."

He blinks, and I catch a flash of—what, disappointment?—in his eyes before he nods. "Of course."

"Of course," I echo.

My heart knocks against my chest as I lead him into the room.

The door clicks shut behind us.

18

Ryan

HERE'S THE THING they don't tell you about the Only One Bed scenario: there are a lot of details to deal with all at once. What side of the bed do you sleep on? Who gets which pillows? Where do you get undressed? What do you wear to bed?

I brush my teeth first, having grabbed my bag from the car, then Josie goes in, leaving me with all these questions. I usually sleep in boxers, but there's no way I'm doing that tonight, so I put on the T-shirt I brought for tomorrow. I pick a side of the king-size bed at random and slide in, then start panicking because what is *Josie* going to wear? I imagine her coming out in lingerie, then smack that away because *duh*, of course she won't. Then I imagine her in something cotton and cozy, which is somehow even more attractive.

She opens the bathroom door a sliver and says, "Um, Ryan?"

"Yep?" I say, stiffening.

"Can you, uh . . . turn off the light?"

Ah. Maybe it's better that I won't know what she's wearing, what Josie Klein looks like before she falls asleep. I flick off my

nightstand lamp and everything goes black. There's a squeak
of hinges as the bathroom door opens fully, followed by a soft
thud and a muttered *oof* as she runs into something (the
dresser?). Finally, the bed sags as she climbs in on the opposite
side.

I'm sharing a bed with Josie Klein. This is so weird.

"Is this weird?" she asks.

"No!" I say, too quickly. "I mean, unless it's weird for you,
and then I'm happy to crash on the floor."

"No, it's fine," she says softly.

We both go silent, and I stare up at the dark ceiling. I can't
stop replaying that kiss, how she tasted like sweet champagne
and the salty ocean. I bet she tastes like spearmint now. It
would be so easy to roll over and kiss her again, to feel the
heat of her hands, the urgency of her touch as she explores my
skin. I want to hear that soft moan again, feel the way she
thrust herself against me.

Fuck, I'm hard just thinking about it. I turn on my side,
away from her, even though she can't see the effect she has
on me.

"I'm sorry," she says, breaking the silence. "I've been so
mean to you over the past few weeks."

My chest tightens with guilt. "I've been just as mean.
Maybe worse."

"I don't know about that. I really wanted to beat you. So
badly."

Wanted? Not sure why she's speaking in the past tense.

"Xander put us in a shitty position," I say, shifting so I'm on
my back. "How about we stop blaming each other or
ourselves?"

A soft chuckle. "I'm always happy to blame Xander."

We're silent again, and the sheets rustle as she rolls toward me. Something tickles my arm—her hair. My skin breaks into goose bumps, and I have to clench my hands into fists to keep from reaching over and touching the soft strands.

"So, uh . . . was it Xander who called my store a bleak existential wasteland?" she says, and I go rigid. In a softer voice, she adds, "And Eddie told me you said there's not enough caffeine in the entire coffee shop to keep my customers awake."

My heart sinks; yes, I said those things. No wonder she was so prickly toward me.

"I've given you grief about not understanding romance, but—" I swallow. "I've done the same to you. I'm really sorry. I was wrong. About your books. And about you."

"I'm sorry, too," she says. There's silence again, like we're both digesting this.

"Do you think we would've been friends?" Josie asks, after a bit. "If we'd given each other a chance before Xander pitted us against each other?"

I think about that. We became friends easily online, but in real life, I'd already judged her for being snooty and unapproachable.

If I hadn't? Maybe I could've gotten to know this side of her a long time ago.

"I think so," I say finally.

She exhales, and I catch a slight whiff of that minty toothpaste I'm dying to taste.

"Have you thought about what you'll do if—if you don't win?" The sadness in her voice settles in the empty space between us. Again, guilt niggles at me; I have another option, even though I don't really want it.

"Yeah, I . . ." I lick my lips. "A friend of mine is opening a romance bookstore in Provincetown, and they're trying to get me to join."

"Oh." The word is a surprised puff of air. "And will you?"

"Maybe. If it comes to that, which I hope it won't." I clear my throat, uncomfortable at the thought. "What about you?"

There's a rustling noise as she shifts her weight. More of her hair brushes against me—my neck and shoulder—and I lift my finger and stroke it. Gently enough that I hope she doesn't notice.

"I don't have anything else," she says in an almost whisper.

"But you could find something." I believe that without a doubt. "Any bookstore would be lucky to have you."

My eyes are adjusting to the dark, and I can make out the shape of her now as I look over. She's lying on her side, facing me, the covers dipping at the curve in her waist. I'm still touching the lock of her hair, and if she can see me as well as I can see her, she knows it. But she doesn't pull away.

"Maybe," she says. "If it comes to that—which I hope it won't."

She's repeating my words back to me, and I chuckle softly. "Yeah."

"So, um . . ." She sighs. "Are we going to be enemies again when we get home? What was it you said—go back to destroying each other's prospects for the future?"

I huff out a mirthless laugh. "Well, you're beating me, so . . ."

"No, Xander said you're slightly ahead."

Startled, I turn. "He told me *you* are slightly ahead."

I feel the bed shift as she rolls onto her back. It moves her hair away from me, and I immediately miss it. "That little sneak—I knew he was trying to manipulate us, but this is . . ."

"Low," I say. "Even for Xander."

Josie groans, lifting her hands and slapping them against the bed in frustration. "I wish we could turn the tables on him."

"Me too, but how? Xander holds all the power here."

I hate feeling like a puppet in his stupid game. But that's exactly what we are.

Josie doesn't speak again, and soon my eyes drift shut.

"Ryan?" Josie says.

My eyes open. "Hmmm?"

"It would be okay if you came over and said hi sometime. When you're not busy, I mean," she adds quickly. "Sometimes my store can get a little . . ."

"Lonely?"

"I was going to say quiet," she says. "But that too."

She sounds so small and sad that I want to roll toward her and scoop her up, pull her against me, and press a kiss to the top of her head.

But of course, I don't. I stay on my side of the bed, as close to the edge as possible.

"I'll come say hi," I whisper.

She yawns, a sweet and intimate sound. "Thanks," she murmurs.

I close my eyes and drift off, too.

I WAKE TO a golden glow behind my eyelids and something warm and soft pressed against my back. My eyes open slowly to see an unfamiliar room, lit by morning light filtering through lacy curtains.

The warm softness against my back? It's Josie, spooning me from behind. One of her arms is draped over my waist, her

fingertips brushing the bare skin on my stomach where my
T-shirt has shifted up.

Who would've guessed that Josie Klein is a cuddler?

I swallow rapidly and try to figure out what to do. She's
asleep—her deep breathing gives it away, plus I'm sure she
wouldn't be doing this if she was conscious. Yes, we made
out last night, and yes, I had my hand under her bra, and
she almost took off my pants—but that was last night, in
the dark on the beach, with champagne fuzzing our minds. It's
morning now, a new day. Somehow, this seems even more
intimate.

My own breathing is shallow. I'm hard and getting harder.

It would be so easy to turn toward her and let nature take
its course. See if she comes to me as easily as she did on the
beach, eager and hungry. But she made it clear that this was
just sleeping, and I would never want to make her feel
uncomfortable.

But I also can't stay here getting more and more aroused,
so I slowly slide away, pulling the covers off my legs and
slipping out of bed as carefully as possible. I glance back as she
sighs and shifts onto her back, still asleep. My shoulders drop
in relief.

Or disappointment?

I pause, taking in the rare sight of Josie Klein utterly at rest.
Her hair is loose and wavy, her cheek creased from the pillow,
her eyelashes thick and full. She's wearing an oversized cotton
T-shirt that has what looks like a dictionary entry printed on it.

Abibliophobia
noun.
  1. The fear of running out of books to read.

My lips twitch in a smile.

Now there's my BookshopGirl. No doubt about it.

IN THE BATHROOM, I grip the edges of the sink and stare at myself in the mirror. My hair is wild, my eyes even more so—I look like a guy whose brain has been thoroughly scrambled.

I started this trip hoping to figure out which side of Josie was real, and now I have my answer: Josie may be icy on the outside, but she's a warm ball of softness on the inside. What still isn't clear is what I do now. Specifically, how do I tell her what I know? And when? We'll be in the car for two hours together this morning heading back to Boston.

But for some reason, my gut is telling me *not yet.*

I will tell her—I just need to figure out the best way to do it, a way that doesn't make her feel ambushed or cornered. She just started barely not-hating me; I need to find a way to bridge the gap between the man she thought was her enemy and the guy she knows behind the screen.

Which leaves one more question. What am I hoping for? Assuming Josie finds out and she doesn't hate me again . . . what do I want to happen between us?

BOOKFRIENDS

July 7, 8:02 AM

BookshopGirl: Hey! Haven't heard from you in a few days. Busy weekend?

RJ.Reads: Hey. Yeah . . . It was pretty busy. How was your weekend?

BookshopGirl: It was okay.

RJ.Reads: Just "okay"? Did you do anything special?

BookshopGirl: Not really. How about you?

11:43 AM

BookshopGirl: So what kept you so busy this weekend?

4:17 PM

BookshopGirl: Or maybe you were busy with someone. Did you have a hot date? Ooh, maybe you're still with them. That's fine, of course.

8:26 PM

BookshopGirl: Sorry for prying. You don't need to tell me. Is everything okay, though? I hope I didn't say something wrong. If so, I apologize.

July 8, 5:18 AM

BookshopGirl: Hi again. I didn't sleep well last night and I've typed a dozen different responses, trying to figure out what to say. I can't help feeling like something has shifted between us. I assume it's because I didn't want to meet in person, and I'm sorry. I'm not the best at connecting with people in real life and I don't have a lot of friends—I'm sure you're shocked, because I'm so delightful online. (That's a joke.)

BookshopGirl: But I deeply value your friendship. Whenever anything interesting or crazy or weird happens at work, you're the first person I think of telling. Whenever I read a book that surprises or excites me, I wonder what you'd think about it. And whenever I get a new message from you, my whole day brightens. Now I feel like I've lost something precious and I know it's my fault but the fact is, I miss you. So much. And honestly, it's rare that I miss anyone.

6:34 AM

BookshopGirl: I'm sorry, that was a lot. Feel free to disregard. Why doesn't this stupid website allow us to edit or delete our messages?

9:33 AM

RJ.Reads: Hi. I didn't mean to leave you hanging but I needed to collect my thoughts. You haven't done anything wrong, I promise. I respect your decision to keep this friendship online, but if that changes, let me know. I'd love to keep chatting here as often as you'd like. I've really missed you, too.

19

Josie

SINCE RETURNING FROM Maine last week, I've decided on a new rule: no more drinking around Ryan Lawson. And no more touching him.

I've never thought of myself as someone whose judgment is easily impaired, but the combination of alcohol and Ryan makes my head fuzzy. And no more getting so close that I can smell him, either.

I've done my best to be polite and distant whenever we run into each other at work. But every time I pass him at Beans, or in our now-combined back room, I get a whiff of his scent. And I'm catapulted back to that beach, to his mouth on mine, my hands shaking as I unbuckled his belt.

I keep imagining what would've happened if I'd reached out and touched him when we were in bed together. If he would've pulled me under him and finished what we started.

Hence the new rule.

I've just unlocked the front door of the store and flipped my sign from CLOSED to OPEN when my phone chimes.

RJ.Reads: Just thinking about you and wanted to say hello.

I grin, happy to see his message—and grateful for the distraction from my confusing feelings for my former nemesis turned . . . whatever Ryan is now.

Still my competition, I remind myself. And I might actually be beating him.

Freaking Xander.

BookshopGirl: Hi!

RJ.Reads: You'll have to let me know when you're ready for another book rec.

BookshopGirl: Ooh! I'm almost finished with the new Zadie Smith (so good btw) so now would be good. But is it one of YOUR favorites or your brothers'? ☺

BookshopGirl: As reader commandment #3 says, Thou shalt share thy favorite books with thy trusted friends, for in doing so thou art baring thy soul and revealing the essence of thy heart.

I cringe; too much? I'm not exactly the "funny" type, and this was RJ's joke to begin with.

Then his response appears, and I relax again.

RJ.Reads: Ha! Your right—don't want to break the commandments. OK here it is: Romantic Comedy by Curtis Sittenfeld.

BookshopGirl: Read it and loved it! I grew up watching SNL and the behind-the-scenes glimpses were fascinating. And such an insightful evaluation of how conventionally unattractive men can date women "out of their league," but it rarely happens the other way around.

RJ.Reads: Agree. (Also: *you're* above, sorry.) And the chemistry and character development—it was my first book by her and I really enjoyed it. (Also also, I'm relieved you liked it! Otherwise I'd never be able to speak to you again.)

BookshopGirl: Oh I'm a huge fan. I've read all her books. I cannot WAIT to hear her speak at IBNE. (And please don't stop talking to me! I'd be miserable.)

RJ.Reads: You'll be at IBNE? Me too!

Heart sinking, I stare at the screen. The email about the panel selection is supposed to come today, so IBNE is on my

mind—but I didn't mean to let RJ know I'd be there.
The thought of running into him sends panic racing through
my body.

Fumbling with my phone, I type a quick response.

> **BookshopGirl:** Forget you read that.
> Please?

> **RJ.Reads:** But it could be great—we
> could meet naturally, no pressure. Just
> two online friends meeting IRL at a book
> conference.

He's right, but my stomach twists. What's wrong with me?
Why can't I be normal and agree to a casual meetup with an
online friend?

Because he's more than a friend. The truth of it barrels
down on me: I care about him. I care about his opinion
of me, too. And I'm terrified that meeting him in person will
strip away the carefully constructed layers I've built about
myself, that I won't live up to the version of me he's come
to know.

> **RJ.Reads:** Hey, you still there?

> **BookshopGirl:** Yeah. Sorry.

> **RJ.Reads:** No, I'm the one who should
> apologize. You told me you weren't
> interested in meeting, and I pushed it
> again. I'm sorry.

> **BookshopGirl:** Please don't apologize—like you said, it's not strange for two people in the same industry to meet at a conference. I'm the one making it weird.

> **RJ.Reads:** What if we've already met? Wouldn't you want to know?

I assume he means we might have already met at IBNE, in prior years. And it's true, we might have, but I didn't know it was *him*. Is it so wrong that I don't want things to change? Is it so terrible that I want to stay in this online bubble where I can choose my words, take my time, keep everything safe?

The thought of meeting him out there, in the real world—of being seen, really seen—makes my chest constrict. It's suddenly hard to breathe.

> **BookshopGirl:** No, I wouldn't.

That sounds so harsh. Quickly, I type a new message.

> **BookshopGirl:** All I mean is that I really love what we have right now and I don't want to mess that up.

> **RJ.Reads:** What if it didn't mess it up, though? What if it made it even better?

And then it hits me: the only thing scarier than the possibility of losing my online friendship with RJ is the possibility of it turning into something more.

> **RJ.Reads:** Sorry, I did it again. From now on, the ball is in your court (so to speak. I never played sports so that analogy doesn't feel right. The library book is now checked out to your account? The bookshelf is yours to arrange?)

"Good morning, darling sister!" Georgia calls as she comes in the door.

I quickly type a response to RJ:

> **BookshopGirl:** Thank you for understanding. I appreciate it.

"Hey! How were your exams?" I say, pocketing my phone.

Georgia's been so busy studying we've hardly seen each other. But one look at her, and I know they must have gone well: she's glowing, her dark hair in a loose braid, big hoop earrings swinging from her ears.

I wait for her to ask why I'm so flustered, but she's not looking at me—she stops in the middle of the store and turns slowly, eyes widening. "Wow! The place looks great!"

"Really?" I say, grinning.

I've noticed that people spend more time in Ryan's store compared to mine—despite the chaotic hodgepodge of mismatched bookcases and shelves. Or maybe even because of them. His customers stick around, hunting for the perfect title or discovering new ones. My customers don't spend a ton of time browsing—they find what they need and head out.

So I've shifted a few bookcases out of their neat rows and

made room for a reading area. I've also highlighted specific books to draw the eye along the shelves and hopefully keep people interested. I'm impressed at how such simple changes can have a big effect. Customers are spending more time here. Buying more, too.

"You're going to kick Ryan's big dumb ass," Georgia says, reaching out her hand for a high five.

My smile fades, and I give her palm a half-hearted slap. "Yeah. That."

"What? Do we not hate Ryan anymore?" Georgia leans her cane against the counter and plops into a chair. "You haven't told me much about your trip to Kennebunkport."

As if summoned, Ryan walks from his store to the counter at Beans. He's framed in the gap between the two bookcases that form the wall. When he catches my eye, his entire face brightens. My stomach does a weird flip.

"Hi! Good morning!" he calls, brushing his hair off his forehead.

"Morning," I say, smiling in a way that hopefully says, *How do you do, fellow bookseller,* and not *I'm having filthy thoughts about what's underneath your cardigan.*

"See you later?"

"Sure."

With another smile, he grabs his coffee-flavored milkshake and heads back to his store.

"Ohhhhh," Georgia says.

I look up. "What?"

She's staring at me knowingly. "Classic body language of attraction: Prolonged eye contact. Mirrored facial expressions. Preening gestures."

"*Preening?*"

"He brushed his hair back. You licked your lips." She leans forward. "Something happened between you two."

I want to protest, to insist I'm not attracted to *him*, that we definitely still hate him. But there's no use in lying to my psychologist-in-training sister.

"We, uh . . . may have made out on the beach after his parents' party."

Though I've never gotten so hot and bothered making out. I'm not sure I've had actual *sex* that got me so hot and bothered.

Georgia's eyes widen. "My sister, making out with a guy on the *beach*? Like, in the sand?"

"Yeah," I say, grimacing. "It was . . . gritty."

I decide not to tell her about the sharing-a-bed part. That feels like something I want to keep for myself.

"He is *so* not the kind of guy you go for. You usually go for men who look like sickly Victorian orphans."

This is true; my MFA-candidate boyfriend had a birdlike bone structure and skin so pale it was nearly translucent. And everyone I've dated since college has been a smaller guy, not much taller than me, which is fine—though for the first time, I wonder why. Maybe because I hate being looked down on.

"Do you like him?" Georgia prods.

I wave my hand dismissively. "I'd had a bunch of champagne."

Her body stiffens. "He took advantage of you?"

"Of course not. Ryan would never do something like that."

Georgia grins, triumphant. "You defended him! You do like him." Then she pauses. "But a week ago you loathed him?"

"We got caught up in the moment," I say, which isn't an

answer, but if I analyze this too much, I may not like what I discover. "We kissed. It won't happen again. Okay?"

"I mean, you're both adults. And he's cute, in a bumbling giant kind of way, and he likes books . . ."

She raises her eyebrows at me, then turns thoughtful. "But you're right, it's not a good idea to get involved with the competition. At the end of the summer, only one of you can win."

A customer walks in then, saving me from the conversation. But Georgia's comment sticks in my brain.

Before last weekend, the idea of *me* winning and Ryan skulking off in shame would have made me giddy with excitement. Now it leaves me unsettled.

Maybe because I know there's a solid chance I could lose—Xander lied to both of us, so who knows who's really ahead. Or maybe because I now understand how much Ryan loves what he does—and how protective he is of his staff and customers.

And all that nice-guy behavior? It's not an act. He actually *is* a good human. It's terrible news for me; a complete disaster. Humanizing your enemy makes it difficult to destroy him.

Plus, there's the undeniable fact that I'm attracted to him. Intensely.

Ryan's laugh echoes through the store, and I sneak a look between my bookcases. He's helping a tiny, white-haired woman reach something on a top shelf marked KISSING AND KILTS. The top of her head is level with his elbow, and when he hands the paperback to her, she beams up at him. Then he holds out an arm and leads her toward his register.

As they disappear from view, his laugh booms through the air again. My eyes unexpectedly fill with tears.

Again, Georgia's comment echoes in my mind: *Only one of you can win.*

I want that winner to be me, of course. But for the first time, I realize that I don't want Ryan to lose.

That's how this stupid competition works, I remind myself. Xander wants to see which manager can make him the most money, and I doubt he'll be amenable to the winner hiring the loser when his entire goal is to increase his profits.

Unless . . .

An idea sparks, and I pull open my laptop and start brainstorming.

A COUPLE HOURS later, I'm in the back room heating up my dinner and working through this potential plan. My phone buzzes with an alert: an email from the organizers of IBNE.

> Dear Ms. Klein, we're delighted to offer you a spot on a panel . . .

I jump in the air, whooping and fist pumping. I did it! My first impulse is to tell RJ—which I stifle immediately. He could figure out who I am by looking at the conference schedule.

"Are you okay?" It's Ryan, in the storage room behind me. "I heard you shouting?"

I clear my throat and face him. "Yeah, I . . ." I shrug and hold out my phone. "I just got word that I'll be on a panel at IBNE."

His face bursts into a grin like sunshine. "What? Josie! That's *amazing.* Congratulations!"

He takes a step forward, like he's going to scoop me up in a hug, then seems to think better of it and stays put. Probably a good thing.

"What's the topic of the panel?" he asks.

"I don't know yet—they'll let me know soon. But I'm excited. I've been applying for years, and I've never made it."

"We should celebrate," he says. "We could get drinks—"

"I can't." That would be breaking *all* the rules. "I, uh . . . need to run some errands after closing. But thanks for being excited for me."

His eyes track across my face. "Of course. Congrats again."

Someone calls his name, and he disappears. I pull out my phone to read the rest of the email about the panel, but then he's back with one of his employees—a dark-haired woman wearing all black.

"Hey," Ryan says, sticking his hands in his pockets.

"Ask her," the woman whispers, poking him.

"I am," he mutters to her, then turns to me again. "So, uh, I have a question for you."

My curiosity is piqued. "Okay . . . ?"

"Do you . . ." He brushes his hair from his face, then mumbles something under his breath about going on a date.

I blink. A flicker of warmth lights in my chest, like a candle being lit. "A . . . date?"

"Not with me," he says quickly, and the candle is snuffed out. "We're hosting a speed-dating night, and Indira"—he motions to the woman in black—"just told me that one of the women canceled."

Oh. Not with him, obviously. Not that I even want that. Totally against my new rule. So why do I feel . . . disappointed?

"We can't have an odd number," Indira adds. "It'll mess everything up."

"You can't do it?" I ask Indira. There is nothing I'd rather do *less* than struggle through a bunch of conversations with strange men.

"I'm in charge of the event, and I have a girlfriend," she says, shaking her head.

"I'm sorry, I really can't," I say to Ryan. "I have to run the store."

"I'll watch it for you," Ryan says.

I bark out a laugh. "You can't be serious."

He makes a face like, *Excuse me?* I didn't mean he's incapable of watching my store; I meant, *You really want me to meet a bunch of other men?* If the situations were reversed, if Ryan was joining a speed-dating event while *I* had to sit a few yards away and listen . . .

I wouldn't be so eager. In fact, the thought makes me queasy.

But apparently, it doesn't bother him one bit. Good to know.

"Fine," I say eventually. "But now *you* owe *me.*"

I follow Indira over to Happy Endings, and as I sit down with my first date, a knot tightens in my stomach. I force it down and muster a smile. But I can't stop wondering:

Why did Ryan ask me to do this?

And why does it bother me so much that he did?

20

Ryan

I'VE BEEN TALKED into a lot of bad ideas in my life, but this might be the worst.

Josie's over at Happy Endings now, sitting across from someone who isn't me. Telling a story or making a joke to someone who isn't me. Smiling at someone who isn't me.

I may not know what I want with her, but I do know this feels . . . terrible.

To quote Miss Taylor Swift—in my defense, I have none. Except that Indira looked like she was about to cry when she begged me to ask Josie to sit in. I offered to find an eligible bachelorette over at Beans or even on the street outside, but she said a "rando" was too risky. And in her words, "We don't like Josie, but at least we know her."

Except I think I do like her.

I haven't been able to stop thinking about this past weekend—although to hear BookshopGirl tell RJ about it, her weekend was nothing special.

Anyway: I caved.

It'll probably be fine. I mean, what are the chances Josie

hits it off with one of these guys? They have to be minuscule. Right?

But so were the chances that my online crush and my IRL nemesis would turn out to be one and the same.

Stupid, stupid, stupid.

I SPEND THE next two hours stewing in misery, cursing myself for putting Josie in this position, and trying not to analyze every sound coming from Happy Endings. Only a few customers come in, so most of the time I can hear *everything*.

No wonder Josie gets lonely.

A laugh rises above the rest of the noise—a laugh that could be hers? I peek around the bookshelves she's positioned between her store and Beans, trying to catch a glimpse. Her back is toward me, so I can't tell if she's enjoying or suffering through her current conversation.

I'm certainly suffering enough for the both of us. My mind flashes between images of Josie with ten other men (laughing, chatting, leaning in and putting her hand on their arm) and memories of Josie with *me*: her head resting on my chest as we danced, her eyes glinting on the beach, her breath hitching as I slid my hand under the cup of her bra and felt her hard nipple against my palm.

I had this woman in bed next to me and I *kept my distance*? I woke up in the morning to find her plastered against my backside and I fucking *rolled away*? I told myself I was being respectful, but that wasn't the whole truth.

While my body knows exactly what it wants, my heart and my mind aren't so sure yet. But right now all I can think is:

What if she ends up going home with one of these assholes and I never get another chance with her?

I will hate myself for the rest of my life.

As the painful minutes tick by, it hits me: what I thought was a complication—BookshopGirl and Josie being one and the same—might actually be the most incredible opportunity of my life. Ever since I read my first Harlequin at fifteen, I've been looking for a woman I could connect with both physically and emotionally, and now I've found both in the same person.

Except that the last person I felt this way about destroyed my ability to trust my own feelings when it comes to any of this, and I promised myself I'd never again fall for someone who doesn't feel the same way.

Especially not someone who has specifically stated that she doesn't want to meet me in real life.

Putting my head in my hands, I let out a soft groan; what the fuck am I going to do?

"SLEEPING ON THE job?"

I bolt upright, rubbing my eyes. Josie's standing like a vision before me, a playful smirk on her lips. "It was so slow over here, I had to get Eddie to bring me a triple-shot frappe," I say.

She rolls her eyes and straightens a book no one touched.

"So, uh . . . how were your dates?" I ask.

She shrugs, walking to inspect another table. "Fine."

"No sparks?" I ask, trying not to sound too hopeful.

"Just one." Her eyes meet mine, and she holds my stare for an unbearably long second. "Did we make any sales?"

We. Things would be so much easier if we could join forces and be on the same team, against Xander.

"Just one," I say, echoing her. *"Remarkably Bright Creatures*—but it took me fifteen minutes to find it."

She gives me a confused look. "It's shelved under the V's. For the author's last name. Van Pelt, Shelby. Where did you think it would be?"

"Maybe on a table with books about unexpected friendships, or books set in the Pacific Northwest. Or even books with charming characters that also happen to be marine animals."

Josie cringes. "That would be utter chaos."

"Well, it's a lot more inspiring than the letter *V*," I snap, offended on behalf of my creative shelving system.

She tilts her chin up in challenge. "How do you organize romance? Enlighten me."

I have a flash of picking her up, carrying her to the back room, and spending the rest of the night showing her what I've learned from reading romance novels. She probably thinks it's all smooth moves and sexual antics, but really, it's listening. Paying attention.

I'm dying to know what makes Josie's panties wet, what'll make her lose control—even more than she did on the beach. But that's not what she asked me.

"Well," I say, conjuring up a mental image of Happy Endings' myriad corners. "There's YA, new adult, and adult. There's contemporary and historical. Romance that merges with fantasy—romantasy. Think Sarah J. Maas or Rebecca Yarros."

"Faerie smut and dragon riders," she says. "Got it."

If I look shocked that she knows these authors and their books, it's because I am.

"I keep up with trends," Josie says. "Although if I carried those books, they'd be comfortably tucked in with the other M's and Y's."

Shaking my head at her traditional thinking, I continue on, describing all the other ways I might organize the store: by subgenres, tropes, historical eras, or heat level.

"Sounds complicated," Josie says, looking genuinely surprised.

"And fun," I say. "Imagine a hypothetical book about two men on rival hockey teams who fall in love. Where do I shelve it? Contemporary, sports romance, LGBTQ+, or enemies to lovers? And what if one of the characters has an adorable pet cat—"

"Okay, okay," Josie says, resting her hand on my forearm. The feel of her skin on mine sends a jolt through my body, bringing back memories of the beach, the way her fingers trembled as she struggled to undo the buttons on my shirt.

My breath stills. Her bottom lip is caught between her teeth, and when she releases it, I move closer. My eyes are asking permission, and hers are granting it—

When the goddamn door opens and a customer walks in.

Luckily, Josie has him in and out in less than ten minutes, after locating *Demon Copperhead* among the K's (for Barbara Kingsolver).

"That would have taken me an hour," I admit, once the customer has gone.

Josie turns back toward me, but she's put distance between us, like the bridge has gone up and there's no chance of crossing the moat to rescue the princess from her strictly regulated world.

"I wouldn't be able to handle the way you have it," she admits.

"Does it come back to having control?" I ask. "Your intense need for organization."

"It's not *that* intense," she says. I arch an eyebrow. "Okay, maybe it's a little intense. But it's efficient."

"Clearly." Maybe *too* efficient. Yes, the customer found what he was looking for, but he didn't have a chance to stumble over anything else he might have fallen in love with.

"Well, my mom—"

"The reader of bodice rippers," I say.

Josie tilts her head. "Did I tell you about her?"

Shit, shit, shit.

"You must have mentioned it," I say. "In the car when we were talking about our families."

Josie nods, but looks uncertain, and I curse myself for mixing up the conversations. I've got to be more careful—she's made it clear she doesn't want to meet RJ in person, and I shouldn't press the issue until I'm *really* sure this is something worth exploring. I'd hate to blow up my friendship with BSG for nothing.

"Mom has some hoarding tendencies," she says. "She loved going to yard sales, thrift stores, finding 'super fun treasures,' bags piled on boxes piled on trash."

Josie shudders, as if the memory's reached out and wrapped its icy arms around her. Her left hand is resting on the counter, and I bring mine up next to it, not touching, but almost. "So that's why you keep the store so organized?" My fingers are itching to slide between hers, to hold her hand.

"That, and it's my job," she says.

At the mention of her job—the one she might lose at my expense—she pulls her hand away, and all traces of BookshopGirl disappear. The ice queen is back, her posture stiff, her eyes dark and intense.

A couple weeks ago, this would've intimidated me, but now I know that underneath the cool exterior, Josie's filled with insecurities and worries, just like anyone else. Just like me.

"So, um, there's something else I've been wanting to talk to you about," Josie says.

I look up. "Yeah?"

"Remember what we were talking about that night . . . in Maine? About how Xander's playing both of us and we wish we could turn the tables on him?"

"Yes," I say, intrigued.

"Well, I have an idea. I need to figure out a few details, but maybe we could chat tomorrow?"

She raises her eyebrows and shrugs, a gesture that feels vulnerable and hopeful. Whatever she wants to talk about, it's important to her. Which means it's important to me, too. If I'm going to figure out these complicated feelings I'm having for her, I need to get us out of our usual routine at work, where we're both so stuck in the roles we've been playing all summer. Rival booksellers. Competitors.

And I think I know just the spot.

"Sure," I say, and she lights up. "What if we get dinner?"

She blinks, the light dimming slightly. I need to tread carefully.

"Just as colleagues," I say, and she nods. "But you know I'm going to be in suspense all day tomorrow, wondering what you want to talk about—can you give me a hint?"

She gives a nervous smile. "You're going to have to be patient."

"I'll try," I tell her.

And I mean it, in more ways than one.

21

Josie

RYAN MADE RESERVATIONS. At a restaurant. This doesn't feel like two colleagues meeting over food to discuss an idea. This feels like a date.

He won't tell me where we're going, either, just called us an Uber after closing. Now we're in the back seat of an immaculate Subaru, heading toward Back Bay. Across from me, Ryan looks squished, his long legs drawn up to his chest. No cardigan tonight—he's wearing a blue button-down, collar unbuttoned, the sleeves rolled up. It's taking all my effort to not stare at his forearms, thick and veiny with fine brown hair. I'm also trying to breathe through my mouth because his scent is making my head feel fuzzy.

I need to focus on the purpose for this outing: sharing the idea I've been contemplating. What if we can figure out a way for both of us to keep our jobs? I think I have a solid plan. I just have to convince Ryan to give it a chance.

I force my attention out the window. This area is all too familiar. My muscles tighten involuntarily.

The driver turns down Boylston and there it is: the Boston Public Library. Imposing granite exterior, arched doors, copper trim along the eaves. As much a museum as a library—filled with murals and sculptures, rare original books and manuscripts—and arguably the most beautiful library in the country.

Instead of driving past, continuing toward any of the dozens of restaurants in the neighborhood, the Uber pulls up out front.

"I don't go there," I blurt out.

Ryan brushes his hair off his forehead, his eyes concerned. "How come?"

"My college roommates and I . . . we used to come here to study. We'd go into Bates Hall and work on our papers and . . ." Deep breath. "I loved it there."

The hushed voices, the huge domed ceiling, the rows of tables filled with people reading, studying, researching. The private thoughts and quiet conversations of all those booklovers filling the space like radio waves.

"I had to drop out of school," I say in a rush. "And I haven't been back here since."

Ryan's face softens, his eyebrows pulling together in concern. "Shit. I'm so sorry. I had no idea. We can leave if you're not comfortable. But there's a place here I want to check out, and you're the only person I know who will appreciate it."

I'm intrigued; I can't help it. "What place?"

He hesitates, then says, "I know this is a crazy question, given our history over the past few weeks, but here goes: Do you trust me?"

"Yes," I say, surprising myself.

His face breaks into a delighted smile. "Really? Okay— great news. Shall we?"

I nod, and he leads the way.

"SO, WHAT DO you think?" Ryan asks once we're seated.

"It's amazing," I say, looking around.

He's brought me to the Map Room, a tea and cocktails lounge just off the main entrance of the BPL. It's all warm, dark wood and industrial brick accents, with cozy tables perfect for conversation—a hidden gem at a public library, of all places.

Despite the cozy atmosphere, I'm fussing with the menu, mentally rehearsing my rule: *no drinking around Ryan Lawson*. When our waiter comes by, Ryan orders a Summer Wind cocktail (the menu describes it as "fizzy, jammy, floral") and a bunch of small plates to share. I order an oolong tea called the Iron Goddess, hoping it will bring me strength.

A month and a half ago, I'd never have predicted this. Me, sitting across from my nemesis. About to propose something that could change our lives forever.

"So, uh—how did you end up becoming a bookseller?" I ask, not quite ready to launch into my idea. "You said you weren't a big reader as a kid."

"Yeah, I didn't read until third grade. Before that, letters and words looked like hieroglyphics. I couldn't believe they meant anything." He sits back, one arm extended across the empty chair next to him. "You were probably reading chapter books at that age."

"Well . . . yeah. In third grade I read *The Hobbit* and started *The Lord of the Rings*."

"Seriously?" He whistles. "I was struggling with *The Cat in the Hat*."

"How did you go from Dr. Seuss to romance novels?"

His eyes spark with mischief as he leans forward. "Would you believe me if I said it had to do with a lonely parrot and a stack of Harlequins?"

Soon I'm laughing, imagining Ryan as a teenage hooligan shoplifting (badly) from a bookstore, then working off his debt by reading to the owner's pet parrot.

"Nothing like erotic literature to motivate a teenage boy to read," he says, grinning.

"I can imagine," I say, then think about my mom and her habit of disappearing into her romances. "So reading all that . . . did you ever confuse reality with fantasy?"

"You mean, did I believe I was an eighteenth-century princess betrothed to a Scottish laird who is rough around the edges but remarkably tender in bed, and the first time he growled the words 'my wife,' I literally swooned?"

I snort a laugh and cover my mouth. "Yes?"

"No. But you can see how ridiculous that question is, right?" He leans forward, elbows on the table, his eyes bright. "When you were reading Tolkien, did you believe that you were a hobbit or an elf or a—a shieldmaiden riding into battle?"

"I *wanted* to be a shieldmaiden riding into battle."

"I bet you did," he says, grinning. "Donning your armor, brandishing a sword, sacrificing yourself to save the ones you love."

I shrug, a little surprised by how accurate that is. "I guess so."

Our waiter appears with our drinks and food, and I'm so hungry I dive in, closing my eyes in delight when I take my first bite of lobster mac and cheese. Ryan's doing the same, tasting the fig and prosciutto flatbread.

After we've taken the edge off our hunger, he looks up again.

"So you wanted to chat about something?"

"Uh—yeah." I take another sip of tea, regretting not ordering booze for liquid courage. "Remember how, at the beginning of all this, you said if you won, you'd hire me as your assistant?"

I sneak a glance at him; his brow is furrowed. "Yeah, sorry, I can see how that would be insulting, implying that you should be under me." He coughs. "*Work* under me," he corrects, but it's too late; I'm already remembering what it felt like on that beach. His weight over me, his hand sliding up my ribs and under my bra.

I swallow and start over. "What I mean is: maybe you were onto something. What if we could both keep our jobs?"

"How? Xander only wants one manager."

"Xander knows nothing about running a bookstore. And he has no idea that we have very different strengths in bookselling."

His eyebrows shoot up. "Is Josie Klein admitting I have strengths?"

"You're great at creating an inclusive, welcoming environment. Customers adore you. Your staff respects you." I'm surprised at how easily the list comes to me. "Remember how Xander said he wanted people to get their parenting books and their Harry Potters and their spy thrillers all in the same place?"

He shakes his head. "I must have blocked that out—I know nothing about those genres."

"Neither do I. Which is my point. The new store is going to have *everything*. Think about it: thrillers and baby board books and how-to books. And a good manager knows the products they sell."

"I'm stressed out just thinking about it," he says. "But I'm not sure what you're saying."

"I'm saying we should convince Xander that he needs two managers."

He stares at me for so long I start to get nervous. Our waiter stops by again, bringing us a plate of lemon meringue tart, which I promptly start devouring.

"What are you thinking?" I ask Ryan. He's being mighty quiet.

He takes a bite, chewing thoughtfully. "I'm thinking that Xander's priority is making money."

"Yeah, and he's delusional—no one gets rich owning an indie bookstore. But—here, take a look at this."

I grab a napkin and pen and start doing rough calculations. "If Xander keeps only one of us as manager, the store will be woefully understaffed. You can't sell books without booksellers, so sales will take a hit—and the new store will have more overhead expenses. Xander could end up in the red. I estimate that the new manager will have to hire more staff—two, maybe even three people to compensate for the loss of one of us, since they won't have the experience we do.

"So it would be in Xander's best interests to keep us both," I finish. "We just have to prove it to him over the next six weeks."

"How?"

"We'll have to significantly increase our profits—by a lot, so he can't ignore that we make more money when working together. We can brainstorm ways to do that. I already have a few ideas, but first, I wanted to see if this is something you're even interested in."

There's an unexpectedly guarded expression on Ryan's face. And I find myself leaning forward again, hoping he says yes.

"Can I think about it?" he asks.

I sit back, disappointed. Maybe I've been reading him wrong. Just because he took me to one of the most bookishly charming places I've ever seen doesn't mean he wants to work with me.

"Of course," I say. "Just let me know."

WHEN WE FINISH our food and drinks, Ryan tries to take the check, but I badger him into splitting it. We head out of the lounge, and I notice a sign for Bates Hall.

"Do you think it's still open?" I ask, nodding in that direction.

He glances at his phone. "We have a few minutes. Do you . . . want to go in?"

I hesitate; being here, so close to this place I loved all those years ago, has made me realize I've spent too much time avoiding anything that reminds me of my college experience. I want to push myself.

"Could we?" I say. "Just for a minute?"

We climb the stairs in silence, but when we get to the threshold, I freeze.

Ryan's hand comes to my shoulder, warm and steady. He leans down, putting his mouth an inch from my ear. "You got this."

And, taking a deep breath, I walk inside.

The reading room is exactly as I remember: domed ceiling, arched windows, rows of wooden tables with green-shaded lamps. The vast space is mostly empty, just a few people finishing up their work for the evening.

We sit at a table near the end, across from each other.

"We came here for a field trip in elementary school," Ryan says in a low voice. "Imagine thirty rambunctious kids, the librarians hushing us, and our teachers reminding us to *be respectful, children.*"

I smile, imagining Ryan at that age. A head taller than everyone else, his hair a bird's nest.

"What were you like back then?" I ask.

"I was the kid at the back of the line who had to be assigned my own chaperone to keep me from wandering off," he says, which makes my smile grow. "Let me guess—you were the girl who sat at the front and raised her hand before anyone else. Who had all the stars on the star chart and got the 'Best Reader' award."

His description is pretty accurate. "Yeah. I guess so. I loved the structure of school.

And I loved the positive feedback: *Josie is a delight. Josie shows real talent for reading. Josie is going to go far in life.*

"Meanwhile, I was the kid with one star that the teacher only gave me because she felt bad." He softens his words with a smile, but I never thought about how demoralizing that could be. To me, the stars were motivating.

"I'm sorry," I say.

He shrugs. "My brothers were great at school, so the teachers were shocked when I wasn't. But after a while, I'd disappointed everyone so thoroughly that their expectations were on the floor."

"I guess that's the thing about expectations," I say. "High or low, they can screw you up. I was totally focused on academic success, you know? And then when I got to college . . ."

I trail off. He's leaning forward, listening intently. When his eyes meet mine, I get that bubbly, effervescent feeling I had on the beach, like I'm tipsy. Like everything I say is fascinating, and the world is warm and kind, and baring my soul to him feels like the most natural thing I could do.

Except I'm *not* tipsy. So maybe it's not alcohol and Ryan.

Maybe it's just Ryan.

Blinking, I refocus. "Anyway—that's part of why I never finished my degree."

I say the words casually, though they feel like shards of glass in my mouth. Thankfully, there's no surprise or—worse—pity in his expression. Instead, he just nods and says, "Do you ever think about going back?"

"No," I say immediately. "What would be the point? I don't need it for my job."

"What was your plan for a career, back when you were in college?"

I shrug. "No idea. I was an English major—"

"Of course."

"—and I had this vague idea of spending my life reading Big Books and having Important Conversations."

"Which is what you do now." He nods. "And you're great at it—if we had a sticker chart, your row would be filled with gold stars."

I laugh—then stifle the sound as a patron glances our way.

"If we're going strictly by books sold, you'd have more gold stars."

"But there's so many other ways to get gold stars." He leans forward on his elbows, and I do the same, like we're co-conspirators. "Gold star for each organized shelf. Gold star for your efficient stock tracking system."

"Gold star for helping tiny elderly ladies reach the top shelf," I say. "And another for having a staff that genuinely respects you."

He smiles; my stomach goes *flip*, and I look down. His left hand and my right are resting flat on the table, a millimeter of space between our fingertips. My palm tingles, remembering how it felt to slide under his shirt, his skin fever hot. The broad span of his back, the cords of muscle flexing beneath my fingers.

My breath quickens, and I slide my hand forward a fraction of an inch.

He does the same. Our fingertips graze. My nervous system is going haywire, the touch of his skin on the sensitive pads of my fingers sending golden light darting up my arm. He turns his palm over, an invitation, and when I slide mine into his, his thumb sweeps across the back of my hand, then down each finger one by one, like he's committing their size and shape to memory.

I've never considered the aesthetics of a man's hands before, but Ryan's are near perfect: thick fingers, a palm as comfortable as a well-worn baseball glove, knuckles that are just a bit knobby. I starfish my hand flat against his, then curl it, stroking his palm with my fingertips, feeling the scrape of calluses. When I sneak a glance at his face, he's focused on our hands, too, but then his lashes lift, and his gaze meets mine for the span of one shaky breath. It's too intense, the eye contact and the hand contact, so I look back down as his hand slides up and wraps around my wrist.

I swallow. He's pulling me toward him, or maybe I'm pulling myself—but either way, his hand is sliding upward until he's gripping my elbow and we're leaning together across the table and—

"We're closing soon, dears." A librarian gives us a smile before moving on.

My breath rushes out and I pull my hands into my lap. My entire right arm is tingling.

"Ready?" Ryan says, standing.

I nod, gripping the strap of my crossbody bag as I follow him out. He sticks his hands in his pockets, which is probably good. I clearly can't be trusted around him. Even when I'm stone-cold sober.

WHEN WE PULL up in front of my building, Ryan asks the Uber driver to wait while he walks me to the door.

"So, um . . . thanks for tonight," I say. "It was fun."

"Thanks for coming." In the light of the streetlamp, his eyes are shadowed, and I can't read his expression.

"You want to think about it overnight?" My voice squeaks on the last word. "My proposition?"

His eyebrows lift, and I laugh nervously. The point of this evening was not to get all giggly and touchy-feely with Ryan Lawson. It was to talk business.

"About convincing Xander that he needs us both as co-managers," I say.

"No."

The disappointment hits me like a rock. "Oh."

"No, I don't need to think about it overnight. I'm in."

"Yeah? Amazing!" A balloon of excitement rises in my chest—and I pull out a mental thumbtack and pop it, especially after what just happened in the reading room. The more time I spend with Ryan, the more I realize how much I enjoy his company. Add that to the attraction we clearly both feel . . . and that's a complication I cannot afford right now. "Um—there's one more thing. You know what happened after your parents' party?"

He leans toward me the slightest bit. "Yes."

"I think . . . if we're going to be working together . . . we should keep things professional." I'm unable to maintain eye contact, so I stare at the buttons on his shirt, the fabric pulled tight across his chest. "I'm going to put my entire soul into convincing Xander we both deserve this. I know you feel the same way. It would be best if we didn't let ourselves get . . . distracted."

Maybe he hasn't been distracted, but I sure have, and tonight isn't going to help matters.

"Sure," he says after a beat. His voice hovers in the air above me. Stiff. A little strained. "If that's what you want."

Then he says good night and turns to go, leaving me with a question: *Is* it what I want?

22

Ryan

LAST NIGHT'S "DATE" with Josie was worthy of a gold star. If it was a book, I'd have given it a four point five, rounded up to five.

There was one beautiful moment where I thought the night might end with a kiss. It didn't—which is what knocked it down half a point. Not that every date has to end in a kiss, but I was hoping this one would.

I was caught up in the moment, picturing us working together and growing even closer, until she burst my bubble with that one little sentence: *We should keep things professional.*

Last night proved that what happened in Maine wasn't a fluke—we *do* get along well (when we're not in competition) and we *definitely* have chemistry. But I'm not clear about what Josie thinks—or wants to do—about it.

I've read enough romance novels to know that a happy ending needs to be earned. Like I've said for years, it's not realistic to go directly from enemies to lovers. It makes more sense to go from enemies to friends, *then* to lovers.

The only problem: I'm still keeping a giant secret from her.

BookshopGirl has been *very* clear that she doesn't want to know who RJ is, and I promised I'd leave it in her hands. But would Josie want to know?

"Hey!" Josie's voice breaks through my thoughts like a siren song.

"Hi!" I say, straightening. I'm at the front register, working through my to-do list.

"Are we still on for later?" There's a spark in her eyes, like she's as excited about our plans to start working together as I am.

Although I have a feeling she's more excited about the "working" part, while I can't stop thinking about the "together" part.

"Can't wait."

"Me neither!" Josie's smile is so wide, she looks like a kid on Christmas morning. Or Chanukah evening? I'm pretty sure she's Jewish. "I've already started thinking of some ideas."

"Awesome," I say, even as my stomach twists. The only ideas I've had are of the unprofessional variety.

"What're you working on?" she asks, following my gaze to the computer screen.

"Oh, just an order from Ingram."

"Ooh!" She lights up. "What's your strategy? Your method?"

"My . . . method?"

Josie laughs. "You don't just blindly guess how many of each book you'll need, do you?" Her smile fades when she sees my blank expression. "Oh, you do."

"Show me how you do it," I say.

She hesitates, then seems to remember we're working *with* and not against each other. "Come with me."

FORTY-FIVE MINUTES LATER, I have even more respect for Josie. She has a whole system to log her inventory and sales, analyzing the data to project how many of each title she should order. Mind. Blown.

Another reason working together makes sense—I'm terrible at the business stuff. Seeing how much work Josie puts into that aspect of her job, I realize how over my head I would be managing the new combined bookstore without her.

When I get back to my side of the store, Cinderella is on the leather couch, reading, Persephone curled up on her lap.

"Sit," she commands, closing her book.

A cursory glance around the store is enough to tell me the few customers we have don't need any immediate attention, so I join Cinderella, taking a seat in the purple chair beside her.

"What's going on between you and that stuck-up girl next door?" she asks, eyes blazing.

"Nothing."

Cinderella arches an eyebrow.

"We're just friends," I say. "Friends who went out to dinner last night."

Cinderella grimaces. "You need to be careful—she might be trying to use her womanly charms to loosen you up and steal your secrets."

"I don't have any secrets to steal. Unless you count the mantra of 'What would Elaine do?' that runs on a loop in my head."

"Elaine was one hell of a woman, but you need to give yourself some credit here, boss."

So she does know I'm her boss . . .

"I might have decent gut instincts, but Josie has real knowledge. You should see her system—"

Cinderella whistles, shaking her head. "A month ago, that woman was Satan incarnate, and now you're complimenting her? You've got it bad."

"It doesn't matter how I feel," I say. "She wants to keep things professional."

Cinderella rolls her eyes. "Yeah, right, and I'm a natural redhead. You should know that sometimes people lie about their feelings to protect themselves. I've seen the way she looks at you."

"How does she look at me?" I ask, intrigued.

"Like she wants to peg you."

"Jesus Christ," I say, flushing.

Cinderella stops petting Persephone and presses her lips together. "Now listen—I don't trust that girl, and I have no clue what you see in her. But there's a lot on the line here, so bang her if you have to, then move on."

I gasp in mock shock. "Are you telling me to sleep with the enemy?"

"Just once, to get it out of your system."

"Yeah, because that always works so well in the books."

LATER THAT EVENING, Josie and I are sitting across from each other in a booth at the Burren, an Irish pub down the street. It's a cozy, welcoming spot to grab a beer and a bite to eat, and tonight there's even a pickup band playing Irish folk songs.

We've been here for more than an hour, brainstorming and

building off each other's ideas. Now the server clears our dinner plates, and we start looking through the books we brought to consider for our collective book club—another of Josie's ideas to start bridging the gap between our customer bases.

I have two historical romances (the historical aspect might appeal to her crowd), a romantasy (this genre has broken every single barrier people tried to set on it), an enemies-to-lovers story (for obvious reasons), a romance novel that leans literary, and a few other faves (mine, not my brother's).

At the last minute, I added my personal copy of *11/22/63* to the stack. I genuinely think the book will appeal to both our reader groups, but it's also a subtle hint to help her see me for who I am without breaking my promise to respect her decision not to meet RJ in real life.

The stack of books Josie brought is . . . overwhelming. It's full of big, thick tomes. I've only read one of them—*A Little Life*—because it was on BookshopGirl's Favorites bookshelf. It took me more than a week to get through the thirty-three-hour audiobook and left me ugly-crying on the T.

The one I'm currently flipping through might make me cry of boredom. It's about a man who spends a decade in his garden, contemplating the way grass grows, as he loses everything in his life that he thought he loved.

But I'm not a quitter, so I turn the page and persevere.

"You're reading out loud," Josie says. It's more of an observation than a question.

I look up, brushing my hair away from my eyes. "Sorry, is it bothering you?"

"No."

"Good—otherwise we might have to read at separate tables."

Josie raises an eyebrow. I suppose now is as good a time as any to tell her. Maybe if I share something vulnerable with her, she'll see that she can trust me, Ryan, as much as she seems to trust me, RJ.

Here goes. I blow out a breath and tell her what I've only admitted to a handful of people. "I told you I wasn't a good reader when I was a kid," I say. "Well, it can still be a challenge for me. Reading out loud helps me understand the words on the page because, well . . ." God, I'm starting to sweat. This shouldn't be so hard. I look back down at the page, and the words come out in a rush: "I have dyslexia."

There's a slight pause, then she says, "Oh, okay."

I glance up, nervous to see her expression. She seems completely unfazed. Even still, all the residual shame left over from my childhood bubbles up and I say, "It's just . . . booksellers are supposed to be good readers. And Lawsons are supposed to be smart—you met my brothers."

"Yeah, they're intimidating," Josie says. "But I don't think having dyslexia means someone is less 'smart.'"

I shrug. "No, you're right. But that's how it felt growing up—because it's more than just reading problems, my brain's just wired . . . differently." Probably why I struggle with organization and time management, too. "Getting diagnosed was a game changer, and I learned methods to help."

"Like reading out loud," Josie says.

"And listening to audiobooks," I add.

"Would it be better to download samples of these on audio?" Josie asks, nodding toward the giant stack of books beside me.

"The hardcovers are fine—as long as you don't mind my whisper-soundtrack."

"Not at all." She smiles before going back to the book she's reading.

And that's that. I exhale, feeling my shoulders relax. A month and a half ago, I never could've imagined confessing a weakness—much less *that* weakness—to my bookish rival. And I definitely wouldn't have imagined her reacting like it was no big deal. No pity or shame, just acceptance of this new information and moving on.

But I didn't know her back then. I'd invented a persona for her that had more to do with my own insecurities than reality—and if I hadn't figured out that she was BookshopGirl, I never would've given her a chance. And that would have been a tragedy, missing out on getting to know the real Josie Klein.

I return to my book. But after reading the same sentence four times, I give up and look across the table at Josie. Her cheeks are flushed. She's only had a few sips of her Irish Flower cocktail, not enough to bring that much color to her face.

It must be the book.

"Good part, huh?" I ask.

"No," Josie says, too quickly. "I mean, it's okay."

"Which one?"

She holds up a copy of a beach read from a few summers ago, and I wonder which part has gotten her all hot and bothered. I don't remember it being super high on the spice scale.

"Read it to me?" I ask.

"No," Josie says, closing the book. But she still has her finger on the page, holding her spot.

"It'll be fun. Here, I'll read mine out loud first."

Josie doesn't look convinced, but I clear my throat and begin reading. "*Within its slender frame resides a mosaic of life—dewdrops clinging delicately like jewels.*"

Josie's lips part as she listens to me read. Who knew a blade of grass could be so erotic?

"*Each blade, a testament to resilience and endurance, whispers tales of forgotten kingdoms and ancient battles fought silently under the watchful gaze of the sun.*" Okay, this is getting weird. I close the book again. "Your turn."

Josie gulps and looks around, taking in the crowd—everyone's talking and laughing, and the Irish band is playing a lively jig. There's no way anyone could overhear us.

"No one's paying any attention to the two nerds who brought a stack of books to the bar," I tell her.

Josie shakes her head but opens her book. "Okay, but here's the thing: I don't read romance. So this probably isn't even that steamy . . ."

"Then it shouldn't be a big deal to read it."

Josie's eyes spark—she doesn't like to back down from a challenge. Clearing her throat, she starts reading, her voice low. "*A beam of moonlight through the window casts silvery shadows on his torso—shoulders, chest, abs—and the trail of darker hair that disappears into his waistband. Lust pools in my belly.*"

She looks up, wide eyed. "This is ridiculous. Why can't these authors just imply that sex happened and skip to the next scene?"

"Because it's not just 'insert tab A into slot B.' Sex reveals things about a person that can't be shown in any other way. It's not just about the mechanics. And if you believe sex can be *implied*, as if it's always the same and the details have no impact on the relationship . . . that might say something about how you think about sex."

I'm getting worked up, so I grab my beer and take a long sip. When I set it down, I catch Josie's face—she's staring at my throat. Her comment as BookshopGirl pops into my mind, about watching a man's Adam's apple bob as he swallows. Interesting.

Then she shakes herself. "I can't read this out loud. I can barely read it in my own mind."

"Come on," I say.

Taking a deep breath, she looks at the page again. My pants grow tight in anticipation.

"*He crawls over me until he's caging me in with his arms, gazing down at me, and I'm desperate to feel him inside me.*"

This isn't even close to the most explicit book I've read, but the words on her lips, the urgent whisper of her voice—it's so fucking hot. I'm rock hard, grateful she can't see from her side of the table.

My foot inches forward until it comes into contact with hers. Her arch nestles against mine. Josie doesn't move it away, but she stops reading and looks up at me. There's a question in her eyes.

"Keep going."

Josie bites her lip, then takes a deep breath, her chest rising and falling, calling my attention to the hint of cleavage I can make out in the V of her blouse.

She starts to read again. "*He slides inside me*"—she hesitates, but to her credit, she doesn't stop—"*and I roll my hips, inviting him deeper. We move together slowly, learning each* other's rhythms, *the unique way our bodies shift and slip against each other."*

She continues, reading about how the intensity builds between them, their defenses finally dropping after two hundred pages of keeping each other at a distance.

Under the table, I feel Josie's foot slide up to my ankle, then back down—and I realize she's slipped her foot out of her shoe. Josie Klein's bare foot is brushing against my pant leg as she reads words that grow increasingly sensual, and how is this the hottest thing that has ever happened to me? I'm gripping the edge of the table with both hands, trying to keep my breathing under control as her foot slides against my leg again.

"He kneels next to the bed, wrapping his hands around my thighs. 'Please,' he says, 'I've been dying to taste—'"

The band stops playing, and Josie's voice breaks through the silence before everyone starts applauding. She closes the book; her pupils are dilated, her cheeks flushed highlighter pink.

I shift in my seat, adjusting myself subtly. She does an identical wiggle in her seat, and I'm positive she's feeling it, too.

"What do you think?" I ask, hoping my voice sounds normal. "Would your customers be okay with turning up the heat?"

"I think . . ." she says, her foot pressing ever so slightly against mine. "I think we should go with that book."

I follow her gaze to *11/22/63*.

"The Stephen King one? You haven't looked at it yet."

"I've already read it," she says.

"You have?" My heart rate quickens; here it is, the moment I've been waiting for.

"A few weeks ago, actually. A friend suggested it."

"I listened to it a few years ago," I tell her. "On a road trip with my family."

It's almost exactly what RJ told BookshopGirl. She glances up sharply, and my mouth goes dry. Her eyes narrow as she studies me, and I try not to blurt anything out.

Let her figure it out in her own time, I remind myself.

"It would be good for a long trip," she says slowly.

I force the next words out. "You know my brother Robert? It's his favorite book."

She's still staring at me, eyes narrowed, and I wait for the flash of realization to hit her, the way it did me when I saw her reading *The Princess Bride.*

Instead, she blinks and looks down. "I guess it is a really popular book," she says, mostly to herself.

I exhale and down the last sip of my Cloud Candy IPA. Cinderella was right: I've got it bad. But is she right about how Josie feels about me? Playing footsie under the table while reading a sex scene aloud isn't exactly *keeping things professional*—but does she want what I want? I have no interest in a "just once to get it out of our system" situation. I want something real, even if it takes longer to get there.

Which means I need to stay focused. Eyes on the prize. Head in the game. All those sports-related phrases I grew up hearing around the dinner table, things I never related to.

But I've never wanted anything as much as I want Josie. Which means that if things don't work out, I'm in for a hell of a crash.

BOOKFRIENDS

July 21, 9:01 PM

BookshopGirl: Okay, I've got a major whammy of a bookish pet peeve today. Ready?

RJ.Reads: Always.

BookshopGirl: All the bizarre and disturbing descriptions of sex in romance novels.

RJ.Reads: Um . . . disturbing? More details, please.

BookshopGirl: I'm reading a whole bunch of romances to prep for an event. And I keep asking myself why we need so many euphemisms for penis? Why? WHY? Dick, cock—okay, fine, utilitarian if not terribly creative. But then we get throbbing member, velvet-wrapped steel, hungry rod of lust, thrusting sword of desire?

RJ.Reads: So you'd prefer anatomically correct terms? Just plain old penis?

BookshopGirl: I'd prefer not to hear about any of it. And don't even get me started on words for the female anatomy. We don't even get a nice, sturdy word like "cock"—we get pussy and cunt, which just rub me wrong.

RJ.Reads: Definitely don't want to rub those wrong.

BookshopGirl: And then there's all the euphemisms. Like "slippery tunnel of heat" and "slick pearl of desire" and "moist folds."

RJ.Reads: You'd rather the folds be dry?

BookshopGirl: I NEVER WANT TO READ ABOUT FOLDS.

RJ.Reads: I hate to say this, but . . . are you . . . a prude?

BookshopGirl: No. I'm perfectly comfortable with my sexuality. Anyway, my issue isn't just the body parts. It's the noise level. Why is everyone always moaning and groaning and grunting and screaming?

RJ.Reads: I assume because they're experiencing intense pleasure.

BookshopGirl: Yes, but screaming? Anyone who is THAT loud during sex is faking it. I don't think I've ever made anything more than a deep sigh.

RJ.Reads: A deep SIGH? I'm starting to worry that you've had extremely mediocre sex. Not to toot my own horn (how's that for a euphemism?) but plenty of my partners have been loud.

BookshopGirl: And I hate to break it to YOU, but they were probably faking it. Which brings me to my next point: What's with all these men in romance novels who are thrilled to go down on women for a ridiculously long amount of time? Have these authors ever been with a straight man? Because they're doing the bare minimum down there before moving on to what they really want.

RJ.Reads: There are men who enjoy that, you know. Some men love it. It's their favorite part of the whole experience.

BookshopGirl: Eh, I think that's a myth. Like the Loch Ness Monster. People swear they've seen it but there's no objective evidence. Like all the so-called photos of Nessie that end up being an oversized eel.

RJ.Reads: There's a sex joke somewhere in there but I feel like now's not the time.

BookshopGirl: Or an underutilized euphemism in romance novels. "His oversized eel slithered in . . ." Never mind.

RJ.Reads: Gross. That's worse than the moist folds.

23

Josie

A WEEK INTO Operation Save Our Jobs, working with Ryan feels natural—maybe too natural. It's becoming more difficult to remember why I was so insistent on *keeping things professional*.

Each morning before we open, we meet at the newly renovated Beans. Whoever arrives first puts in our orders, then we sit at one of the tables and discuss that day's game plan (while Eddie sneaks glances at us, smiling).

After that, we separate to open our doors and start the day. But our stores are feeling less and less separate—the "wall" of bookcases I put between us is gone (Ryan moved them, and this time, *I* watched). We're constantly bumping into each other in the back room, eating lunch together, sharing ideas about how to prove to Xander that we both deserve to stay.

And yet . . . it's been a struggle.

Every night, I lie in bed and relive our interactions. The whiff of Ryan's scent I caught when he reached above me to grab something in the back room; the way his eyes dip down my body when he thinks I'm not looking; the glimpses of his hands, his mouth, his ass. If I'm being honest, my mind wanders like a naughty child to a few specific memories: his body over mine at the beach; his hand touching mine at the library; my foot sliding up his leg at the bar.

And if I'm being *really* honest, my vibrator has been getting plenty of use as I replay those memories. Over and over again.

Tonight, thankfully, I have something else to focus on: we're hosting our inaugural Bookstore Date Night. For a fee, couples can rent out the store after closing for a romantic evening.

Tonight's couple, newlyweds Brigitte and Sam, are celebrating their one-month anniversary. Ryan and I have been setting up all afternoon. We arranged a cozy table for two on the Happy Endings side, and I went back to my apartment earlier to fetch table settings. Ryan picked up the wine and some candles. A delivery guy dropped off the meal Sam ordered, and Ryan plated the food while I lit the candles in time for the couple to arrive.

As they walk inside, Brigitte gasps and jumps into Sam's arms. There is *much* embracing and kissing, and Ryan and I fade into the back room.

"So . . . now what?" I ask. We can't go far—we'll need to clean and lock up when they're done.

"We could go on a walk?" Ryan suggests. "Maybe stop by J.P. Licks?"

"I could go for a scoop," I say, smiling.

We stroll while we eat. I got a cone with two scoops— salted caramel and cookies and cream—while Ryan got a giant waffle sundae made with an actual waffle. It's a sticky, warm evening, bikes zipping by, crowds gathered in front of bars and restaurants, couples walking hand in hand.

"Random question," he says. "What does *Tabula Inscripta*

mean? Or is it just Latin words designed to make everyone else feel dumb?"

I laugh as he grins over at me, eyes twinkling, and I'm struck by how things have changed between us since that first meeting with Xander, when he made similar comments with a completely different tone.

"No, it's a reference to another Latin phrase, *tabula rasa*, which means 'blank slate,'" I say. "The original owner—Jerome—told me that it's a theory that we're born without any built-in knowledge, and all our experiences shape who we become."

"So I'm guessing *inscripta* means something like 'inscribed'?" he says.

I nod. "Jerome wanted to capture how every book leaves its mark on us, constantly adding new ideas, stories, and insights. A mind continually in progress, he said, with infinitely more to be added."

"I like that. And now that I know it"—he flashes me a smirk—"I can feel intellectually superior to everyone who doesn't."

I laugh again and take a bite of my ice cream. "Tell me about the original owner of your store. Elaine, right?"

His face lights up. "Oh, she was great. She opened the store back when most bookshops kept romances to one shelf in the back, like they were a dirty little secret—even though they'd been keeping the publishing industry afloat for decades."

I nod, remembering the first bookstore I ever worked in, in Newburyport. Like Ryan's saying, the romances were shelved in the far corner.

"Back then," Ryan goes on, "Elaine mostly stocked 'mainstream' romance, heteronormative relationships written by white authors. It's not that she wasn't supportive of diversity, but that's what was available then."

"What changed?" I asked. "Because it's definitely more diverse now. Your store and your clientele."

"Um. It's kind of a long story."

"Brigitte and Sam have the store for two more hours, so we have time." I nudge him. "Go on."

"Well, the industry changed, for one thing. But for me, it's more personal." He hesitates, then goes on, telling me about his best friend growing up, JR, who was gay. "His parents were really religious, and he grew up feeling like a fundamental part of himself was unacceptable. Unwanted."

"So he inspired you to stock more diverse reads?" I ask.

"Yeah."

"He must be proud," I say.

Ryan hesitates, looking at the ground. "I hope he would be. He died when we were seniors in high school." He pauses. "An overdose on prescription medication—his parents said it was an accident, but . . ."

My heart sinks. "But you think it was intentional?"

He blows out a long breath. "I don't know. I don't think he could imagine a positive future for himself. Maybe it's trite, but if he could have seen *one* example of a happy, healthy gay relationship, even a fictional one—maybe he'd still be here."

I take his hand, lacing our fingers together. In contrast to the hand touching that happened at the library, this feels natural, comfortable, fingers interlocking, palm against palm.

"I'm sorry about JR," I say.

"Yeah. Me too." He clears his throat. "Anyway. If I can help other people who feel like they don't fit in see themselves in a love story . . . I think it matters."

"It does matter," I say. "You're doing good work."

He squeezes my hand. "Thanks. That means a lot coming from you."

"Why—because I'm usually such an uptight bitch?" I soften my words with a smile, but this is a sore spot for me, and he's accidentally pressed on it with his thumb.

Ryan stops, tugging on my hand to make me face him. "Josie, absolutely not." His expression is dead serious. "Because you're good at what you do—I'm in awe. You're deliberate about every decision you make in your store. You're wicked smart, and I could watch you for a year and learn something new every day. So when you tell me I'm doing good work—it means a lot. More than you understand."

I'm momentarily speechless.

"Thank you," I say softly.

He turns and we start walking again, our conversation drifting to other topics, a peculiar feeling unfurling inside me. It's as warm and comforting as Ryan's hand in mine; as sweet and irresistible as the ice cream melting on my tongue. I'd call it *friendship* . . . except I never think about friends while reaching for my vibrator. I'd call it *attraction*, except he has absolutely nothing in common with anyone I've ever been attracted to before.

Maybe I'm just confused. I'm in a state of heightened stress, my job on the line, and here's this big, kindhearted man who listens to my ideas and says lovely things and treats me like I'm not just a college dropout who spends her days unpacking boxes and ringing up purchases and trying to prove that she's made something of herself while battling the ever-present fear that she hasn't.

WE RETURN TO the store an hour later, and I let us in the door to my side so we won't disrupt Brigitte and Sam. Music is playing, and as we slip into the back room, I catch a glimpse of them, dancing in the flickering candlelight, gazing into each other's eyes.

"Dance with me?" Ryan asks, and I look up to see him holding out a hand.

There's no way I can resist. I take his hand, allowing him to fold me against him. *God*, he's warm. Just a sturdy wall of gentleness. And every time I inhale, my nose is filled with that scent I can't describe other than *Ryan Ryan Ryan*. I think back to dancing at his parents' party, the strangeness of being close to him after weeks of animosity. This is different: being held by him is like coming home after a long day, kicking off your shoes, and falling into bed with your favorite book.

My cheek presses against his chest, and his chin rests on top of my head, my hair rustling slightly with each breath. Persephone slinks between our legs, purring, and I spot Hades up on a shelf, peering down at us suspiciously. I close my eyes.

One of Ryan's hands spreads wide across my back, the other holding my hand as he rocks us back and forth. His heart is a drumbeat against my ear, and there's definitely something stirring below his belt. I make sure to keep hold of his hand because that's my lifeline right now, my proof that I'm not plastering myself against Ryan Lawson because I want him so fiercely I'm having trouble breathing.

We're just dancing.

A noise out in the store distracts me—a low groan. I lean

away from Ryan to peek through the partially open door into Happy Endings.

"Oh my god," I whisper. "I think they're—"

"What?" Ryan says, and we're now cheek to cheek, two Peeping Toms gazing into the store.

Sam's in an armchair, Brigitte straddling his lap, his mouth on her neck and her hands in his hair. Quickly, I pull us both into the back room. Now Ryan and I are inches apart in the darkness, staring at each other with wide, shocked eyes.

"You told them the security cameras were running, right?" he whispers.

I nod. "I guess . . . they don't care."

We wait, scarcely daring to breathe, until another sound makes us jump: the squeak of something heavy being shoved across the floor. I reach out to shut the door and accidentally get another glance: Sam's got Brigitte up against a bookcase, her dress around her hips. A tiny, scandalized squeak comes out of me, and I put my hands over my face.

"What?" Ryan whispers, alarmed.

I open my fingers and peek at him between them. "I'm pretty sure they're doing it."

"Here? Now?" He scrubs a hand through his messy hair. "What do we do? This has to be against some kind of health code. Right?"

"I'm not going to interrupt," I say, holding up my hands. "Are you?"

He shakes his head. "I guess we . . . wait it out?"

And that's what we do, both of us putting our hands over our ears when the moaning gets louder. For someone who was so willing to have me *read* a sex scene out loud, Ryan is remarkably flustered by an *actual* sex scene. I can't help wondering what he'd be like in bed—if he'd be pink cheeked and flushed, eager to please but a little awkward. Or like he was on the beach—intense and focused, his mouth and hands demanding *more more more.*

My body flares with heat.

A rhythmic thumping echoes from the store, followed by the unmistakable sound of trade paperbacks falling to the floor.

"What. Are they doing. To my *books*?" Ryan whispers, aghast.

We hear male grunting, joined by a higher-pitched moan. It reminds me of my last conversation with RJ about noisy sex, and my admission that I've never made more than a loud sigh. *I'm starting to worry that you've had extremely mediocre sex.*

Brigitte cries out, a piercing scream that goes on and on and *on.*

"Gold star, Sam," I murmur.

Ryan squeezes his eyes shut, his shoulders shaking with silent laughter, and then I'm doing the same, both of us stifling giggles and struggling to breathe. I make a mental note to delete the security camera footage ASAP.

Finally, Sam and Brigitte head out the door, and Ryan and I go survey the scene. One bookshelf has been shoved a good two feet from its original location, and most of its books are on the floor. I also discover a suspicious damp spot on the chair our two lovebirds were sharing. I'm about to mention it to Ryan, then decide he's had enough sexually traumatizing experiences in his beloved bookshop and flip the cushion over.

Together, we clean up the remains of dinner, and I stack the dirty dishes in a box to bring to my place.

Ryan takes it out of my hands. "I'll walk you home."

It feels so natural to head back out into the warm summer night, to smile up at him and see him smiling down at me. Like this is something we do all the time, walking home from work together. When we get to my building, it feels just as natural to fish out my key and unlock the door, to have him follow me up the stairs.

When he steps inside my apartment, though, it no longer feels so natural, maybe because he's taking up half the space in my kitchen, sucking the oxygen out of the room. My bedroom is twenty steps away, and my knees feel wobbly, my brain playing a slideshow of possibilities: *Ryan. Bed. Naked.*

"Your place is cozy," he says, setting the box of dishes on my counter.

I turn and see it through his eyes: my small kitchen with two stools pulled up to the counter; sofa and armchair in the living room; two big bookshelves against one wall.

"Were you expecting some kind of ice castle?"

He chuckles. "Maybe."

I'm not sure what to do now. After the night we've had— deep conversation, holding hands, dancing, listening to vigorous sex? I ought to be shoving him out the door.

"Want some tea?" I say instead.

"Sure."

I'm turning to grab the mugs when something vibrates on my counter.

"My phone!" I gasp. I must have left it here when I came home this afternoon to get the dishes for the dinner. It's a clear sign of how distracted I've been that I hadn't even realized.

MOM is flashing across the screen. I send her to voicemail—and notice that my screen is filled with messages from Georgia. Her most recent text:

> We're about to take off. I'll call you when I land. Hope you're OK??

My sister is on a plane? What's going on? I immediately call her. No answer.

Confused, I scroll back to the first message she sent— nearly six hours ago.

> I just heard from Mom. Darrell left and she's alone in Puerto Vallarta. Give me a call as soon as you can.

Twenty minutes after that: I talked to Mom again. Call me? Then a series of texts:

> Maybe your phone is dead. I'll try the store.

> No answer there either. Where are you?

> Jojo, please call me. Mom's upset and I don't know what to do.

> Are you okay? Please tell me you're okay.

> Where are you??

A few minutes after that:

> I'm looking at flights to PV. Mom's freaking out.

"Shit," I whisper. This is why I can never truly relax—no matter how much time passes, at any moment, my mom could self-destruct.

And I'll be damned if I allow my innocent sister to suffer the consequences.

"Everything okay?" Ryan asks, but I'm reading the next message from Georgia, sent four hours ago.

> I've found a flight tonight. Call me when you can, ok?

"I—I need to call my mom." I glance up at Ryan, who's watching me with concern. "I'll just . . . One second."

I step into my bedroom and call; Mom answers—and she's crying. All the ease and comfort I've felt this evening vanishes. I'm a ball of tight muscles, gripping the phone and bracing for impact.

"Mom? Mom, are you okay?"

"He's gone," she says through sobs. "I woke up and Darrell was gone; he took all his things, and no one knows where he is."

"I'm so sorry," I say, and I mean it.

"We were having a wonderful time, Jojo. I don't know what happened."

Probably the same thing that's happened all the other times with all the other men. Except this time, she's in a foreign country, and my sister is flying to her rescue.

"Mom, why did you ask Georgia to come? She has classes and exams."

"I didn't ask! She offered."

But what kind of mother would *want* their daughter to do

something like this? Decades of resentment are churning inside me, and I try to stuff them down.

"Okay," I say, thinking through the logistics. "I need you to offer to pay for her flight—"

"I don't have the money!"

I take a deep, calming breath. "I know, but I do." The money I set aside every time Georgia helps at the store. "I'll pay you back. Just don't tell her it was from me, okay?"

"Fine," she says sulkily. "But maybe you could come with her? I need my girls by my side."

"You know I can't, I have a store to run."

"It's obvious where *your* priorities lie," she mutters.

Her words are a stab to the heart. I haven't told my mom what's going on at work—and this is why. She wouldn't even try to understand.

"Mom. That's not—" I take another calming breath. "Let me help you get home. I'll go online and book your flight. Okay?"

"No!" The word is a horrified screech. "I need to find Darrell."

"Find him? He left you!"

"Because he's scared! Things are moving quickly with us, and he got scared, that's all—"

"Would you ever leave *him* alone in a foreign country with no explanation?"

"Of course not! I love him!"

I hate saying this to her, but it's necessary. "Mom. Listen to me: if he loved you, he wouldn't have left."

There's a pause. Then a stifled sob. My heart cracks; she deserves better than this.

"That may be true," she says in a shaky voice. "But I have to find him and ask him myself."

I sigh. That's my mom: ninety-five percent desperation, five percent undaunted hope.

"Now what's this I hear about *your* man?" she says, her voice oddly upbeat. Forced.

"I don't—"

"Georgia said you're seeing the guy who runs the bookstore next to yours?"

"Ryan?" I spit out, shocked. My mother is delusional; no way Georgia said that. "No. We're not involved."

"Georgia said you're spending a lot of time together . . . and it sounded like you're falling in *love*."

"We're not—" I pinch the bridge of my nose, my frustration growing. "He doesn't matter. This isn't about— Listen, Mom. When Georgia gets there, please come home. Don't drag her all over the city looking for this guy, okay? I'll pay for your flights—"

"I better go, sweetie! I'll let you know when Georgia arrives."

And then she's gone.

"Shit," I whisper. "Shit, shit—*oh my god!*"

Ryan's in my bedroom doorway.

I clutch my heart as my pulse slows. How long was he there? Did he hear me say his name?

But all I see on his face is that same gentle concern.

"Sorry," he says. "Everything okay?"

My throat is tightening up. "I—I need to figure some things out."

"Can I help? If nothing else, I can listen."

Part of me wishes I could pour my heart out to him, but that would mean revisiting the whole messed-up saga, and Ryan hates complicated stories with sad endings. He said so himself. He prefers the ones that end neatly, tied with a bow, happily ever after, the end.

He wouldn't want to touch this situation with a ten-foot pole.

Ryan is still waiting, his forehead furrowed. "Josie," he says gently. "What can I do?"

I sigh—a deep, defeated sigh from the bottom of my exhausted, eldest-daughter soul. "Nothing. I'll handle it. Thanks for helping me bring everything home."

"Of course," he says. "But you're *sure* I can't do anything to help?"

"I'm sure."

He stares at me for a moment, his mouth opening and shutting, then turns and goes.

The door clicks shut behind him, and I immediately regret it. Why did I tell him to *leave*? The last thing I want is to be alone with my spiraling thoughts. What can I do but wait until my mom or sister contacts me? Nothing.

That's when I walk back into my kitchen and see that Ryan's taken all the dishes out of the box, washed them, and set them in the drying rack.

If I wasn't so upset about my mom, I'd melt. Now all I can do is berate myself: *A kind man with huge hands, who's a good listener and gives wonderful hugs, offered to stay and I told him to leave.*

What's wrong with me? I'm so tired of carrying this by myself, this heavy burden of responsibility, worry, and shame. Maybe I couldn't have found the words to explain, but at least if Ryan were here, I wouldn't be alone.

And then I realize: I don't need to be alone.

I pick up my phone and send a message to RJ.

24

Ryan

I DIDN'T MEAN to eavesdrop. I was looking for the bathroom when I heard Josie say my name. It stopped me. Not just that she said it, but *how*. Almost with a sneer, like she was talking about something—someone—she despised.

If this had been a month ago, I wouldn't have given it a second thought. But earlier tonight, when we were dancing in the back room, when her head was on my chest and her hand was in mine . . . her breath actually hitched. A person can't fake that.

And yet.

He doesn't matter.

As I walk down Highland Avenue, away from Josie's apartment, my head and my heart battle it out, each making its case.

My head: She was talking to her mom. Based on everything I know about their relationship, they're not close. I shouldn't read too much into what she said.

My heart: But she could have easily said we were just friends. She didn't have to say something so cruel. I don't matter?

My head: Something else is clearly going on.

My heart: I shouldn't have left her alone.

Up ahead, I see the pink and orange light of a Dunkin' Donuts, glowing like a beacon in the night. While sugar won't solve whatever problem Josie's having with her mom, it could make her feel better.

And it's the perfect excuse to go back and try again.

If she wants to talk, I'll stay. If she wants space, I'll give her the donuts and go. Either way, she'll know I was thinking about her, that she doesn't have to be alone. Maybe then she'll realize we can be a team in and out of the bookstore.

I'm about to head back to her apartment, a box of twenty-five assorted Munchkins in my hands, when my phone buzzes in my pocket. My heart leaps when I see her name on the screen, but it falls when I realize it's a message for RJ.Reads.

Me, but not me.

> **BookshopGirl:** Hey. Are you there?

Crestfallen, I pull up a chair at an open table. Even though I'm dying inside, I type out a happy little message, because that's how far gone I am for this girl.

> **RJ.Reads:** Hey, I'm here! And I was just thinking about you 😊

Not a lie.

> **RJ.Reads:** How are you?

A normal question, even if I already know the answer.

> **BookshopGirl:** I've been better.

> **RJ.Reads:** Who do I need to beat up?

I picture Josie sitting alone in her apartment, staring at her phone with a soft, sad smile on her face. Did she ask me to leave so she could talk to RJ? Not knowing she could have the real me, sitting there with her?

> **BookshopGirl:** Oh, it's nothing like that.
> Just family stuff.

> **RJ.Reads:** Want to talk about it?

> **BookshopGirl:** I don't know . . .

> **RJ.Reads:** It could help.

Her three dots appear and disappear, and I can picture her trying to find the right words. Weighing how much she wants to get off her chest, and how much she wants to hold close to it.

Finally, her message appears.

> **BookshopGirl:** It's my mom . . .

In a series of messages, Josie pours it all out, how hard it was growing up with a lovesick mom who chased the wrong men, leaving her young daughters to fend for themselves.

My heart aches for her. No little kid should have to go

through that. And it's clear Josie tried her best to take care of her younger sister, absorbing their mom's dysfunction so Georgia could have a more carefree childhood.

I open the box of donut holes and pop one in my mouth. It doesn't feel right going back to Josie's now—she chose the person she trusts enough to open up to. She has my number; she could have called or texted the actual me.

Instead, she's opening up to this nameless, faceless guy online.

It's a strangely painful experience, being jealous of yourself.

> **BookshopGirl:** Anyway, she's done it again. Picked a real gem this time—the guy left her stranded in Mexico.

> **RJ.Reads:** Oh no! Is she okay?

No wonder Josie was upset.

> **BookshopGirl:** That's debatable.

> **BookshopGirl:** I'm sure she'll be fine. My sister is on her way there now, which makes me irrationally angry. Not at her, but at my mom.

> **RJ.Reads:** Doesn't sound that irrational to me. Parents are supposed to protect their kids, not the other way around.

> **BookshopGirl:** YES! Exactly.

> **RJ.Reads:** Have you talked to Georgia about it?

> **BookshopGirl:** Did I tell you my sister's name?

Shit.

Sure, it would be a relief to end this charade, to be fully honest about who I am and how I feel about her—but I don't want her to accidentally find out when she's overwhelmed and stressed.

I'm trying to figure out how to respond when another reply from her arrives.

> **BookshopGirl:** Anyway, I didn't get to talk to her before she took off. But I'm hoping she'll be on board with my plan.

Despite how awful I'm feeling—for myself and for Josie—I smile, popping another Munchkin in my mouth. Of course she has a plan.

> **RJ.Reads:** What's your plan?

> **BookshopGirl:** For Georgia to turn back around and bring Mom home. And delete every dating app on Mom's phone. Maybe put her in a nunnery. Think a convent would take a crazy Jewish lady?

RJ.Reads: In real life, I have no idea. But if that was the plot of a novel, I'd read it.

BookshopGirl: Same. We could buddy read it.

RJ.Reads: I'd love that.

I stare at the screen, waiting for Josie to say that she's changed her mind about meeting in person, that she wants to read a book *together* together, sitting side by side or across a booth from each other, the way we did the other night.

Maybe that's exactly what she's thinking of. Of me—Ryan.

BookshopGirl: Although, any book about my mom would be unsatisfying.

RJ.Reads: How so? Sounds like a real page-turner.

BookshopGirl: Nah. In fiction, readers want the character to grow or change. My mom keeps making the same mistakes over and over.

RJ.Reads: You're right—that wouldn't make a good novel.

RJ.Reads: One star.

BookshopGirl: DNF.

I laugh, loud enough to distract the girls studying at the next table over. One of them shoots me a glare before going back to quizzing her friend on the ventricles of a plastic heart. I consider asking if they want to dissect the complicated feelings of a very real heart, but I know the answer I'm looking for isn't in any book, medical or otherwise.

Even the most skilled romance writer would have a hard time capturing the situationship I've found myself in. For one thing, it's impossible to condense the essence of Josie—her personality, her beauty, her intelligence—into black words on a white page. It would take a whole series to get to the bottom of what makes her tick.

Then there are my messy feelings: the elation of Josie opening up online to me (well, RJ); the crushing disappointment that she had no intention of opening up in real life to me (Ryan); the overwhelming hopelessness that comes with the realization that the closer we get online *and* in real life, the more complicated it'll be when she finds out the truth.

The sick feeling in the pit of my stomach returns when I remember that I'm not being honest with her. But as much as I want her to know who I am, it feels wrong to drop a massive truth-bomb on her. Especially right now.

I stare back at the screen. Maybe if I can understand where the fear comes from, I'll know how to convince her it's worth the risk of breaking anonymity.

> **RJ.Reads:** If you could write your mom's story, what lesson would you have her character learn?

BookshopGirl: That real life isn't like a romance novel, that you aren't guaranteed a happy ending and you should be careful who you give your heart to. I'm so tired of her sacrificing everything for men who won't sacrifice anything for her.

RJ.Reads: Now that sounds like a five-star read.

BookshopGirl: Shoot—my sister is calling. I've got to go. Thanks for listening, for being here.

RJ.Reads: Anytime.

Anytime, Josie Klein.

THE NEXT MORNING, I'm at Happy Endings early for a staff meeting. My team deserves an update on this new alliance with Josie.

"Who wants to pick the prompt?" I ask as everyone takes their seats.

"I will!" Indira says with more energy than anyone should have at this hour. I've never been a morning person, and I barely slept last night, thanks to a toxic combination of worrying about Josie, feeling sorry for myself, and however much sugar is in an entire box of Munchkins.

Indira reaches into the fishbowl and chooses a slip of paper. She reads aloud: "'If you were to get dropped into a romance novel, what would you want to experience?'"

"Let's make this a speed round," I say. "Eliza, want to start?"

Eliza sits up taller in her seat. "I'd love to get dropped into the Bridgerton world . . . just for a few days. Then I'd want to come back to our world, where women have at least some human rights."

We continue moving around the circle:

Cinderella: "No question: secret billionaire with a heart of gold."

Indira: "Put me in the Omegaverse and give me a lady werewolf."

Nora: "I'd choose the third-act breakup."

Everyone stops and stares at her, aghast.

"That's bananas!" Eliza says.

"Why would you want to experience the saddest part of the whole book?" Cinderella asks.

"Seriously," Eliza agrees. "That's my least favorite part of a romance."

"But the dark moment is an important part of story structure," I say, although I agree it can be painful to read.

"And it's important for character growth," Indira adds, nodding.

Eliza scoffs. "It's emotionally manipulative and predictable."

"Not when it's done well!" Indira says, her voice rising.

"All right, all right," I say, but then Nora raises a hand.

"May I?" she asks, and I motion for everyone to listen.

"You're all right, in a way," Nora says. "Falling in love is something that happens *to* you, sometimes even against your will—like being struck by lightning or catching the flu. But *staying* in love? That's a choice."

She pauses, glancing around our circle. Everyone is quiet, digesting her words.

"Maybe don't think of it as a third-act breakup," she says. "Think of it as a decision point. Will the lovers allow themselves to be torn apart by outside circumstances or their internal fears? Or will they fight for each other?" She smiles. "That's a decision anyone in any relationship will have to make, over and over again."

"Huh," Eliza says thoughtfully. Cinderella seems to be digesting it, too.

I'm up next, and our senior staffer has given me a hard act to follow, so I say the simple truth: "Friends to lovers."

Cinderella rolls her eyes and mutters something about enemies under her breath, but I bite my tongue. The last thing I want is to call more attention to myself and Josie.

Especially given the news I'm about to share.

"Moving on," I say. "I wanted to share an update about the competition."

Everyone stills. The store is so quiet you could hear a condom drop. Eliza looks like she's about to cry; Nora and Indira are holding hands.

"There's no real news yet," I say, and the group collectively exhales in relief. "But we do have a shift in our strategy."

When I finish filling them in on Josie's plan, they're all staring at me with shocked expressions.

Indira is the first to speak, her dark eyes flashing. "You want to work with that uptight, snobby little—"

"Hey!" I say sharply.

Indira blinks, surprised. "Sorry. You want to work with . . . *her*?"

"Voluntarily?" Nora adds.

"I thought we hated her?" Eliza says.

"We do," Cinderella says at the same time I say, "We did."

I shoot Cinderella a glare. "We don't anymore. Josie has a lot of great ideas and—"

"How do you know she's not trying to sabotage us?" Indira cuts in. "I don't trust her."

Eliza folds her arms. "Me either."

"Ryan, why in the world would you consider this?" Nora asks, her wrinkled face full of confusion.

Under her breath, Cinderella mutters, "Because he wants to f—"

"Okay, okay," I say loudly, then take a breath. They're saying all the same things I would've said a month ago. "I hear your concerns, and I understand. But if we keep treating each other like the enemy, the only person who wins is Xander— and no one wants that."

"Cosign," Eliza says, scuffing her sneaker on the ground, and after a moment the others mumble their agreement.

"If we can show Xander how much higher our collective profits are over the next four weeks, he'll have to admit that Josie and I make a good team—along with the rest of you, of course."

"What if he doesn't go for it?" Nora asks, her voice small.

I don't want to admit I'm worried about that very thing. But Josie's plan gives me two things I desperately want: a chance to be with her, and the opportunity to keep my store and my staff. No other option gives me both. If I win, she'll never want to be with me, and if she wins, I lose the store that feels like home and the staff that feels like family. No romance store in P-town or anywhere else could compare to the history I have here.

But I'm not going to burden my staff with my fears. Instead, I pretend to be as confident in our plan as Josie is and say, "He'll go for it—the man speaks dollars and cents; he'll see this option will make him the most money."

I'm not sure if any of them believe me, but we wrap up the meeting so Eliza can get to soccer practice and everyone else can get to work opening the store.

I leave them to it and head over to Beans. Josie is standing at the counter, and she greets me with a smile even bigger than the frappe she hands me, the straw unwrapped and ready to go.

It feels like the sun coming out: Josie came in this morning and thought about *me*. Ryan.

"Sorry about last night," she says. Her eyes fall away from mine, and I get the sense she's embarrassed that I saw her in a less than perfect moment.

She's back to being the woman she lets the world see: cool, calm, and collected. And gorgeous. Not a hair out of place, crisp green blouse, gray pencil skirt—and sky-high heels, of course.

I hated seeing her upset, but I have to admit, I loved getting a glimpse beneath her armor. I want to be there for her in all the moments of her life. Especially the flawed and imperfect ones. The real ones.

"Nothing to apologize for," I tell her. "Is everything okay now?"

Josie shakes her head as she says, "It will be."

"Are . . . is . . . your—" I shove the straw in my mouth and take a big sip in an attempt to stop myself from asking her about all the things I'm not supposed to know: if Georgia made it to Mexico, if she was able to convince their mom to come home, if Josie slept okay last night, if the conversation with RJ—with me—helped her feel better.

A hot flash of pain hits and I cringe and close my eyes. *Brain freeze.* Too much, too fast. Why is it that the things I love always cause me so much pain?

When I open my eyes, Josie is looking up at me, a playful grin on her face.

"I'll be fine," I say, rubbing my temple. "Thanks for your concern."

"I'm sorry," she says, barely concealing a laugh. "It's just . . . seeing a big, strong man get taken down by a froufrou drink. You have to admit, it's funny."

"Hilarious," I say, taking a smaller sip. "But back to you . . ."

Her smile fades, and I know the brief window of her being willing to open up is over. The page has turned; the book has closed.

"I really am okay," she insists. "But I won't be if I don't get the store open—we can't sell books if we don't open the doors!"

I give her a salute and turn to start my own opening rituals. Before I disappear around the corner, she calls out, "Hey, Ry?"

Ry. I like the sound of that, a nickname, on her lips.

"Yeah?" I say, turning.

"Thanks for washing the dishes last night—it was a nice surprise."

"Oh, sure," I say.

What kind of surprise will it be when she finds out I'm the

anonymous stranger she's been confessing her secrets to online?

I have to tell her. I'm going to tell her. Right now. If she knew what I know, then maybe she wouldn't have said that she doesn't want to know. It'll be easier to explain and ask forgiveness for that than it will if I keep on not telling her. Lying to her.

It's time. I take a deep breath and—

"Excuse me?" It's a customer, walking over from Josie's side of the store.

Immediately, Josie turns on her polished smile. "Hi there. How can I help you?"

Then she's gone, and I've lost my chance.

TWENTY MINUTES LATER, I'm ringing up a customer when my phone chimes.

> **BookshopGirl:** Hey, just wanted to let you know that everything is good now. My sister and my mom got home safely earlier today.

Exhaling, I head over to a chair and sit. She must be done with her customer. But instead of coming over to talk to me again, she's retreating into the safety of this online world.

> **RJ.Reads:** I'm glad to hear that. It must be such a relief!

> **BookshopGirl:** Yeah.

> RJ.Reads: You don't seem super relieved though . . . ?

BookshopGirl: I am. Really. It's just that Georgia keeps saying I need to talk to Mom, but I haven't been able to bring myself to reach out because what's the point? My mom is never going to change. And then I start berating myself, because why can't I do something as simple as call my own mother?

> RJ.Reads: Probably because she never took care of you or your sister the way you both deserved.

She deserves someone who puts her first—this I know for sure.

BookshopGirl: I know, and maybe that's ruined me. She broke my trust so many times that maybe I'll never trust anyone. Maybe I'll never be able to open myself up to anyone, not really.

> RJ.Reads: You've opened up to me.

BookshopGirl: Because it's anonymous. If you were standing right in front of me, I couldn't. You've been so patient with me after I said I didn't want to meet in real life, and I keep wondering what is wrong with me because I'm just so terrified.

My heart pounds, and I fight the urge to walk over to her side of the store and find her so we can have this conversation face-to-face.

RJ.Reads: Terrified of what?

BookshopGirl: Of meeting you and being a disappointment.

RJ.Reads: You wouldn't be. I know that for a fact.

BookshopGirl: How do you know?

This is my chance, the moment of truth. My heart lodges in my throat and I'm about to type it right in the box—Because I know you, Josie—when a new reply arrives.

BookshopGirl: Never mind, that wasn't me fishing for compliments. I brought this up because I wanted to thank you for understanding that I need time.

I blink. Well, now it feels wrong to tell her. But I can't keep waiting around indefinitely, either. So I carefully type a message and press send:

RJ.Reads: I do understand, but I think we have something here. Something that could be real. But we won't ever know unless we give it a chance. Unless you don't feel the same way?

There's an excruciatingly long pause as I wait for her reply.

BookshopGirl: No, I do.

My breath rushes out in relief.

BookshopGirl: But again—I'm scared, RJ. Could you give me a little more time?

I'll give her anything. Even if it's killing me. Even if I'm starting to worry that this whole thing is going to end with my heart shattered, that I've gone and done it again, letting myself fall for someone who doesn't feel the same way.

Sighing, I stare at the phone. The only thing I know for sure is that nothing can happen between us in real life until she knows the truth. I'm going to have to be patient—but she's worth it. No question.

RJ.Reads: Of course. But please, not forever.

BookshopGirl: No, not forever. I promise.

Josie

NEVER IN A million years would I have imagined I'd have the time of my life talking to a group of teenagers in outlandish costumes about a fictional dystopian world. But here we are.

The event is part of our plan to bring in a new demographic to the combined bookstore: a discussion about the *Hunger Games* series, inviting participants to dress up—and these kids delivered. I underestimated how *awesome* teenage book nerds are. Some came in gray and brown clothes to represent the districts, others in colorful feathers and sequins to represent the Capitol. And they were all fully engaged, expanding on the topics I brought up with insightful comments. It was exhilarating and fascinating.

Plus, those kids spent money—or their parents' money; we sold thousands of dollars of stock tonight, and not just from our new YA section. I wasn't surprised by the kids who wandered into Ryan's side and found romances to add to their TBRs. I *was* surprised (and thrilled) by how many came over to my side and asked for recommendations.

"That was incredible," Ryan says. Everyone is finally gone, and we're alone. "You were great with those kids."

"It was so much fun! Different from talking with adults—more challenging. But rewarding. Your staff was great, too." I think of the distrustful glances they kept sending my way and add, "Even though they hate me."

He frowns but doesn't deny it. "They'll come around."

"Hope so." I've made it my mission to change their minds about me, and my first step has been watching how Ryan treats them. Not like a boss, more like a friend or a mentor.

"Some of the boys looked like they were developing a crush," he says in a teasing voice.

"And some of those girls were pretty impressed with your height." I'd overheard whispers as they pointed at him and grinned at each other.

He rolls his eyes—playfully, but there's a hint of discomfort.

"You really don't like being tall?"

"I like being able to reach things," he says, easily setting a stack of books back on top of a bookcase. "I don't like not being able to fit comfortably in things."

"Things?"

"Cars. Shoes. Booths. Airplane seats. Clothes." His eyes slide over to meet mine. "Beds."

And just like that, I'm imagining Ryan in my bed, crawling over me, his head brushing my headboard, his feet dangling off the end. My fantasies about him haven't subsided; if anything, they've gotten more vivid. The vibrator isn't cutting it anymore. I'm a horny mess. I keep trying to tell myself that I'm horny in general, but that's a damn lie. I'm horny *specifically*. For the guy I've been spending twelve hours a day with.

"I can see how that would be hard," I say, swallowing.

Hard. Oh my god. I'm a freak.

"I don't like being constantly asked if I played basketball," Ryan goes on, "and when I say no, people act almost offended, like I'm a waste of inches." He pauses. "I was seeing this woman once, and she sent me this meme. 'Is he hot, or is he just tall?' I'm pretty sure she was telling me that I'm 'just tall.'"

I'm offended on his behalf. "That's ridiculous—"

"Is it?" There's a wry smile on his face. "Be honest. If I was a foot shorter, would you have made out with me after my parents' party?"

My cheeks flush. "A foot shorter . . ." I mull that over. "You're what, six-four?"

"Six-seven. And a half."

I gasp. "Fucking hell. Really? And you didn't play basketball?"

He rolls his eyes as we both make our way over to his register to close out.

"Very funny. But answer the question: What if I was five-seven and a half?" He nudges me with his shoulder. "Would you have?"

I have that tipsy feeling I get around Ryan, bubbly and a little flirty. So as I start counting out the bills in the register, I say, "Would I have what?"

When I sneak a look at him, his cheeks are deliciously flushed. "Would you have made out with me. On the beach."

"Definitely."

His eyebrows lift. "Yeah, right."

"I mean, it was your mouth I kept staring at," I say. "And every once in a while, I got a whiff of your smell—"

"My smell?" He looks appalled.

"You smell *amazing*," I say, then realize I used the present tense. And that I'm gushing too much. "That night, I mean. You smelled great that night."

"What if I didn't smell good? What if I had some kind of condition where my lip skin was peeling off? Would you have made out with me then?"

I snort-laugh and cover my mouth with my hand. "That's like me saying, would you have made out with me if I had a big wart on my nose and stinky feet?"

His laugh is pure, radiating joy, and the fact I'm the one who caused it makes me inordinately proud.

"Well?" I say, nudging him. "Would you?"

He's replacing the paper roll on the register, struggling to get it locked in place. "Depends," he finally says.

"On . . . ?"

"If you were wearing the blue dress you had on that night."

"Ah, so it was the dress," I say, matter of fact even though my face is warming.

"It was *you* in the dress. I couldn't stop staring at your . . ." His eyes dip down my neckline and his cheeks flush.

I focus on the cash, sorting the bills into neat piles on the counter. "My what?"

He clears his throat. "Your hair. It was . . . uh, pretty that night. You don't wear it down much."

"It gets in my face," I say, flicking my ponytail over my shoulder. "It's messy."

"Nothing wrong with messy." He's gazing at me with soft eyes. Bedroom eyes.

"Do you . . . think about that often? What happened on the beach, I mean."

"Pretty often." His voice is husky and close. "You?"

"Sometimes, yeah." I straighten a stack of twenties and lay

it parallel to the tens. It's taking all my energy to pretend this conversation is no big deal.

"Do you think about it happening again?"

Startled, I look up. He's inches away. His pupils are dilated, focused on mine, and they pull the honest truth out of me, a halting whisper:

"All the time."

His eyes spark with surprise. "All the time?"

I nod.

"Me too," he says, and leans in and kisses me.

It's a soft, closed-lip kiss, but as soon as his mouth touches mine, I react, a lion pouncing on prey she's watched for weeks. I grip the front of his cardigan and yank him closer. He lets out a surprised grunt, and his glasses slip down his nose, but he recovers quickly, lips parting and tongue meeting mine. Soon we're kissing like we were on the beach—going from zero to sixty like some fancy sports car that's been kept far too long in a garage.

I set his glasses aside as he works one hand into my hair, his fingers fiddling with the elastic holding my ponytail. I help him pull it out, sending my hair falling around my shoulders. Ryan groans like he's in pain, grabbing fistfuls of my hair and tugging down to move my chin up so he can kiss my neck, tilting my head so he can move to the other side. His stubble is rough and his mouth is soft and it's all I can do to hang on to his shoulders. When his teeth scrape my earlobe, my knees give out.

And then I'm lifted off the ground so easily I feel weightless, one of his forearms wrapped under my butt, the other hand still in my hair, fingers rasping against my scalp. He sets me on the edge of the counter, and I spread my legs so he can step between them, my skirt riding up my thighs.

My neat stacks of cash are now jumbles of bills fluttering to the floor, and I have the vague thought that we have a security camera trained right on the register, that the lights are on and it's dark outside and anyone passing by could see us, but those feel like problems for future us to deal with. Here and now, Ryan is kissing me like he's drowning and I'm desperate to inhale as much of him as I can before my brain catches up and reminds me that I'm the idiot who wanted to *keep things professional.*

One giant hand cradles the back of my head; the other slides around to encircle my neck, thumb trailing down my throat and dipping into the front of my blouse between my breasts, sending goose bumps across my skin. When he reaches the first button, he starts fumbling with it, and I let go of his shoulders and help him.

As soon as my blouse is open, he slips his hand inside and then it's all rough callused palms on my skin, and I'm humming with pleasure as he shoves my bra up and out of the way. I wrap my legs around him and pull him against me; his breath rushes out and he dives in for another deep kiss. He's rock hard, and I get a flash of him buried inside me, gasping and unraveling.

"Condoms?" I say. "Do you have one?"

He kisses my mouth, hard. "In the—" Another kiss as he waves a hand in the direction of the register. "Jar."

Of course they have a jar of condoms next to their register. I'd laugh if I wasn't so turned on.

I reach for the jar with one hand, the other grabbing for his belt, but he shakes his head and kneels in front of me. Flushed cheeks and bright eyes. Gazing up at me like I'm the most beautiful sight he can imagine.

I'm breathless, wanting him to get going, but he's looking at my feet, dangling in front of him. He lifts one and inspects it. "These shoes," he murmurs. "So many fantasies about these fucking shoes."

"My shoes . . . you have a shoe fetish?"

His mouth quirks. "I have a Josie Klein fetish. You, wearing nothing but these shoes. Or pressed against a bookcase with my hand up your skirt. In bed with your hair loose. In the shower. Bent over my desk. All the time. Everywhere. I can't stop thinking about you." He presses a kiss to my ankle, then the inside of my knee, kissing his way up my thigh, spreading my legs wider and pushing my skirt out of the way as his mouth moves *up up up* until he's right there, heat and softness pressing through the thin fabric of my panties.

"*Ryan*," I gasp. I'm acutely aware of the front window twenty yards behind me. My back is to it, and I hope to god Ryan isn't visible, because I'm physically incapable of stopping this.

"Tell me." The words are a vibration. "Tell me what you want."

"This." My hands grip his hair as I move his mouth where I want it. I'm so wet it would be embarrassing—except it's obvious that he wants me just as badly. His fingers are digging into my thighs, sliding up to squeeze my ass. "More. Harder. *Yes*."

I hold his head and grind against him and he's right there with me, allowing me to ride his face with wanton abandon. My vision goes hazy, and for a second I think I might actually die of pleasure, and wouldn't that be a terrible shame when I still have my panties on?

I reach for my underwear, tugging it down, and again he's

right there, hungry and hot, tongue sliding and lips sucking, pulling me closer with one hand so he can slip two fingers inside me with the other. A sharp, sweet ache spreads through my body. My eyes roll back in my head and my legs tremble and I let out a sound I've never heard from my mouth, wild and unrestrained.

RJ was right: all the sex I've had has been mediocre. There really are men who love to do this, men who can't get enough.

"I guess it's not a myth," I say, gasping.

Ryan freezes. "What?"

I shake my head, pulling him closer. "Nothing, sorry . . ."

But he rocks back on his heels. I look down at him, catching my breath. His hands are gripping my hips, and he's gazing up at me with desperate eyes.

"I can't do this," he says. His lips are shiny, wet from me. "Not now. Not like this."

"What?" I'm perched on a counter, my skirt around my waist and my underwear down my legs, the imprint of his mouth burning through me, and he's telling me he *can't do this*?

His expression is pure misery. "I'm sorry. I—I need to stop."

My stomach bottoms out. I've never behaved like this with a man, so needy, so blatantly desperate. And he's . . . stopping?

"I don't understand," I whisper.

Slowly, he releases his grip on my hips and gets to his feet. There's such obvious reluctance on his face, and my confusion grows—did I do something wrong? Did I come on too strong?

I reach down and pull up my underwear, then slide awkwardly off the counter, smoothing my skirt. My face is hot with shame; I can't look him in the eye. I would have let him do anything he wanted with me . . . and he stopped.

I have never been so mortified in my life.

He starts buttoning my blouse, straightening my collar, tucking a lock of hair behind my ear. It's so sweet—which makes everything worse. Tears prick my eyes and I blink furiously. No way in hell am I letting him see me cry.

"Let's get you home," he says quietly.

He finishes closing down his register, and somehow, I hold it together as he walks me to my apartment. No talking, no touching, no smiling. When we reach my building, he waits a few feet away as I get out my key and open the door.

Before going in, I muster what's left of my dignity and face him.

"I don't think I've ever been walked home after a rejection," I say. "So thanks, I guess."

His eyebrows pull together. "This isn't a rejection."

"Then what the hell is it?" It's obvious I'm hurt. And that makes me feel even stupider.

"It's an invitation," he says.

"To what?" I demand. This man pulled away seconds before he would have given me the orgasm of my life, and he's telling me it was an *invitation*?

"To make this something more. Something real."

"That wasn't *real*?" I choke out a laugh. "What are you saying?"

He takes a step forward. There's something in his eyes that surprises me—determination.

"I'm saying that I'm falling for you, Josie. Hard. You're the smartest person I've ever met, we have the best conversations, and you're so beautiful I could look at you for hours and never get tired of the view. I think—" He clears his throat. "I think you could be endgame for me. But I'm not sure you feel the same way, and if that's the case, I'll deal with it and try to move on. Eventually. Hopefully." He swallows. "But I care too much about you to have casual sex. This isn't casual for me."

"And you think it is for me?" This is all such a revelation that I'm having trouble digesting it, his words splintering as I try to grasp them. *Falling. So beautiful. Endgame.*

"I'm not sure. There are things you don't—things I can't—" His jaw clenches, as if he's trying to decide what to say next. "I get the sense that you're holding back."

I scoff, disbelieving. "I wasn't holding back tonight, Ryan. You were."

He winces. "I mean emotionally. I don't want you to do anything you don't want to do."

"I wanted to do *you*," I say. "That wasn't clear?"

He smiles slightly, then shakes his head again. "It's not enough. Not for me. Not with you."

And he turns and walks away.

ONCE IN MY apartment, I immediately text Georgia. SOS.

Within fifteen seconds, she's video calling me. "What's up? You okay?" She's sitting in bed, her glasses on, a pencil tucked behind one ear—probably doing some late-night studying.

Tears fill my eyes and roll down my cheeks. My face in the corner of the screen is blotchy and red, my hair a frizzy mess. This is exactly why I read books that make me cry—to get all these emotions out so I don't have to experience them in real life.

Georgia's forehead wrinkles in concern. "Jojo? What's going on?"

I take a breath, grateful for my sister and her big, soft heart.

Even after our disagreement about our mom—who I still haven't called, despite Georgia's urging—she's here for me unconditionally. "Something happened with Ryan."

"Tell me everything."

I do, spilling it all in a messy jumble, and she listens without interjecting any sisterly asides. Maybe that therapy training really is paying off.

"Wow," she says when I finish.

"Right?" I shake my head, wiping my eyes. "I just—I don't understand what he wants."

"It sounds like he cares about you," she says. Then, more carefully, "It sounds like he's . . . maybe in love with you?"

"How? He hardly knows me!" The words burst out. "Six weeks ago, we hated each other, and yeah, we've been spending a lot of time together, but not enough to say I'm *endgame* or whatever the hell that means."

"So you don't feel the same way?" Georgia says.

I freeze, running a hand through my hair. How *do* I feel about Ryan?

"I'm insanely attracted to him. Physically."

"Do you like him? As a person?"

"Yes." *So much.* "He's kind and funny and thoughtful."

"But . . ."

"But I'm confused about tonight! He wanted it as much as I did, and then he's pulling away and saying he *can't do this*?"

"Sounds like he was trying to communicate his personal boundary. He doesn't want to have sex without a deeper connection. Contrary to what many people believe, men crave emotional intimacy just as much as women do."

"Thank you for that fascinating point, Dr. Klein," I say dryly.

But I'm thinking of what Ryan told me about the customer

who used him to act out her romance novel fantasies. Or the one who implied he was *just tall*. Does he think I'm doing the same?

"We *do* have an emotional connection," I say. "More than any other guy I've been involved with."

"How so?"

I think back over our interactions—once we got through the hostile phase. "I can relax around him. Like I don't have to try so hard, if that makes sense? I feel . . . looser, I guess, when we're together." I sigh, shaking my head. "That sounds silly—"

"Not at all. How comfortable you feel around a partner is a huge indication of the success of a relationship."

"We're not in a relationship, though! Which is a good thing, because look how I'm acting, and nothing even happened."

"I mean, I wouldn't call tonight *nothing*." Georgia smirks. "But that's an interesting point. I can't think of any guy you've been this shaken up over, even after dating a while. I've never seen you have much of an emotional response at all."

"Maybe I've never liked anyone that much," I say, which makes me wonder what's different about Ryan.

Or maybe I'm different with him.

"Or you never let them get close enough to you to matter." Georgia gives me a supportive smile. "Which makes sense, with what you saw growing up. Mom's terrible relationships, all those boyfriends who dumped her and left." She pauses. "But Ryan didn't leave you, Jojo. He's asking for *more* connection."

My eyes fill with tears again. "Maybe I don't know how to connect with anyone. Maybe I've spent so much time with books that I never learned how to handle real life, real relationships."

Just like Mom. I hate considering this; I've always tried to *not* be like her.

"You had to handle more 'real life' at age ten than most people at age twenty-five," Georgia says. "You're just careful about who you let in, and that's understandable. Is there anyone you *have* connected with deeply? Besides your favorite sister, I mean." She grins teasingly. "Doesn't have to be romantic."

My mind instantly goes to RJ. *I think we have something here*, he wrote. *Something that could be real.*

"There's a guy I'm friends with on this book forum. I've opened up to him about some fairly deep stuff."

"But only online," Georgia says, and I nod. "Not even a phone call or a video chat?"

I shake my head. "He wants to talk face-to-face. But I keep . . . chickening out."

"Interesting." She takes off her glasses and rests them against her chin. "So there's a man in real life that you're physically attracted to, but you're holding back emotionally. And there's another man online that you feel a deep connection with, but you won't meet him in real life. Why?"

She's definitely therapizing me now, but I think I'm okay with it?

"Because it's scary!" I shake my head. "What if I meet RJ in real life and we have zero chemistry and it's super awkward? I could lose him as a friend."

"I don't think that's what you're scared of. I think you're worried that you'd have *tons* of chemistry in real life—and then you'd have to face the question of what happens next."

She's hit the nail on the head, and my eyes fill with tears
again. There's no turning the page and moving on when it's
your own life. No closing the book and choosing a new one.
I'd have to face my own feelings, and that's the scariest thing
of all.

"RJ's coming to IBNE," I say, wiping my eyes. "He wants to
meet up, and I've been avoiding it. But maybe I . . . maybe I
should."

Georgia studies me through the screen. "What would you
do if you met RJ and the connection was there—physical,
emotional, mental, all of it—and he felt the same way?"

"I think . . . I would want to go for it with him." Even
though I don't know where he lives, or if our lives even make
sense, I'd want to try.

"And what would happen with Ryan?" Georgia asks.

My stomach knots. The thought of hurting Ryan is
physically painful. Not to mention, how could I show up at
work every day and ignore the blazing-hot attraction between
us? Would I spend the rest of my life thinking about what
almost happened?

I wish I didn't have to choose. I've gone thirty years
without allowing myself to feel a connection with any man,
and now I've gone and gotten attached to two. But as much as
I don't want to lose Ryan, my connection with RJ feels deeper.
I need to give that a chance.

"I'd have to tell Ryan there's someone else I'm interested
in," I say finally.

"Okay. And what if you meet RJ and you have zero
chemistry?" Georgia asks.

My heart feels like it's in a vise. I've built RJ up so much in
my mind, but she's right; there might be nothing there.

Just a wonderful online friendship—which I would still be grateful for.

And if that's the case?

Ryan's face fills my mind, the sight of him kneeling between my legs, gazing up at me and confessing everything he's fantasized about. It must have nearly killed him to step away. Yet, he did, because what he wants is something more, something deeper.

Am I brave enough to give that to him? I'm not sure, but I want to be. I want to have the courage to step out of my bookish little world and embrace the possibility of something real, even if it means risking my heart. Because continuing to let fear hold me back feels like the biggest risk of all.

"I think I know what I need to do," I tell Georgia. "Thanks for listening."

"Anytime," she says, smiling.

After saying goodbye, I pull up my chat with RJ, take a deep breath, and send a message.

> **BookshopGirl:** I would really like to meet you. In person.

26

Ryan

SHE WANTS TO meet me. In person.

Correction: she wants to meet *RJ* in person.

I wrap the towel tighter around my waist and toss the lotion back in my nightstand drawer. I can't stop thinking about my view from between Josie's legs, looking up at her perched on the counter, her head thrown back in ecstasy.

Stopping was one of the hardest things I've ever done. But thank god I did—it would've been worse if she'd sent RJ that message after we'd slept together.

I leave the message unanswered while I brush my teeth and get ready for bed. Bed, where I won't be going anytime soon with Josie.

I wish I didn't know how fucking perfect she tasted.

It was her moaning that ruined everything. Under normal circumstances, it would have turned me on, knowing she was enjoying herself, that I was doing a good job. But tonight, it brought me back to that conversation with BookshopGirl when she told me she was a quiet lover. Josie even brought up the stupid myth thing.

It screwed with my head, being intimate with Josie while I

was thinking about BookshopGirl and she was thinking about RJ. Plus, I promised myself that nothing would happen between us until she knows the truth. So instead of fucking the smartest, most beautiful woman I've ever met and living out my fantasy, my fingers (the very ones that were inside her just moments before) buttoned her blouse and walked her home.

I know she was hurt and confused—and so was I. It's not like I've been exclusive with every woman I've slept with—but I've never known how deep and real a woman's connection with the other person was. Because I've never also been the other person.

This whole situation is so fucked up, and I wish I'd told Josie the truth the day I discovered it. Of course, back then she hated me, Ryan, so she would have stopped talking to me, RJ. She wouldn't have gone to Maine with me, and she *never* would've suggested we work together. I'd be almost exactly where I am now, jerking off to thoughts of my fantasy girl.

Except my fantasy girl, the woman who was riding my face a few hours ago, just said she wants to meet another man. In person.

FML.

THE NEXT MORNING, I wake with a sense of dread. I don't know how I'm going to face Josie—and I still haven't figured out how to reply to her message on BookFriends.

I should feel relieved. Elated. BookshopGirl is finally ready to meet in person. It's what I've been waiting for. But the timing . . . she didn't just turn down my invitation, she turned around and offered it to someone else.

I reach for my phone and reread her message: I would really like to meet you. In person. Followed by: You'll be at IBNE, right?

She knows RJ is going to be there. But she knows Ryan will be there, too.

Frustrated, I close out of the app right as my phone buzzes with a text from my mom: Almost at the restaurant! See you soon! xoxoxo

I groan. Normally, I love the chance to spend one-on-one time with my mom—but today, I don't think my tender heart can handle it. And it's not like she made the drive down to see me; she's here for a hair appointment, even though there are plenty of high-end salons in Kennebunkport.

I type out a reply:

> Was just about to text you. I'm not feeling great. Rain check?

> Nonsense, you'll feel better after a good breakfast.

I shake my head and throw back the covers. After raising four boys, my mother can sniff out a lie, even if it's over text.

Fifteen minutes later, I walk into Rosebud, a restaurant near the bookstore where you can sit inside the dining car of a train from the 1940s. My mom is at a booth by the window, her hair looking pristine. I shouldn't be surprised that the woman who cleans before the cleaning lady comes would do her hair before going to the hairdresser.

"Hi, Mom," I say, giving her a kiss on the cheek before sliding into the booth across from her.

"You don't look good," she says.

She reaches across the table to put a hand on my forehead, and I feel a pang for early childhood, the days when my mom had the magical ability to make everything better.

She frowns before taking her hand back, studying me. "Did you and Josie break up?"

I lean back and sigh. I knew she'd be able to tell something was wrong, but I didn't think she'd zero in on a version of the truth so quickly.

She won't let this go, so I tell her the most truthful thing I can bear to share: "You can't break up with someone you aren't dating."

My mother purses her lips.

"What?" I ask, an edge to my voice like I'm fourteen years old and about to get busted for saying I made my bed when we both know I didn't.

"You can lie to yourself, sweetheart, but you can't lie to your mother. I saw the way you two looked at each other—and Officer Dan told me he caught you in flagrante on the beach."

"Mo-o-om."

She tsks playfully, but my parents have never treated sex like it's something to be ashamed of. The only two things that concerned them were safety and consent, something I heard repeatedly growing up.

"Whatever you want to call it—hanging out, hooking up, friends with benefits—the label doesn't change the feelings."

"It's complicated," I say, even though I know she won't let it rest at that.

"Then uncomplicate it. Do you have feelings for her?"

"Yes," I admit. "But *my* feelings aren't the problem."

It's my mom's turn to sigh, a sound that says more than a thousand words. Before she can explain herself, our waitress arrives. I order the Masala Chai French Toast and a side of extra-crispy bacon.

I wonder what Josie would order—something more savory than sweet, maybe? And probably not bacon because of the whole Jewish thing. If it mattered to her, I would give it up, too. Out of solidarity and respect for her culture. I would give up anything for that woman.

My mom clears her throat, and I realize the waitress has come and gone.

"You know," she says, "in some ways, I think all those romance books you've read have done you a great service. I imagine you're a kind and considerate lover"—I dry heave at the thought of my mom thinking of me as any kind of lover— "but I also imagine it gave you an unrealistic idea of how fast and easy love is in the real world."

I shake my head. "C'mon, Mom. It's never fast or easy in the books. If it was, they'd be thirty pages, not three hundred."

"You're making my point—no real love story wraps up in three hundred pages. Real life doesn't follow plot beats, and real love isn't like your books."

"Says the woman who married her high school sweetheart. If you wanted me to have a more pessimistic view of romance, you and Dad shouldn't have been so happy for so many years."

My mom goes quiet, looking down at the small diamond on her right hand—the original engagement ring my dad got her when they were in college.

"It wasn't always easy. There were several—"

"I know," I say. I lived through the blips—Dad had a bad

habit of working too much, and Mom didn't have great boundaries with her family. "I know your life wasn't always sunshine and roses. But I also know that when you were sixteen years old, you knew he was the one. When you know, you know, right?"

Another sigh, but this time, she's acknowledging that I'm right.

"The thing is, Mom, none of that matters if the knowing is one sided."

"Are we talking about Kate?"

"No," I say, too quickly. But then I meet her eyes, so full of love and understanding. "Maybe."

But it's not Kate, specifically—I got over her years ago. What I'm not over is how it felt. The sickening realization that the person I'd given my heart to didn't want it. And the way it made me question everything I thought I knew about love.

"Here you go," our waitress says, setting our plates on the table.

I'm grateful for the distraction, although I know it's temporary. It would take someone bleeding out on the floor to distract Merrie Lawson from making her point.

"Your beautiful heart has always been one of your biggest gifts," Mom says, once the waitress has left.

"And one of my biggest curses," I say, shoveling a bite in my mouth.

"I wasn't finished. You were so open to love when you were young. In fact, the first time you told me you'd met the girl you were going to marry, you were in third grade."

"So you're telling me this bad judgment is a lifelong pattern?"

"No, I'm telling you that these ups and downs are part of

your journey—it's growth, not failure. Every time your heart was broken, it healed even stronger. But after Kate you just . . ."

"Stopped trying," I say, setting down my fork. I've lost my appetite.

"Listen, sweetheart—I know your dad makes it sound like our story was love at first sight. And it might have been for him; I was pretty cute back then. But you should know that he asked me out every week for four months before I said yes. And even then, I only did it so he'd stop asking."

I sit up straighter; she did not just say that.

"You're telling me the story at the heart of our family is a lie?"

"It's not a lie." Her voice sounds faraway, like she's talking to me from the past, not from across the table. "I had that 'knowing' moment, it just took me longer." She sets her fork down and looks up at me, like she just had a literal lightbulb moment. "Love is like swimming in the ocean. And you, my darling—and your father, for that matter—want to cannonball right in. But some people, perhaps like your Josie"—*my Josie*— "need to dip their toe in the water and ease in. Slowly."

Great, now I'm thinking about Josie in a bathing suit, a bikini that shows off her curves and her generous tits.

"But she'll get there, and if she doesn't—"

"Don't say there are other fish in the ocean."

"Fine," my mom says, cutting into her egg-white omelet. "I won't. But it's true, even though I'm holding out hope for the two of you."

"So am I," I say.

We're both quiet for a moment, and the silence is comfortable. Comforting. Maybe you never outgrow needing your mom, I think, and as I do I feel sorry for Josie and her sister, who never got to experience this kind of love.

"If—*when* Josie comes around, don't hold the time it took against her," my mom says. "I know it feels personal, but trust me, it's got more to do with her than it does with you."

We spend the rest of the meal covering safer topics: a trip she and my dad have planned, how much everyone loved their party, and of course, the latest accomplishments of my gold-star brothers and their families.

It's not until I've hugged and kissed my mom goodbye that her words sink in.

This isn't about me.

Josie Klein is one of the most cautious, deliberate people I know. If she feels even a little spark with RJ.Reads, which I know she does, then of course she wants to explore that. So who am I to get in her way?

I pick up my phone and open the BookFriends app, where Josie's message has been sitting, ignored, for far too long. I take a deep breath and type a response.

> **RJ.Reads:** I'll be at IBNE. And I'd love to meet you there.

For the rest of the week, Josie is so busy we barely have time to be awkward around each other. I do my best to focus on my store and not what she's doing on her side. But my best is nowhere near good enough—I'm constantly aware of her.

It doesn't help that she's hardly talked to RJ once they— *we*—decided on our/their plans to meet. Since I, Ryan, knew Josie would be nervous and focused on her panel the first afternoon, I, RJ, suggested meeting for a late dinner. I thought about suggesting the Map Room, but that's such a special memory for me, Ryan, that I don't want to share it with me, RJ.

God, I can't wait for the truth to be out.

In the end, I picked the Parish Café, a restaurant close enough to the hotel that we can walk, but not so close that it'll be overrun with other conference attendees.

I'm walking into the lobby of the Boston Park Plaza now, impressed as always by the way the hotel manages to be both understated and elegant. The library to the left, with its mahogany walls and leather furniture, is the stuff of a booklover's wet dream. Then straight ahead, past the white, flowing curtains, is the bar, already crowded with hundreds of booksellers from all around New England.

We're an eclectic crowd: young and old, some stern and reserved, others bubbly and animated; some with pink or purple hair and piercings, others wearing tweed jackets with reading glasses tucked in the pockets.

The one type I don't see is a curvy bookseller with a bun on top of her head. I assume Josie is in her room, drilling herself on all the points she hopes to make on her panel this afternoon.

The line for check-in moves quickly. When it's my turn, I collect my swag bag and get oddly emotional when I see my name tag. For the last dozen years I've been coming to this conference, it's read, RYAN LAWSON, HAPPY ENDINGS / SOMERVILLE. Next year, who knows what it will say. Xander's Books?

Only if Josie and I are successful in our scheme. If she even wants to keep working with me after today.

I slip the lanyard around my neck; it feels light without any crazy buttons—although maybe I should have brought a few. That STFUATTDLAGG one would have been an interesting icebreaker with the literary elite. Josie's crowd. Although I think the last few weeks have taught us both to be more open minded to other genres.

The thought of Josie reignites my nerves, and I distract myself by heading upstairs to the exhibition floor where publishing companies have set up tables featuring their upcoming releases. I load my swag bag with as many romance ARCs as it'll hold, stopping every few minutes for a hug and hello from booksellers I've met at conferences past.

After the fifth conversation about my height (really, you'd think book people would have something more interesting to say!), my phone buzzes with an alarm reminding me to make my way to Salon B for Josie's panel.

"Ryan Freaking Lawson!"

I freeze, then turn and see Kimberly, a bookseller from Rhode Island that I've hooked up with at past IBNEs. There's a reason it's called I-BONE.

"Hey, Kimberly," I say as she throws her arms around me.

"It is *so* good to see you," she says, giving my cheek a big kiss, complete with a *mwah!* sound. "Are you coming to the 'I Like It Nasty and Neurodivergent' panel?"

"No," I say, taking a step back. "It was on my list, but I'm heading to 'Literary Fiction and Gen Z.'"

She pouts, looking disappointed and more than a little confused.

"Got to go," I say with a wave before she can ask me anything else—including what I'm doing later.

JOSIE'S PANEL IS packed—standing room only. I claim a spot in the back and notice with pleasant surprise that Josie is wearing her hair down. I wonder if she decided to forgo the bun because I told her how much I liked her hair down, or if she's wearing it that way for RJ.

RJ, who she's meeting for dinner in a few hours.

My stomach churns, and I try to quiet the what-ifs circling my head and focus on the panel, which is in full swing. Josie is the only woman, and the only one under fifty.

"Have any of you had any luck getting Gen Z interested in literary fiction?" the moderator is asking.

Josie straightens. "The other night, we held an event for—"

"How are they going to sit still and read anything worthwhile if they're stuck on their phones all day?" an old white man—one of four on the panel with Josie—says, interrupting her for the third time in five minutes.

Josie tries again. "I actually think—"

"Their attention spans have been decimated," another man says, nodding. "It's a real shame, and—"

"I'm interested in hearing what Ms. Klein has to say." The room goes quiet, and all eyes dart to the woman in the audience standing up. It's Penelope Adler-Wolf, Josie's hero, coming to her rescue. I'm grateful, and a little pissed at myself for not doing it first.

"Go on, Josie," Mrs. Adler-Wolf says.

Josie flushes—both from the attention and, I bet, from the fact that her idol knows her name.

"I—I was saying that the other day we had an event with a group of teenagers." Josie's eyes flit toward me before she looks back at Penelope. "And a lot of them were interested in literary fiction. These kids are *so* smart—yes, they're on their phones, but that means they have the whole world at their fingertips, exposing them to complex issues. They have strong opinions and real insights to offer. I think we need to do a better job listening to them instead of talking over them."

Penelope Adler-Wolf smiles and nods in approval. "I agree wholeheartedly," she says, and Josie glows.

The conversation moves on, but for the rest of the hour, Josie is given the space to talk. Soon, everyone in the room is as captivated by her as I am. When the panel ends, she's swarmed by people asking her additional questions.

I hang near the door, waiting my turn. It takes almost twenty minutes, but I don't mind. This is her moment, and I want her to soak it all in.

By the time she's finished talking to the last person, her cheeks are flushed, and she's practically floating down the aisle toward me.

"Eeek!" she says, raising her balled fists in celebration. "I did it!"

"You did it," I say, swooping her into a hug. She feels so good in my arms, I almost forget what happened the last time we touched. I almost forget what we're doing tonight.

"You were amazing," I say. "We should celebrate."

Josie's smile fades.

"I have plans," she says. Then her gaze turns icy. "And maybe you do, too?"

She motions toward my cheek.

Fucking Kimberly. I wipe away the evidence of her red-lipstick kiss, grateful it's at least on my cheek and not my lips. I already have more than enough to explain later.

I can barely swallow past the lump in my throat, but I manage to squeak out, "Maybe we can grab breakfast before the first panel tomorrow?"

Josie's lips press together. "Sure."

She turns to go, and I drink her in, knowing the next time I see her, everything will change.

I can only hope for the better.

BookshopGirl: We're still on for tonight, right?

RJ.Reads: I wouldn't miss it for the world.

BookshopGirl: Good. Can we talk logistics? How will I know who you are? I mean, technically speaking, we're strangers. We could have walked by each other a dozen times today or sat next to each other in a session. I really hope you weren't the guy in the tweed jacket who was flossing in the row ahead of me during the welcome address.

RJ.Reads: That wasn't me, I promise. And I think we'll know when we see each other—but if it helps, I'm wearing a dark blue suit and I can put a crimson rose in my lapel.

BookshopGirl: Just like the movies . . . Shoot, I have to get moving. How weird would it be if I was late to meet you because I was busy talking to you? I'll see you soon!

27

Josie

MY HEART POUNDS an erratic rhythm as I head to my hotel room. All day, I've been scanning faces at the conference, knowing that any of the men here could be RJ. Even during my panel, I couldn't stop searching the audience, wondering if he was there, if we'd make eye contact and feel a zing of connection.

Instead, my eyes kept snagging on Ryan. His concerned frown when I was interrupted by the old guys up there with me, his proud smile when Penelope Adler-Wolf stood and silenced everyone so I could talk. But also catching glimpses of him around the conference, always surrounded by hordes of women. I'm sure they all think he's just the best thing ever, this tall smiling man with his cardigan and tortoiseshell glasses who loves all their favorite books. Every time I saw him shining his smile in another woman's direction, my insides crackled with envy.

He's probably having dinner with that woman who left her lipstick on his cheek. Maybe they'll end up back in his room afterward, and I bet he won't stop right before giving *her* a mind-melting orgasm.

The thought makes me nauseous. Truly sick to my stomach.

Forcing my mind away, I let myself into my "Wicked Small" room (which is literally what the hotel calls them—they're barely big enough for a queen-size bed) and change into the dress I picked out to meet RJ, my body tingling with fear and anticipation. I wish I could skip to the ending of this night, like I used to skip to the end of books as a kid, skimming the final pages because I couldn't stand the tension. Will we connect as much in person as we do online? Or will our spark fizzle?

Only one way to find out.

I don't need to leave yet, so I sit on the bed and pull out my phone, staring at the last message from RJ. My eyes catch on his profile picture, that familiar image of his hands holding a small, leather-bound book.

Feeling like a stalker, I click on the picture and zoom in, scanning the pixelated image for clues about this man I know so well but have never met. He's wearing a light blue T-shirt, and I can make out some kind of pink strap around his neck. Maybe a lanyard.

The skin on my arms prickles. How many men wear a pink lanyard?

With shaking fingers, I zoom back out, now noticing the edges of what looks like a gray cardigan. A wave of dizziness hits me, but I force myself to stare at his hands again. Wide palms and thick fingers and knobby knuckles.

I know those hands. I've watched them handling books, carefully—almost tenderly. I've felt them in my hair and deep inside me.

It can't be. Can it?

My vision is going black around the edges, my rib cage tightening as my breathing goes shallow.

A new message pops up.

RJ.Reads: Just got to the restaurant. Can't wait to see you.

My entire body goes rigid. I don't have time to sift through my prior conversations with RJ or mentally analyze my interactions with Ryan. I don't have time to call my sister and get her advice. And I certainly don't have time to sit here and freak out.

I need to go. Now.

Teetering in my heels, I hurry down the street to the restaurant. My legs are wobbly, my mind a whirling tornado— shock and confusion and a thousand questions.

How is this possible? Does he know? If he does, why didn't he tell me? If he doesn't, will he be happy? Am *I* happy? What if I'm wrong? Do I want to be wrong?

A rush of impending doom overwhelms me, and I falter. But it's too late. I'm at the restaurant, and my eyes are scanning the crowd gathered at the entrance. There: Dark blue suit. Light blue shirt. A red rose in the lapel and a bouquet of daisies in his hands.

I slowly lift my eyes to his face and—

All the breath rushes out of my lungs. It's Ryan.

He's pale and fidgety and nervous looking. But none of the shock I feel is written on his face.

"You knew," I whisper.

He blinks. "Wait—did you know?"

I nod, dazed. It was one thing to stare at my phone and put the pieces together. Quite another to stand here, facing him, knowing it for certain. My throat tightens with a feeling somewhere between anger and betrayal.

"Why didn't you tell me—is this some kind of weird game?"

"No. Of course not." Ryan takes a step forward, eyes flashing with panic. "Josie. I—I've been trying to tell you, I swear, but every time I asked about meeting in person . . ."

I said no. I kept asking him to be patient, to wait until I was ready—and he did. *He did exactly what I asked.* So why does my chest hurt so much? Why am I fighting tears and struggling to catch my breath?

"It's really you?" My voice is faint.

He nods, the bouquet drooping in one hand. "It's me. Ryan James Lawson."

"How did you figure it out?" I ask, staring up at him in disbelief.

"I saw you reading—"

"*The Princess Bride,*" I say, gasping. "You knew before we went to *Maine*?"

He winces.

"And you knew my sister's name." I can't believe I didn't make the connection before. "You knew my mom read bodice rippers. Things I didn't tell RJ, things I told Ryan. Or vice versa. Whatever. Fuck. I can't—" My voice is getting hysterical. "He's been you the whole time? You've been him? The whole fucking time?"

The world tilts, and I look for somewhere to sit. To calm myself down so I can approach this rationally.

"Wait, don't go—" Ryan puts out a hand and grabs my arm. "Can you give me ten minutes? Five minutes? I don't blame you for being upset, but let me explain. Please."

The rawness in his voice jolts me out of my dizziness and confusion, and I force myself to look at him. Really look at him. He's an absolute wreck, his eyes teary, his hand still clutching the daisies. The expression on his face is complete and utter despair.

And then it all crystallizes.

The two men I've been torn between are one and the same. RJ is Ryan and he's standing in front of me, staring at me like his heart is cracking in pieces. That ache in my chest? It's the pain of realizing what I've missed out on all these weeks. I could've had him—all of him—if I'd been brave enough to meet him the first time he asked.

And I'll be damned if I miss out on a moment more.

Without a word, I put my arms around him. He hesitates briefly before wrapping his arms around me in the best hug I can imagine, like being wrapped in a blanket fresh out of the dryer. He's rubbing my back, whispering that he's sorry, that he wanted to tell me but didn't know how, that he's crazy about me, that he'll do anything to make this up to me. My hands clutch his suit jacket, my eyes leak tears onto his shirt, and I inhale his scent in deep, calming breaths. It's my favorite smell in the entire world.

"Don't cry, BookshopGirl," he whispers, so quiet I almost don't catch it. "Don't cry."

"Can we go somewhere?" I say, my face still buried in his chest.

"I put our name in for a table. We can talk more. I know this is all such a mess, but I'll try to explain everything."

That's the smart thing to do. Sitting down for dinner and hashing it all out, discussing what this means for our partnership at the bookstore, if we should let our relationship go further. This is my usual approach: keeping my distance, avoiding my feelings, compartmentalizing everything into manageable, safe categories.

But if I've learned anything from the books I love to read, it's that life is full of misunderstandings, raw emotions, and hard truths—and so are relationships. I've sometimes wondered if spending too much time lost in fiction has left me unable to face reality, but maybe it's done the opposite. Maybe it's been preparing me all along for this very moment: messy and complicated and real.

And now? I'm finally ready.

I look up at him. "I don't want to go to dinner."

"Oh," he says, disappointment in his eyes. "I understand—"

"You have a room, right?"

He blinks. "At the hotel? Yes."

"Then let's go."

I grab his hand and start marching back the way I came, no longer wobbling in my heels.

"Wait—what's going on?" he says, tugging on my hand to turn me around.

"What's going on?" I repeat, facing him. "This is the best news I've gotten in years."

It takes a moment for that to hit him, but when it does, his entire face changes, confusion morphing into hope. "It is?"

"I've been an absolute *mess*, torn between RJ and Ryan, wishing I could somehow keep you both. So yes, we're going to need to talk at some point, but all I can think of right now is picking up where we left off the other night."

"I—" He shakes his head, a smile spreading across his face. "Then let's go."

We hurry down the sidewalk, hand in hand, grinning like kids on their way to the Scholastic Book Fair. When we reach the hotel, though, he starts tensing up, sneaking shifty glances at me in the elevator. And when we reach his door, he fumbles with the key card and drops it.

I stoop to pick it up, then pause and touch his cheek. "Hey. How you doing up there?"

He looks like he's stuck his finger in an electric socket: eyes wide, glasses askew. "I'm having trouble believing this is happening. Is this happening?"

I hold the key card to the reader. "I sure hope so."

The card registers, I turn the handle, and we both enter. And as the door clicks shut behind us, all his nerves swoop right into me.

It's the sight of the bed, crisp and white, his suitcase open on the floor next to it, the cardigan and jeans he wore earlier draped over a chair, the warm glow of the lamp on the nightstand. The intimacy of it. We are alone in a hotel room and nothing is going to interrupt us.

"Hey," he says, touching my cheek. "How you doing down there?"

"I'm . . . nervous," I say.

"Why?"

"Because this matters to me."

It never has before, I realize. Not with anyone else.

He's looking at me with pure sweetness. "You know I've got you, right?"

I know he doesn't just mean physically—he means in every way possible. And I believe him. I take his hand, leading him into the room, and he sets the bouquet on the desk. With trembling fingers, I reach for the top button of his shirt and undo it, working my way down.

"Good god," I whisper.

"What?"

"Your chest." It's official: my new kink is a sturdy, six-foot-seven-inch man wearing a suit with the shirt unbuttoned to reveal peachy skin, scattered freckles, light brown hair fanning across his chest and diving into his waistband. "I want it."

"It's yours."

"All of it?" I reach for the fly of his pants—there's already a bulge—but he catches my wrist, and I have a moment of panic that he's pulling away like last time.

He must see it on my face, because he says, "Don't stop. But can we go slow?"

I nod, even though I'm aching to get going. He shrugs off his suit jacket and drapes it over a nearby chair.

"Ryan Lawson, now you're worried about wrinkles?" I say, smiling.

"I'm trying to prove that I'm not just a messy ball of chaos. I remember your face when you saw my car the first time."

His hair is way too perfectly combed, so I reach up and mess it with my fingers. Now he looks more like my Ryan.

"I'm learning to appreciate a little chaos," I tell him. Then I reach for his glasses, setting them behind me on the desk, never taking my eyes off him.

I slide my hands under his dress shirt. His shoulders are broad, his arms thick, and he has these big, rounded pecs that make my eyes go wide as I spread my palms across them. No six-pack or V-cut abs here—his stomach is just the right amount of soft, which means this man doesn't deny himself delicious things, like his beloved sugar-loaded coffees. I'm grateful; I have plenty of soft areas, too. If he was built like some action hero, I'd be intimidated.

I mime pulling a sticker off a sheet, then press it over his heart.

"Uh . . . what was that?" he says.

"A gold star." I glance up at him; he's smiling fondly. Then I glide my hands down his torso and start working on his belt.

"Josie, wait," he says, tilting my chin up. I stiffen again, and he kisses my forehead. "Slow, remember? Please, I want to look at you."

His eyes are almost feverish as he gazes down at my body. Big, warm hands come to my shoulders and my neck, searching for the zipper for my dress, so I turn around. He brushes my hair over one shoulder, and I swear he presses his nose to my head and inhales. Then he's sliding the zipper down, fingers trailing along my back.

The dress puddles at my feet so I'm wearing nothing but my pale pink bra and panties and red high heels. Only an hour ago I put these on, wondering if RJ might see them—and the truth hits me again: RJ is Ryan and Ryan is RJ and somehow I'm here with them both.

The pad of his finger presses between my shoulder blades. "Gold star," he whispers.

Another gentle press of his finger, below my bra strap, then another, star after star running down my spine, sending goose bumps across my skin.

He reaches around me from behind in a bear hug, cuddling me against him, and it would be sweet if there wasn't a bulge pressing against my backside. I push back against it, and he clucks his tongue like he's disappointed in me.

"What?" I say innocently.

"Slow," he reminds me.

Then he takes my hand and turns me, guiding me toward him as he backs up and sits on the bed, facing me.

"I . . ." His face goes slack. "You're so . . ." He licks his lips. "Josie, I'm . . ."

He's glitching like a radio coming in and out of range, so I take his hands and place them on my waist. He was so urgent before—at the beach, in the store the other day—but now he's tentative, sliding his hands up and down my hips, stroking my stomach with his thumbs. My body is lighting up, shivers running down my legs. He slides his hands up to encircle my ribs just below my bra, his fingertips teasing the clasp in back.

"May I?" he asks. So polite. As if he wasn't the same man who roughly shoved my bra out of the way and palmed me like a dirty-minded teenager.

I nod, smiling.

"Say it." His expression is grave.

"Yes," I say obediently.

Slowly, he unclasps my bra, his eyes darkening as he takes in this new sight. His palms are warm and deliciously rough as he cups my breasts and leans forward, his mouth giving attention to one nipple, then the other. I run my hands through his hair and hum with pleasure. Everything is hazy and golden, sweet as honey on a summer morning.

Hands drift down to my hips, fingers playing with the elastic hem of my panties. "May I take these off?"

"What do you think?"

"I need to hear the word."

He waits, and when I say "yes," he starts sliding them down.

I step out of my panties, leaving my shoes behind, too, and then it's just me, standing naked on the carpet as Ryan sits in front of me, almost fully clothed. I start to shrink into myself, but he catches my wrists and holds them out, turning me one way, then the other, letting his eyes linger.

"The most beautiful thing I've ever seen," he murmurs. When I can't stand this lazy perusal any longer, he looks up. Sharp eyes. Laser focused. "May I take you to bed?"

"*Yes!*" I shout, and he breaks into a smile and bends forward and throws me over his shoulder.

I yelp as I'm lifted in the air, inches away from the ceiling, but soon enough I'm being lowered, my back gently hitting the mattress as Ryan comes over me, grinning.

"You sounded pretty eager," he says.

"You left me so hot and bothered the other day—"

"I know." His smile disappears, lips dipping in a frown. "Let me make it up to you?"

"You better."

He kisses my forehead, then my lips, moving down—neck, chest, stomach, hip. I need no encouragement to let my thighs fall open, and I gasp when I feel his wet, warm tongue as he tastes me, sucking, sliding two fingers to stroke inside me. It feels as wonderful as it did the other day in the bookstore—but now there's nothing between us, no holding back, no unwilling deception. He was right; this is infinitely better, and I'm so damn grateful for him, grateful that he was patient when I wasn't ready . . . and grateful that he made us wait until we could be fully open with each other.

He's still going slow, and I shift myself to guide him where I want him. When he hits the right spot, I suck in a breath. I'm about to say, "Do that again," but he's apparently gotten the message, because he repeats the same motion, circling and stroking, and the rhythm is perfect, the friction exquisite.

Somehow, he manages to continue exactly the way I want.

Time stretches and twists until I have no idea how long we've been here, but I'm squirming and my legs are trembling and I'm making the kind of noises I've mocked in the past, gasping and groaning, pleading for him to keep going, don't stop, just like that, *oh my god oh my god yes yes yes*. He's relentless, holding me in place as the intensity builds and builds, waves on a stormy sea, until I crest the highest peak and tumble down, head over heels, crying out over and over again.

I'm shaking when I open my eyes to see his face over mine, blurry.

He's smirking down at me. "I seem to remember someone suggesting that women don't make noises like that in real life."

"Apparently that's because I've only had mediocre sex."

He chuckles. "Not anymore. Only the best for BookshopGirl."

I laugh, shaking my head in amazement. "I still can't believe you're RJ. That I've been talking to *you* all this time. It's going to take me a while to get used to it."

"But it's a good thing? You're sure it's good?" The vulnerability in his voice surprises me, and I put my hand on his cheek, gazing into his dark-honey eyes. All the times he confided in me that he felt like he didn't measure up, that he was the participation trophy kid—I want to erase it all, every doubt in his mind that he is anything but extraordinary.

"So good," I say. "The absolute best."

He exhales and settles next to me on the pillow, putting one arm around me so my head is on his chest, my cheek resting on his unbuttoned shirt. "I didn't know how to handle this when I first found out," he says, his voice a quiet hum.

He's still fully clothed, just his shirt open, and when his hand rests on my bare stomach, I feel suddenly exposed.

"You probably didn't think it was such a good thing, huh?" Now it's *my* voice that sounds vulnerable.

"Not at first. But it didn't take long before I knew I had to do whatever it took to convince you to give us a chance."

"I didn't make it easy on you."

He trails his fingers across my stomach. "Someone once told me that the effort is what makes it worth it—like mining for jewels. If they were out in the open, they wouldn't be so precious."

He's repeating my words about my favorite books, but he's saying them about *me*. It makes me feel, for the first time ever, that my protective shell isn't a character flaw; maybe I'm not too difficult to get to know. Maybe I've just been waiting for someone who's willing to put in the work.

Before I can respond, he slides his hand down between my legs, where I'm still sensitive. My breath catches. His fingers start drawing a slow, whisper-light circle that feels so good I can't help sighing again.

Still, I feel like I should tell him. "Just so you know, I never have more than one orgasm during sex."

"That's fine." But he doesn't stop, and it does feel great, so I try to relax and enjoy it.

"Just don't want you to be disappointed," I murmur.

"Never."

But as the minutes tick by, I start to worry. He's used to romance-reading, sex-positive partners, not an aloof ice queen. Plus, he's already given me a top-notch orgasm, and I don't want to be greedy. What if he's getting impatient? Or bored? This is why women fake it. But if I tried that, he'd know—he just saw the real thing.

"We really can do something else," I say after a while.

He presses a kiss to my temple. "Josie. If it doesn't feel good, just tell me."

My breath hitches as he increases the pressure. "It feels good. So good. I just . . ."

"What?"

"I feel bad taking so much time and . . . and effort."

Another brush of lips on my temple. "I'm in bed with my fantasy girl, and she's naked and warm and soft, and I'm touching her exactly where I've been dreaming of touching her. I'm having the time of my life."

A warm glow settles in my chest. "Fantasy girl?"

"You have no fucking idea." The words are a deep rumble, and another wave of pleasure rolls through me.

"Tell me."

He lets out a chuckle. "You want me to talk dirty?"

"Sure." It's not something I've liked in the past, but Ryan is getting me to believe in the power of change.

"Let's see . . . the day you moved those squeaky bookcases, I *was* watching your ass. Trying not to think about how I wanted to pull your skirt up and pull your panties down and bend you over and bury myself inside you." His fingers pick up the pace, and I feel a rush of heat. "Even when we were fighting, I'd have these impulses to press you against a bookcase and kiss you until you squirmed. Dreams, too. I'd wake up so hard I couldn't function."

My legs begin to tremble. He keeps talking, keeps touching me.

"I've imagined waking up with you in that bed at the inn, and we're spooning and I get harder until you let me slide inside you, both of us lazy and sleepy, my lips pressed to the back of your neck and my hand between your legs."

My fingers find his open shirt and I clutch it, bracing myself against the intensity of this feeling. It's more than the building arousal—it's his words. This isn't simple dirty talk. These are his most intimate thoughts, murmured in my ear like confessions.

"At work I find myself listening for your voice and thinking about how your lips look like a perfect bow, and how your neck starts flushing when you get riled up. Like right now."

I can't respond; I'm on the edge, and he lowers his mouth to my ear and says, "Of all the books I've ever read and all the fantasies I've ever had, none of them hold a candle to the reality of being with you. You are what I've been waiting for." He presses his lips to my jaw. "Please trust this: I will do whatever it takes to give you every single thing you have ever wanted."

I'm starting to believe him. He's so patient, and it's paying off—my legs are tense and I'm breathless. My grip tightens on his shirt, and I squeeze my eyes shut and arch my back and—

This climax is a rolling wave, tossing me up and under, and when I resurface, I feel like I'm floating in warm, calm water. Slowly, I become aware of my body's weight against the mattress, the sheet covering my bottom half, the scratch of Ryan's shirt collar against my cheek. The press of his lips against my hair and his voice murmuring, "Watching you fall apart is the sexiest thing I've ever seen."

"Fuck," I whisper. I am in so much trouble with this man.

"Is that an exclamation or an instruction?"

I blink. "Huh? Oh. Both."

Without further ado, I reach down and grab his belt. We've had plenty of *slow*—I'm ready to speed things up. I bat his hands away and whip that belt off, then unbuckle his pants to reveal baby blue boxers and a bulge veering to the left.

I palm him and he groans. It's clear that Ryan is a giver, but now I'm desperate to see him take it, to watch him unravel and know that I'm the cause.

"My turn," I say.

I'd like to say I have as much finesse as he does, but I'm a trembling mess as I pull his shirt off him, then struggle to get his pants down. He helps me, tossing them on the floor. I reach into his boxers and wrap my hand around him.

"Oh, thank god," I whisper.

"What?"

"I was terrified that you'd have some monster giant dick."

An awkward laugh. "I'm not sure how to respond to that."

"I'm thrilled," I say honestly. "I know women in romance novels want to be knotted or split up the center or get their backs blown out—and good for them—but this woman is ecstatic to see a penis that appears to be proportional and manageable."

"That's . . ." He pauses. "Good?"

"It's great. Perfect. Wonderful. I mean, nothing about you is small." I tug his boxers down; he helps me take them all the way off and send them in the direction of the rest of his clothes. "On your back."

He obeys without a word. It's almost comical, how much space he takes up in the bed, his legs sprawled out so his feet don't dangle over the edge. Finally, I have him completely naked. Thick thighs and muscular calves, all covered in curly golden-brown hair. The skin near his upper thighs and hips is creamy and soft and I have half a mind to make him roll over so I can see that view. Instead, I make my way down, kissing

the smooth skin near his hip bone, running my hand down
that nice happy trail until I get to where I want to be. I wrap
one hand around him and lick the tip.

"Fuck," he hisses.

"Is that an exclamation or an instruction?" I say, then take
him deeper. His hips jerk, but then he stays still, allowing me to
get to know him. For the first time in my life, doing this doesn't
feel like a chore or an expectation. It's a privilege, a pleasure, a
joy. To give this to him, to hear his breathing quicken and
watch his hands grip the sheets as he struggles to stay in
control.

But all too soon, he's pulling me up and shaking his head
and throwing me back against the bed.

"That's all I can take for now," he says, grinning.

I scoot back against the headboard, and he comes up on
his knees.

"Condom?" I say hopefully.

He opens the nightstand drawer and fishes one out. "I also
have some in the pocket of my pants, just in case."

He's blushing, and those pink cheeks on this large naked
man are so cute I can't stand it.

I take the condom package, and he watches as I open it
and roll it on him. His eyelids flutter in pleasure, and then he
grabs my waist, pulling me under him.

There's a moment of shock as our skin touches. He's warm
as a radiator on a winter's night. And the scale of him—

"God, you're so . . ." Big, I almost say, and stop. "Perfect," I
say instead. Because there's so much more to him than his
body, though I am a fan. He's the man I've been pouring my
heart out to online for months, the man I've worked side by

side with for weeks, the man I've come to respect and admire for his passion, integrity, and dedication.

No longer my nemesis or even my competition—somehow, he's become my best friend.

And now we're skin to skin and he's gazing at me, warm brown eyes and dilated pupils and soft eyelashes. He dips closer, and his lips find mine. Deep, searching kisses, still slow, savoring every taste. He parts my legs with his knee, and I feel him nudging against me.

"Josie. Do you want to do this?"

I can only nod, and he punishes me with a bite of my bottom lip.

"Words," he says. "I need words."

That feels like a big ask right now, but I search for one—"Please."

His eyes spark as he presses inside me, just an inch.

"Please, what?" he says.

I struggle for more words—the right words to capture how I feel. "Please be mine, Ryan."

His smile is pure sunshine. "I already am," he says, and pushes all the way inside me.

We both exhale—in pleasure, in relief. I've been waiting my entire life to want someone this much. To feel safe enough to drop my defenses. He pulls out partway and drives in again, and I'm along for the ride, letting him take the wheel. My heart is swelling and warming, like it's too big for my chest. He's locked in, thrusting slowly and watching me, changing his angle or his pressure, and each roll of his hips is better than the last.

"I take back everything I said about your books"—I gasp with another thrust—"if they taught you tricks like this."

"Tricks?" A vein on his forehead is popping; he's working hard to stay in control.

I wave in the direction of our hips. "This. You're good at this."

He thrusts again and I groan. "No tricks."

"So you're naturally gifted?"

"Nope. Just paying attention."

And god, if that isn't the sexiest thing I've ever heard.

"For example . . ." He bends my knee up against him, lifts my hips off the bed an inch, and presses inside me again, a new angle that makes me whimper. "You seem to like that." He leans down and puts his teeth on my earlobe; I shiver. "And that." Then his hand moves up to my hair and makes a fist; my eyes roll back in my head. "And that, too."

"Do you like it?" I feel like I'm not contributing much, but it's difficult to participate when I'm melting into the bed.

"I like everything about this. Fantasy girl, remember?"

He closes his eyes and rolls into me again. Over and over, slow and steady—until it's not. He quickens his pace, pressing his forehead against mine. Every muscle in his body is tense and taut. I run my fingernails down his back and bite his shoulder and kiss his neck until finally his rhythm falters and he tenses and shudders, holding on as long as he can to this moment before collapsing on me.

"Oof," I say.

He springs up, rolling off me. "I'm sorry, did I—"

I tug him back over me. "Crush me, please."

Shaking his head, he pulls me on top of him and I sprawl out, my cheek on his chest, listening to his heart rate slowly coming down. Every speck of tension in my body dissolves until I'm rag-doll limp and drifting toward sleep.

"Stay with me tonight?" he asks.

My eyes pop open. The thought of leaving hadn't even occurred to me. "I might as well. Don't want anyone to swoop in and take my place at breakfast with you tomorrow. By the way—where the hell did that lipstick on your cheek come from?"

I sound like a jealous harpy, but Ryan chuckles and wraps his arms around me. It's like being in a straitjacket; I love it.

"All I was thinking about all day was you," he says, kissing my forehead. "And now I'm thinking you must be hungry. I didn't feed you dinner."

There's no way I'm leaving this bed. "We could get room service?"

"Sure. And then should we . . . talk?"

I know we need to talk—about everything that's happened and what it means for our partnership at the bookstore and our future together—but there's something else on my mind. Only problem is, it's up in my room.

"Don't take this the wrong say," I say, "but I, uh, got an ARC from one of my favorite authors today—"

"Same!" He shifts so we're facing each other. "It's for the next book in this series I'm obsessed with—"

"And I keep thinking about it—"

"I read the first chapter over lunch—"

We're talking over each other, and we both stop. Then we burst out laughing.

"You won't be mad if we read tonight for a while?" I ask.

"Mad?" He laughs again. "I cannot think of anything better than hanging out in bed with you and reading."

So that's what we do. Ryan puts in a room service order. He cleans up and gets dressed, then takes my key card and goes to my room to fetch my roller bag and tote full of books from the convention. After we eat, he strips down to his boxers and I put on my pajamas, and we prop ourselves up in bed and open our books. He pulls my legs over his lap and lazily strokes them with one hand, pausing only when he needs to turn the page.

And as we lose ourselves in our stories, I find myself hoping, for the first time in my life, for a happy ending.

28

Ryan

HOLDING JOSIE KLEIN'S hand is my new favorite thing to do. And kissing her. Being on top of her, beneath her, inside her, hearing the sharp little noises she makes when she's about to come. Lying in bed afterward, talking or reading or talking about reading. Everything with Josie is my favorite. She's my favorite.

I spent so much time worrying she'd be furious and never want to see me, Ryan, or talk to me, RJ, again, that I didn't think about how good it could be. How good we could be.

Based on this last week, we could be great.

Saturday: I woke to the sound of Josie's sleepy sigh. Pure bliss. Then I got to live out my fantasy of leisurely morning sex, which was even better than I imagined, followed by room service, which was not as good as I expected. Turns out avocado toast really is just avocado and toast.

Later, we went around the conference together, meeting reps at new-to-us imprints and talking up our vision for the new store. Every few minutes, I'd look over at Josie, and she'd blush, which would make me grin. By the time the conference ended, we were both ready to run back to our room and spend more time together (naked).

Sunday: (After another round of sweet and slow morning sex) we played tourist and walked down to Fanueil Hall. We took our time reading every quote on the glass columns at the Holocaust Memorial, then went to the North End and did a taste test between the cannoli at Modern and Mike's. (Mike's won.) From there, we Ubered back to her place and had every intention of going our separate ways, but our goodbye kiss got so heated that Josie dragged me upstairs and had her way with me. Which I didn't mind at all.

Monday: We tried to act like everything was normal, but Cinderella knew as soon as she saw the smile on my face. It didn't take long for everyone else to figure it out, too. After we closed the stores, I took Josie out on a proper dinner date.

Tuesday: I woke up in Josie's bed, which is as soft and lovely as she is. It's a queen, which meant it was too small for me. But I'd take being squished with Josie over being alone in my king-size bed any day. We ate takeout Thai and stayed up most of the night, making love and making plans for our final meeting with Xander on Thursday.

Which brings us to Wednesday.

Today.

"Morning, lovebirds," Eddie says as we walk in the door— one door for the entire store now.

Josie drops my hand. I miss the feel of her fingers, but I don't take offense. I'll be patient while Josie dips her toe in the water, getting used to the temperature. Damn it if my mom's cheesy metaphor doesn't make perfect sense.

"Things are looking good around here," Josie says.

She's right. Construction officially wrapped up this weekend while we were at the conference, but it took the crew a few days to load everything out.

"It's so . . . quiet," I say. "No more clanging or banging."

"From here on out the only banging I want to hear about is between the two of you," Eddie says.

Josie's eyes go wide, and she turns, speed walking to her side of the store.

"Sorry." Eddie shrugs. "She makes it too easy."

"White mocha frappe with extra whip for you," Mabel says, handing me my drink. "And an Americano for your lady."

"Thanks," I say, taking the drinks. The store isn't the only thing that's changed in the last three months. It feels like a lifetime ago that Mabel was mixing up our drink orders. Back when Josie thought my name was Brian.

When I bring Josie her coffee, she isn't alone. Georgia's there, leaning on her bedazzled cane with both hands. Her head perks up as Josie's falls. From our conversations, I know Josie's been dreading this introduction as much as I've been looking forward to it.

"Georgia," I say, extending my hand. "It's nice to officially meet you."

"He really is shockingly tall," Georgia says, as if I'm not standing right there.

Her mouth curves into an open smile that lights up her face, reminding me of Josie—except it took me weeks to coax that kind of smile out of her sister.

"Nice, firm handshake," she says, making eyes at Josie. "So tell me, Ryan-slash-RJ, what are your intentions with my sister?"

I choke on my frappe.

"Okay, I'm out," Josie says. "Georgia, take it easy on him, please?"

"Yes, dear sister," Georgia says, smiling sweetly.

But as soon as Josie disappears into the back room, Georgia turns back to me, her expression dead serious. "Listen," she says, "I've never seen my sister this happy with anyone in her life."

I give a tentative smile. "Thanks, that's really—"

"It's not a compliment, it's a warning," she says, and I shut my mouth. "Josie has spent her life sacrificing her own wants and needs for other people—especially me, and I can never repay her." Her voice cracks, and she clears her throat. "She's busted her ass to get where she is, and I'd hate to see her get screwed over by some guy who's riding on the coattails of her brilliance and hard work."

All the blood drains from my face. It's like she's speaking my fear aloud: that Josie doesn't need my help to run this bookstore. Georgia's right. Josie has worked her way up to her position against all odds, while I lucked into mine. Most of the time, I can barely keep my own staff in line.

"I would never do that to her," I say. "I adore your sister, Georgia. She's the most—"

"I know," Georgia cuts in. "And she deserves someone who will put her first, for once. Do you understand?"

"Of course," I say, nodding for emphasis.

"You better mean that," she says, narrowing her eyes. "My sister deserves to have every single thing she wants. And apparently, right now, that includes you."

I blow out a breath, grateful that Josie's sister—the person who knows her better than anyone else—sees it, too. "I won't let either of you down," I promise.

THE NEXT MORNING, I wake in Josie's bed, feeling like there's a dark cloud hovering above me. I barely slept last night. And not in the fun, staying-up-and-having-sex-and-deep-conversations way. No, I was up in the anxious, tossing-and-turning, going-over-all-our-plans, thinking-and-rethinking-every-single-thing way.

Josie seems to be feeling optimistic, and I'm doing my best to pretend I am, too.

"I can hear you thinking," she says. Her head is on my chest, and she looks almost ethereal in the early morning light.

"Oh yeah?" I say, trailing a finger down her arm. "What am I thinking about?"

"Peanut butter."

I don't know what makes me laugh harder—the contemplative tone of her voice or the words themselves. "I wasn't, but I am now," I say, remembering around three a.m., when my sweet tooth got the best of me. I wandered, naked, into Josie's kitchen and was disappointed to find her pantry nearly empty. The only thing she had that came close to satisfying my craving was a jar of peanut butter. So I introduced her to one of my favorite childhood delicacies: a peanut butter lollipop—a.k.a. a spoon dipped in peanut butter.

It hit the spot, and so did the sex we had afterward on her kitchen counter.

"Want me to get the jar?" she asks.

"I thought you said no eating in bed? Besides, I want to make you breakfast. A real breakfast—not that instant oatmeal crap."

"Oats are nutritious," she says. "They're rich in fiber—"

"—and they taste like cardboard. Let me cook for you."

"Fine." Josie sighs, but she looks pleased. "I suppose it's not every day a tall, naked man offers to cook you breakfast."

"It could be," I accidentally say out loud.

In a pathetic attempt to distract her from my lovestruck blunder, I kiss her on the nose and pop out of bed. I'm trying not to be all the way in until I know Josie knows, too, but it's hard when she's literally everything I've been looking for.

It's unsettling, knowing none of what happens next is up to me. Whether or not she becomes my business partner is up to Xander, and the rest is up to Josie.

One thing at a time, I remind myself, as I run down to the corner store to grab a few ingredients. How can I love a woman who doesn't have butter in her fridge?

Thirty minutes later, Josie emerges from her bedroom, smelling like gardenias, her hair wet from the shower. "Wow, you went all out," she says, surveying the array of dishes.

"I forgot to ask how you like your eggs, so I made them all the ways." I place the last plate on the table. "I've got sweet and savory bagels, too, with butter, jelly, cream cheese, and lox. Sorry, the bagels got a little burned."

"Mmm, lox," Josie says, reaching for a well-toasted sesame bagel. "I'm not religious, but my taste buds are very Jewish."

"And how do you like your eggs?" I ask, looking over the bounty: scrambled, fried, poached, and omelet style.

Josie winces. "I don't," she admits. "I'm sorry—but the bagel is perfect. I never eat much when I'm nervous."

"You're nervous?" I ask cautiously.

"Of course. I mean, I feel good about our plan, but I don't trust Xander."

My stomach clenches; she's voicing the very thing I've been

afraid of. Josie's plan is brilliant, and the presentation we've prepared is bulletproof—but logic and common sense don't matter when you're dealing with a money-hungry, manipulative piece of shit like Xander.

"If he doesn't . . ." Josie shakes her head. "I don't have any other job prospects."

"Any bookstore would be lucky to have you," I say, feeling a pang of guilt that I *do* have another job prospect, even if it's one I don't want. My heart is here, with Josie and our store, and I've made that very clear to Gretchen. Which hasn't stopped them from spending the last month trying to change my mind.

"I don't know," Josie says. "It's not easy to find a manager position at an indie bookstore. I might have to look in other cities, and I'd hate to leave Georgia. It feels like everything is on the line."

"Everything," I agree, wondering if she's including our relationship in her equation. "So, let's focus everything we've got on this meeting. We can't control the outcome, but we can give it our best shot. Right?"

The spark is back in Josie's eyes, and I smile. If we've got a chance, it will be because of that fiery spirit. The thing that drove me crazy, then made me crazy *for* her.

AN HOUR LATER, we're heading into work. After we grab our coffee at Beans, I make my way to the Happy Endings side of the store. There are a million things I could be doing, but I'm too anxious to do anything but pace.

"Morning, boss," Cinderella says, startling me. I didn't see her, curled up on her favorite reading couch. Her hair is platinum blonde today—one of the most ordinary colors I've ever seen on her. Between that and her bright blue eyes, she looks like an older, more exaggerated version of the character she named herself after.

"Aren't you fresh off the pages of a storybook," I say.

She blushes and runs her hand through her hair. "A new look for the new store."

"Hey, guys!" Eliza walks up to us.

I glance at my watch. "Shouldn't you be at practice?"

Eliza shrugs. "I wanted to come wish you luck."

"We all did." I turn to see Indira and Nora, who worked her weekly shift yesterday, and my eyes well up with tears. "You guys, I . . . This is . . . Thank you for being here."

"We couldn't let you cross the finish line alone. What time is your meeting?" Indira asks.

"In about five minutes," I say, blowing out a nervous breath.

"No matter what happens with Xander," Cinderella says, "we want you to know how proud we are of you and how hard you've fought."

"Working here has kept me young," Nora says.

"And hot," Eliza adds, bumping her shoulder against Nora's.

"You didn't just give me a job," Cinderella says, getting choked up. "You gave me a home, a safe space when I needed it."

Indira puts her arm around Cinderella's shoulder, and Eliza steps in on her other side. We all move together in an awkward group hug that I wish didn't feel so much like goodbye. Because no matter what happens, everything is going to change.

The alarm on my phone chimes, and my stomach clenches. Cinderella offers me a sad smile. "Go give 'im hell, boss."

XANDER IS TEN minutes late. He walks in, looking out of place in a white linen suit. I wouldn't be surprised if he's hopping a jet for a private party on a yacht in Bimini after this meeting.

"Lawson. Josie," he says, approaching our table in the newly remodeled café.

"Xander, good to see you." I stand and shake his hand, filling my voice with false cheer.

Josie remains seated in a counter–power move that I admire. More proof of her badassery.

"We're going to have to make this short," Xander says, grabbing the power back. "But I know you're both eager to hear the results. And I'm happy to say both stores had impressive sales this quarter—"

"About that," Josie says. "Ryan and I would like to make a counterproposal."

Xander laughs, although he isn't amused. "You don't know my decision yet."

Hades appears from wherever he's been hiding and makes himself at home in Xander's lap. I expect Xander to freak out—black cat, white suit—but instead, he starts to pet Hades. And my cat—the damn traitor!—starts to purr, tilting his head back in an invitation for Xander to stroke the fur between his ears.

Without hesitation, Josie launches into the speech we prepared, explaining how our numbers went from good to great because we started working together; that the combination of our strengths surpassed anything we could do alone.

Then it's my turn: "That sharp increase you noticed in my sales over the last month—that's because of Josie. She had incredible ideas for maximizing Happy Endings' efficiency, from our organizational structure to our strategy for placing orders. It's been a game changer."

"And Ryan has a knack for bringing people together and creating spaces where they want to stay and spend their money." Josie takes the spreadsheet we prepared and slides it across the table to Xander. "The numbers speak for themselves. If Ryan and I manage the new store together, you'll get the best of us both and the profit margin will more than make up for any additional overhead."

Xander takes the piece of paper in one hand, continuing to pet Hades with the other. The silence is torture, and I slip my hand under the table and give Josie's leg a comforting squeeze. She places her hand on top of mine and links our fingers while we wait for the verdict.

Finally, Xander sets the paper down and narrows his eyes, studying us. Josie unclasps our hands and brings hers above the table, folding them in front of her.

She breaks the silence: "What do you think?"

"I think," Xander says, "that it was incredibly stupid of you to give up your competitive advantage."

"Stupid?" Josie repeats. There's a laugh in her voice, but I know it's covering hurt.

"Idiotic," Xander says, directing that venomous word toward her. My hands clench into fists under the table. "Honestly, Josie, I thought you were smarter than that. Helping the person you're competing against? The person you could've beat with your hands tied behind your back?"

His words sting—and not only because he's berating the

woman I love. It's my worst fear coming true: that I'm not good enough, that I've ridden Josie's coattails like Georgia suggested.

"You were ahead all summer," Xander says to Josie. "Until the past few weeks, when Ryan pulled ahead—because of you, apparently." He shakes his head and makes a *tsk*ing noise. "I thought you wanted this job."

"I did . . . I do," Josie says. Her voice wavers, and it takes every ounce of my self-control not to lunge across the table at Xander.

"Such a shame." His sinister smile pushes me over the edge.

"The only shame is you, missing the point," I snap.

"Am I?" Xander turns to address me now. "Interesting, since I was about to give you a compliment—this is the smartest thing I've seen you do since I bought your silly little bookstore. Befriending the competition, playing nice so you could steal her business plans? Very sly."

"He didn't steal anything," Josie says, her voice sharp.

"We worked together," I tell him. "We make a good team. And if you hire me, I'll just hire Josie as my co-manager—"

"No, you won't." Xander's eyes narrow. "I'm underwater because of this renovation—I'm putting you on a hiring freeze. The whole point of this competition was to eliminate one of your salaries, not this kumbaya bullshit."

"This really is just a game to you," Josie says, more to herself than to Xander.

"Business is a game, sweetheart," Xander says. "And you just lost. As for you"—he moves his gaze toward me—"I suppose that makes you . . . 'the winner' seems like a stretch, but here we are. Congratulations, Lawson, you're the new manager."

Josie won't look at me, but I can't tear my eyes away from her—this complicated, beautiful, smart, passionate woman. Even at my best, I know I'm not good enough for her or this store. And I intend to keep the promise I made her sister: to put her first.

Fueled by fury and justice and yes, love, I stand and look down at Xander. A glimmer of fear crosses his face, and for once, I'm grateful for my size.

"I don't care if your dick is small, or your mother never loved you, or whatever wound you're trying to heal," I say, "there is no excuse for this bullshit."

I keep my eyes trained on Xander, who's scowling. If I look at Josie, I might break. And I can't—because it's about damn time someone stood up for her. She's going to get her dream, even if it means I have to lose mine.

"If I didn't care so much about this fucking bookstore, I'd say we should both walk out and leave you scrambling. But this store, our staff, our customers, our community—they matter more than anyone's ego, yours or mine. And there's only one person who should be running this place."

Xander's face is beet red; he looks like the devil he is. But I'm not done yet.

"In case it's not clear, I quit. The job should be Josie's." I risk a glance down to see her looking up at me with a dazed expression I can't read. "The job should be yours."

And with that, I walk out the front door with my heart broken but my head held high.

29

Josie

I'M ROOTED TO my chair, trying to grasp what just happened. I've never seen Ryan so furious. And now . . . he's gone?

"That was intense," Xander says, and I whirl to face him. He's flustered, smoothing the nonexistent hair on his shiny head. "I guess you're the manager, Josie. Congrats."

"Huh?" I gape at him.

"Let's talk next steps." He launches into an explanation, but I'm too dazed to pay attention. All I can think about is finding Ryan to make sure he's okay.

"I've carved out Monday mornings from nine thirty to nine forty-five for us to check in," Xander is saying, "so save nonurgent items until then. It'll streamline things for me, having one manager to deal with. Let's gather the staff and let them know."

"Wait, I don't—"

But he's already standing, clapping his hands. "Everyone! I have an announcement."

Ryan's staff comes over, and Eddie joins us from behind the counter, bringing Mabel. Xander gives them all a bland smile. "I'd like to introduce your new manager. Josie Klein."

Cinderella's eyes spark with alarm. "What? Where's Ryan?"

Xander shrugs. "He quit."

"Why would he do that?" Nora gasps.

Another shrug from Xander, more impatient now. "If you have questions, direct them to Josie, and she'll contact me if needed." He emphasizes the last two words. Then he faces the staff again. "Thanks for all your, uh, hard work. Let's make some money, okay?"

On that uninspiring note, he heads out.

I'm immediately mobbed by the Happy Endings staff, asking why Ryan left.

"I'm calling him," I say, pulling out my phone. No answer, so I leave a voicemail and text him to call me. As soon as I hit send, Eddie tells me that Mabel is starting cosmetology school soon and will be cutting her hours, so he'll need to hire another barista. Also, he needs a new espresso machine.

"Order what you need, but be mindful of the cost, okay?" I tell him. "And can you draft a job description for me to review?"

"Sure thing."

Then the door chimes, and in comes the contractor. He says there's an issue with the lighting and he's going to get the electrician back in here tomorrow to fix it.

"Sure, okay," I tell him.

The rest of the day rushes by in a whirlwind of responsibilities, but underneath it all, worry gnaws at me—and guilt, too. This is all my fault. My plan failed, I couldn't convince Xander, and now Ryan's out of a job. Is he angry? Does he blame me? What does this mean for *us*? I try calling again, texting—nothing. I even send him a DM on

BookFriends, but the silence stretches on, making the knot in my stomach twist tighter.

Finally, as I'm locking up the store, my phone pings with a text. From Ryan.

> Hey, sorry for disappearing on you. Just needed some time to clear my head and figure a few things out. Want to come over?

All the tension of the day rushes out of my body. He's fine. We're fine. Everything is going to be fine.

I reply:

> Sounds great. I'm leaving the store now. Send me your address?

He does, and I take a bus toward Charlestown. When I reach his building, he buzzes me in, and I race up the stairs to his apartment. The door opens before I can knock, and there he is, all big and broad and sturdy, wearing sweatpants and a T-shirt, his hair adorably messy. I launch myself into his arms, breathing in his familiar scent. Tears well up in my eyes and soon I'm sniffing, trying to hold myself back from crying.

"Hey, it's all right," Ryan murmurs, running his hands down my back. "What's going on? Wait—" He pulls away; his forehead is wrinkled with concern. "Xander gave you the job, right? That asshole better—"

"Yes, he did—not that he had any choice," I say, then bury my face in Ryan's chest again. "What were you thinking?

Quitting your job for me? Why would you ever think that's a good idea?"

He exhales and holds me tighter, kissing the top of my head. "Because you deserved to win, Josie. You're the reason we started working together in the first place—otherwise you would've crushed me."

"But I can't take your job!" I hiccup, wiping my eyes. "You love that store—you've worked there since you were fifteen years old!"

"And I think it's time for me to move on."

Alarm flickers through me, and I look up at him. "What do you mean, move on?"

"Come in and I'll explain," he says, taking my hand. He closes the door behind me and leads me to his couch, where we both sit. He leans forward, elbows on knees. "Remember when I told you about my friend who offered me a job at their new bookstore in Provincetown?"

Yes, but he told me about it way back in Maine, before we agreed to work together.

"What about it?"

"I called my friend and . . ." He hesitates, then presses on. "I'm going to drive down there to check it out this weekend. See the space, meet some of the other booksellers, talk details with Gretchen."

Shock ricochets through me, and I straighten. "Wait, what? You're taking that job?"

"It's the perfect opportunity for me," he says, not meeting my eyes. "There aren't any other romance bookstores in Boston."

"But it's two hours away! Would you just . . . move there?"

He gives a slow nod, and my heart plummets. "My lease is up at the end of next month. Gretchen has a room I can rent until I find my own space. But I'll come here on my days off, and you can visit me anytime. Plus we can always chat online like we've been doing for months, and we can FaceTime, too."

I blink; it sounds like he's worked all this out. Has this been his backup plan the whole time? The thought makes my lungs constrict. While I was putting everything into us working together, he had a safety net?

"And I—" He hesitates before clearing his throat and continuing. "I think maybe it'll be good if I'm out of your way as you get the new store up and running. You need the freedom to run things according to your vision—"

"We had a vision *together*, Ryan. Remember?"

"I know, but unfortunately, that didn't work out."

The regret in his voice makes my tears well up again. This whole thing is my fault. "I'm so sorry, Ryan. I really thought it would work. I tried my hardest, I gave this everything I had, and—"

"Shhh," he says, pulling me against him. He kisses my head; strokes my hair. "It's not your fault. Let's just be glad I have something else to fall back on."

I hear his unspoken words: *Because you don't.*

It's true; I have nothing else, no other job, no direction, and it's so completely *Ryan* for him to consider that. But nothing will be the same if we're separated—with both of us in new positions, launching new stores, we'll be lucky to get the same day off at the same time. That's no way to start a new relationship. Surely he knows this.

Unless . . . maybe he *wants* some distance from me.

I try to brush the thought aside, but it sticks in my mind like a splinter. Since our first night together, we've had countless discussions about our future as it pertains to the bookstore—

but nothing about us. Our relationship. Now here we are, facing a crossroads, and he's taking a detour.

He'll only be a few hours away, I remind myself. He's trying to do what's best for both of us. Ryan Lawson is the kindest, most generous person I've ever met; he would never hurt me on purpose. *I know this.* But my logical brain doesn't stand a chance against the old, familiar feelings of abandonment bubbling up. The feeling I used to get when Mom would disappear without warning, leaving me to figure everything out alone.

The same tightness grips my chest now, making it difficult to breathe. I know Ryan isn't Mom, but the scared kid inside me is panicking, terrified of being left behind again. I'm spiraling, drowning, and I can't seem to stop. *Ryan's leaving.* He's leaving the store, he's leaving me, and my heart feels like it's ripping apart.

My mother's face flashes in my mind. Her desperate need to prove that permanence and stability and everlasting devotion aren't just plot devices. I've never believed in any of that. Why would I? I've never seen any evidence that it's real. Like I told Mom when she was in Mexico, left behind by yet another man: *If he loved you, he wouldn't leave you.*

If Ryan loved me . . .

Abruptly, I stand and walk toward the windows. Tears blur my vision. Georgia pointed out that I've never had much of an emotional connection to anyone I've dated. Well, there's a reason for that—I've never *allowed* myself to care too much.

And god, it's so much easier that way.

Maybe I had the right idea all along, burying myself in books so I don't have to feel all this. Some distance from Ryan might be good—I've started relying on him, and that's never a good idea. I learned that with Mom. Now it's happening again—I'm letting myself need someone, handing them the power to break my heart.

So I do what I've always done: pack up my emotions—confusion, hurt, abandonment—seal them in the farthest corner of my heart, and ice them over so they'll never, ever thaw.

"When are you leaving?" I ask without looking back at Ryan.

"I was thinking I'd drive down tomorrow. Do you want to come with me? We could stay the night at a bed-and-breakfast—I'd love to get your opinion on everything."

The thought of seeing him in some other bookstore makes my eyes flood with tears again. But I know this isn't how he wanted things to turn out, and I never want to make him feel bad for trying to do what's best.

So I blink away the tears and smooth my hair before turning around. Ryan's sitting on the edge of the couch, watching me with a concerned expression.

"I don't think so," I say, "I have so much to do at the bookstore this weekend. I'm overwhelmed as it is."

"I don't have to go tomorrow; we can find another time—"

"No, you should go," I say, and give him a smile that I hope looks genuine. Supportive. "You can call me and tell me all about it."

He looks disappointed, but nods. "Yeah, of course. I understand."

"I'm really excited for you," I say. "Congrats on this new opportunity."

If he catches the lie in my voice, he doesn't let on. "Thanks. I wish . . ." He pauses, and I wait for him to say more: *I wish our plan had worked*; *I don't blame you*; *I don't want to go*. But instead, he clears his throat. "Thank you."

"Can I help you pack?" I ask.

"You don't have to—"

"I want to spend time with you." If he doesn't let me stay a little longer, I really might start begging, and that would be a disaster.

His face softens. "Sure. I'd love that."

TEN MINUTES LATER, we're packing a duffel bag in his bedroom, a place I never even got the chance to spend time in. There's a king-size bed with a blue comforter covered in an insane number of pillows—more than I've ever seen on a man's bed, but it's so Ryan. Big, comfortable, inviting. One entire wall is a bookcase, bulging with messy stacks and rows of paperbacks.

I'm over by his dresser, which is littered with odds and ends. Including the pink lanyard covered with colorful romance-related buttons with their inside jokes I'll never understand. I assume he'll get a new one at his new store, where he'll probably meet women who share his passion for romance.

He deserves someone like that. The thought wriggles into my mind, and I try to push it away, but I can't. Ryan deserves someone softer than me. Someone sweeter, warmer, easier.

What do I know about happy endings, anyway?

"I guess I don't need that anymore," he says, coming up behind me. He's close enough that if I lean back, he might wrap his arms around me. Maybe he'd take me to bed, and I could stop thinking about what's happening.

My eyes land on one button in particular: STFUATTDLAGG.

"You never told me what this means," I say, touching the letters.

There's a pause. A long pause. I turn around; he's awkwardly shifting his weight.

"It's, uh, something that got popular on social media," he finally says. "The romance community picked it up, and . . . it's stupid, honestly."

The evasiveness in his voice sparks a jolt of anger. Okay, he's leaving, and I have no say in the matter, and he didn't even tell me until after he'd decided. But can't he tell me *this*?

I face him. "I want to know what it means."

"No, you don't." There's a stubborn edge to his voice.

"You don't get to decide what I want."

That's the crux of it: he's made a choice that affects my life, and I don't have a say. And just like that, all the feelings I stuffed down surge up again, a red-hot flame bursting to life. Because guess what? It's so much easier to be angry than sad.

He's inches away, looking down at me, his eyes memorizing my face—my lips, my hair, my neck. There's a pained expression in his eyes, a tiny crack in the mask he's wearing. I want to rip it off.

"Tell me, Ryan." Heat crackles between us, like it did during those first few weeks of our battle.

"It's nothing," he says, sharper.

"What does it mean?" I'm egging him on, poking his chest with my index finger. "Shut the fuck up and . . . ?"

"I am not saying those words to you." His voice is a growl.

"Tell me."

"No."

I stick my finger in his face. "I swear to god, if you don't tell me—"

"Shut the fuck up and take that dick like a good girl."

And my knees hit the floor.

30

Ryan

MY FANTASY GIRL is on her knees in front of me, tugging down my pants. I stumble backward and hit the dresser behind me.

"Josie, wait, I didn't mean you had to—"

But she's already reaching into my boxers and wrapping her hand around me.

"Please," she says, gazing up at me, her eyes so big and bright they almost hurt to look at.

I can't deny this woman a single thing, so I nod, and she slides her tongue up my shaft. She circles the tip before taking me in her mouth, warm and wet. Gasping, I grip the edge of the dresser as she works me with her hand, sliding up and down in rhythm with her lips, taking me deeper each time.

Flashes of the last three months play like a movie sequence in my mind: that first day, when she called me Brian; when she stormed over to Happy Endings, all fiery and gorgeous, accusing me of sending the Book Club Sluts to sabotage her event; the moment I realized she was BookshopGirl; dancing in Maine; Josie reading steamy scenes out loud at the bar;

kissing her on the beach; kissing her at the store, in her apartment.

But as incredible as this feels, something is missing. It's like she's tucked all her tenderness back inside, the hidden softness I've spent weeks trying to uncover, the warmth between us, all the sweetness of our past week together.

Somehow, I've fucked this up. But all of this, everything, was for her. I just want Josie to get everything she's dreamed of. Everything she deserves.

Even if I could find the words to say any of that right now, I'm not capable of speaking. So I lean back and close my eyes, surrendering myself to the mercy of this woman and her magic mouth.

"Josie . . ." Her name on my lips feels like a prayer. I don't know if I believe in God, but I believe in Josie, and I believe in us. "Josie, Josie, fuck, Josie—wait."

I need to be closer to her, to feel her body next to mine and see her gorgeous green eyes. So I reach under her arms and haul her up. She's startled and flushed, and I catch a glimpse of something—sadness?—in her expression.

"What's wrong?" she asks. "You don't . . . want this?"

The hurt in her voice is another dagger in my chest. "Josie, I will *always* want this. I'll always want you, but can we—"

She comes up on tiptoe and puts her mouth on mine, silencing me. Message received: she doesn't want to talk. I'm not sure exactly what she wants, but I'm desperate to make this better, so I return her kisses, hard and deep.

Soon we're tearing at each other's clothes; she's yanking my T-shirt up and off and I'm fumbling with the buttons on her blouse, popping one off as I rip it open to reveal her glorious cleavage against a black bra. So beautiful. I want to fall to my knees and worship her for hours, but she's still kissing me with a fervor that takes my breath away.

Josie unclasps her bra, and my brain goes hazy. All I can think about is touching her, feeling her soft skin and hard nipples under my fingertips.

She moans, then stifles it by pressing her lips to my shoulder. I hate that she's quieting herself with me after I've heard the sounds she makes when she feels safe and uninhibited. I reach down and pick her up, spinning so her back is against my bookcase. A few paperbacks fall from the shelves, but I hardly notice. Josie's skirt rides up her thighs as she parts her legs so I can step between them.

I'm living out the fantasy I've had for weeks, but it feels like there's an emotional mountain between us, and this physical connection just isn't enough.

I know she's not happy about this other job, but she's got to see this was the only option. She has to understand that I'm committed to us. Is this her way of thanking me for giving it all up for her? Or is she trying to show me what I'll be missing when I go?

I cup her face in one hand and force her to meet my eyes. "Josie, please tell me what's wrong."

Tears are caught on her eyelashes, and I hate myself for making her cry. But I still don't understand why, because she won't fucking *talk* to me. "Words, remember? I need words." I lean my forehead against hers, breathing hard. "Baby. Talk to me. Please."

My voice is ragged, desperate. And when I pull away slightly to meet her eyes, I see the same desperation reflected in hers.

"Just give me this moment, Ryan. Give me tonight before . . ." Her voice cracks and it breaks my heart in two.

"Josie, I . . ."

She swallows my words whole, her kiss hungry and urgent. It feels like a goodbye—and a flash of terror hits me. I never want to say goodbye.

We discard the rest of our clothes and fall into bed together. If she doesn't want to talk, I'll just have to show her how I feel. As I press my lips to her jaw and down her neck, I hope she knows I'm saying, *You're everything I want.* And as I skim my hand down the curve of her waist, I hope she hears, *You're beautiful.*

My other hand sliding into her hair is me saying, *I never want to lose you,* and my lips pressing right above her heart mean, *I'll do anything for you.*

Somehow, I think she understands, because she's opening up to me like a flower, relaxing and unfurling as I touch and taste and stroke. And by the time she's rolling on the condom, her expression is open and her eyes are fixed on mine, unguarded and trusting and so beautiful my own eyes fill with tears.

I roll her on her back and she parts her legs for me, eager and ready, and as I press inside her I hope she knows I'm saying, *I love you,* even though I haven't dared to say it out loud yet. We move together and I can't tell where I end and she begins—we're one body, warm skin and mingled sighs.

And even though she doesn't want my words, I need to say them anyway.

"Josie." My voice is rough, and I interlace our fingers, holding her in place. "Josie, look at me."

She does, and goes completely still.

Gazing into her bottomless eyes, I say the words I hope she's ready to hear. "No matter where I go, if I'm two hours or two thousand miles away, I'm yours."

Her eyes fill with tears, and she looks away.

"Josie," I say again, and she slowly lifts her eyes to meet mine. "I'm yours. Always."

The tears roll down her cheeks, but this time, she doesn't look away.

"Always," I whisper.

She doesn't speak, but I see her lips form the word: *Always*.

AFTER, WHEN JOSIE'S asleep in my bed, I lie awake, staring at the ceiling, my thoughts a jumbled mess.

I thought I was doing the right thing, the brave thing, putting her needs and wants over mine. I thought I was sacrificing *for* her. But what if I'm sacrificing *her*? Us. The future we could've had together.

I look down and watch her sleeping. She's curled on her side, her hair a cascade of chestnut-brown waves across my pillow. How did I ever consider moving more than a hundred miles away from this woman? It's madness. Sure, we could try to make long-distance work, but why would I even want to?

I thought it might be good to give Josie space and time, like my mom suggested. But maybe that's not what Josie needs. Maybe she needs to know—really know, down to her core—that I'm not going anywhere, so she can trust her heart with me.

Josie stirs in her sleep and says something that sounds like my name.

"I'm here," I whisper.

She exhales, her eyes still closed, and mumbles, "Oh, good."

I hold my breath, hoping she'll say more. That she'll tell me what I can do to make this right. But she's asleep again, and I know it's unfair of me to expect her to fix this. I made this mess—because I've been terrified the girl I love wouldn't be able to love me if I was the one who stole her dream.

For years, I've been happy to facilitate love stories for customers or read love stories about fictional characters. But all along, I've been trying to protect myself. Wanting the guaranteed happy ending without any of the risk.

This is a decision point, like Nora said. I can choose to let circumstances or fears come between us, pulling us in different directions, allowing us to slowly drift apart despite our best efforts to stay connected.

Or I can choose to fight for *us*. I don't want our story to end like those tragic novels Josie loves, where the author tries to console the reader by insisting that sorrow and despair are more profound and meaningful than joy. I want a different kind of ending, the kind that's like another beginning, a story that will hopefully continue for the rest of our lives.

I'm tempted to grab my phone and text Gretchen that I can't take the job after all, but I won't make another rash decision without talking to Josie. I'll find another job in Boston, beg Xander to reconsider—anything. I owe it to Josie to try. I owe it to *myself*, too.

I yawn, suddenly feeling bone tired, and slip my arm around Josie, who sighs and curls closer.

As I close my eyes, I promise myself I won't leave this bed without talking to her. I'll be brave and honest and tell her how I feel—that all I want is to be with her—and then I'll listen while she tells me what she wants. And we will figure it out together.

31

Josie

I WAKE TO a soft buzzing sound and open my eyes, slowly remembering where I am: Ryan's bed, warm and comfortable. He's behind me, his breathing steady and deep, and my entire body feels at peace.

Then everything from yesterday comes rushing back: the awful meeting with Xander, Ryan storming out, everything he said about this new job. The confusion and hurt, all my old fears of being left behind resurfacing.

But then, the words he whispered later: *No matter where I go, if I'm two hours or two thousand miles away, I'm yours.*

He all but said he loves me, and I want to believe him. But does he *understand* me? If he did, he'd know that moving, even just a couple hours away, is the worst thing he could do.

I know it's ridiculous, but the thing that keeps popping into my head is all those books he recommended to me on BookFriends—I read every single one, but he never asked me for any of my recommendations in turn. I've always believed that the best way to truly know someone is by reading their favorite books, and he hasn't made any effort to do that.

I shake my head, trying to shrug it off. I'm being silly, right? But the thought nags at me as I try to drift back to sleep.

The buzzing starts again, and I realize it's my phone on the nightstand. I reach over to grab it; my mom has sent me a text. At 6:14 a.m.

> Hey sweetie pie! Sorry for the whole mess in Mexico. Call me when you can, we should catch up!

My stomach sinks at the brightness in her tone—it feels forced. Georgia's been trying to get me to reach out, but our mother never reaches out unless she needs something. What does she want?

My finger slips and I accidentally hit the video call button.

"Shit," I whisper—I don't want to disturb Ryan, and I'm also not in the mood to deal with my mother.

But it's too late, she's already answering, and I slip out of bed and quietly shut the door behind me.

"Jojo! How are you!"

"Um, I'm okay." I hurry through Ryan's living room and let myself out to his tiny balcony, shutting the sliding glass door behind me.

When I glance back at my phone screen, my mom's face comes into view: she looks worried. "What's wrong?"

I open my mouth to tell her it's nothing, but the words catch in my throat. I try to hold it in, but within seconds it all bubbles over, and soon I'm crying as I tell her everything about Ryan, that my plan to save our jobs didn't work and now he's moving and I don't know if I can handle it.

When I finish, she sighs and says, "Oh, Jojo. I'm so sorry."

I wipe my eyes, surprised at my outburst—I've never broken down in front of her—but also because she's never seemed to care much about my emotional state. "Yeah. Same."

"But it doesn't make sense—it sounds like he cares about you! Why would he leave? I think you need to ask him what's *really* going on."

Before I can explain that he thinks it's best for both of us, she continues:

"You know how I wanted to find Darrell and ask him why he left me in Puerto Vallarta? Well, he showed up on my doorstep last week. He said he took off because he was scared, just like I thought. He apologized and begged me to give him another chance."

My heart sinks. "So you're back together."

"Goodness, no!" Mom laughs, shaking her head. "I told him that I understand being scared, but I can't be with someone who'd abandon me in the middle of a foreign country."

I blink at the phone screen, shocked. "Wait—you're *not* with him anymore?"

"No, I'm not." She pauses, presses her lips together. "Sweetheart, I know you saw a lot of unfortunate circumstances when you were growing up, with some of the men I dated."

Maybe more like unfortunate choices—on her part. But I bite my tongue. This is the closest she's ever come to taking any kind of accountability.

"And I—I regret it," she continues. "I know I wasn't there when you needed me." Another pause. "Especially after Georgia's accident. You deserved so much better. You still do. I let myself get caught up in trying to find happiness in someone else and lost sight of the two little girls who needed me most."

My throat feels tight, and all I can do is nod.

"Why did you do it?" I ask, swallowing. "Why did you always chase after those guys?"

She frowns. "I guess it's because I couldn't stop hoping. And I'm not ready to give up—"

"But where's the evidence, Mom? Falling in love doesn't magically make everything work out perfectly. Maybe it's time to put away the hope, stop reading silly books that feed into unrealistic expectations, and be practical."

"That's not what I mean by hope," Mom says, her voice surprisingly calm. "And that's not why I read those books."

"Then why?"

"Because you know what happens to the characters in a romance novel?"

I sigh. "Yes, Mom. They fall in love—"

"They *change*. They grow." Her voice goes serious. "Even when they have painful pasts or have made mistakes. Those 'silly books' show me that anyone can be brave and try again. It's not that love makes everything work out perfectly—but love can create the perfect environment to face our fears."

I'm stunned; she's speaking in a way I've never heard before, with confidence and conviction. Georgia was right— our mom is doing better.

"I used to think I'd never be able to stand up for myself with a man, but I did it with Darrell. For the first time, I asked for what I deserve, and when he couldn't give it to me, I walked away." Mom smiles, her eyes soft. "And for the first time, my independent, successful older daughter has trusted me with her heartbreak, and I'm able to give *her* support. So yes, I think that's cause for hope."

My eyes fill with tears. This is exactly what Ryan's been

trying to get me to understand about his beloved books: the point isn't the sex, or the fantasy of the perfect partner, or even falling in love. It's about being willing to be vulnerable, to dig deep, to confront your shadows, embrace your own story, and become a stronger, braver version of yourself.

It's not about the happy ending—it's about believing that you're worthy of one.

"Thanks for sharing that, Mom," I say, and I mean it. It may take some time for me to trust her, but for the first time in years, I'm willing to give her a chance.

"Enough about me," she says, smiling brightly. This is a classic Liz Klein tactic, changing the subject when she's uncomfortable, but I understand. Baby steps, for both of us. "Do you want my advice?"

"Sure," I say, surprised that for the first time ever, I do.

"First, you need to tell him how you feel about him moving away."

She's right. I didn't share my true feelings about his plan, his new job, and Ryan deserves better. He deserves to know just how deeply I care about him, that I'm desperate to find some other solution because the thought of him being anywhere else is tearing me apart.

A flicker of hope sparks, and I'm about to tamp it down, but I stop myself. Hope may be dangerous, but just like a fire, it can also be warm and comforting.

"I will," I say. "Thanks, I should—"

"Wait!" She tilts her head, studying me. "One last piece of advice. Something I wish I'd learned years ago. No matter what he says, do you know what *you* want?"

I want him to stay. But if he doesn't?

"I—I'm not exactly sure," I say.

"Well then," my mom says, smiling. "I think you need to figure that out first."

After ending the call, I lean against the railing and consider that. *What do I want?*

Three months ago, I was hell bent on beating Ryan. Then I joined forces with him and laser-focused on us winning together. But I've never stopped to ask myself: Is this truly what I want to do with my life?

I close my eyes, letting an image of my store fill my mind, the way it used to be before construction started. Neat and orderly, cozy and safe, the perfect place to rebuild my confidence after my life fell apart. But recently, it's started to feel a little . . . small?

I think back to the months after Georgia's accident, when she was relearning how to walk, using her brace and cane. She was confident getting around our apartment, but she refused to go outside—too scary, she said, and every step reminded her of how much she'd lost.

I told her she couldn't spend the rest of her life stuck in an apartment, that even though she was scared, she needed to get out. She was frustrated, at first, but eventually she listened. And now she's living on her own, rocketing toward her goals.

Meanwhile, I've done exactly what I didn't want Georgia to do. I've gotten comfortable, focusing all my efforts on the bookstore so I don't have to face what scares me.

How many years did I spend avoiding the Boston Public Library because of bad memories? How many years did I refuse to even talk about how devastating it felt to leave college? But Ryan's been a safe space to share all this—

whether behind the scenes as RJ or in real life. He's encouraged me, cheered me on as I stepped outside my comfort zone, hosting events, presenting at IBNE.

Like my mom said, love creates the perfect environment to face our fears.

I think of my little bookstore again: Tabula Inscripta, and how Jerome explained why he chose that name. He wanted to capture the way each book leaves its mark on us, inscribing new perspectives and ideas on our minds like a well-worn page. All the stories I've read have been my teachers, sheltering me when I needed comfort, making life richer, showing me how to face adversity. It's never been a choice between fiction *or* reality, books *or* people, it's both. I am the product of every book I've ever read and every experience I've had, each heartbreak and failure, every moment of sadness and joy. The people I've met and the characters I've encountered, the events that challenged me and the narratives that have stretched me—all this is inscribed on my soul. They are the stories that shape who I am today and give me the strength to reach for more.

Turning, I head inside, back into Ryan's apartment. I wish I could go in his room and wake him up, tell him my plan, but I stop myself. He isn't going to like what I'm about to do—he'll try to stop me. But I need to do it anyway.

I find a pen and paper and leave a note on his coffee table: *I have some things to take care of today. Meet me at the bookstore at closing tonight?*

Heart pounding, I hesitate before adding: *Love, Josie.*

Then I gather my things and head out into the brilliant sunshine of a new day.

AN HOUR LATER, I'm at my own apartment. I've completed
my first step of the plan: asking Cinderella to cover the store
today. She hesitated, until I promised her I'll do everything
possible to get Ryan back as manager.

Now it's time for step two.

I pull out my phone, take a steadying breath, and call
Xander.

"It's not Monday," he says when he answers.

"I know," I say, ignoring his irritated tone. "But this can't
wait."

"What is it?"

"I quit."

A long, shocked pause. Then: "What? This is ridiculous!
Why does nobody want to work anymore? Do you realize how
inconvenient this is for me? How much time and effort it's
going to take to find a new manager? I—"

"That's why you need to convince Ryan to come back." My
heart is pounding. This has to work. Everything relies on it.

He harrumphs. "Why should I have to convince him?"

"Because he's the best person for the job," I say. "And
because a bookstore is more than just a store that sells books.
It's the heartbeat of the community, a place where stories and
ideas come alive, where people come to explore new worlds,
to challenge their thinking, to feel seen and welcomed. Ryan
understands that better than anyone. He knows how to
connect with readers in a way that builds trust and loyalty.
He's created something here—something real—and without
him, this place loses its soul."

Xander scoffs, and I know I need to bring this down to his level.

"And let's be honest," I say, "hiring and training a new manager takes time you don't have. If you want to keep the store running smoothly and profitably, you need him."

"True." Xander seems to be mulling this over. "But how am I going to convince him? He made his feelings pretty clear."

"First, you need to give him a raise," I say. "He's taking on more responsibility with this new position, and he should be compensated appropriately."

Xander snorts, but he doesn't say no. And after a moment, he adds, "What if that's not enough to change his mind?"

"I'm going to tell you exactly what you need to say to him."

After ending the call with Xander, I turn off my phone. I'm sure Ryan will call me when he hears what I've done, and I need more time to set things in motion.

I hear my mom's words: *Anyone can be brave and try again.* And Jerome, talking about a mind in progress, with infinitely more to learn.

Finally, I hear my own voice, telling my sister to walk out the door and into the big world, even if it's scary.

It's time I listened.

HOURS LATER, WHEN I head back toward the store, the sun is setting and I'm exhausted—everything took much longer than expected, and now I'm running late. I've been practicing what to say to Ryan, to convince him to accept Xander's offer and *stay with me*. I'm not sure I have the right words, but at least I'm allowing myself to hope. That feels like a pretty big deal.

I round the final corner to the store, and the windows are dark.

My heart crashes and shatters. He's not here. He didn't come.

Tears fill my eyes. I imagine him driving to Provincetown, away from me and this bookstore where all my memories will forever be filled with him. If that's truly what he wants, then I'll have to accept it. We'll visit each other as often as we can, talk on the phone every night, text during the day. We'll make it work, somehow.

Even still, it feels like a piece of my heart has been torn away. My chest aches and I try to hold in a sob—though I would've thought I'd cried enough today. I head into the bookstore to find a corner where I can sit and weep before heading home. There's a warm glow inside—Cinderella must have left a lamp on.

Only when I unlock the door and step inside, I realize it's not a lamp.

Candles cover every surface—the shelves and tables, even the floor. I'm awestruck, slowly turning in a circle, drinking in the magical sight of candlelight glinting off the spines of books.

The spark of hope I've carefully tended roars to life, a vibrant flame inside me. This has to be good, right? Not even Ryan Lawson would do something this wonderful if he didn't mean it.

I step closer to one of the candles, safely contained in a jar, and notice that there's an open book right next to it. A line on the page has been highlighted.

"He now viewed a successful relationship as one in which both people had recognized the best of what the other person had to offer and had chosen to value it as well."

Confused, I blink at the cover. *A Little Life*, by Hanya Yanagihara. I might've mentioned this book to Ryan—or rather, RJ—but what is it doing here, on his side of the store, with this obscure passage highlighted?

Then I notice another open book on the next shelf, also illuminated by a candle, and as I come closer, I see a line highlighted here, too.

"We would be together and have our books and at night be warm in bed together with the windows open and the stars bright."

I lift the cover: *A Moveable Feast* by Ernest Hemingway. I read this for an Honors seminar focused on Hemingway's work, junior year of college. I loved it, but I've never mentioned it to Ryan, either in person or online.

On the next shelf, there's another: *"I loved her against reason, against promise, against peace, against hope, against happiness, against all discouragement that could be."* *Great Expectations*, Charles Dickens. My favorite book from AP English.

Another: *"The moment I saw her, a part of me walked out of my body and wrapped itself around her. And there it still remains."* *The Ministry of Utmost Happiness*, by Arundhati Roy. Jerome recommended it to me my first year working for him.

Footsteps echo, and I look up to see Ryan, emerging from the back room, filling the doorway. He's wearing his tortoiseshell glasses and a gray cardigan, his hair falling across his forehead, Persephone curled up in his arms.

"Ryan," I breathe. "What is all this?"

"It's my grand gesture." His voice holds so much regret and gentleness that my eyes fill with tears.

"Your what?"

"It's, uh, something people do in romance novels? I'm not sure what characters do in literary fiction when they make a massive mistake."

"Usually they dig themselves into a deeper hole until their entire world falls apart."

His lips quirk in a smile. "Well, lucky for us, I don't read many of those books."

I let out a shocked laugh, looking around at the highlighted passages. "But—what are these?"

"You don't recognize them?" He looks concerned.

"I do, but—"

I glance at another open book, the highlighted words: "*To love or have loved, that is enough*." I don't even need to look at the cover; I know that one by heart. *Les Misérables*, the book I stubbornly read in its unabridged form, all fourteen hundred pages of it.

"Why are these here?"

Ryan sets Persephone down and walks over to me. "I've been tackling all the books on your Favorites shelf on BookFriends. Some of them are ridiculously long, so I've been listening to them, and I'm not through all of them yet, but . . ." He shrugs. "I'm trying."

A lump forms in my throat. All those times I saw him with earbuds in, I assumed he was listening to some steamy romance. "You're reading *my* favorite books?"

"Well, yeah. Someone told me it's the best way to get to know a person."

He says it like it's a no-brainer. Because he's Ryan Lawson, a man who knows how to pay attention.

"I'm not sure if you've noticed," he says, "but a lot of your favorite books have something to do with love. It's almost like you've been a closet romance fan all along."

I let out a disbelieving laugh. Maybe he's right. Maybe all stories are love stories at their core. The search for belonging, the ache of grief, our fumbling attempt to find purpose and connection in this big, confusing world.

Ryan takes a few steps toward me, his expression turning serious. "Listen, Josie—you can't quit. Not for me—"

"But *you* can quit for *me*?" My voice wavers, but I force myself to say what I should have said yesterday, instead of pushing down my feelings and icing him out. "The thought of you leaving . . . it's unbearable, Ryan. I want you here, I want you *with* me. But if that's not what you want . . ."

His eyes soften, and he comes closer. "Not a single part of me wants to leave. I thought . . . I thought if I stepped back, you could have everything you've ever dreamed of—"

"But—"

"I know, you must have felt like I was abandoning you, even though that's the last thing I wanted." His voice is gentle, earnest. "Which is why I'm here. Grand gesture. Candles and quotes about love from your favorite books. My heart on my sleeve. Asking you to forgive me."

"Of course I forgive you," I say, putting my arms around him. His arms come around me, too, and I close my eyes and breathe him in. For the first time, the ache of all the past abandonments is fading away, replaced by the warmth of knowing that I'm right where I belong.

Finally, we separate, and I wipe tears from my eyes. "What did you tell Xander?"

"I told him he owed you a fucking apology." His voice is all growly, which makes me smile. "And that I won't come back without you as my co-manager—"

"Oh, I'll be too busy for that."

He pulls back, startled. "What?"

I smile up at him. "Can I finally tell you what I've been doing all day?"

"Of course. Let's sit. Your neck has got to be aching."

He sits in the big armchair and pulls me onto his lap, my feet dangling like a kid's. I explain this morning's epiphany, how I knew what I needed to do—and fast, before I lost my nerve.

"I went to Emerson and talked with an academic adviser," I say in a rush.

His jaw drops.

"I was so nervous," I continue. "But she looked up my records and said my enrollment can be reinstated. Some of my classes are outdated, and I'll need to retake the ones I failed that last semester, but it should only take me about a year and a half to graduate."

"Graduate," Ryan repeats. He looks flabbergasted. "You're going back to school?"

I nod. "To finish my degree. And before you ask, no, I don't know exactly what I want to do yet. Maybe I'll end up teaching. Or library sciences? Or maybe I'll end up back here, working with you. I don't know. But I think the point is being a mind continually in progress, you know?"

"That's . . . that's wonderful. And so brave, Josie. I can't tell you how impressed I am."

"Don't be too impressed yet. I'm going to need even more bravery to show up my first day. I'll be in classes with people a decade younger than me."

"You're starting soon?"

I nod. "Next week. Three classes I need still had space."

"I'm thrilled for you," he says, kissing me. Then the light in his eyes dims slightly. "But I can't do this without you. I don't know anything about other genres, I have no business sense, I—"

"So you'll learn," I cut in. "It'll be challenging, sure, but you can do it. If you don't have the confidence in yourself yet, you can borrow some of mine."

As my words hit him, his eyes turn shiny, and he swallows. "Deal," he says.

"Plus, you won't have to do it without me—I need a part-time job," I say. "Hopefully I can convince my manager to work around my class schedule."

He laughs. "I think we can make that happen." Then he presses his forehead against mine and closes his eyes. "So . . . now for the most important discussion. If it isn't clear already, I love you."

I startle upright. "Did you just say that? Just like that? Shouldn't there be more ceremony? I don't know—I've never actually had a guy tell me he loves me before."

"All this isn't enough?" he says, looking around the store. He's smiling, though, amused. Then he takes my chin in his hand, forcing my eyes to meet his. "I'm all in, Josie. One hundred percent. Always and forever. But if you need more time, that's fine, too. Just know that I'm not going anywhere."

As I look into his eyes, flickering with the reflection of dozens of candles, I realize that I have a choice. I can keep my armor, keep him at a distance for weeks or months, slowly allowing him a little more of my heart.

Or I can be brave and do what I should have done the first

night we spent together, when I learned that the two men I loved were the same person.

"I—I need you to be patient with me," I say slowly. "I don't know how to be in a good relationship, I've never experienced one—"

"I can recommend a few books to learn from," he cuts in, grinning.

I smile back, then take a deep breath. "I know you've spent years thinking you didn't measure up, that you weren't enough, but you *are*. You're more than I ever expected, more than I ever dreamed of. You deserve someone who loves you without hesitation, and I—" My voice cracks. "I'm not going anywhere, either. No more holding back, no more hiding. I'm all in, too, one hundred percent. I love you, Ryan."

Relief washes over his face and he folds me against him, tucking my head under his chin. He lets out a long, shaky exhale, like a weight has finally lifted. "Thank you," he whispers.

And that has to be the most quintessentially *Ryan* thing I've ever heard—thanking *me* for loving him, as if it's not the best thing that's happened to me.

"I knew we'd get our happy ending," he says.

I sit back to look at him. "This isn't our happy ending."

His forehead creases in confusion. "Seems pretty happy to me."

"Yes, but think about it. Even after a book ends, whether it's happy or tragic, the characters have more life to live—and so do we. So much happens beyond the pages that we never get to read. That's what I'm looking forward to—living it all, the good times and the tough ones—wherever the story takes us."

"Beyond the pages," he says, smiling. "I love that."

As I kiss him, unshakable certainty fills my heart. I may not know exactly what will happen next, for the bookstore or our relationship or our individual lives, but I know one thing for sure: I want Ryan by my side as we find out.

The battle is over. But our story is just beginning.

One Year Later
Ryan

WHEN MY LOVE lamented about the happy endings in romance novels, she forgot about the epilogue. The glimpse into the future—maybe one year, maybe more—to let the reader know that the happiness of the characters they've come to love was not short-lived. That in the space between the end of the last chapter and the end of the book, the characters have continued to grow and live their full, complicated, beautiful lives.

Our lives have definitely been full over the last twelve months. Going back to school has been an adjustment for Josie, but she's rising to the challenge with the same badassery and grace she brings to everything she does. She added a business minor to her degree, so it'll take her longer to graduate, but the things she's learning will set her up for success in whatever she decides to do next.

And I'd be lying if I said it didn't feel good to take care of her, keeping her fed and watered with plenty of Americanos and the occasional Munchkin.

Between studying and reading (for pleasure!), Josie's been

working a few hours a week at the store. She's helped me implement a lot of her systems and strategies so I'm no longer making decisions based on my gut alone. More than that, her support and belief in me have helped my anxiety go down and my confidence go up.

The new, expanded bookstore is organized and efficient, but we've maintained the personality of my old store, the coziness that invites customers to feel at home. And of course, our romance selection is still the largest and most diverse in the city.

Josie's here now: moderating an event with author Luke Duncan about the second book in his *Camp Shadows* YA series, which our teen readers have been devouring. Josie and Luke—who used to write under the name William Lucas Duncan (I always thought the three-name thing was a bit pretentious)—are having a lively discussion about why it's so important to let kids with disabilities be the heroes of their own stories, and the teenagers in attendance are rapt. Although it's hard to say if that's because of the conversation, or because Luke looks like a modern-day Paul Newman— which also explains why Eddie's been lingering by the event space for the last hour.

"Hey, boss—I've got something for you."

Cinderella's smile is as bright as her hair, which is currently blue. She says she's still trying to figure out who she is, but I think she's a human rainbow: full of color and quick to make people smile.

She's been smiling more lately, ever since she started "talking" to a very nice man. Carlton was the foreman of the construction crew that worked on our stores, and he kept coming in after the job ended. Cinderella insists they're just friends, but I see the way she lights up when he walks in.

"Should I be nervous?" I ask.

"Don't be silly," she says dismissively. "Put your hand out."

I oblige, and she places a sparkly pin in my open palm. It says: BOOK ~~BOYFRIEND~~ HUSBAND.

My eyes go wide, and I close my fingers around the pin, slipping it in my pocket next to the velvet box I've checked and rechecked a dozen times today.

"She hasn't said yes yet," I whisper.

"She will," Cinderella says, patting my shoulder. "She's a smart girl."

The compliment makes me smile. Josie has managed to endear herself to all my OGs, which wasn't the easiest task. Everyone made the transition to the new store except Eliza— and that's only because she's studying and playing soccer at the University of Florida. We miss her, but she's promised to stop by whenever she comes home for school breaks.

In her absence, Nora has added a few more shifts— including leading story time on Saturday mornings. She bristles at any comparison to a sweet grandmother, but the role fits her. Indira's here almost every day. She still wears all black—but she's got a bright pink ribbon on her name tag that lets people know she's an assistant manager. She's done an amazing job familiarizing herself with the new genres we carry, and it's been nice to have an assistant manager who actually assists.

Georgia isn't on staff, but she might as well be with how much time she spends studying and hanging out in our café. She still makes incessant jokes about my height, but I put up with it because I love Josie and Josie loves Georgia. I kind of love her, too. In that annoying-kid-sister way. It's nice not being the youngest in this little found family of ours.

I've met their mom a few times; she's working to earn Josie's trust back, holding down a job, going to therapy, and staying out of the dating world for now—but it's Georgia whose blessing I asked for. She also helped me pick out the ring. There are two small diamonds (Georgia made me make sure they weren't blood diamonds) and the center stone is an emerald. According to my future sister-in-law, emeralds are the stone of intuition and foresight, and throughout time they have been seen as symbols of truth and love. I couldn't think of any better symbolism for my relationship with Josie.

A smattering of applause calls my attention to the event space; the conversation is over. I head up front to help people check out, but Henri, one of our new employees, has it under control. They're moving faster than the credit card machine can approve the purchases, handing customers a multicolored bag printed with our new store name: Beyond the Pages. Thanks to Josie's coaching, I was able to negotiate my involvement in the naming of the new store as a condition for accepting the job. Xander surprisingly agreed, which shows just how desperate he was.

Kind of like how desperate I am to get this crowd moving, so I grab a pad of sticky notes and help write the names for Luke to sign.

An hour and a half later—one superfan bought twelve books!—we say good night to Luke and his very pregnant wife, Jessie, and lock the door behind them.

We're finally alone.

My stomach knots up. After participating in hundreds of

bookish proposals, it's my turn. For so long, I thought I'd never find my love story, that I was meant to help other people find their beshert (a Yiddish word Josie taught me, which means the person they were destined for). Never in a million years would I have thought my own beshert would end up being the prissy girl who worked at the highbrow bookstore next door.

"What are you smiling about?" Josie is looking at me suspiciously, her hand on her hip.

"Aren't I allowed to be happy?"

She steps closer and gives me a quick kiss. "Let's go home and we can be happy there."

Home. I love that word—and the fact that we moved into a two-bedroom apartment near Porter Square a month ago.

"In a minute," I tell her, my stomach uneasy with nerves. "I got you something—sit down and I'll be right back."

Josie moves to her favorite spot, the reading nook on what used to be the Tab side of the store. The old leather couch from Happy Endings is there, and we've added a rug and a lamp to make it feel homey. When I return, her shoes are off, and Persephone is purring in her lap. She looks like the BookshopGirl I always imagined.

"Here you go," I say, handing her the wrapped package. My hands tingle in anticipation.

"A blind date book?" Her eyes light up. "It feels pretty thick . . ."

"Just read the clue. Out loud."

She gives me a soft smile. It took Josie a while to warm up to what she calls my acts of adoration, but as she says, there are worse things than being in love with a practicing romantic.

"'Enemies to friends to lovers,'" she reads, then looks up. "I didn't know that was a thing?"

"Keep reading."

" 'Witty banter, slow burn, online epistolary, Jewish representation, tall fetish'—this sounds like it could be our story." Josie laughs, but I'm too nervous to join in.

"Open it."

She unwraps the brown kraft paper slowly, like she knows what's inside is precious. As she takes in the cover—an illustration I had commissioned—her eyes grow wide. The two of us, standing back-to-back in front of our respective old stores. Josie has her nose in a book, but I'm only pretending to read mine. Instead, my eyes are on her. The title is *BookFriends to Lovers*.

"There's a blurb from Penelope Adler-Wolf," Josie says, confused.

Josie's mentor and friend was more than happy to give our story an endorsement: "A true testament to the power of love and good literature."

"Take a look inside," I say.

She does, and her breath catches. "It's our messages," she says, awe in her voice.

As she flips through the pages, all the conversations between RJ.Reads and BookshopGirl, I slip off the couch and onto one knee. Josie doesn't notice—she's reading, laughing and smiling at the notes I left in the margins: pointing out when I started having feelings for her, when I first realized who she was, when I knew I loved her.

It's all there, captured in the pages of our story.

"This is . . ." She looks up and freezes when she sees me on bended knee, holding out the open ring box.

"Josie Anne Klein," I say, my voice shaky. "I think I fell in love with love stories because I knew one day, they would lead me to you—a woman who thought my name was Brian." She laughs, her eyes filling with tears as she smiles down at me. My voice gets stronger. "From the moment I met you—both on BookFriends and in person—something about you captivated me. Whether we were bantering online or sparring in real life, I couldn't get you off my mind."

She's glowing, and tears escape her gorgeous green eyes.

"I grew up hearing my parents say, 'When you know, you know,' but I didn't really know what love was until I started loving you. What we have is deeper, and richer, and more beautiful than anything I ever could've imagined. So, Josie—" I take a breath, my own eyes brimming with tears. "Will you—"

"I know, too," Josie says, kissing me. I taste the salt of her tears—or maybe mine.

"Is that a yes?" I ask between kisses. "Remember, I need words."

"You can have all the words," Josie says, pulling back to look at me. She's sitting on my knee, her hands on either side of my face. Her smile is the most beautiful thing I've ever seen. "Like fiancé."

"I like that."

"And husband. Or partner?"

"Either is okay with me," I say, giving her another kiss. "But there's one more word I need—hopefully a three-letter one. Will you marry me?"

"Yes!" Josie shouts. "Yes, I will marry you, Brian and Ryan and RJ." She throws her arms around me, and I hold her, silently thanking whatever fates conspired to bring us right here.

Eventually, she pulls away, narrowing her eyes in a way that tells me her mind is working through a plan. "I just have one condition."

"Okay . . . ?"

She sits back on the couch, pulling me up to sit beside her. She takes the ring box from my hands and admires it before looking back at me. "After I graduate, I want this bookstore to be ours."

"It already is," I say, confused.

"Technically speaking, it's Xander's. But I want to buy it from him. Together."

My laugh dies on my lips when I see how serious she is.

"No way Xander will agree to that," I say, shaking my head. "He put too much money into the renovation. He'll never sell."

"Well, it's a good thing neither of us is afraid of a fight."

Josie's got a gleam in her eyes that I remember from our early weeks of competition.

"Another battle?" I say.

"Think of it as the fight for our future."

I blow out a breath, but something in my gut tells me she's right. "And this time we'll be on the same side from the start."

"Oh, Ryan," Josie says, picking up the book of our conversations—our love story. "We were always on the same side. It just took us a while to figure it out. So, what do you say?"

I nod.

"Words," Josie teases. "Will you be my life partner *and* my business partner?"

"Yes," I say. "Always and forever yes."

And with that, I slip the ring on her finger, and I kiss her.

My former enemy.

My fiancée.

My everything.

Acknowledgments

Book people really are the best people, and we are fortunate to know the best of the best. First and foremost, this book is a love letter to indie bookstores. We've been lucky in our career as co-authors to visit so many across the country, meeting booksellers and doing events.

Like Josie, we know that bookstores are more than just stores that sell books; they're a vital part of a community. Thank you to the booksellers, the unsung heroes of the literary industry, for your tireless work in spreading the love of books and matching readers with their perfect story. A special shout-out to: Anne Holman and the team at the King's English in Salt Lake City, Stephanie Skees and the team at the Novel Neighbor in St. Louis, Rebecca and Kimberly George at Volumes Bookcafe in Chicago, Zibby's Bookshop in LA, Hyphen and the team at FoxTale Book Shoppe in Atlanta, M.Judson Booksellers in Greenville (the inspiration for the Pages and Pairings event at Josie's store!), Melody Wukitch (and Sarah!) at Park Books MD, Elizabeth Bosscher and team at Schuler Books in Grand Rapids, Litchfield Books in Pawleys Island, and Sundog Books in Seaside. Much love to Pamela

Klinger-Horn (the inspiration for PAW!), Maxwell Gregory, and Mary Webber O'Malley. We also want to thank all the librarians who read and recommend our books—especially "Uncle Ron" Block and the Cuyahoga Library in Cleveland.

Before a book ever reaches the shelves, it requires a massive team of incredible people working in the background. We wouldn't have a writing career if not for our literary agents. Thank you, Amy Berkower and Joanna MacKenzie, for your support, guidance, and wisdom. Thank you to the entire team at Writer's House and Nelson Literary, and special thanks to Genevieve Gagne-Hawes for her expert feedback and sharp editorial eye.

We're so grateful for the entire team at Berkley—our book could not have been in better hands. Thank you to our editor, Kerry Donovan, for helping us bring this story to life, and to Cindy Hwang for suggesting that we make our male character the romance lover. Thank you to the rest of our wonderful team, including Jessica Plummer, Elise Tecco, Chelsea Pascoe, and Genni Eccles, for all your hard work and dedication.

A special thank-you to Ana Hard for the beautiful cover. You captured our characters and setting perfectly!

Many thanks to Julie Carrick Dalton for walking ALL over Boston with us and suffering through the painstaking cannoli taste test. It made the single line in the book so much more believable. We're grateful to the Boston Park Plaza for being so welcoming—especially the guy at the front desk who encouraged us to take advantage of our free drink credits. Thanks also to Blythe Colyer and Lara Zelman, who joined us for our difficult research at the Burren and bearing witness as we read a sex scene out loud in honor of Josie and Ryan.

One of the best parts of being an author is getting to know other authors. Much love to the Berkletes, the Women's Fiction Writers Association, Ink Tank, Every Damn Day Writers, the 2022 Debuts, the Eggplant Beach Writers, and our Featuring Banana! and Noods and Balls crews (you know who you are).

And a huge thank-you to our incredible author friends and mentors: Suzanne Park, Kathleen West, Kimmery Martin, Lainey Cameron, Lyn Liao Butler, Leah DeCesare, Lisa Barr, Renée Rosen, Emily Henry, Colleen Oakley, Nancy Johnson, Julie Carrick Dalton (our Boston tour guide), Kathleen Barber, Kristin Harmel (Alison's literary godmother), Mary Kay Andrews, Kristy Woodson Harvey, Patti Callahan Henry, Amy Mason Doan, Jennifer Klepper, Jamie Beck, Kerry Lonsdale, Tiffany Yates Martin, Orly Konig, Rochelle Weinstein, Kristan Higgins, Barbara Claypole White, Jennie Nash, Julia Whelan, Abby Jimenez, KJ Dell'Antonia, Christie Tate, Christina Clancy, Heather Webb, Liz Fenton, Lisa Steinke, Camille Pagán, Ali Hazelwood (special thanks for teaching us about knotting!), Zibby Owens, Shelby Van Pelt, Chloe Liese, Lynn Painter, Katie Gutierrez, Jill Santopolo, Ali Rosen, Kate Spencer, and Anabel Monaghan.

We would also like to thank the bookstagrammers, BookTokkers, bloggers, and everyone on social media who put our book in front of potential readers. Special thanks to the Bookish Ladies Club; Annissa, Bubba, Dawn, Reca, Aileen, and everyone else in the Beyond the Pages Book Club (the inspiration for the name of the new bookstore!); Andrea Katz of Great Thoughts Great Readers; Kristy Barrett of A Novel Bee; Sue Peterson; Robin Kall of Reading with Robin; Kate (@RomanticallyInclined); Lauren Margolin, "The Good Book

Fairy"; Ashley Hasty; Ashley Spivey; Cindy Burnett of Thoughts from a Page; Courtney Marzilli with Books Are Chic; Sara with Harlequin Junkie; Megan from the *Well-Read Podcast*; Jean Meltzer and Jannete Djemal from Jewish Joy; and of course, Meg Walker, Ron Block, and the Fab Four of Friends and Fiction.

Thank you to our incredible readers! We've loved connecting with you on social media and at events—and special love to the Ali Brady Bunch on Facebook. Thank you to our beta readers, who provided valuable feedback on an early draft and helped us shape the story (including adding the Only One Bed scene), offered guidance on living with dyslexia, checked our Boston-area facts, and cheered us on: Dallas Strawn (first one to read!), Danielle Medina, Sarah Van Cleve, Elizabeth Buttrick, Olivia Jackson, Shay Tibbs, Blythe Colyer, Jessica Silfen, and Michelle Charles.

From Alison:

Bradeigh—or should I say BSG? I can't believe how long it took us to realize that you share initials with the heroine of our story. And what a heroine she is. I know I've already told you this, but I am so proud of how you kept pushing yourself, digging deeper and deeper to bring Josie fully to life. She's got your spirit and your passion, and that's probably why I love her! I'm grateful to be on this journey with you, and I can't wait for whatever happens next.

Thank you to my amazing family: my mom, Kathy Hammer; my dad, Dr. Randy Hammer; my little/big sister, Elizabeth Murray; plus Carlene, Nick, Dylan, Alex, and Louie. And I can't forget the Lewins, Bergers, Blocks, Hammers, and Kirbys. I'm lucky to have friends who are like family—My Girls, Meg

McKeen, D.J. Johnson, Kristie Raymer, Julie Johnson, Krissie Callahan, #LibbyLove, Michelle Dash, Katie Ross, Mia Phifer, Jenna Leopold, Shana Freedman, Robbie Manning, Christina Williams, Pierrette Hazkial, Beth Gosnell, Mary Chase, Peggy Finck, Leah Conner, and Stephen Kellogg. Thank you to the Rock Boat Family, the Rock by the Sea Family, and the *BoatCast* podcast crew for all the support.

Thank you to Becky Thomas for telling me about the pickle book (it's in here!), to DJ and Chardy for the perfect wedding toast that inspired a line in the book, to Carlton and Jen for throwing the finest literary salon in Chicago, and to everyone who's been patient with me this year as I've tried to balance working what sometimes feel like three full-time jobs.

This last year has not been easy for the Jewish community—but I know we need darkness to appreciate the light. And I've been surrounded by so much light. I've strengthened friendships and developed new ones, and I'm particularly grateful for Jill Santopolo, Ali Rosen, Courtney Sheinmel, the AAA Founders group for giving me a place to feel safe, the Jewish Bookstagram Chat, and the whole Artists Against Antisemitism Board. I'm honored to be on this journey with you all.

Last, but certainly not least, thanks to the whole Godfrey family—Nate, Isaac, Eliza, Everett, Nora, Merrie, Jim, Ginger, and Beans (who I think is cute no matter the haircut). Thank you for sharing Bradeigh with me and making me feel like I'm part of the family. I'm the luckiest.

From Bradeigh:

Alison, there's no one else I'd rather embark on this writing journey with—thank you for being my partner in this story and so many others. Together, we've navigated every twist, turn, and plot hole crisis with countless texts, Zooms, and so many rewrites. I couldn't be prouder of the story we've brought into the world, and I'm excited for more to come! I'm blessed to be surrounded by so many booklovers in my life—thanks to the Physician Mom Book Club and my IRL book club for surrounding me with a community of kindred spirits who understand the thrill and solace of a good story. Thank you to my parents, Merrie and Jim, for raising me in a home with plenty of books and lots of discussions. I'm endlessly grateful to my wonderful friends (including but not limited to Amanda, Amy, Suzanne, Erin, Stephanie, Kellie, Susan, and Ashley) for the conversations, laughter, and unwavering support. To my kids—Isaac, Eliza, Everett, and Nora—I'm so lucky you cheer me on even when my head is buried in a manuscript. My furry sidekicks, Ginger and Beans, thank you for curling up beside me during long writing hours. And finally, Nate—thank you for being my anchor, for believing in my stories even when I doubt them. Without you, none of this would be possible.

Last, but not least, this book would not exist without the magic that Nora Ephron created when she wrote and directed one of our all-time favorite movies, *You've Got Mail*. For that, we thank her.

　—Alison & Bradeigh
　a.k.a. Ali Brady

PS: We love hearing from readers—find us online at www .alibradybooks.net and on Instagram @AliBradyBooks.

Battle
of the
Bookstores

Ali Brady

Discussion Questions

1. What did you think of the authors' decision to flip the gender stereotypes, having the man be the romance fan and the woman be more into literary fiction?

2. If you could attend one of the literary events held at Happy Endings or Tabula Inscripta, which one would you go to?

3. Why do you think romance is sometimes looked down on as a genre? Do you enjoy reading genres other than romance?

4. Do you have a bookish pet peeve like the ones Josie and Ryan share?

5. Ryan and his staff have strong opinions about the third-act breakup. What's your opinion on it, and did their discussion change your mind at all?

6. "Do audiobooks count as reading?" is a big debate in the literary community—did hearing Ryan's experience with

dyslexia and listening to books make you think about it differently?

7.   How many books do you usually read at one time? Do you have purse, bathroom, kitchen, and bed books like Josie does?

8.   What did you think of Ryan's decision to quit and sacrifice his job without talking to Josie about it first? And what did you think about Josie's decision to quit and go back to school?

9.   Both Ryan's and Josie's views on love were influenced by their parents (Josie is distrusting of love, and Ryan believes when you know, you know). Could you relate to either of their beliefs?

10.   Do you think Ryan should have told Josie who he was sooner?

11.   Could you be friends with someone who hates your favorite book?

Continue reading for a preview of

UNTIL NEXT SUMMER

Available now!

Jessie

August

WHEN I WAS a kid, I had a button on my backpack that read I LIVE TEN MONTHS FOR TWO. When people noticed it, I'd get one of two reactions: total confusion (*Ten months of what? Does this poor girl have a terminal illness?*), or a knowing smile.

The ones who smiled would inevitably ask one question. A question that let me know, without a doubt, that they were my kind of people:

"So where'd you go to camp?"

No matter the age gap or difference in our backgrounds, we'd start swapping stories, sharing memories. The gruff custodian at my elementary school bragged about winning Color Wars when he was fourteen. A bus driver sang his favorite camp song (*The Princess Pat . . . lived in a tree*), complete with hand motions. My pediatrician told me she once caught her marshmallow on fire and then, panicking, waved her roasting stick in the air, causing the marshmallow to fall onto her bare foot. She even showed me the burn scar, taking her shoe off in the middle of her clinic room while I waited for my twelve-year-old vaccinations.

Here's what I took from those conversations: there's something magical about summer camp. Those days stick in your mind like pine sap in your hair, like the scent of campfire smoke on your clothes. Even decades later, the memories remain vivid.

Which is why I decided that I didn't want to spend ten months slogging through what everyone else called Real Life only to spend two months living what felt like *my* real life.

I wanted it all the time.

It's sometimes still hard to believe I achieved that childhood dream. That this is my full-time, year-round, always and forever job. I am the head camp director at Camp Chickawah, and we've just completed another successful summer session.

The big lawn in the middle of the property is abuzz, hundreds of campers milling around, duffels and sleeping bags heaped in messy piles. Counselors try their best to wrangle the kids as they exchange tearful hugs with their cabinmates and friends, promising to see each other next summer. Then we herd them onto buses, double-checking that their gear is safely stowed below, and wave as they take off down the road.

I gather my summer staff—the counselors, lifeguards, kitchen crew, sailing and archery and tennis instructors—and thank them for working so hard. I remind them that camp people never say goodbye; we say "see ya next summer." So that's what they do, exchanging phone numbers and hugs before taking off.

And then everything goes silent.

The only signs of the three hundred people who called this place home for the past eight weeks are the trampled ground, scraps of trash, and whispers of memory floating through the air: campfires and songs, pranks and crafts, friendships to last a lifetime. I take a deep breath, thinking how grateful I am to be part of it.

At the same time, I'm exhausted. Each day at camp feels like a week, and each week feels like a month. I haven't had a full night of sleep since May—I'm always listening for the knock on my cabin door. This summer, I drove two people with broken bones to the emergency room in the middle of the night (one camper, one counselor), calmed a pack of terrified ten-year-olds when a tree fell on their cabin's porch during a rainstorm, and stayed up all night cleaning vomit after a stomach bug ran through camp.

And most importantly: I kept a calm, reassuring smile on my face the entire time. After all, I set the tone for the summer. The former owners, Nathaniel and Lola Valentine, taught me this.

"Welp, made it through another year," a gruff voice says, and I turn to see my assistant camp director, Dot.

Like me, she's dressed in Camp Chickawah gear—khaki shorts, a polo shirt, and a wide-brimmed hat. Dot is five feet tall and stocky, built like a human bowling pin with short gray hair. I'm nearly a foot taller, with strawberry blonde hair in two braids and skin that freckles or burns within minutes of sun exposure.

I smile. "It was a good summer, right?"

"It was Chicka-wonderful. Nathaniel and Lola would be proud."

Dot's been a staple of Camp Chickawah since my days as a camper, and now she's looking at me for direction—something I still haven't gotten used to, even after four years of being her boss.

"Let's do a sweep of the grounds for lost items," I say. "Then we call it a day. Sound okay?"

"Sounds great!" Dot says, and off we go.

THE NEXT MORNING, after sleeping for ten glorious hours, I head toward the lake. The air is cool, faintly scented with pine, and full of birdsong. I pull my favorite canoe from the shed— it's hand-carved birchwood and nearly a century old—and slide it halfway into the water, sending ripples across the shimmering surface. After discarding my hiking boots and wool socks on the dock, I pop my earbuds in.

It's time for some Broadway magic.

I press play on the original cast recording of *Hadestown*. The iconic trombone begins wailing, joined by the inimitable André De Shields, and as I wade into the cool water and transfer myself into the canoe, I can't help dancing. Luckily, no one's around to see.

After stowing my phone in a dry bag near my feet, I shove myself out with my paddle. Our camp hugs the west side of the lake; the rest is ringed with pine trees. The rising sun paints a golden streak across the water, and I follow it, paddling until my shoulders burn.

Canoes can be tricky to navigate solo, especially an old wooden one, but I love the nostalgia, the knowledge that countless campers and counselors have sat where I am now. Soon I relax into the rhythm and pull of paddle on water, and my exhaustion melts away.

I've spent every summer at Camp Chickawah since I was eight years old. My parents divorced when I was a toddler, splitting custody fifty-fifty because they both "loved me so much." I believe them—but the fact is, packing up and moving to a different house each week does a number on a child's sense of stability. It's not only adjusting to a different home— it's an entirely different culture. Different food in the fridge, different neighbors, different rules and expectations. Every week, just as I'd settled in at one home, I'd have to readjust all over again.

Which is why that first summer at camp felt revolutionary. Eight whole weeks sleeping in the same bed. Associating with the same people, following the same routine. Camp was the stable home I'd never had. Every summer I returned, and when I was sixteen, I applied for the counselor-in-training program, where I was able to teach and mentor the younger campers.

More than anything, I wanted to become a real counselor during my summer breaks in college. My best camp friend and I were going to do it together, but in the end, she bailed on me. It was painful—the kind of hurt that takes years to heal—but I took the job anyway. When I graduated (with a bachelor's in recreation administration—yes, it's a real degree), Nathaniel and Lola offered to keep me on as an assistant director, one of the few year-round positions at Camp Chickawah. When they retired, I became head director.

Nathaniel and Lola were more than my mentors—they were like an extra set of grandparents who instilled in me the values of hard work and integrity, who taught me the importance of giving our campers a place to learn skills, make friends, and grow. Even though they've passed away, it feels like they're still with me. And like Dot said, I think they'd be proud.

An hour later, I'm pulling the canoe onto the shore when I hear footsteps. Turning, I see Dot and two other people: Jack and

Mary, Nathaniel and Lola's son and daughter. He's short and stocky, with his dad's square shoulders, and she's short and soft, like her mother. They inherited the camp, but neither of them has any interest in running it, so they've left it in my hands.

"Hi!" I say, putting my earbuds away. "So nice to see you both. What brings you to camp?"

Jack gives his sister a quick glance. "We're wrapping up Mom and Dad's estate. Can we talk?"

"YOU'RE SELLING THE camp?" I say, dumbfounded.

The three of us are sitting in the Lodge, a rustic two-story building overlooking the lake.

"The camp hasn't made a profit in years," Jack says, which of course I know. But making money was never Nathaniel and Lola's goal.

"But—but it's been in your family since 1914!" I protest. "Parents depend on this place for their kids each summer."

Mary gives me a sad smile and her eyes crinkle around the edges, just like Lola's. "I've tried to find a buyer who wants to keep operating it, but no one's interested—"

"I could reach out to the camp community," I say, my voice tinged with desperation. I'm part of a huge online group of summer camp directors throughout North America. There has to be someone who understands how important this place is. How irreplaceable.

Jack shakes his head. "Mary's already tried that."

"I'd buy Jack out if I could," Mary says. "But there's no way I can afford it—"

"And your health, Mary," Jack cuts in.

Mary closes her mouth and nods. "Yes. Well, that too."

I don't know what they're referring to, and it doesn't feel appropriate to ask. But Mary looks thinner than I remember, the shadows under her eyes deeper.

Panic is rising in my chest. This can't be happening.

"So . . . what does this mean?" I ask.

Mary and Jack exchange glances again. Mary's eyes fill with tears, like she's silently pleading with him, but Jack gives a shake of his head before turning to me.

"We're listing the property as residential real estate," Jack says, his voice brisk. All business.

I know what this means—I've seen it happen throughout our area. Luxury vacation developments, condos, and town houses crowding the lakefront, rustic cottages torn down to make way for huge, fancy lake houses.

"Of course, you'll get a portion of the sale, Jessie," Mary says brightly.

I startle. "Wait—what?"

Mary turns to her brother. "I thought you sent her a copy of the will, Jack?"

"I'll send it when I get home," Jack says, shooting his sister a peeved glance. Then, to me: "You get one percent. Should be a tidy sum with a sale this large."

He seems offended by this, as if losing a fraction of his own profit is a profound injustice.

For my part? I don't care about the money. I'm not sure I even want it—it would feel tainted somehow, though it was thoughtful of Nathaniel and Lola to think of me.

"But what does this mean for my staff?" I say. "Do you want us to just . . . clear out?"

"No, no, of course not," Mary rushes to say. "The whole process will take a while."

"Probably not as long as you think," Jack mutters under his breath.

Anger flares inside me. I want to grab them by their shoulders and shake them, ask how they can do this. Don't they understand how much this place means? To their parents, to all our campers. To me.

I remember Dot saying Jack *hated* camp as a kid, that he resented how his parents spent all their time and energy here. Mary loved camp, apparently, but she's never been strong enough to stand up to her older brother.

Now she smiles gently. "Don't worry—we haven't even listed it yet. And whenever we get an offer, we'll make sure to delay closing until next fall. We're not going to just toss you out on your keister, you know?"

She gives a little laugh, but I can't join in, even half-heartedly. My camp is closing. After twenty years, this summer will be my last.

Photo by Robin Facer

ALI BRADY is the pen name of writing BFFs Alison Hammer and Bradeigh Godfrey. They are the *USA Today* bestselling authors of romantic, heartwarming, funny novels including *The Beach Trap, The Comeback Summer, Until Next Summer, Battle of the Bookstores,* and the novella *One Night, Two Holidays.* Their books have been "best of summer" picks by *The Washington Post, The Wall Street Journal, Parade,* and Katie Couric Media. Alison lives in Chicago and works as an advertising creative director. She's also the founder and a co-president of the Artists Against Antisemitism and the author of *You and Me and Us* and *Little Pieces of Me.* Bradeigh lives in Utah with her husband, four children, and two dogs. She works as a doctor and is the author of psychological thrillers *Imposter* and *The Followers.*

VISIT ALI BRADY ONLINE

AliBradyBooks.net

AliBradyBooks

AliBradyBooks

AliBradyBooks

Ready to find
your next great read?

Let us help.

Visit prh.com/nextread

Penguin
Random
House